Copyright © 2024 by Anthony L. Crawford, Jr.

All rights reserved. No part of this book may be reproduced or used in any manner without written permission of the copyright owner except for the use of quotations in a book review. For more information, address: alcrawfordjr2@gmail.com

SPECIAL EDITION

linktr.ee/krawfpravurb

Anthony Crawford, Jr.

Black Pain't, Vol. I

I write and speak from the deepest and darkest depths of my heart. I write and speak for myself, and I write for you. I write and speak for those that have dreams, goals, and visions. I write and speak for the thinkers and those that know that something is wrong with our society. This is for those that are ready for a change through truth. This is for my family. This is for the writers who are not afraid to take people through dark places through artistic expressions. Most importantly, this is for those that are willing to make a difference for melaninated people.
-Anthony Crawford, Jr.

Anthony Crawford, Jr.

Introduction and Acknowledgements

    I kept all my writings. First and foremost, let me express my gratitude towards you and the millions of others that will be reading this novel. It means more to me than you or anyone else will ever know. This was just a dream and now it's a reality. Thank you so much for supporting this movement onto universal self-love. Thank you to my father, Anthony Crawford, Sr., and my mother, April Taylor-Crawford, who supports me throughout this blissful journey. Family matters, and I am thankful for the bond I have with my brother, Aaron Crawford, and my sister, Aaliyah Crawford. Thank you so much to my girl and future wife, Kieara and our beloved family. To my daughter, AKiera Crawford.

    Thank you to Ms. Latasha Timberlake for editing this book the first time I published it. Thank you for teaching me how to be a better writer and educator. Thank you for watching over me throughout my time in Oklahoma. The blessings that you all have bestowed on me will never go in vain. Thank you to my people in Oklahoma. You all taught me so much about myself and my potential. Thank you for your continuous support.

    I realized at a young age that I loved telling stories. That's probably the reason why I used to lie a lot. I'm not justifying my actions, but just imagine what we could do if we turned our "flaws" and "faults" into art. Whatever we consider an imperfection is just what the word says, I'm perfection. Everything is perfect about you because you were made from and out of Love. God is Love.

    I remember I was writing poems, raps, and stories since I the fifth grade. I wrote in notebooks, compositions books, and any type of paper that I can get my hands on. I still have those writings till this day. One summer, when I was 13 years young, I had got hit by a car. I really couldn't be as active as I was because my body needed to recover, so I was in the house most of the time. Bored and tired of playing video games, I spontaneously had written five movie scripts using William

Black Pain't, Vol. I

Shakespeare's methods of play writing. I don't know what inspired me to do them, but I diligently worked on them. I don't know where those stories came from, but I got them out of my system. Long story short, I lost four of the scripts as time went by. So maybe I haven't kept completely all my writings, but the synchronicity of me finding that one that was not lost, is an astonishing story to tell.

After graduated high school, I went on to college and sort of stopped doing the things I was naturally gifted in. I kept of all my writings in my parents' closet in a crate. While in college, I got actively involved in the Student Government Association and traveled the United States through the services it provided for its members. I remember I would write poems out-of-the-blue and didn't understand why I was writing them. I kept all those writings.

I began writing *Black Pain't* at a time when I was enduring my own pain. I would write poems and post them on my social media pages, and I gained a grand following. People were reaching out to me letting me know how much my poetry was helping them internally. Then, one day, an abundance of ideas surrounded my thoughts. Characters, settings, plots, and messages came to me as if it something was downloading. I was in a different zone. It felt like I was out of my mind and something else was writing while using my body to do so.

After writing the first draft of the book and giving it my editor, I started having revelations and visions of freedom and prosperity. I was becoming happy. It was as if I founded myself. Throughout the wait, I started going back to my childhood to reflect on the lessons and on the things that made me feel free. I went back to Los Angeles one December and went through that crate that I had placed in my parents' closet. I was reading all my old poems, raps, and writings. I still write with the same concepts, topics, and word play. Pay attention to your childhood. We leave ourselves clues. That's why I kept all my writings.

Anthony Crawford, Jr.

Chapter 1:
Signs

"Hello, this is Rayven. How may I help you?" she says professionally after picking up the phone.

While leaning on a desk in the classroom, he flirtatiously says "Oh my Rayven! You sound sexy."

Firmly, she says, "Sir, how may I help you?"

Noticing the tone in her voice, he says, "Lighten up sweetie. It was a compliment. My name is Darryl Jones and I want to pay my monthly insurance payment over the phone." He tells her his account information while he straightens the desks in the classroom.

"Thank you, Mr. Jones. I'll be sure to send you your receipt via email. Was there anything else that you needed help with today, sir?" She says in a proficient manner.

"No ma'am. Thank you."

Black Pain't, Vol. I

"Thank you, Mr. Jones. Have a wonderful day, sir," she says as she quickly hangs up the phone.

He softly says, "You, too," under his breath as he proceeds to straighten the desks. He walks towards the last row near the windows and notices sun rays shining in through the blinds. He then stands by a window, pulls down the string to lift the blinds and stares out into the bright sky. He's stands still for a moment soaking in the peace.

Suddenly, he sees two white doves flying across the soothing sky. He feels like it is a sign. He begins to feel this ounce of joy traveling within him. He crosses his arms feeling an enticing love that gives him the goosebumps.

A woman and a young man slowly walk in the classroom and notice photos of *Huey P. Newton, Malcolm X,* and *Martin Luther King, Jr.* above the class' smart board. They then look across the room to see the teacher's desk standing horizontal in a corner with photos of *King Tut* and the *X-Clan* above it. Looking towards the back of the classroom, they see more photos of *Dr. Yoseph Ben Jochannan, Neely Fuller, Jr.*, and Egyptian Pyramids pinned on the walls. They observe how the desks are lined.

While the young man continues to view the classroom, the woman notices a groomed man in a grey suit staring out the window, and with a country tone she says, "Excuse me, sir. Are you Mr. Jones?"

Turning proficiently around noticing the woman and her son, Mr. Jones innocently says, "Yes, ma'am. And excuse me, you are....?"

Discerning his nice haircut and thick beard, she says, "My name is Mrs. Tabitha Thomas. This is my son, David Thomas, Jr. He will be in ya class this school year and I just want to formally intaduce myself to ya and let ya know that if ya have any trouble out of him to please give me a call." She grabs a pen and a small writing pad out of her purse and writes down her contact information. "Here's my cell. Call or text me if ya have any issues outta dis one."

Clutching on his shirt and moping, David Jr. says "I'm not going to act up! Why do you always do this?"

Anthony Crawford, Jr.

Mr. Jones interrupts and says, "I believe you young man. Relax on your mama. She just cares about you. There are too many young brothers who do not get the privilege to have the type of mother that will bring up to the school to meet their teachers. Appreciate her."

"He's right, DJ…… and let go of ya shirt before ya wrinkle it," she says gently. He can get a bit disruptive. Just call me and I'll set him straight," she says.

"There will be no need for that, right king?" Mr. Jones asks while staring at David Jr. waiting for his response.

"Yes, sir," David Jr. says irritably. He looks at his mother and asks, "Can we go now?"

"Okay, hold on," she says. She then turns to Mr. Jones and says, "Thank ya, Mr. Jones. It's good to see a black man as a teacha these days. The kids need someone who they can relate to."

"Ase'. This is my way of paying it forward."

"Nice, nice, very nice."

"I can tell by your accent that you're not from here. Where are you from?"

"I wa' born 'nd raised in Iberville Projects in the lost state of Louisiana, sir. Right before *Katrina* hit, me and my family moved right along to find a place where their be good negros and some southern hospitality. Went to college, met my husband, had some chillren' and been doin' this motherly wife thing ever since, don't judge me I don't look like what I've been through," Tabitha comically concludes.

Mr. Jones laughs, saying, "You are hilarious!"

"Why thank you Mr. Jones! Ya seem like an awesome good teacher, yaself..."

Humbly, Mr. Jones says, "I believe this is a part of my purpose, Mrs. Thomas. The children are the real teachers. They teach me more than I teach them. I really believe this next generation of children will be the ones to change this world. I want to help inspire their revolution," he says humbly.

While nodding her head in agreement, Mrs. Thomas says, "Amen to that, Mr. Jones, my husband is heavily involved ina church and, som'times, he doesn't have the time to be there for DJ like I would like him to be. Do ya think ya can kind of help my son? Ya know, just be like a mentor to him?" She leans in and whispers, "He was bullied at his last school. He may com' off a bit antisocial. I told him he need to learn how to fight and fight those bullies but his daddy just don't want him growing up dat way.... but all kids needs to fight or how else will they learn to take up for themselves right? I don't know......."

Darryl pauses for a moment to ponder on Mrs. Thomas's statement and firmly says, "I don't tolerate bullying. That's a pet peeve of mine. I would do my best to ensure that he's getting the guidance and lessons that he needs in life. I'd be a fool to pass up on this opportunity." He enthusiastically says as he walks them to his door. "Which church do you all attend?"

"We attends 18th St. Missionary Baptist Church; my husband is the Deacon there," she says devotedly.

Smiling, he cheerfully says, "I heard they have a nice choir there." After his statement, he notices her energy shift as if he said something or reminded her of something that she does not want to think about. A brief and awkward silence fills their distance. To break the tension, Mr. Jones says, "Hey! Ummm...... It was nice meeting you, Mrs. Thomas."

"It is nice meeting ya too, Mr. Jones." As she's walking out the door she says, "Rememba to call me when he bein' a pain in da butt."

After laughing out loud, he says, "I will remember that, Mrs. Thomas. Thank you! Have a good day."

After they walk out, he turns to stare out the window in attempt to catch the previous feeling he felt before Mrs. Thomas and David Jr. walked in. He then sits at one of the desks and ponders on the lesson plans he constructed for next upcoming week. He starts looking around his room in grace. Feeling happy and excited about the new semester.

He looks at the time on his phone, remembers that he and his best friend were meeting at a Kemet for their Happy Hour and Appetizers event later this evening. He gets up, grabs his lap top bag,

Anthony Crawford, Jr.

walks to the door, looks around his room, and turns his classroom's lights out. He then closes his door and locks the classroom door.

While walking to the car, he sees the science teacher, Ms. Luna Hall, talking with the principal.

"You two have a good weekend!" Darryl yells.

"Have a good weekend, Mr. Jones!" The principal replies, but Ms. Hall stays silent as they both catch eyes.

(Last year, Darryl and Ms. Luna Hall dated for a few months. Luna was new to the school and city. Darryl helped her get adjusted to the school, hung out in her classroom during lunch, and helped organize her room.

They conversed about Luna's hometown, her childhood, her education, the reason for becoming an educator, her ultimate life goals, dreams, and aspirations. She felt comfortable and not as nervous about moving to a new city, because of Darryl's interest in wanting to know more about her.

They instantly connected. He took her out on dates to many of the black owned restaurants in the city. He would always say, "This is the heart of the city." He introduced Luna to many of the local community leaders in an effort that she would get involved and become a mentor for the young women. He helped make her new beginning feel like home.

She was fascinated by his service to the youth, his love for the arts, and how encouraging he is towards everyone. His outlook on life kept her intrigued and in wonder. She learned a lot about herself through his analytical views on the issues that Black people endure. She developed strong feelings for Darryl.

One day at school, Darryl walked into Luna's classroom with lunch he made from home. He greeted her with charm and said, "Hola Miss Luna."

Smiling, she said, "Hola Darryl," while he handed her a warm plastic container with food inside it, a couple of small napkins, and plastic fork. They hugged and, in that moment, she was taken into an

Black Pain't, Vol. I

abyss by his scent. He sent chills up her spine while gently rubbing her lower back.

As they slowly released from each other's embrace, he asked, "How's your day going? What did you teach today?"

She broke free from her thoughts and removed the lid from the container laying it on her desk. She stuck her fork in the middle of the food and stirred it around allowing the noodles to wrap around its teeth. She then lifted the fork near her jaw and said, "It's going great. I am teaching them the fundamentals of stem cells." She blew on the fork to cool the food and slowly rammed it in her mouth savoring the taste.

"Stem cells? What about stem cells? The only thing I know about science is that I am here, I take up space, and I matter!" Darryl said as they both laughed.

She said, "Stem Cells are the atoms in your body that are able to travel through any and all parts of your body to heal, fix, duplicate, speak, enlighten, build, create, grow, move, transform, transcend, and perform miracles."

He hesitantly asked, "Oh, okay. Well, since we are cells, and cells can duplicate themselves then is there another me out there in the world, or is that an analogy for soul mates, or what?"

"I don't know. That's an interesting question. I know you are not a twin, so technically there can't be another one of you out there. Umm, if it was an analogy for soul mates then that would disrupt society's views on relationships and dating."

He sat down in a desk and asked, "Why?"

She thought for a second, smiled, and said, "Because the only way to tell if someone is your soul mate is to court with that someone. Courting means seeing if the two are God's choice. It means no sexual activity until marriage." She shrugged her shoulders and continued eating.

"Are you able to be with someone and not have sex with them until marriage?"

She smiled and confidently said, "Yes. Yes, I can."

Anthony Crawford, Jr.

He smiled admiring her confidence. She put her head down in embarrassment as he graciously stared at her. His loving energy sent her waves. He asked, "Why are you going in your shy-shell, turtle?"

"I'm not a turtle," she said as they laughed. "Stop staring at me. You're just making me blush."

He smiled and said, "My bad." They ate their lunch and conversed more. Luna thought about Darryl heavily for the remainder of that school day.

That weekend, Luna found herself at her apartment feeling lonely and homesick. She was missing her family. She cooked pasta and called Darryl to see if he would like to join her for dinner and a movie. Darryl showered and rushed over to her apartment.

When he arrived, he knocked on the door, and she instantly walked to the door to open it. As soon as she opened the door, he melted while gazing at her golden skin. She had on a white tank top and one can tell that she did not have on a bra. She wore some pink shorts that stopped at her upper thighs. She was shaped like a spoon. He thought to himself, "Damn, her body is perfect," while watching her put a robe on and wrapping her braids into a ponytail with a rubber band.

Walking through the doorway and closing the door, he noticed the dimmed lighting in her apartment. She had elephant souvenirs lying around the room, pictures of her with other women making a triangle symbol with their hands, and lit candles on her counters. He said, "You have a beautiful home. Care to give me a tour?" She gave him a tour around her small, quaint apartment. He joked about how much of a neat freak she was.

They sat on her sofa to eat dinner. They joked and laughed about the things that were going on at work. He brought her up-to-date on everything like who didn't like who, the "bad kids," the white teachers that aren't able to reach the "bad kids," and curriculum that doesn't contribute to the advancement of a young Black man and woman. They were drifting from conversation to conversation hardly watching the movie.

Black Pain't, Vol. I

He was a different vibe to her. She was attracted to his intellect, his pro-blackness, and the way he would look into her eyes and down to her lips when they conversed. She loved his stature, the fact that he wore a shirt and tie, slacks, and dress shoes every day during the week at work. She loved the fact that he was a gentleman. She felt a strong physical attraction, but never expressed her feelings to him.

While he was talking, she got lost in his words. He spoke in a zealous tone about how we all live in a system that is set up for black people to economically, mentally, physically, sexually, and internally suffer. She got so lost in his words that she fell into a slight trance. While in her trance, he yelled her name three times to snap her out of it.

"Are you okay?"

"Yes, I'm sorry. I was just visualizing what you were saying," she said. "Didn't you say that you write poetry?"

"Yes. Yes, I do. I usually don't share it with others."

"Why not?"

"I don't like the attention I get from them. Plus, most of them are a bit erotic. I wouldn't want anyone looking at me like I'm some sort of freak-a-zoid," he said innocently as they both laughed.

"Can I hear one? I promise I won't judge you."

He nods his head and reaches for his phone in his front right pocket. He scrolls down the screen clicking on apps to get to the notepad on his phone. He looked at her as if he was undressing her with his eyes.

"Okay, I'll read just one poem. This one is called Making Flowers." He romantically read:

"We walked into the room,
immediately melted into the Divine.
The sensations of mental penetrations were aligned,
we stared at each other, eye to eye.
We allow the light to light our flame that gave us a burning desire
I put my everything into her everything, and we became everything.
It's amazingly crazy knowing that she's the girl in all my dreams.

Anthony Crawford, Jr.

I can feel her heart beating fast as she gasps.
She holds her breath while looking up to the ceiling.
Something that's beyond nature is in her, she embraces the feeling.
I whispered in her ear, I grab her fiercely
she held on, and, for the goodness of sake,
she bloomed like flowers, from the love that we make."

While Darryl was reading, she felt a wave of wetness dripping from her vagina that almost went through the pink shorts that she wore. She switched her position on the couch and crossed her legs so he wouldn't notice. She began to sweat a little.

"What you think? Don't lie." He asked inflexibly.

"It was……good. Real good, actually. Is it hot in here to you? Is my air conditioner on?" She asked as she got up to go check the thermostat. He followed right behind her.

"I don't know why it's so hot in here. It never gets this….." she paused when she turned around and saw him standing tall with his wide shoulders and toned torso. He pinned her against the wall. She moaned while closing her eyes. He began kissing her on her neck, down to her breast, and eventually got on his knees to kiss her stomach. She began moaning and groaning while he was kissing her body. He pulled her shorts off. He noticed the wetness dripping down her leg. He licked the stream from her leg to the inside of her thighs. He pulled her panties off, lifted her leg against his right shoulder, and began to lick and suck on her vagina lips. The moaning became more intense. She was biting her bottom lip and grabbing his head with her right hand while using the other hand to hold herself up against the wall.

Two minutes went by, and he could feel the grip that she had on his head getting stronger. Her breathing was getting deeper and deeper. She grabbed his head during her orgasm. Her legs vibrated as she pushed his head away. He carried her back to the sofa and took off his pants. She was startled by how greatly endowed he is.

He spread her legs and spit on her vagina. He rubbed the saliva with his right hand around her vagina and put his finger inside her to

Black Pain't, Vol. I

see how wet she was. He whispered, "Damn, you're wet," in her ear and gently put his penis inside her. She grasped for air. She closed her eyes and tried to visualize those flowers he recited to bloom all around her living room until it formed a lovely garden.

 For about fifteen minutes, they engaged in multiple positions before she told him that she couldn't take anymore. He slowly and gently pulled himself out of her. Confidently, he asked, "Are you okay?"

 "I think so. I can't move," she said while lying on the edge of the sofa motionless. They both laughed and laid there for the rest of the night.

 During the "wee" hours, he carried her to her bedroom and left without a trace. When she woke up, she checked her apartment and wondered where he went. She quickly tried to contact him but didn't get a response from him. She texted him and left voicemails on his phone throughout the day, still no response. She felt confused and played but gave him the benefit of the doubt.

 "Maybe he lost his phone," She thought. "Or maybe he's busy doing something important."

 That Monday, at work, Darryl didn't go to her classroom to say good morning like he usually did. He didn't go to her room during lunch. She felt her heart aching and her mind racing back and forth about his actions. She saw him during a staff meeting after school. He never looked her way or acknowledged her existence. When she got home, she cried her eyes out.

 Vulnerable and hurt, Luna felt used. She didn't understand Darryl's actions and secret motives. She thought they shared a great friendship. She felt ashamed for opening herself up to him. During school, Luna would stare at Darryl searching for an answer and the truth from Darryl.)

 Walking up to the bar in Kemet, Darryl sees his best friend waiting and says, "Wassup Alvin!"

 While shaking hands, "Ahh, man, wassup Darryl, how was work?"

Anthony Crawford, Jr.

Darryl sits down on a barstool and says, "Same shit, different toilet, brother. How's Corporate America treating you?" He begins looking around at all the people inside the restaurant.

"It's perfect if I stay in my lane and do my job. The white folks leaves me 'lone," Alvin says wittily. "You know how it goes."

While they are at the bar, they are talking more about work, going back to college for their doctorate degrees, and they are discussing the unjustified police shootings and beatings that millions of Black people are protesting and marching against.

As they eat the bar's special wings and drinking their usual Old Fashions, their usual waitress walks in and walks behind the bar. Wearing black tank top, black shorts that come up to the middle of her thighs, and some black tennis shoes. She greets them, saying, "Wassup, gentlemen? How are we this evening?"

"Wow, you're usually here when I get here. Where you been, Trina? Trouble in paradise?" Alvin comically asks while she is clocking in.

"Some things came up, boys. Y'all know how that goes, right?" She says sarcastically.

Confusedly, Alvin says, "Ahh, man, what you mean? We're good guys."

"All those ratchet stories you two tell me about and the women you two have done wrong, please don't come for me unless I send for you," she securely says flipping her hair and rolling her eyes.

"Dang, our bad. We were just worried about you. This will be the last time we check up on your mean ass," Darryl says candidly.

She sarcastically says, "Oh, please. Spare me. How was the work week?"

"If it was any better, I'd have to pay taxes," Darryl says spontaneously as he takes a sip of his drank.

Looking around the bar at the beautiful women, Alvin bluntly says "Just trying to make it."

Their typical conversations with Trina are about relationships, religion, 'white supremacy,' and reminiscing about past events and incidents from their life. Trina remembered when Darryl was telling her about.

Trina asks, "Are you two still attending that event you told me about?"

"Which one?" Darryl asks.

She tries to remember and can say, "Something by someone name James or something."

"Oh, you're talking about Aaron James's Remove that Ribbon speech," Darryl says.

She outspokenly says, "Yes."

"If anyone's going to be there, you know Darryl's going to be there. You should attend, Trina," Alvin encouragingly says.

"What's it about again?"

Darryl says, "Remove that Ribbon is an evening event featuring Aaron James. Aaron James travels across the world speaking about self-love, forgiveness, societal issues, relationships, the importance of being happy, and living out our dreams. A lot of college students, political leaders, teachers, community activist, church members, parents, and teenagers attend his event because of his views and outlook on life."

She contemplates and says, "I'll think about it. I know my sister would probably love to go. She loves those types of things."

"How is she doing?" Alvin asks keenly. "I hear a lot of great things about her in the community. Especially about her dance program. My company is looking to make a nice donation."

As Trina is serving drinks to other customers, she says, "She's good. Still getting on my damn nerves."

Usually, Alvin would stay until the bar closed to talk to Trina. Darryl always leaves a couple hours early to go to the bookstore near his apartment to buy a good book to read over the weekend. Darryl loses track of time and notices that he has less than forty minutes to make it to the bookstore. He hastily leaves Trina a large tip and daps up Alvin as he departs.

While pulling up to the bookstore, he notices more cars outside in the parking lot than usual. He could not park in his usual parking spot, so he parks on the side of the building. He hops out of his car, closes the door, locks it, and walks towards the store.

In the store, he makes his way towards the African American section where he usually chooses his books. On the way there, he notices a beautiful, mocha latte-skinned woman standing in aisle of the section. He observes her while she skims through a book. He glances at her natural hair, her dark-red glasses, and the afro-centric style of clothes she has on. He traces his eyes through her hourglass shaped body.

Time seems to have stopped as he walks towards her, which gave him enough time to detect the book she's holding. Once he gets near her, he asks, "Hey, Queen, how are you?"

She looks at him with a dark shimmer and candidly says, "I'm fine, Thank you." She proceeds to skim.

Noticing the blunt tone in her voice, he cautiously asks, "What are you reading?"

She takes an irritably, deep breath and replies, "*The Fire Inside: The Story and Poetry of Nikki Giovanni.*"

Darryl, being very intrigued, notices her unfriendly body gesture and says, "Nikki Giovanni's poems are like feeling the pain of many Black people, especially black women. I love how she forms her words. So unfathomable and influential for only a conscious mind could understand. She's a Queen worth getting to know and worth reading. Those that understand and read works like hers have a great deal of consciousness. Wouldn't you agree?"

"Yes," she says uninterestingly.

He looks away to quickly think of another question to ask and asks, "Do you write poetry?"

She swiftly closes the book, gazes at him to observe his demeanor, and quickly speaks. "I write a little bit of poetry. I'm more into reading, blogging, and exercising. Well, bye."

As she begins to walk away, he enthusiastically asks "What do you normally blog about?"

Black Pain't, Vol. I

She stops herself, instantly think then impatiently replies, "Liberation, injustice, the Feminisms of today's society, and altering the minds of young girls that idolize these women on television that portray women as trophies, strippers, sex-toys, and bitches."

Darryl, with an impressive expression, says, "I feel and understand where you're coming from. Too many Nicki Minaj's and not enough Nikki Giovanni's, huh?"

Zealously and affirmatively, she replies, "Exactly! That's why it's psychologically important that we teach our young ones these things or we're doomed."

He grins in amusement as she speaks with such passion about the topics that he has an interest in. He says, "It's very interesting to hear that. I believe that the women and the youth will be the two driving forces that will change this world. I don't meet too many that have your type of mind set."

"It's interesting that you say that sir," she says sardonically.

"Why don't I ever see you here?"

"I don't come here. My protégé from the school that where I work at asked me if there were any books on Nikki Giovanni. Her teacher told the class to choose someone from history that they would want to do a presentation on. She chose Nikki Giovanni. Funny thing is that our library doesn't have many books on 'African Americans' being the true Natives of this country. Just the same old lies and conceptualisms about Dr. Martin Luther King, Jr., slavery, and the underground railroad, Nat Turner. So, I took the liberty in getting a few books for her to help her with her research so she can complete her assignment."

"Wait a minute, wait a minute...... what lies were told about our history?"

"That's a different conversation for another time."

"Well, give me one lie."

"Okay............ remember, you asked for it!"

"Try me...."

"Okay, which one stood out to you the most?"

Anthony Crawford, Jr.

"Out of the ones you mentioned?"

"Yes."

"Nat Turner for sure. I seen the movie, *Birth of a Nation*! The one with Nate Parker as Nat Turner. Best shit on television since *The Watchmen Series* with Regina King!"

"Okay......" she says, giving him a squinting look. "Nat Turner never existed......"

"Whoooooaaaaaa.......hol up, now, I know...."

"Hey, you ask for the truth, I know the truth is hard to handle, but I'm just giving facts about someone that never existed."

Talking over her, he says, "That's just a crazy statement to make! They're books, documentaries, and movies over this man's life."

Interloping, she says, "First off, who is 'they?' and second, you know Willie Lynch didn't exist, but 'they' have books, documentaries, and movies over this man's 'life.'"

"I'mma need some evidence or your sources on that," he says skeptically, feeling internally defeated but finds interest in wanting to know the truth. He continues, "Look, I'm not surprised. A lot of school curriculums doesn't even have many of our ancestral history or our true leaders in them. Our education system wasn't built to educate our own anyway, so it's expected. Then they taint the history that they do put in the school's history books. They're even rewriting history saying that our ancestors wanted to work those slave-shifts. Like we weren't forced to integrate into this bizarre democracy. I commend you on what you're doing. What do you do at the school?" He asks stimulatingly.

She peeks at her watch and says, "I'm the librarian."

"I'm sorry, I'm not meaning to hold you up, Miss......." he says while holding his hand out, waiting and hoping she'll shake it and tell him her name.

She looks at his hand to see if his nails are dirty. Since they are not, she doubtfully shakes it, and says, "..........Patricia."

"Miss Patricia. I'm Darryl Jones. I'm a history teacher at George Washington Carver Middle School," he says politely with a charming smile.

Black Pain't, Vol. I

"That's good, Darryl. I'm pretty sure the kids love you. What brings you here at this time of the night on a Friday?"

He grins and says, "I come here every Friday night to get a book or two so I can read over the weekend. I tend to trap myself in the house to escape from the realities of this world."

"What or who is it that you're hiding from?" She asks inconspicuously.

"Me," he says instantly.

Confusedly, she asks, "You? Why are you hiding from yourself?"

For a moment, he ponders on many of his darkest secrets. He stops himself from telling her his first thought of interior conflicts that he battles with and says, "Because everyone has their flaws and battles that they must deal with internally. I just embrace mine and live a private life until they are completely under control and there is peace and understanding within me. I choose to deal with my battles alone."

She notices his change in tone and sarcastically asks, "You seem like the type that waits on 'Jesus' to come and save you?"

"No, I'm not. Matter of fact, I sort of struggle with religion, so, no, I'm not waiting on 'Jesus.' I only want a wondrous woman to come and save me. Not man," he says flirtatiously.

"Oh, I'm pretty sure you have a lot of wondrous women in your life," she says mockingly.

He chuckles and says, "Naw, I don't. I've had my share of breaking of the hearts and had my heart broken to know what I really want and what I value in a relationship. So, I choose to be alone until I can find that."

Irritably, she says, "Yeah, yeah, yeah. Whatever you say sir. Funny how you don't know me and bring up relationships. And then you say you're waiting on a wondrous woman to come and save you? That says a lot about our men. Why don't you put a bib on and go back to live with your mama?"

Noticing her irritation, he says, "If I believe women and the youth will be the ones to change the world, I might as well get one that

Anthony Crawford, Jr.

will change my world, too." He watches her as she marinates on his statement. He can tell that she feels a mental sensation while listening to him. "What about you? Why don't you have a ring on your finger? Someone as smart and beautiful as you shouldn't be single."

Calmly, she says, "That's because our men don't know what it means to be a man. Most have to grow up and do some soul searching themselves. It takes years for them to do so. I don't have time to train, teach, tolerate, or baby someone from the male species."

Confidently, he says, "Understandable."

"There aren't really any good men left. That's why most women are single, miserable, lesbian, independent, or transferring to white men."

Nodding his head in agreement, "I agree and respect your point of view, Queen. Have you ever read the Willie Lynch Letter?"

"Of course," Patricia inauthentically says, knowing that Willie Lynch never existed, but she wants to hear his ignorance, so she allows him to speak. She drifts off thinking about how being around men makes her feel.

Darryl's blabbing internally sends her back through time…....

(A few ago Patricia's boyfriend began to change after she graduated from college. He always seemed angry. He complained a lot, became jealous when guys would look at her, and became very territorial. She wouldn't make anything out of it because he was struggling in trade school and was getting overworked at his job. He became very defensive.

She used to come home late from hanging out with her friends. It would make him angry, but he let it boil up inside. She wanted to enjoy her life and didn't always want to be in a negative space with him.

One night, she was out a little later than usual. He was up waiting on her to come home and, as soon as she walked through the door, he raised up from the couch he was lying in. He asked her, "Where have you been all night, Patricia?"

"I was out with my friends."

Black Pain't, Vol. I

"What friends?" He asked angrily.

"The only friends I have," she mockingly said while going into the bathroom to wash the make-up from her face.

A few minutes went by, and he walked into the bathroom to question her about where she was, what she was doing, and who she was with. She ignored him and walked into her room taking off her clothes to put her pajamas on. He went back to the living room to calm down but got angrier. When she went to the kitchen to get some water, he got up from the couch, smiled and calmly asked her, "Where were you, Patricia?"

"Dennis! What's wrong with you?" She irately asked as she tried to walk pass him. He instantly punched her across her face. She flew against the counter and grabbed her face in shock. She hopelessly frowned at him with fear in her eyes. He grabbed her shoulders and slammed her against the wall making a few pictures fall and break on the floor.

She blacked out for a quick moment as her heart began beating fast. She slowly fell to floor crying in disbelief. "You hit me, Dennis," she said screeching.

He stood over her with his fist bald up and yelled, "MUTHA FUCKA, WHEN I ASK YOU A QUESTION, YOU TELL ME! I'VE BEEN WAITING ON YOU ALL NIGHT. I CALLED AND TEXT YOUR ASS!"

She cried and flinched whenever he would raise his hand. She helplessly lied on the floor. He repeatedly took deep breaths, bent over to Patricia, and remorsefully said, "I'm sorry, Patricia. Please forgive me. I'm sorry. Don't leave me. I'm sorry."

She looked at him with despair and said, "You hurt me! Why would you hit me? What did I do?"

"I'm sorry. I love you, Patricia. Please don't leave me. I need you. I'll die without you. We've been arguing a lot lately. Things aren't going right for me at school. My job is treating me like shit. I just feel scared that you're going to leave me," he said as a horrifying

Anthony Crawford, Jr.

atmosphere filled the room. He began to cry and said, "Please, please! I'm sorry Patricia. Don't leave me baby."

She felt sorry for him. She scarcely asked, "Why would you think that I would leave you?"

"I don't know. Who wants to be with someone who can't even handle his responsibilities as a man?" He said picking her up off the floor. He carried her in the bedroom and laid her on the bed. He went into the bathroom and grabbed a washcloth to wipe her tears.

Patricia couldn't sleep that night. She was so fearful for her life. She felt like she needed to tell someone, but the love that she had for him kept her from getting him in trouble. He had never put his hands on her before and she prayed that it was the last time.

Their relationship got worse. Some mornings, he would kick her out the bed because she took a few seconds to turn her alarm off. He would aggressively pin her against the wall and slap her for not cleaning their apartment. He hated hearing stories of her and her male co-workers; he would always accuse her of cheating. She hated going out with him because he would threaten her in public.

Some days, Patricia had to cover her face up with a lot of make-up and would wear dark shaded glasses to hide the lumps and bruises by her eyes from the many times he would punch her. She had to wear hair wraps to hide the scars on her head from when he banged her head against the bathroom mirror. She wore turtleneck sweaters to hide the bruises on her neck.

They lived together and she wanted to leave, but he would always say that he loved her and that he would kill himself if she was to ever leave him. The fear and the pain were so damaging that she felt that no one else would understand, help, want, or respect her. When she built up the strength to leave, she felt that no one else would look past the pain that he inflicted on her, and that no one else could love her the way he did.

He made her stop talking to some of her friends and she was too embarrassed to reach out to her family. Their sex wasn't meaningful, the words, "I love you," didn't mean the same; she heavily cried most nights and was very fearful of her life. She felt as though he was going to kill her whether she stayed or left.

At work, some of the teachers noticed the bruises, but never said anything to her about them. One day, at work, Patricia was feeling nauseated and dizzy. She went to the bathroom and sadly stared into the mirror. She removed the glasses and took the scarf off her head. She began to cry. She didn't know the woman she stared at in the mirror. Suddenly, a little girl in a school uniform came in. The little girl's hair was frizzy, and her shoes looked old. She saw all the cuts and bruises on Patricia's face and head.

The little girl softly and innocently asked her, "Are you okay?"

Crying heavily, Patricia was able to mumble, "Yes," out and tried to get up from the floor but couldn't because her legs were very heavy and weak like someone had broken them.

The little girl sat close to her, wrapped her arms around her, held her tight, and said, "My mama had those same black paintings on her face. I tried to wipe them off her face, but the paint was hurting her."

"Where is your mother now?"

"She's an angel now."

Patricia observed the girl's eyes and noticed that she was crying, too. They both found the strength to stand up from being on the bathroom floor while holding hands. Patricia felt a sense of hope and urgency for herself for the first time in months. She eventually went to the police and told the police everything that had been going on with her and Dennis. She moved out that day leaving a lot of her things behind. That same week, she got a restraining order against Dennis.

Patricia later learned that the little girl's mother died from domestic violence. The little girl was forced to live with her aunt and her six cousins in a three-bedroom house. Ever since that day, Patricia decided to mentor the little girl and has been totally committed to being in her life.

Patricia met with the aunt during a parent-teacher conference. The aunt asked, "What made you want to mentor my niece?"

Anthony Crawford, Jr.

Patricia said, "She saved my life.")

"She saved my life," Patricia says out loud.

He confusedly asks, "What?"

She snaps out of her daydream and says, "I read it once when I was young. Obviously, I need to read it again. That's what you were going to suggest right?"

He smirks and says, "Yes, please do. It'll be a good source to have knowledge of as to why most men are 'no good.' Though Willie Lynch is a myth, the concepts, and methods that the letter mentions was still used against our ancestors. Our condition takes us all the way back to slavery. That's why we need to be patient and compassionate with our people. After you finish reading it, let me know what you think."

"Oh, wow, he does know that Willie Lynch isn't real." She thinks to herself as his knowledge supersedes her feelings. "How am I supposed to tell you what I think?"

"Well, we can exchange numbers, we can schedule a time for us to have lunch, we can meet at a coffee shop... or..."

She interrupts him and says, "Or......... we can allow the synchronicities of life bring us back around one another to discuss the letter. How about that?"

He smiles and says, "What are the odds of that happening?"

"Oh ye' of little faith?" She cleverly asks as she walks to the counter to pay for her books.

Darryl, in delight, stares at her while she walks away to pay for her book, hoping and praying that they will soon meet again somehow, some way. He then proceeds to the African American section to select a book. He chooses *New Dimensions in Black History* by Dr. Yosef Ben-Jockannan. He pays for it at the counter and walks out of the bookstore.

While walking to his car, he looks to the nightly sky noticing that there are more stars out tonight than any other night. It was as though angels were trying to communicate with him. He takes it as a sign and continues to walk to his car. He gets in slowly while staring at the nightly sky. He then shakes his head, starts the car, and drives away.

When he pulls up to his apartment, he checks the mailbox and grabs the mail along with a small package. Before walking into the apartment building, he stops to view the rare constellations in the sky. He feels as though it is a sign and proceeds to walk inside. He says, "Peace and light," to the receptionist and walks to the elevator. He pushes the bottom by a closed elevator door, and, within seconds, "*BING*" goes the elevator. It opens and he gets on pushing Floor 20.

While on the elevator he can't help but to think about Patricia and what would it be like to be with her. The elevator stops on his floor and the doors split apart. He walks up to his door, unlocks it, and opens it. He walks in, hangs his keys on the key rack that was pinned on the wall in the front hallway. He turns on a light that lit the balcony area of his huge studio apartment. He walks towards the windows and looks out towards the city's lights.

Then he looks around his studio apartment just to get a sense of homeliness. He walks to the kitchen area to put his new book on the kitchen table. He unties his tie and removes it from his shirt. He walks towards the bedroom area unbuttoning his shirt and sits on the edge of his bed. He takes his shoes off, slides the shoes under his bed, and falls back on the bed.

So many thoughts going through his mind, he thinks about his family, work, sex-life, and the responsibilities he must handle. These are the hours when he feels a sense of loneliness and vulnerability, so he tends to write poetry to ease his mind and fight the illusions of being alone.

He starts to think about the two white doves he saw flying across the sky. Then he thinks about Patricia and their conversation. He wondered about what it would be like to be with someone as dynamic as her. He admires her beauty and how she embraces who she really is in this world. She serves as his muse this evening.

He takes his wallet out of his left back pocket, his chap sticks out of his left front pocket, and places them on his nightstand. He then

Anthony Crawford, Jr.

takes off his clothes and tosses them onto the floor. He takes his phone from off the nightstand, scrolls to the notepad, and begins to type:

Saw her at a bookstore
in the small African American book section.
I noticed her natural hair and her melaninated complexion.
I walked past the aisle hoping she'll see me and my intellectual ways,
because it's rare seeing a black man buying books these days.
She was too much into her book to notice me,
so I stepped up to her and said,
"Hi, I'm Darryl, and your aura is potent."
She smiles and says,
"Hi, Darryl. I'm flowered and flattered, but you can call me Lotus."
Her title made sense,
but I had to stay focused.
"Do you come here often?"
I asked as I stuttered over my words,
staring into the secrets of her eyes,
I couldn't help but to absorb.
We were walking around the store conversing,
she did not blush from my flirting,
but she knew that I was an interesting person.
She didn't even mind my cursing,
I noticed that she's not the type to run game on,
so I didn't.
I wanted to express my attraction to her,
but I kept it hidden.
I wanted to give her my card hoping she'd use it and call,
but I hadn't heard from her at all.

Black Pain't, Vol. I

Chapter 2:
Night Light

The professor passionately says, "You see class... we come from Kings, Queens, Gods, Goddess; we were Pharaohs. We were here first. Our ancient ancestors roamed the earth. They build nations. The Ancient Egyptians developed governments, an education system, and spirituality. Matter of fact, long before the Jesus Christ's story, there was Horus's story. Before the cross, there was the Ankh." The professor sees a student raising his hand. Noticing the student's unstylish dress and nappy, dreaded hair, he acknowledges him by saying, "Mr. Givens?"

"Dr. Carson, did the Ancient Egyptians have slaves?"

Dr. Carson replies, "No, they didn't."

"So who built the pyramids?"

Anthony Crawford, Jr.

While the professor begins walking around to the classroom podium,

A student yells out, "It could have been their servants or their prisoners of war that could have built the pyramids…...."

Another student says, "Servants? Prisoners? That sounds like a caste system similar to the mass incarcerations of this country. Is that why Moses came to free them?"

"Son, first off, the Nephilim built the pyramids. Second, I can assure you they are not the same. The Ancient Egyptian's society had people like you and me in control and in power. It could not have been ruled the way that Europeans colonized and ruled because they were absent of light, we are the light."

"Dr. Carson, you always talk down on society and how it limits the people's natural born abilities. You say that society divides people into classes based off of their finances, skin color, and keeps them divided amongst one another. Did the Ancient Egyptian's society do the same? Am I supposed to disregard the ancient Pharaoh's power over people because they were Black? You talk down on religion, but the Ancient Egyptians had a religion."

An incomprehensible silence filled the room as tension begins to flare. "Alright, class! Please check your syllabus for next weeks' assignments that are due. This is graduate school. I shouldn't have to keep reminding you all about work that you're responsible for in this course, any questions?" The professor stands on the side of the podium and patiently waits for any questions.

Mr. Givens raises his right hand again and Dr. Carson says, "Yes, Mr. Tony Givens. I should have known you would be the one with the question." The class laughs at the professor's comment.

"Dr. Carson, first off let me tell you that your light grey suit is sharper than a tat! Your tie compliments it," he says comically.

Dr. Carson looks around the room with a fake smile while the class laughs and walks away from the podium. He bluntly says, "Kissing ass for a better grade, Mr. Givens?"

Black Pain't, Vol. I

"Yes, sir! And I was just going to ask you about your plans for the weekend, sir," he says modestly.

Dr. Carson rudely says, "That's none of your business young grasshopper." He begins to mumble under his breath, "I shouldn't have to sit here and tell my personal life." He walks back to the podium and shuffles the papers that were on it.

"He was just asking a question," another student says aloud.

Dr. Carson gives the student a blight stare and says, "Ms. Knight, now if you want to get on my list of 'Reasons Why I Shouldn't Fail This Student' along with Mr. Givens, then I suggest you stay out of this and worry about next week's assignment! Class dismiss."

As all the students hastily grab their book bags, Dr. Carson announces, "Oh, and any student who attends Aaron James' speech next month will receive extra credit. I will be there with a sign-in sheet."

The students got up from their seats and walk out the door in an orderly fashion. Feeling disrespected, Jazmine Knight takes her time to leave the classroom. Tony Givens is waiting for her by the door. She passes by him not even noticing that he is there. "Jazmine!" He yells as she cringes and drops her books on the floor. He bends down to pick up her books and says, "My bad. Thank you for sticking up for me back there. I really appreciate you."

She irritably says, "Uggggh! Someone gotta stand up to him. He's an asshole!" She puts her books in her book bag, puts the straps over her shoulders, and continues to walk with Tony.

Noticing her anger, he says, "It's all love. I saw him last weekend. That's why I asked that question."

"Huh?" She says perplexedly. "For real? Where? Doing what?"

While walking beside her as they leave Carver Hall, he says, "He was with some sexy, BAD woman at my store. The girl looked around our age too. She was being loud and obnoxious; he seemed to be enjoying it. That was the weird part. They were being all hugged up and affectionate."

Shocked at what she just heard, she says, "He's rude and disrespectful, why would any woman want that?"

Anthony Crawford, Jr.

Showing understanding, he says "He's not rude and disrespectful, that's just his form of love. Plus, there's somebody out there for everyone. No matter how they act."

Pondering on his statement, she rhetorically asks, "If that's true, why are you still single, Tony?"

He slyly says, "I'm practicing self-control."

She thinks for a moment and asks, "Why self-control?"

Confidently, he says, "We all deal with at least one deadly sin, and mine just happen to be lust. I'm very sexual. I learned that early sex could ruin a relationship if the friendship isn't strongly built first. So I'm practicing self-control, so I won't hurt anyone."

"So you're saying that if two people are truly feeling each other, but then have sex early, you don't think that they will work out?" She says instantly.

He unpretentiously says, "Based off my experiences, it will not work out. Sex blinds us from our reality and drains us of pure energy, which eventually pushes us off of our individual paths. Or it could just be the challenge in the relationship aspect."

"That's the first time I have heard that. Especially from a man.... Good luck, because most women do want a man that knows how to touch her body and not just their mind," she says while patting him on his back.

He instantly asks, "What about her soul?"

She hesitates to speak, but can say, "Of course her soul; that's the obvious."

"But you didn't mention it."

She stops between the parking lot and the library to playfully mean mug him. After he notices that she wasn't walking with him, he turns around, and Jazmine scoffs, rolls her eyes, and sarcastically says, "MEN......"

"Anyways, what you got up for the rest of the day?"

"I have humanistic therapy in the next twenty minutes actually, and then I haveta-"

"Wait, wait, wait, humanistic therapy? What's that?"

Black Pain't, Vol. I

"It's like when it's a one-on-one session with you and a person and they're asking you questions so you can come to your own conclusions."

"I just thought that was called therapy," Tony says as he chuckles.

"Hmph.... typical.... but there are many different types of therapy, not knowing that the actual term 'therapy' is a medical treatment to help with some type of health problem. But humanistic therapy is the one I just explained, sir."

"Interesting....... I learn something new every day... thank you so much, Jazzzzz-mine."

"Whatever Tony!" Jazmine comically but snappishly says."

"What you go to 'huma-nistic' therapy for?" he comically but curiously asks.

"I'm a single mother, I'm in school, and I'm working; I pay my own bills...... I at least need a moment to see if I'm okay from a therapist's point of view. Someone who can ask the right questions."

"I ain't tryna be funny, but do you know, if you break up the word therapist, you get the-rapist?"

After a second of Jazmine giving him a blank stare, she politely says, "That was corny Tony."

"I wasn't trying to be funny or nothing...."

"Ummm hmph..."

"Okay, tell me about your therapist?"

"Mrs. Townsend," Jazmine blushingly says, thinking about all the times she reminded Jazmine about how beautiful and real she is. She really pushes Jazmine to be her best self. "Debra Townsend, she aight.... I mean, she keep me from spazzin'...... She's the only one who knows who Miracle's sperm donor is. Why? You want her number?"

"I might need it......"

"I'll send it to you or whatever," Jazmine gladly says. "You just make sure you take care of your assignments for next week, Tony."

As she continues to walk forward with him on the side of her, he says, "I always do my work ahead of time. I just wanted to see what

Anthony Crawford, Jr.

he was going to say to me due to our little run-in last weekend when I saw him with that woman. I spoke to him, and he looked at me like he couldn't believe I was there. I slid my assignments under his office door before I came to class today."

"Oh, wow, Tony! You're the asshole!" She hilariously says while they both laugh.

"So what are you doing this weekend? Any plans?"

She responds, "I have to work. What about you?"

He nods his head and says "I have to work all weekend too. Shit, gotta work tonight! I'm going to head there and just read over the assignments before I have to clock in. They just promoted me to assistant store manager which means more hours. But hey, if you and your daughter need some clothing or household appliances, just let me know and I got you."

"I appreciate the offer, Tony. I'll be sure to. Hey, when was the last time you talked to Rayven?" She asks as they begin to stroll down a sidewalk.

"It's been a minute," he says. "I haven't really heard from her since she moved back from college."

"That was damn near a couple of years ago, Tony. You helped her move into her apartment, right?"

"Right," he says grippingly. "That's your sorority sister, when was the last time you spoke with her?"

While exhaling, she says, "I haven't heard from her since last year. She doesn't even come to church anymore."

"Didn't you two sing in the choir together?"

"We did but I removed myself from out of that choir."

He interestingly asks, "Why?"

She thinks of the incident that occurred, but internally refuses to disclose it. She cautiously says, "The leadership there doesn't sit well in my spirit. I just go enjoy the service, praise God, and leave. Plus my daughter is in their daycare program. I must be a member of the church in order to have my daughter in the daycare program. Hey, are you attending Aaron James' speech? It's at my church."

Black Pain't, Vol. I

"Yes, I am. Though I don't need the extra credit, I heard about Aaron's perspectives on society and religion are worth listening to."

They walk to a stoplight, and she says, "You will love it. I can almost tell that's what you will be doing. Your views on life, society, and people are one of a kind. Many people need to hear your heart."

He smiles hard and says, "Thanks for prophesying on my life. I accept. Alright then Jazmine, I'll holla at you next week."

"Bye Tony," she says as they go their separate ways. She checks her text messages while walking to her car. She has an unread text message from her daughter's father. (She refers to him as her daughter's sperm donor). The text says, *"Hey, Is there anything you and Miracle need? I just got paid."*

She replies, *"No."*

By the time she arrives to the car, he texts back saying, *"Why do you never let me help!? That's my daughter too!"*

She ignores it by tossing her phone in her purse. She calmly puts her keys in the ignition and drives off from the parking lot.

When she gets to the 18th Street Missionary Baptist Church's Day Care Center, she sees the Deacon from her church. She observes his white button-up shirt, his black slacks, and shiny, black dress shoes. Knowing what she knows, she inconspicuously says, "Hey, Deacon Thomas."

Deacon Thomas guises at her in despair and replies, "Hey Sister Jazmine."

"How are you?" She scornfully asks while signing Miracle out in the day care's attendance sheet.

"I'm blessed and highly favored, Sister Jazmine. What about you?" he asks with a strong and articulate voice.

She sees through his rehearsed mannerisms and gives him a sly smile. Then she contemptuously says, "I'm blessed as well, sir," while shaking her head. "I'm looking forward to hearing your sermon this Sunday. Oh, and thank you for accepting Miracle into the church's day care center at the last minute."

Anthony Crawford, Jr.

Deacon Thomas begins to gradually sweat and says, "Jesus didn't turn the kids away when they approached him, why should we? That's how all the churches should be. Service to the people. Especially to their members."

One of the instructors walks in from a classroom with Miracle holding her hand. Miracle eagerly and happily runs to Jazmine and jumps into her arms.

While holding Miracle, Jazmine says, "Hey beautiful! How was your day?" in her motherly voice.

Soft and innocently Miracle says, "Good."

As they're walking out the day care, "What did you learn today?"

"1, 2, 3, 4, 5, 6, 7, 8, 9, 10!" Miracle says while Jazmine opens the door.

In shock, Jazmine says, "OH MY GOD! GOOD JOB PRINCESS!" She puts Miracle in her car seat. After safely strapping Miracle in her car seat, she closes the door, hastily walks to the driver's side door, gets in, and drives off heading to their apartment.

Once they got home, Jazmine's mother calls her on her cellphone. Jazmine takes a deep breath and answers the phone, "Hey, Mama."

"Hey, baby! How's my grandbaby?"

"She's fine Mama. Growing up so fast and she's very smart."

"Sounds just like how you were when you were a baby. Have you heard anything from that nigga, and you know who I'm talking about?"

Irately, Jazmine replies, "No mama!"

Instantly, Jazmine's mother says, "I'm glad you put his ass on child support. How did you two meet again?"

Jazmine takes a deep breath because she knows where this conversation is heading, and she doesn't want to discuss it. She says, "Mama, I told you......"

Black Pain't, Vol. I

(From Jazmine's perspective, a few years ago, during her senior year of college, she went home while the school was out for spring break. Her high school friends wanted to take her out to celebrate her upcoming graduation. They discovered a new club downtown called RED'S and decided to go.

While at RED'S they all sat in the V.I.P. Section, had a few drinks, and danced. One of her good friends, Ella, invited one of her "Fuck Boys" to come and told him to bring some friends so her girlfriends can have some masculine energy. He showed up with a group of guys and they all joined them in the V.I.P. section.

After an hour or so, Ella, wearing a short black dress with light green pumps that complimented her almond skin, sat by Jazmine, and whispered in her ear, "Girl, the one in the white thinks you're cute."

"Who is he?"

"His name is Alvin, girl. He's Darryl's best friend. He's almost down with grad school. He works as a manager for a corporation that specializes in distribution. He's making a lot of money and he's also single and ready to mingle, girl! I can get him to come over here for you," Ella said urgently.

"I don't know about that. I'm tipsy. And I'm......" as Jazmine tried to finish her statement, Ella stood up, walked to Alvin, pulled him to the side, and said something in his ear. Alvin looked up at Jazmine lusting over the dark blue sequin party dress that she wore with the black heels that toned out her legs and her caramel complexion. While Ella was talking to Alvin, Jazmine swiftly turned her head away hoping he didn't see her staring.

Alvin, wearing a white button up with white pants, a black corduroy blazer, and black dress shoes, walked up to her and said, "Jazmine.... is it?"

She noticed his tall, athletic physique and dark skin. She friendly said, "Yes that's me."

"I'm Alvin."

"Nice to meet you, Alvin."

Anthony Crawford, Jr.

"Congratulations on obtaining your degree. What are your plans after graduation?"

"I'm going to get my Master's in Higher Ed."

"Why?"

"I love college. I had an awesome undergrad experience. I always kept good grades; I pledged a sorority, and I was very active in Student Government. I see myself working at a Historically Black College or University. I want to be a professor one day, too," she said enthusiastically.

"What is it that you want to teach?"

"Either Feminism or African American History."

"I think that's amazing!" He said smiling and eyeing her lustfully.

While everyone else danced, drank, and socialized they got to know each other's passions, goals, strengths, weaknesses, and hobbies. A few times, they danced but stopped every time their friends would hype them up. She was shy and didn't like the attention.

When the club was closing, everyone gathered. They started walking outside acting vulgar and wild. Alvin walked Jazmine to her car letting her know how much he enjoyed celebrating her new endeavor. Their friends were yelling out embarrassing comments about them out of fun and causing them to blush.

"What are you about to do?" He asked.

"Go home and go to sleep, I have to be up for church in the morning. I'm trying to sing in the choir when I move back here."

"For which church?"

"18th St. Missionary Baptist Church."

"Oh, that's good. Church girl that knows how to have fun! What a perfect combination."

"Thanks, Alvin. It was nice meeting you," she said while getting in the car.

He politely said, "It was nice meeting you too, Jazmine." He walked away from her car looking for Darryl and the rest of his friends.

Black Pain't, Vol. I

He thought to ask her for her number and ran back to her car as she was backing up.

"Are you forgetting something?" She asked.

"Yes, your number," he said smoothly.

She smiled and blushed. She pulled her phone out of her purse and Alvin said his number aloud. She texted his phone and said, "Store me in."

"Aight, cool. You know I will."

After their encounter, he would call and text her consistently during her last couple of months of college. He surprised her by driving out to her school to attend her graduation. While there, he watched as she interacted with certain people, especially the men. He noticed her strange attitude the entire time he was there.

When she moved back home, their proximity grew. They would go out to eat, to the movies, to the gun range, swimming, to the fair, and Alvin even went to church with her on a few Sundays.

One evening, Alvin went to dinner with Jazmine, her mother, and her stepfather who really wanted to meet Alvin. Jazmine's mother did not like Alvin. She felt that it was something malicious about him that she couldn't quite figure out.

After dinner, Jazmine and her mother got into an argument about Alvin. Jazmine's mother didn't trust him but couldn't explain to Jazmine why she didn't trust him. "It's something in my spirit," the mother would say though Jazmine didn't care what her mother thought. She continued to date Alvin.

One night, they were at Jazmine's apartment watching movies and eating snacks. He kept staring at her pear-shaped physique and glaring into her eyes in a seductive way. Jazmine told him that she was a virgin and he wanted to take her virginity.

While they were cuddled up on the couch, he began to inappropriately touch Jazmine's perky breast. She removed his hand and held it against her shoulder. He strongly grabbed her up to his chest and tried to kiss her, but she refused. He tried again and she bluntly said, "I'm not ready for that, Alvin."

Anthony Crawford, Jr.

Alvin, being forceful, pulled her closer to him and tried to kiss her again. When she denied, he shoved her off the couch and she almost hit her head on the coffee table. She looked up at him feeling confused and disheartened. He got up to lock the door and turned the lights out with the television illuminating the living room.

Jazmine, being scared, got up off the floor and ran to her cellular phone to call the police. Alvin grabbed the phone out of her hand and threw it against the wall. Jazmine curled up.

Aggressively, he said, "TURN AROUND AND BEND OVER!"

She began to cry and said, "Please don't do this, Alvin. Please! What's gotten into you?"

As he stood there straight faced, he struck her with his fist against the side of her face, knocking her onto the floor. "GET UP and bend over! I ain't playing with you," he said demonically.

"NOOO!! ALVIN!! NOOO," she squealed while crying and holding her face.

He picked her up, turned her around, and laid her forward on the kitchen table with her butt facing him. He pulled her shorts and panties down and spread her legs. He pulled his pants down, spit on his hand, rubbed the saliva on his penis, spit on his hand again, and rubbed the saliva on her womanly secret. He roughly inserted his penis in her and began stroking.

She cried, trembled, and screamed in pain the entire time. She saw a towel lying on the kitchen table and tightly gripped it to help fight the pain. When he finished, he laid on her for a few seconds as she lied on the kitchen table motionless with tears running down her face. He got off her, pulled himself out of her, and pulled his pants up to his waist.

She slowly fell onto the floor with tears racing down her face and hoping that Alvin would not do anything else to harm her. He grabbed a towel that was on the table and tossed it on her lap. He grabbed his keys from off the coffee table and left.

She hurriedly stood up to lock the door and fell right back onto the floor next. She looked around her apartment and fixed her eyes at a

Black Pain't, Vol. I

picture of her and her mother on her bookshelf. She stood and painfully walked to the bathroom. She stared at herself in the mirror crying and noticing the bruise on the right side of her forehead.

Her thoughts overwhelmingly rambled. She did not see any light or reason for Alvin's actions. She felt a fear of him returning and killing her. She turned the water and soaked the towel. She grabbed the soap and used it to foam the towel. She hesitantly wiped the trails of blood from her legs enduring the pain.

She thought about all the things her mother said about Alvin and the mystery that covered him while she went back to the living room to clean up. While cleaning, she felt her body tense from the energy in the room. She stopped cleaning to find herself in the silence.

She eventually looked to her coffee table and saw her book bag lying next to it. She walked over and grabbed it. She unzipped it and took a pen and a notebook out of it. She opened the notebook, skipped a few pages until she came to a blank page and began to write:

What right gives you the right?
To steal so painfully that which was mine to freely give?
Which version of me fit your tastes the best?
You left my consciousness with no days off for rest.
I gotta keep reminding myself no Testimony comes free comes free of test. But what right gives you the right?
To label me monster when I began to act like that which became the single constant in an unstable life?
It is not my fault that this occurrence made me turn off the turn on.
Underdeveloped chest to love on? Man, come on.
Undeveloped morals never knew it to be wrong.
What right gives you the right? To take and take and take and take.
I shudder to think you were my friend, great.
Four years it felt like forever enlisted in this fucked up fate.
Until along came a boy to show me the difference between how friends and family play. What right gives you the right?
To you know what? Pause that……you no longer dictate my life.

Anthony Crawford, Jr.

Because of you, I now have the drive to strive far past this current position of mine and thrive. How does it feel? To know you've taken the intimacy out of making love; No room for sex, all I want is straight fucks. Like it makes no matter,
we can get down with teeth, fingers, or tongue.
But no eye gazing. Because of this predicament I'm no longer the one to chasing; after intimate relations for the sake of love; Fear of the imminent obliteration of all my trust. And yet,
what right gives you the right to sate. Your wicked hunger through unsuspecting flesh in this horrendous act of rape. - Alanna Rivera, R.I.P., Oklahoma City, Oklahoma 2015)

"……and that's how it happened," Jazmine expresses to her mother.

Her mother says, "Now I told you that you should have left that boy alone."

"MA-MA! Okay! I don't want to talk about this. I got the restraining order like you said! When I'm done with graduate school, Miracle and I are moving so we won't ever have to worry about any of that!" She says furiously.

"I hear you, honey. You know mama love you. I know you're grown, but you're always going to be my baby. I love you. Bring my grand baby over here whenever you need some time alone."

"Alright, Mama. Thank you. I love you, too."

"Alright honey, bye."

While at home, Jazmine prepares dinner for her and Miracle while Miracle spends time at the dinner table practicing her ABC's and numbers. While eating, Jazmine sits and stares at Miracle thinking of her innocence and admiring the perfection of her little girl. She feels so blessed and lucky to have her but is fearful for her. She shelters Miracle. She's very strict on what she can do, the questions she asks, what she can watch on television, and the food she eats.

Black Pain't, Vol. I

    Jazmine repeatedly tells Miracle how beautiful and smart she is. Jazmine thinks that the world is cruel to women. So she teaches Miracle to be aware, strong, wise, and ready for anything.

    Jazmine's mother doesn't agree with many of Jazmine's motherly tactics on raising Miracle, because she didn't raise Jazmine that way. Miracle loves being over her grandma's house. She gets to be a kid. She gets ice cream. She gets to roam free around the house and outside. On weekends when Jazmine needs some time for herself, Miracle and her grandma watch movies and eat popcorn.

    After dinner, Jazmine bathes Miracle. During bath time they laugh uncontrollably. After playing and bathing, they put on their pajamas and get in the bed with the night light on.

    While in bed, Jazmine stares at Miracle as she falls asleep. Jazmine's creative juices begin to flow, so she grabs a pen and pad out of her backpack. She flips through her pad of poems and devotions. She stares at Miracle again for another minute or so and begins to write:

> I'm in awe,
> I realized that I was the first to hold you.
> You selected me to nurture and mold you.
> It was love at first sight,
> I thought that only happens in movies.
> We shared each other's eyes, but yours moved me
> You introduced me to the angel that was inside me,
> the one I tried to cover up, because I tried to hide me.
> but I came out of me in the form of you
> and everything about life I'm about to learn from you.
> You are so beautiful and
> I want you to always know that, so I'll say it again and again.
> I'll give you the game, so you won't ever get played by man.
> You'll grow into a beautiful Goddess, a gorgeous Queen.
> You'll inspire others and speak life into them.
> It's in your genes.
> Your name and the essence of who you are is spiritual,

… Anthony Crawford, Jr.

and you came as an aspect of divinity in the physical.
I love you,
You are the Miracle.

Jazmine reads the poem to herself, tosses the pen and the pad by her bag, admires the night light by her dresser for a moment, and lies down to sleep.

The next morning, Jazmine is getting Miracle dressed so she can take her to mother's house while she's at work. They both love listening to Beyoncé's music to get energized and inspired for the day. They both sing and dance all around the house until it is time to leave.

While in the car on the way to her grandma's, Miracle recites her ABC's and the numbers that she knows to Jazmine. Jazmine is very animate about Miracle's education. They pull up to Jazmine's mother house and she parks her car in the driveway. As Jazmine helps Miracle out of her car seat, she excitedly runs into the house. Miracle runs in her grandma's arms saying, "Grandma! I miss you!"

"Grandma misses you too, baby. Ready to have fun?" Jazmine's mother says while picking Miracle off the floor.

"Yes!" Miracle says innocently.

"Good. Give your mother a hug and a kiss so she can go to work," Grandma says while putting Miracle back on the ground.

Miracle runs to give Jazmine a hug and a kiss. Jazmine gives her mother a hug and a kiss on the cheek thanking her for watching Miracle. She tries to give her mother some money, but her mother refuses. She leaves the money in the bible on her mother's bookshelf and walks out of the house. She gets back in her car and listens to Trey Songz's music on her way to work.

Jazmine works at a nursing home as a Certified Nursing Assistant. She distributes medication to the residents that live there. All the elders love her because she's young, pure, and full of life. She always has something encouraging to say to the elders.

Black Pain't, Vol. I

She always eats her lunch with one of the elders named Mrs. Mary Ann Ethel-Williams. She reads her poems to Mrs. Williams, and they talk about her daughter, Miracle. She admires Mrs. Williams's short size and how beauty she is, especially being in her late-50s. Jazmine loves hearing about Mrs. Williams's love stories about her deceased husband and stories about her children.

Mrs. William's husband died from a stroke because blood clots moved through his heart. The blood thinners could not lower his cholesterol levels enough to keep him alive. His passing left Mrs. Williams's heart broken.

During their usual lunch discussions, Mrs. Williams's son walks in. Full of delight, she says to him, "Hey, Baby! What are you doing here? I thought you weren't coming until you got off work?"

Jazmine immediately observes her son's brown skin, the navy-blue scrubs he was wearing, and his vibrant smile. She feels a wave of optimism running through her veins. She admires his short and curly afro.

Her son says, "I'm on my lunchbreak, Mama. I had to come up here and surprise you for your birthday." He pulls out a present that he was holding behind his back.

"Mrs. Williams, I didn't know today was your birthday! Happy Birthday!" Jazmine frantically says.

"Ahh baby, when you're this old, every day seems like your birthday. Jazmine this is my baby boy Jules Jr. Jules this is Jazmine," Mrs. Williams says softly.

"Nice to meet you, Jazmine," Jules says gently.

"It's nice to meet you as well Jules. Your mother tells me a lot about you."

"Oh, yeah? Mama, what you be telling her?" Jules asks in a joking manner.

"Oh, baby, you know. Nothing bad. I didn't tell her about how you used to pee in the bed and cry all the time!"

"MAMA, STOP!" Jules says while they all laugh.

"Open your gift, Mrs. Williams!" Jazmine says anxiously.

Anthony Crawford, Jr.

"Hold your horses, baby. Seen one gift, you've seen them all," Mrs. Williams says while opening the small box her son gave her. When she opens it, she's instantly stunned at what it is.

"It's the original wedding band Dad got you when he first proposed to you. He gave it to me a few months before he died," he says.

Mrs. Williams silently stares at it for a moment. She gets up out her chair and lies down in her bed nearby. Jazmine and Jules stare at her in disbelief.

Softly, he asks, "Mama, are you okay?"

A dark silence entered the room as Jazmine benevolently says, "Mrs. Williams?" She gently rubs on her shoulder.

"I'm fine, babies. Just need to get some rest," Mrs. Williams says in an aching manner.

"Alright, Mama. I have to get back to work. Happy Birthday, I love you."

"Love you too now. Don't ever forget it," Mrs. Williams says resolutely.

"Okay, Mrs. Williams. Get you some rest birthday girl. We're turning up tonight," Jazmine says in a joking manner in an attempt to cheer her up.

They both leave the room and Jazmine shuts the door. Jazmine sees Jules walking down the hallway towards the elevators. She feels a sense of earnestness to stop and talk to him. She calls his name, "Jules!"

He stops by the elevator, turns around to her, and respectfully answers, "Yes, ma'am?"

Concerned, she asks, "Hey, what happened back there with Mrs. Williams?"

He notices the uneasiness in her eyes and says, "My Mama truly loved my Father. They were so in love with each other. They would always listen and dance to *Marvin Gaye, Al Green, ConFunktion, Prince,* and all the other old school artist." They both laugh as he pushes the elevator button.

Black Pain't, Vol. I

"He would take her out on dates. He rubbed her feet every night. They spent more time cuddling and showing affection then they would do anything else. They were best friends. She told me stories of when my father was arrested and beaten for fighting against injustice and racism. She was right there fighting with him. He went to jail for nine months one year for fighting police officers and when he got out, he wasn't the same. He seemed a bit traumatized from his jail experience."

"Awww," she says admiring his radiant eyes and soothing voice tone. "Sounds like true love."

He says, "I know, right. He died from a stroke. Doctors said that blood clots shot through his heart. That's when my Mama started to go downhill. She didn't smile or talk as much. She would never go out anywhere. That really took a toll on her life. She just spent her days working, cleaning, and taking care of me and my sisters. My sisters don't like Mama for some reason. I lied and told mama that they are in another state, married with kids."

"Why would you lie to her?"

"I did not want to break her heart even more. Matter of fact they're living in this city. My mother is actually healthier than what she seems to be. She's just suffering from depression. She lost her best friend; I know she's hurting from the disconnection between her and my sisters, and she really hates being alone."

With her eyes teary, she says, "Awww man, that's hard on you, huh?"

As the elevator door opens, he sadly says, "Very; I can't even talk to my sisters about whatever it is that happened between them without them going off on me. Seems like they hate mama."

"I'm sorry to hear that."

"It's all good. We all have our battles. Hey, it was nice meeting you, Jazmine. I have to get back to work. You're not the only one who take care of our elders. Thank you for everything that you do for my Mama. With just your presence alone, you're probably keeping her happy." He says as he gets on the elevator.

Anthony Crawford, Jr.

"See you later, Jules," she says as the elevator door starts closing. As soon as she turns around, she catches one of her co-workers staring and smiling at her.

Inconspicuously, Jazmine asks, "WHAT?"

Her co-worker says, "I have been watching you work here for the past two years, and I have never ever seen you look at man with that look that you just gave him." Jazmine rolls her eyes, walks away, and the co-worker yells, "I'm just saying!"

Jazmine clocks back in and continues her job. Throughout the rest of her shift, she was thinking of some supplies she needed for Miracle, the house, and she wonders about Jules.

Occasionally, at work, she texts her mother to see what her and Miracle are doing or have done. She checks her emails to see what assignments are due for her graduate classes. Before she gets off, she goes to the elder's rooms to say something inspirational and gives them hugs.

Before she drives to her mother's house, she stops at the grocery store to get some food. She buys fruit, noodles, cases of water, some canned items, and vegetables. She also buys Miracle some fruit snacks for her to have after supper.

Jazmine then drives to her mother's house. When she arrives, Miracle is sleep. She carries her to the car, straps her up in the car seat, and gives her mother a hug. She whispers, "Thank You," to her mother and drives home.

While at her apartment, Jazmine puts the food away in the kitchen. She does some of her assignments for her graduate class while Miracle is asleep. When finished, she puts on pajamas and sits on the edge of her bed thinking about Jules. She begins to wonder if he feels the same connection for her that she feels for him.

Her body feels different, and her mind begins to race. She does not want her past to interfere with the way she was feeling for Jules. She turns around and sees Miracle sleeping. She turns on the night light, turns off the room light, and crawls backward to get under the sheets. She falls fast asleep.

Black Pain't, Vol. I

Anthony Crawford, Jr.

Chapter 3:
Proverbs 7, Proverbs 31

She wakes up early in the morning admiring how well-groomed he is. She watches him as he puts on his clothes. She's taken by his dark-brown skin. She calmly asks, "Will you be preaching tomorrow, David?"

After putting on his shirt, he takes a quiet sigh. He turns around and stares at her with discontentment. He says, "I don't know yet, Rayven," and continues to gather his things from off the floor in her bedroom.

"Are you going to let me know, so I can come hear you?" She asks tentatively.

Black Pain't, Vol. I

His cellphone starts vibrating in his pocket. He pulls it out and sees that it's an incoming call from his wife, Tabitha. He ignores it and inserts the phone back in his right pocket. He turns to Rayven and says, "The next time I get the chance, I'll let you know."

As an awkward silence fill the room, she shyly asks, "Does Jazmine still go to the church service on Sundays?"

"Yes, she does. Her daughter is in our church's day care center too, so we're good," he says while watching her eyes fall in disappointment. "I have to go. I'll call you." He walks out of her apartment and makes his way to his car.

While in the car, he takes his phone out his pocket and calls his wife. The phone rings a few times and she graciously answer, "Hey boo, how was the conference?"

"It was good. I met other pastors and youth directors that gave me some insight on getting more involved in the community."

"That's fascinating. I really hope I can attend one of those conferences one day. I'm glad it went well. Have ya eaten?"

"No, and I'm on my way home. I'm going to need a hot shower."

"Alright honey, I'll see ya when ya make it home. Remind me that I have to talk to you about DJ, too."

"Alright, see you in a minute." As they both hang up the phone, he looks up to see Rayven staring at him through her bedroom window.

(Several year ago, David Sr. and Tabitha were married at their home church, 18th St. Missionary Baptist Church. Their six-year-old daughter, Talitha, was the flower girl and their four-year-old son, David Jr., was the ring bearer. Their wedding was overflowing with friends, family, and members of their church. Everything was perfect and everyone had a great time during the wedding and reception.

Tabitha's parents watched Talitha and David Jr. while David and Tabitha went on their honeymoon in Jamaica for a week. While in Jamaica, Tabitha and David went site-seeing, shopping, wine tasting, went to a few night parties to dance, ate at different restaurants, and

Anthony Crawford, Jr.

had wild and romantic sex. They spent some time on the beach soaking up the sun and conversing while listening to the waves hitting the shore. They had a magnificent time celebrating their love together.

When they returned from their honeymoon, everyone was considering them to be "a power couple." They were the two that all young couples and single church members envied and aspired to be. They both obtained their college degrees, purchased a house, drove nice cars, had two beautiful kids, and were very active in the church. Everyone thought they were just the perfect match for one another. However. Just like any match, they burn.

One Wednesday night, the choir director called David in to give the choir a vocal lesson because of David's singing gospel group that he was a member of when he was in college. David attended choir practice. He observed the two lead singers that were practicing. One of the lead singers caught his attention the most. She appeared to be in her early 20s. She was beautiful and had the most beautiful nutmeg skin he'd ever saw. She stood out to him.

After the choir finished practicing their song, David asked the director if he could work with the two lead singers. While the other choir members were practicing in the risers behind the pulpit, David and the two main singers walked to the back of the sanctuary. He said to one of the singers, "Sister, what's your name?"

She said, "I'm Jazmine."

"Jazmine......" he waited for her to say her last name.

She stuttered and said, "Jazmine Knight, sir. Sorry."

"Okay, Jazmine, you have to just go higher on your pitches. Whenever you hear sister......" He said while waiting for her to say her name.

After she caught her cue to say her name, she confidently said, "Rayven Little."

"Rayven......yes, Rayven. Jazmine, whenever you hear Rayven come in, start adlibbing, you and your section have to go higher. Your section follows your lead, so you have to go higher. Rayven?"

Anxiously, Rayven said, "Yes, Deacon Thomas?"

Black Pain't, Vol. I

Humbly, he said, "Please call me, David. I'm no bigger or better than anyone here." As Jazmine looked on suspiciously, he said, "Okay, Rayven, stop being scared. When you feel like going in, GO IN! The congregation needs to feel your passion for the Lord. Don't be afraid."

Inspired, Rayven said, "Okay, David. I will."

Making sure that they were all on the same page, he asked, "Okay?"

Smiling, Rayven said, "Okay."

"What about you Jazmine?" He asked her.

With a sly gesture, she said, "Yeah, I got it."

"Okay, that's what I'm talking about. You two are the heart and the soul of the choir. With you two, y'all can really heal some members with your voices. Use them. Rep for Christ. Sing for our Lord, Amen," he said motivationally.

The two singers went back to the risers to finish rehearsal with the rest of the choir. While Rayven was singing, David lustfully stared at her admiring her beauty and her singing. Rayven caught eyes with him a few times intensifying the connection that they shared.

While the choir was singing, it was time for Rayven's solo. She didn't do as well as David would have liked. While everyone was still singing, David stopped rehearsal and said, "NO! Bring that part back." He walked on the stage, grabbed Rayven's abdominal and her lower back, and sensually said, "Come from here."

Tabitha walked in before the choir started singing again and noticed where David's hands were placed on her. When it was time for Rayven's solo, she sung like she had never sung before. The choir director and the choir members were impressed and commended her.

David let her go in the mist of the praises and compliments. He felt a firm stare coming from Jazmine. He turned around to see her glaring his way. He then walked off the stage, made eye contact with his Tabitha, and waved. Tabitha waved and smiled back with a slight grin.

Rehearsal ended on a positive note. Rayven began to grow fond of David. She admired him and would always find opportunities to

Anthony Crawford, Jr.

speak to him during church service and bible study. She would always ask for help with her singing, even when she didn't need it. They would sneak off to his office, talk about his old singing days as a gospel artist, and motivate each other to do better as Christians. They often secretly flirted. He spent more time at choir rehearsal than he would attending his bible study class.

Rayven became jealous of Tabitha. She would never speak or acknowledge Tabitha. There were times when she would roll her eyes at Tabitha while in the choir stand during church service or every time, she would walk in at the end of choir rehearsal to get David.

Tabitha sensed Rayven's negative vibes and rude gestures. Every time Rayven would give a rude gesture to Tabitha, Tabitha would tell her cousin. Tabitha really wanted to talk to David about everything but hesitated to.

One evening after choir rehearsal, an overwhelming urge to ask David about his role with the choir captured her. She wanted to tell him about Rayven's actions. He got angry, denied all accusations, and said, "You're going to let this young 22-year-old get you all worked up? Come on now Tabitha, you're grown. Most of all you're a woman of God. Why are you worrying about her? I don't want to hear anything else about it. I work with the choir because the choir director asked me to. Plus, you know how I feel about music."

Tabitha didn't feel any truth behind his words because of his actions. Her emotions became imbalanced. Something deep down inside her was telling her that he's lying and that he has been very deceiving.

Later that year, the choir went out of town for a gospel music competition. The choir director and David served as chaperones for the trip. There was sexual tension between David and Rayven. They would catch eyes constantly on the bus. During the trip's pit-stops, they would horseplay. Jazmine observed David and Jazmine's interactions throughout the trip.

That evening after the competition, in the hotel, all the choir members paired up and shared rooms. David and the choir director shared a room together. The choir director stepped out to have dinner with a few of his college choir friends that he pledges with. David stayed in the room to talk on the phone with Tabitha.

Rayven text David, "WYD?"

While Tabitha was talking, David texted back saying, "Nothing at all. Watching television. You?"

She texts back, "Sitting here with some choir members, bored. Where's Kenneth?"

"He went out with some friends that he went to college with," he texted.

"You're alone?" She asked.

He replied, "Yes."

"David.... David……DAVID?" Tabitha yelled over the phone.

He recognized that Tabitha was calling his name over the phone and said, "I'm sorry, baby. I dozed off. Let me get some sleep. I'll call you in the morning." He hangs up with Tabitha while waiting on Rayven's response.

Rayven text back asking, "You want some company?"

"Yes, I'm in room 306," he responded.

Within two to three minutes, Rayven knocked on the door. He hastily turned off the television, got out the bed, and opened the door seeing her wearing pink and green pajama pants, a white tank top shirt, and a black baseball cap. Her beautiful nutmeg skin enticed his erection. He knew what was about to go down and time was wasting.

"Hey Miss Little, come on in," he said charmingly.

"Hi David," she said innocently as she walked in noticing him still wearing his grey slacks and unbuttoned dress shirt with a white under shirt that he wore during the competition. She adored his red and white polka-dot socks and his black bow tie hanging from his neck.

After she walked in, she stood observably by the door and looked around the room. She noticed which bed was his and jumped on it. She took her shoes off and stared at David admiring his manliness and maturity.

"How long do you think Kenneth is going to be gone, David?" She asked sensually.

Anthony Crawford, Jr.

"Maybe about another hour or so. Does the other choir members know you're over here?" He wondered while he was standing by his bed.

"No, I told them that I was getting some fresh air," she said seductively.

He grabbed her right leg and pulled her to the edge of the bed with her legs in the air. He slowly took off her pants and started kissing the inside of her left leg down to her inner thigh. He pulled her black panties off and began to go down on her. She moaned and groaned while her eyes were closed. She grabbed his head fiercely.

While he had a strong grip of her butt cheeks, he stopped what he was doing to get up and turn the room's lamp off. Then he proceeded to work his tongue around, up, down, and in and out of her.

He removed his head from her inner thighs and lifted. She took off her shirt, he took off his pants. She pulled his briefs down to his ankles and he unhooked her bra. She grabbed his wood, spitted on its tip to watch the saliva stream down and began sucking it. He put his right leg on the bed and grabbed the back of her head. Pulling himself deeper into her throat until she gagged.

He pushed her onto the bed and laid on top of her. Her legs were wrapped around his waist. They passionately kissed while rubbing and grinding on each other. He pinned her arms at the back of the bed and held them with his left hand. He used his right hand to put his wood inside her. She grumped, roughly put her arms around his neck, and unwrapped her legs from around his waist embracing the feeling. He started off slow until he felt her walls loosen.

She said, "Harder," and he began passionately pounding away inside her. The bed started making squeaky noise while he moved up and down on her. "Faster," she whispered as he began to speed up.

After they were finished, they laid on the bed to cool off. As they put their clothes back on, they laughed about each other's facial expressions during their sexual experience. He sprayed some air freshener to mask the aroma that lingered throughout the room.

Black Pain't, Vol. I

While she waited for her cue to leave, he peeked outside to see if there was anyone around. She passionately kissed him before she left the room.

On the way back to her room, she ran into Jazmine in the hallway. "Where are you coming from?" Jazmine asked.

"I had to take a walk. I needed some fresh air."

Jazmine face straightened as she felt the lie. She then said, "Okay, well, good night."

"Good night, Jazmine," she responded as they both parted ways.

When Kenneth returned to the room, David was sleep. He went to the bathroom to take a shower, brush his teeth, and got into his pajamas. On the way to his bed, he noticed some black panties lying on the floor next to his bed. He looked at David, while he was sleep, wondering if David had anything to do with the panties being in the room. He scooted them under his bed with his foot and went to sleep.

The next morning, the choir and the chaperons got on the bus to head back home. Kenneth recognized the looks that David and Rayven were giving each other on the bus ride back home. Jazmine was noticing the same gestures being displayed.

When David returned home to his wife and kids, Tabitha felt that there was something different about him. She couldn't quite put her finger on it, but something was very different. Even though he was acting the same way he always acted, something inside her was chewing on her heart.

When they got in the bed, in the most sympathetic way possible, Tabitha asked, "Hey honey. Are you okay?"

He pulled the cover over their bodies with a straight face and said, "Yes, why wouldn't everything be, okay? I got everything I need right here."

Still curious, she said, "You just don't seem like yourself."

Angered by his concerned wife and her questions, he grabbed a pillow to lay upon his head and crudely said, "BABY! I'm good! We placed 2nd. I'm good."

Anthony Crawford, Jr.

After that night, Tabitha felt a sense of hurt that she couldn't explain. She did not know why she was feeling the way she was feeling. She could not sleep throughout nights. She would usually stay up late to read and watch David sleep. He wasn't vibing with her sexually. She wanted him to hold her and comfort her like he used to do before they got married.

In the mornings, Tabitha would always be the first to wake, make breakfast, get the kids ready for school, and await the love of her life to come in the kitchen to eat with his family. He would not eat with them. He would wake up, take a shower, get dressed, and would hug and kiss everyone before he walked out the house.

David found himself going to a church conference at least once every month; at least that's what he told Tabitha. He missed some of Talitha's dance recitals, missed a few of David, Jr.'s little league baseball games, and would not give Tabitha affection when he came home. When they did have sex, he wasn't as gentle and sensual as he used to be. He was aggressive and corrosive.

Tabitha stopped questioning him on his whereabouts. She'd spend her days crying, cleaning, and reading her bible for answers. Some nights, when the kids were at their grandparents and David was gone, Tabitha would drink wine and watch some of her favorite television shows. She would cry during the romantic scenes and captured butterflies in her stomach.

Church was not the same for Tabitha. She felt miserable every Sunday and Wednesday while not knowing where these obscure feelings were coming from. She knew and felt that David was the cause.)

David pretends he does not see Rayven staring at him through her apartment window. He shakes his head and drives home listening to Travis Greene on the radio. He thinks about all that he must do for tomorrow's church service and all that he has to do to prepare for next month's event.

Once he arrives home, he parks in the driveway, and sits in his car for a moment to shift lifestyles. He gets out of his car and looks around his neighborhood. He walks into his home and sees David Jr. He grabs him from behind, lifts him up, and says, "Hey Junior!"

While laughing profusely, David, Jr. yells, "HEEEEYY DAD!"

David, Sr. gently settles his son on his feet, they do their high five that they've been doing since David, Jr. was a baby. David, Jr. runs off as Tabitha comes into the hallway to greet him noticing an angry look on David Jr.'s face.

"Hey, love...."

"Hey, welcome home!"

Feeling the aggressive resistance from his wife's energy, he vaguely says, "Thanks," and gives Tabitha a kiss on the cheek instead of her lips. "Where's Talitha?"

Tabitha gives David Sr. a hopeless stare and says, "Ha coach picked ha up fa practice."

"Oh that's nice. How is the dance thing going for her?"

As her eyes get slightly teary, she says, "It's goin' well. She seems to enjoys it."

"That's good. I'm about to take a shower and lie down for a minute," he says as he walks to the bedroom.

Tabitha slowly walks back to the living room feeling nauseated from sensing an unusual aroma coming from him. She slowly sits on the couch and pulls a bottle of *pain* relievers from her purse that is sitting on the coffee table. She swallows one, drinks some water to wash it down, and lies on the couch motionless while the television is on.

(Tabitha met David in college. They both were in the school's choir. She was a freshman, and he was a junior. David was very popular. He served as the Chaplain for the Black Student Association and had his own gospel music group called, "The Saints." The Saints consisted of him and three other young men that attended the school. The four young men would travel the country singing and winning gospel competitions on behalf of their school.

David loved Tabitha's country accent and her singing voice. Tabitha's voice grew more beautiful, and David allowed her to record a

Anthony Crawford, Jr.

song with his group. She admired his love for music and the Lord. He admired her voice, her prestigious personality, and courageousness. They became best friends and, overtime, fell in love with each other.

When they became a couple, they were known as the couple that all the other couples wanted to be. They would sneak off campus to a bar that was twenty minutes away. They would illegally sneak off into each other's dorm rooms. They got in trouble in which, at their college, if you were caught breaking school rules you were baptized. David was baptized nine times during his senior year of college.

The beginning of David's last year in college, Tabitha's father passed away from cancer. She was broken. She took the semester off to grieve for the loss of her father. She lived with her mother for the remainder of the semester.

David would drive four hours to her hometown to visit her. He met her courageous mother and her outspoken aunties. He also met her gangster-like uncles and most of her vivacious cousins. Her family grew fond of David and his visits, especially during the holidays. Tabitha loved having David around her family. She would express her feelings to him and how the love she felt just from having him in her life.

During the Thanksgiving Holiday, David spent the week at Tabitha's mother's house with her and her family. At the dinner table, Tabitha rubbed her feet against David's inner thigh. David looked up and noticed Tabitha's smirk and the carnal tautness in her eyes. He was aroused by the vibrancy of her smile. She had not been as effervescent since her father's passing.

After dinner that evening, David and Tabitha drove to a lake that was about fifteen minutes from her family's home. They were cuddled up watching the stars and the moon. They talked and laughed while reminiscing.

She asked him, "Are ya my soul mate?"

"I pray so. I can't picture my life without you in it. Without you, it's just any empty frame."

She noticed the sincerity in his voice and grabbed his face. She said, "I love ya."

Black Pain't, Vol. I

They passionately kissed each other. She jumped in the backseat of the car. He followed right behind her. They continued to kiss. She sat on top of him and unbuckled his belt. He took off her shirt and sucked on her breast. She pulled her skirt up, pulled her panties to the left side of her inner thigh, grabbed his wood, and slid it inside of her.

She slowly and strongly rode him while his right hand was gripping her neck and his left hand held her buttocks. She sped up and bounced on him while grumping and groaning. On the brink of their climax, she aggressively wrapped her arms around his neck, and he wrapped his arms around her waist.

They both caught their breaths while holding each other tight. Into her ear, he whispered, "I love you, Tabitha."

While coming down from the cloud of euphoria, she looked at him and replied, "I love ya, too, Davy."

"I know sex before marriage should be our goal. I hope God forgives us for not abiding by His rules."

"Ya think our love and our sex-life is worthy enough for us to spend eternal damnation?"

"I just know God hates sin. Don't be an Eve trying to give me an apple."

David's comment made Tabitha feel away, but that didn't end their beautiful, meaningful night. A night that Tabitha will never forget, feelings that she felt that will never wither away.

As the months passed and their sexual passions continued to transpire, Tabitha found out some shocking news that she must inform David about. All awhile David had something he was building to ask Tabitha. She was fearful that he wasn't going to take her news too well, and he was panicky about asking his question.

She didn't want to keep him from living his dreams of becoming a Gospel Artist and this well renowned preacher. He didn't want to put too much stress on her during this trying moment in her life of becoming an evangelist while traveling the world studying and teaching the gospel.

Anthony Crawford, Jr.

David flew into her city, and she picked him up from the airport. When they arrived at her home, Tabitha and David both felt anxiety. To calm their spirits, she took him to their get-away-spot at the lake.

"I have something to ask you," he said seriously.

She interrupted and said, "Wait, I have somethin' to tell ya." She took a deep breath and said, "Davy, my period did not come last mont'. Once I realized it, I took a few pregnancy tests……." Tabitha paused for a second. "Davy, I'm pregnant."

Shocked by what he just heard; he sank in the driver's seat looking out into the lake. He got out the car and sat on the hood of the car looking into the sky.

She got out the car, sat beside him, and said "Davy. I don't know if this……"

He interjected and said, "Have you ever felt like things were just too perfect? Like God, why are you blessing me in such a way when I'm unworthy?"

Confused, she said, "No, why?"

He got off the hood of the car and grabbed her by her left hand staring into her eyes. He bent down on one knee. He said "Tabitha, the first time I began to understand Proverbs 31 is when I met you. You're my best friend; you've become my everything. Your love makes me into a better man. You're very supportive and your personality matches mine. I came here today to ask you something……" as he pulled a small box out from his back pocket, she started to cry as he slowly opened it. "Tabitha, will you marry me?"

She nodded her head repeatedly with tears streaming down her face and said, "Yes, Davy. I will marry ya."

He slid the ring on her finger, gave her a strong, sensual hug, and yelled at the lake about him having a baby and getting married. They both were high on love. They felt as though they were in a grand position in life. They spent the next few days coming up with dates for their wedding, children's names, and reflecting on the serendipities of events that led up to this point in their relationship.

Black Pain't, Vol. I

They both cried when Tabitha drove him to the airport. They couldn't wait until they got home to their loved ones to tell them the news. They knew that their families were going to be thrilled and supportive.

When David was at the airport, he was filled with joy and gratitude. He felt an urge to write while waiting at his terminal for his plane to depart. He grabbed his bible, a pen, and some paper from his carry-on bag. He looked around the airport for a moment to soak in all the creative ideas that were flowing through his heart. He began to write:

We went to our getaway spot,
she was expecting the usual beautiful moments we share.
I looked her dead in her soul and said,
"I can be that man for you;
while the world doesn't get you, I'll understand for you;
take your views on men, your last name and your address and make them change for you. You are truly what really matters.
I want to fill your heart with my love just to see your smile splatter.
I don't even have to call you a woman of God, you know it;
I don't even have to tell you 'I love you,' I'll show it.
You don't have to want for nothing;
we'll always be up to something.
You dealt with a lot of boys that claim they're men with no authority;
most that didn't handle their responsibility, some didn't treat you as a priority. You're everything to me."
As I get on one knee she gasps when I asked,
"Will you marry me?"
She said, "Yes."

"We are now boarding flight 2437" was announced over the intercom. He hastily gathered his things, held his boarding pass with his mouth, and stood up to wait in line to board the plane.)

Anthony Crawford, Jr.

David awakes Tabitha from sleeping on the couch and asks, "Tabitha, are you okay?"

Still sore and tired, she says, "I'm fine. How long have I been sleep?"

"About two hours. Are we picking up Talitha or will her coach be bringing her home?"

"Her coach will bring her home. Let me call her to verify," Tabitha says while reaching for her phone.

"Okay, will you be attending church with me tomorrow?"

"Yes, of course. Why ya ask?" Tabitha asks while texting Talitha's coach.

"Just making sure," he yells while walking into the kitchen.

Tabitha runs behind him and grabs him by the waist side, "Let's do something tonight," she says sensually.

Uninterestingly, David asks, "Like what?"

Saddened by his dull response, Tabitha says, "I don't know. Let's go to the movies or something. I haven't really been out to do anything fun lately. I just sit at home, go to the church, or take the kids to their games and performances. I want to go out."

Noticing the hurt in her tone, David holds her, and says, "I'm sorry, honey. Things are really getting tight at the church. I'm doing the Lord's work. Plus, who's going to watch Junior and Talitha?"

Instantly, Tabitha says, "We can pay Ms. Henderson to baby sit. She wouldn't mind......"

Aggressively and irately, David retorts, "Okay, okay. Where? Where would you like to go, Tabitha? Damn...."

In annoyance, Tabitha furiously verbalizes, "Never mind! I'll just go out by myself. Ya act like ya never want to do anything with me." She squalls out the kitchen pouting and whispering under her breath.

While watching her gale, David grunts and yells, "Okay, I'll stay home and watch OUR children!"

Once Tabitha calms down, she says a slight prayer to collect herself. She hasn't been out in years and don't even know where to go.

Black Pain't, Vol. I

She calls the few friends that she still has since her and David got married.

None of her friends were available to go, however. That did not stop her. She is determined to get out of the house and enjoy herself. She googles some nice neo-soul events downtown. She finds a place called Afro-Culture's open mic night. The reviews said that Afro-Culture has a grown and sexy atmosphere with a live band, live poetry, good food, and wine. She decides to go.

Later that evening, Tabitha comes out of the shower to dry herself with a towel and views her nakedness in the mirror. She begins to lotion her body, picturing a strong man's hands massaging her every curve.

She sprays perfume across her neck and on her feet. She goes to her closet, searching for a dress that she hasn't worn since her honeymoon. She chooses some nice heels to color coordinate.

David Sr. is in the living room, watching a movie; not paying Tabitha any attention. He's not noticing the hurt that's about to take her out on a date. He doesn't see the hurt dressing her skin with sexual tension and her scent with sexiness.

When Tabitha is done getting dressed, she's asks him, "What do ya think?" She is in search for a nice compliment or a nice chill to touch her spine. She craves for some type of affection or some butterflies to gracefully fly from out of her garden. She wants any type of affirmation towards her elegance.

David slowly looks away from the television to observe her. He quickly turns back to the television and synthetically replies, "You look nice, sweetie. Make sure you enjoy yourself. Call me if you need anything."

Her eyes fall to the floor in disenchantment. As her veins appear on her neck from clinching her jaws, she tries to calm herself down from becoming internally livid. She prays as she tries to keep herself from crying. She realigns with herself, rolls her eyes, grumps, and leaves the house.

Anthony Crawford, Jr.

While driving to Afro-Culture, she tries to hold her cry while wondering what went wrong with her and David's marriage. *"Everything was so perfect,"* she thinks to herself. She looks at the GPS system on her phone to make sure she is going down the right street.

When she pulls up to the parking lot, she takes a moment to mask her hurt. She practices smiling in the rearview mirror. She finds the courage to get out of the car.

As she walks in the building, she notices all the beautiful, Black people and admires the ambiance. The energy in the building is welcoming. Everyone seems to be supportive and loving.

The live band is playing one of her favorite songs by *Jill Scott*. There were couples on the dance floor two stepping. People were mingling, eating, laughing, drinking, and having a grand time all around the facility.

She discretely sits at the bar where she is greeted by the bar tender. He politely asks, "Hey, Queen, what can I get you?"

Tabitha is immediately taken by his strong voice that she forgot what she is doing. Once she snaps out of it, she confusedly reads the menu. She forgot the last time she even seem a menu as she answers, "I don't know; what do ya suggest?"

The bar tender discerns her, looks at the ring on her finger, and, in a jokingly manner, says, "I'm going to start you off with some Roscato. You look like you need it."

While the bar tender walks away to pour the wine into a wine glass, she sits on the stool. She people watches while the emcee on the small platform announces that there will be some live poetry coming up and encourages everyone to take their seats.

Everyone finds their seat and the emcee allows a heartwarming silence to fill the room. With a smooth, harmonic tone, the emcee closes his eyes and says, "We are about to get into our live poetry section for this evening. You all show some love for my brother from another mother, the doctor of wisdom and knowledge…… PHILLIP!"

The crowd lightly claps while watching suave Phillip step on the platform in his black suit, dark red tie, and shiny black shoes. He

Black Pain't, Vol. I

looks around the facility while noticing the long, but narrow structure. He looks over to the bar and sees that he has the people's attention. He smiles at the people sitting in the front of the stage and says, "This piece is called "Forever." The band begins to play some soft instrumentals in the background while he says:

"What happened to forever?
It was clever what you did and how you pretended.
When I questioned your love, you got silent and defensive.
I felt defenseless, so senseless about what we've become.
What happened to forever?
I had questions and I want answers like,
'When did our love get so stagnant?
What was our cancer?
Why were you so unhappy?'
Help me grasp this,
'Was I not romantic? You didn't see us with a family?'
Love, what happened to forever?
You got me wondering if it's really over and if we are really done.
Tears rushed down my face because you found another man and
I thought I was your lover one, but, to you,
I was never the one.
She slowly grabs me, I roughly push her hands away saying,
'Don't touch me.'
She leaves and both are left thinking that they'll never find better;
we can't just play with hearts like spades and think it'll be forever."

While Phillip is reciting his poem, Tabitha feels her eyes glancing and admiring his tall and wide body. His strong and deep voice captures her, and she imagines herself rubbing his bald head.

He finishes and everyone in the facility starts snapping their fingers. Phillip says, "Thanks, everyone. Once again, my name is Phillip; thanks for listening." He walks off stage giving folks in the crowd high fives. He walks straight to the bar and sits next to Tabitha.

Anthony Crawford, Jr.

The bar tender hands Tabitha her wine and walks away to help another customer.

Tabitha repeatedly looks at Phillip trying to find the courage to ask him a question about his poem. She takes a gulp of her wine and makes a slight, disgusted facial expression. She asks him, "Was that a true story?"

He turns his head to her not knowing what she said and politely says, "I'm sorry. What did you ask?"

She projects, "Your poem. Was it a true story or just something you made up? Sorry if you feel as though I'm in your business. I'm just curious."

For a brief moment, Phillip thinks of his ex-wife……...

(Dr. Phillip A. Carson was married to Shyla Johnson-Carson over eight years ago. They were so in love; however, Phillip was the only man that Shyla ever loved. She never knew what it was like to be with any other man other than Phillip. They met in college and were together throughout their college experience. They ended up getting married after they both received their master's degrees.

Everything just seemed too perfect for Shyla. She became bored and disinterested with her lifestyle with Phillip. There were times when she felt like she forced herself to be happy, while desiring adventure and fun. While preparing to go back to school to get his doctorates, Phillip gave her everything she wanted and, in her eyes, was just too nice. She wanted him to take control, be aggressive, make decisions, and put his foot down every once and a while.

Shyla never got the opportunity to venture out, make mistakes, and to live independently without Phillip. She would never express her feelings to him because she didn't want to hurt him. She would work during the week and party with her girls on the weekends. She found some night club to go with her girlfriends. They loved going to the grown and sexy night clubs to drink and two-step to live music.

She would usually come home around two o'clock in the morning. She would be drunk and wanting rough and wild intimacy.

Black Pain't, Vol. I

Most of the time, Phillip would be sleep or just not in the mood to deal with her aggressiveness.

One night, she didn't make it home. She arrived home around noon while Phillip was in the living room watching a basketball game. "Where have you been all night, Shy?" He asked collectively.

She said, "I fell asleep at Brittany's. I was too drunk to drive home."

"Funny how those same words have come out of your mouth for three consecutive weekends," he said feeling broken by her actions.

They argued and he complained about how they don't spend much time together anymore. He mentioned how she does not seem interested in doing things with him and how they were not vibing physically and emotionally. Their bond became thin.

The negative tension in their home grew and they were becoming more distant. Phillip would sleep on the couch throughout the week just so she would feel at peace when she slept. They would hardly speak to each other. When they did, it was just to go over bills. He wanted to see a marriage counselor, but she refused to. She claimed that she didn't feel comfortable pouring out her heart to a stranger.

Months went by and one of Phillip's friends wanted Phillip to join him one Saturday evening for the grand opening of a new night club called RED'S. Phillip agreed to go to get out of the negative space that he dwelled in. He seemed joyful while preparing to go out. His mannerisms angered Shyla internally because she had no idea as to where he was going. He left without saying a word to her.

The club was packed that night. Phillip and his friend sat on the side of bar where they could people watch. They bought each other drinks and conversed about their whereabouts. Forty minutes later, Shyla walked in with her arm wrapped around another man's arm. Phillip's friend witnessed it first and informed Phillip.

Furious, Phillip walked up to them by the bar, grabbed Shyla by the arm, and started yelling at her. She tried to pull away. Her boyfriend pushed Phillip away from her. Phillip's friend struck Shyla's

Anthony Crawford, Jr.

boyfriend in the face. Phillip grabbed Shyla right before security came and pulled her outside.

As they walked to the parking lot, Shyla belligerently said, "Let me go, Phillip." She pulled away from him and released herself.

"HOW COULD YOU? WHY SHYLA?" He asked desperately.

Furiously and with a confused expression, she asked, "Why what, Phillip?"

His voice cracked while he asked, "Why are you with him? Who is he?"

Her rage made her feel like her heart was about to break out of her chest and punch him in the throat. She said, "Because I do not want to be with you."

"Why? Tell me why."

"Phillip! Stop doing this. You know we're both unhappy. You know we lost our spark."

He swallowed the truth and asked, "So are you done with me?"

"OUR MARRIAGE HAS BEEN DONE! I can no longer feel bad for going home. I can no longer live in a house with a man who just naïve to reality. A marriage should be filled with love and happiness, no grudges and madness," she said while her fists quaked. She watched him as he froze in disbelief. He was speechless. "Why are you acting surprised, Phillip? We have to move on."

"What ever happened to 'Till death do us part?' You are right. We have not been on the same page and things have not been the same between us, but that does not mean quit. I love you, Shyla. You were my best friend, the only woman I could confide in and I gave you my all." He said as tears were falling from his eyes.

His response angered her. She gathered herself and said, "I fell out of love with you, Phillip. I am not nor have been happy. It has been going on for quite too long. I cannot continue to lie to myself and you. We have history together, not chemistry. I am not forcing myself to love you anymore. It is not fair to you and not fair to me."

"So what are you saying, Shyla?" He asked sorrowfully.

Black Pain't, Vol. I

She took a deep breath, folded her arms, stared in his eyes, and said, "I want a divorce, Phillip. I cannot continue to portray this image that you have of me."

Her words sliced through his mind and stiffened his body. He wiped the tears that flowed down his face. He stood up straight, cleared his throat, and said, "I understand. I pray everything works out between you two."

She scoffed and said, "Thank you. Goodbye, Phillip."

As she walked away, he embraced the hurt. He turned around to see his friend witnessing the entire scene by the car. He quickly turned back around to watch Shyla walk away with another man's arm wrapped around her shoulder.)

Phillip unapologetically replies, "It's a true story; I just was not the man for her." He sips his small glass of Whisky and says, "I've been reluctant to love again."

"Why is that?"

He sorrowfully says, "I must learn to love and fully understand myself before I can learn to love and fully understand someone else. Our situation humbled me. It made me stop lying to myself and to always find the truth in a person, no matter how beautiful they are."

Feeling sympathetic, she says, "It's crazy how we always learn that after the *pain*."

He takes a deep sigh, takes another sip, and sings, "Yep, *that's just the way love goes on Love's Train*." They both laugh hysterically. Finishing his last few giggles, he humbly says, "You just learn to move on. You learn that you will learn to live with the *pain* or use it as a survival too of when to detect unhappiness in future relationships. Just remember that no matter what, you have to move forward. You have no other choice dammit! So how do you want to move forward? With no baggage or with baggage? Don't let the hurt cage you; make peace with it. Surrender its purpose within you and let it do what it came to do. Forgive yourself and forgive that person. That's the only way to heal and to let go of that baggage."

"Easier said than dun, Mr. Phillip. We all struggle."

"True… but who said that it has to be hard? Who said that you have to struggle?" He asks rhetorically.

She hesitates and asks, "Is that not the purpose of life though? To experience the *struggle*? Isn't that the fun part? How else do we gain genuine appreciation for the things we have if we don't go through struggle for it?"

"What if we're taught genuine appreciation?"

She instantly says, "Ya can be taught anything, but a lesson isn't learned until it is applied or experienced."

Passionately, he asks, "Who's going to teach it? Who knows how to teach it? You certainly can't get a degree in gratitude."

She ponders on his statement with no counter argument. She asks, "Why do ya think that?"

"Society does not want you to understand your God-given powers, Queen. If you knew about those powers, then cancer and other known diseases would not be billion-dollar industries. You'll be able to heal yourself."

Soaking in the wisdom, she says, "Hmm. I neva thought about dat."

"Oh, yeah? You don't have anyone to challenge your mind?" He asks while glancing down at the ring on her finger. An awkward feeling rubs against his chest. He discontinues his pursuit and says, "Hey, there's a public speaker named Aaron James coming out here next month, you should go to his speaking event. He speaks about society, relationships, and life in general. I think you will enjoy what he has to say."

She smiles and says, "I heard of him. Dat speaking event is at my church."

He gleefully asks, "You attend 18th St. Missionary Baptist Church?"

"Yes, my husband is one of the deacons there."

"That's nice," he says respectfully. "So you're a Christian woman? I can see you as the Proverbs 31-type."

Black Pain't, Vol. I

"Thank ya, sir" she replies frankly. "So ya say ya a doctor?"

"Yes, I am. I am a graduate school professor."

She thinks for a second and says, "I've been thinking about going back to school to get my master's."

"Why don't you?" He asks interestingly while sitting next to her.

"I don't know. I guess I just keep giving myself reasons not to."

Noticing the tone in her voice, he says, "Well if you ever think that you can find the time, I'll be willing to assist you in anyway." While reaching in his right back pocket to grab his wallet, he says, "Here's my card. Please don't hesitate to contact me whenever you have a goal in mind. It was nice meeting you, Tabitha."

"It was nice meeting ya as well, Phillip," she says with her country tone as he walks away to continue mingling within the crowd. The bartender is staring at Tabitha while drying some of the glasses. She notices him staring and guiltily asks, "What?"

He innocently throws his hands up and says, "Sorry, I was just noticing your glare. If you're feeling him, go get him."

She defensively says, "I'ma married woman, sir."

"There are married men and women that come in here all the time without their spouses."

She stops herself to think before saying her next comment. She looks around the room while analyzing what's been happening in her life. She's feeling the buzz from the wine. She sees her reflection in the mirror above the bar. A sense of guilt fills her spirit. She rapidly leaves and drives back home.

~

When she makes it home, she quietly moves through the house, checking on her family from room to room. She goes to Talitha's room, opens the door slowly, and sees Talitha sleeping peacefully in her bed. She slightly closes her door and creeps into David Jr.'s room.

Anthony Crawford, Jr.

She worries for a moment because he isn't in the bed. He's asleep on the floor from playing with his toys. She picks him up and lays him in his bed. She lightly pulls the blanket over him and kisses him on the cheek. She leaves his room and goes to her bedroom where she sees David Sr. sleeping in the middle of the bed.

She sighs and aggressively says, "Scoot over!"

He opens one eye, scoots over while yawning, and says, "I hope you had a good time."

She takes her clothes off and throws them into the dirty clothes hamper. She tautly says, "I had a great time. Definitely going again. Ya should come." As she finishes her statement, she hears David Sr. snoring. She shakes her head and goes into the bathroom to take a hot shower.

After soaping, she starts reflecting on her relationship with David while the water hits her light-skinned body. She cries a little while wishing that their relationship was how it was when they were in college. She sensually lifts her head back to let the hot water rinse her neck.

She thinks of Phillip and his poem. She remembers his attentiveness and his poise. "No, no," she whispers to herself as she turns off the water and grabs a body towel from above a cabinet.

While out of the shower, she dries herself with the towel and begins staring into her red eyes in the mirror. She internally encourages herself to continue fighting for better days. She wonders if she overstepped her boundaries at Afro-Culture.

She closes her eyes and whispers a prayer. "Amen," she says as she grabs the lotion from under the bathroom sink. While she puts on lotion, she thinks about Phillip and how, for a brief second, she felt an attraction for him. She contemplates on whether the attraction she felt was based off her vulnerability or because she truly felt something.

She puts the lotion back under the sink and openly walks into the bedroom. She pulls a t-shirt and some pajama pants from out her dresser drawer. She puts them on and turns around to see David lying down on the bed in the form of a cross. He's still snoring. She stands there for a moment and gets annoyed. She leaves the room and sleeps in the guestroom.

Anthony Crawford, Jr.

Chapter 4:
Ar'twerk (artwork adj.)

"Dammit! Why can't they just score?" He yells while watching the football game.

Walking from the beer fountain, she says, "Calm down, Alvin. It's just a game. Plus, you're scaring the customers."

He looks at her in revulsion and says, "Oh the hell with them, Trina! I had money on this game." He takes his wallet out his back pocket, pulls out money, and hands it to her.

She laughs as she takes the money and says, "I told you to stop betting me on these games. Women love sports too, suga."

"Ahh shut up, Trina," he says while closing his wallet and putting it back in his pocket. "What time is it?"

Black Pain't, Vol. I

Looking at her watch, she says, "Time for me to get off! How long will you be here?"

He takes a deep sigh and says, "I don't know. I'll probably watch the rest of the game."

"Alvin, your team is down by three touchdowns; it is less than five minutes left in the fourth quarter. Let's be real, champ."

He motivationally says, "Anything can happen! You better be ready to give my money back."

"Have fun with that, sir. Are you going to church in the morning?"

"Now, you know I ain't going to nobody's church."

She looks at him in despair and asks, "Why not? What's wrong with church?"

"Have you ever listened to Darryl?" He asks while taking a sip of his drink. "He would tell you about religion and how it all originated, how Jesus never existed, and every verse in the bible that contradicts itself. I can hear Darryl now, *'Be careful who you have these conversations with. Black church members aren't ready to hear the truth about their God, about their bible, about their savior. It's all tainted, Alvin! It's a system of control. It's not meant for people like us to follow.'* I ain't trying to hear all that shit right now."

Assessing Alvin's statement, she asks, "So you don't believe in God or Jesus because Darryl doesn't believe in them?"

He looks at her and says, "I believe in a Higher Source. I can't believe in a God that was forced upon my people. The first time our people even heard of *Jesus* was during the slave trade when they brought us over here on that ship called *Jesus*. Stay woke."

"Were you on that ship?"

"No, but it doesn't matter. They had our great, great, great, great, great, great grandmothers and grandfathers on that ship. They forced the bible on our people. They made us believe in Jesus or it was death. The bible is a white man's bible. Stay woke."

"Why do you keep saying stay woke? What does that even mean?" She asks as she gathers her belongings.

Anthony Crawford, Jr.

"You know, stay woke, like see the truth of what's happening in our society and stop allowing things to distract you from the truth. When you know the truth, nothing or no one can lie to you. You have to see this system that we call society."

"That's it?" She asks sarcastically. "No resolutions? No changes being made? We just have to 'stay woke' to criticize the system and other non-woke Black folk? What exactly do we really need to be woke to?" As he stumbles over his words, she interjects and says, "Good night, Al. I'm about to go home and go to sleep. Stay woke if you want to; you'll develop sleep paralysis."

Trina leaves the bar and walks towards the parking lot. She gets into her car and pulls out a bottle of Jack Daniels from out of her purse. She stares at it to admire the shape and the appearance of the bottle. She twists off the top and takes two huge swigs. She makes a sour face and does the sound effect that one would make after being thirsty and drinking something refreshing. She shakes her head to get rid of the brain-freeze-like feeling that was rushing to her head. She then starts her car and drives home.

When she pulls up to her apartment complex, she puts the car in park. She relaxes for an instant and takes the key out of the ignition. She puts the key chain around her neck and gets out the car stumbling. She slams the driver side door and walks around to get the rest of her things from the passenger seat. She takes the Jack Daniels out of her purse, twists the top off, and launches the top into some bushes.

She takes another huge swig and continues to sloppily walk to her apartment. She gets to the door and searches for her keys to her apartment. She searches for the keys in her purse. Confused as to why her keys are not in her purse, she starts to search for them in her pockets. After noticing that the keys are not in her pocket, she looks over the stairwell at the path that she took to her apartment and recognizes that the keys are around her neck. She laughs unceasingly as she unlocks her door and walks in.

While walking in, her phone automatically connects into her house speakers, she turns on some Hip-Hop and R&B music. She wildly

Black Pain't, Vol. I

kicks her shoes off to the back of the couch and plays one of her favorite songs. She clumsily spins to her living room and takes off her belt. She removes her bra and sits on her couch. She lifts to grab the Jack Daniels, takes a gulp, and places the bottle on the coffee table. She then pulls out a weed tray with a bag of marijuana and a Backwood from under her couch.

She crumbles the marijuana on the tray. While singing, she unrolls the Backwood and removes the tobacco into a small, brown paper bag that is on the floor. She sprinkles the weed in the Backwood. She begins to roll up the Backwood after licking it multiple places. She grabs the lighter from off the table and lights one end of the blunt waiting for it to stay lit. She repeatedly put the blunt to her lips to inhale and exhale.

Then she takes off her shirt and pants. She sits on the couch with just her panties on. After smoking half of the blunt, she puts it out and takes another swig of the bottle. Her song comes on and she begins to twerk. She twerks on top of the coffee table and twerks in front of her standing mirror near the hallway. She stops to stare at her petite body and dark-oily skin. She begins to feel on herself while admiring her perky breast. She feels on her thighs down to her legs. She starts to feel dizzy, so she turns off the music and lies down on the couch. She grabs the folded blanket that's lying on the shoulder of the couch, unfolds it, and covers herself. She falls asleep.

~

It's morning. Someone is at the door knocking to come in. Trina's wakes up grumping. She then hears keys and watches the door fly open.

"Hey wombmate!" She says cheerfully.

Trina mumbles, "Jalisa, why do you always have to do this."

"Rise and shine! You know today is our monthly bonding day!" Jalisa says as she sees the blunt lying on the edge of the coffee table and an ashtray poking out from under the couch. She looks over to see a half empty bottle of Jack Daniels standing on the arm of the chair and her left leg hanging from the top of the couch. "JaTrina Mary Williams! Get up." She pushes Trina's leg and watches her roll off the couch.

"Don't fuckin' call me that! You know I hate that fucking name!" Trina irritably demands. "Uggggghhh! You get on my nerves with your ugly self."

"Another night of drugs, alcohol, and twerk music, huh?"

Wiping the crust out of her eyes while lying on the floor, Trina happily says, "You know it!" She wraps the blanket around her body to cover her nakedness. "How was the dance competition last night?"

Jalisa sits down; watches Trina put away her marijuana tray, and says, "It was lit. Made an easy five-grand from tickets. Wish you would have come."

"I had to work, sis. You're not the only one with bills. I'll be at the next one, I promise." Trina says while standing up from the floor and falling carelessly onto the couch.

"How's that job going? Getting a lot of tips?" Jalisa says impudently.

Trina stops for a moment to give her a look of annoyance and says, "You're teaching young girls how to twerk and getting paid for having them twerk in front of thousands of people. Y'all have them out there doing the splits and shit. You something like a pimp!"

Jalisa instantly and loudly says, "I am teaching these girls more than that! Don't ever try to compare my girls to some strippers!"

"You got them dancing for money, sounds like stripping to me," Trina satirically says.

"That's a competition we do for fun. I teach my girls more jazz dance than anything. Dancing is an art. An art that parents don't mind spending their money on to see their daughters perform. It's my dance studio and I make good money. You used to dance, too!" Jalisa says passionately. "And you can always come back! I can use a lil bit of help you know."

Black Pain't, Vol. I

Trina gets up while Jalisa is talking to get some water out of the refrigerator. When Jalisa finishes, Trina says, "I still dance." She walks in front of Jalisa and twerks in her face.

"Eww dirty booty lil' girl!" Jalisa says as they both laugh.

"Ya mama," Trina says as they both experience an awkward moment.

"Have you talked to Jules, lately?" Jalisa asks.

"Naw, I told him to come to the bar one night, but I think he's still mad that we don't go visit mama," Trina says.

"If only he knew what type of woman, she was to us when we were kids............

(It was in the middle of the night; a slight yell woke Mary Ann from out of her sleep. She noticed that her husband, Jules Sr., was not in the bed with her, so she got up and slowly walked into the hallway. She checked her son's room, and he was sound asleep. She headed towards her daughters' room and saw that the door was already opened. She saw her husband inappropriately touching their daughter's purity while the other daughter watched.

As she trembled into an internal frenzy, she slowly walked back to her room in dismay. She was very confused and did not know what to do. She was fearful for daughters and hated herself for not saving them. She wondered rather it was JaTrina or Jalisa that she saw him fingering. About 30 minutes later, her husband came back to their bedroom, lied down on his side of the bed, and went to sleep.

The molestation lasted for nearly a year or so. Dreadful silence surrounded the house all throughout the days. The best time of the week was when Jules Sr. was at work. Within those years, her husband's cholesterol kept rising. He became very ill and had to quit his job. When he went to the doctor, they prescribed Coumadin and Warfarin for his condition. The doctor told him to take either pill at least twice a day. The doctor also gave his wife a list of foods that would help keep his levels low. He continued to experience terrible chest pain and shortness of breath. He died months later.

Anthony Crawford, Jr.

Jalisa and JaTrina hated their father. His death made them happy because he wasn't coming into their room anymore. They hated their mother. Though Mary-Ann and her three kids received monthly checks from the government from Jules Sr.'s death, it was only enough to cover the rent. She was also determined to put money into a college fund account for each of them. She worked ten hours a day to buy them clothes, food for the house, other bills, dance lessons for the girls, school supplies, and trips for Jules Jr.'s traveling basketball team. Jalisa and Trina used to dance for their school, however, Mary-Ann never came to watch their performances. She attended most of Jules Jr.'s basketball games.

After Jalisa and Trina graduated from high school, they moved out and never talked to their mother. Jules Jr. told Jalisa and JaTrina that their mother sold the house and put herself in a nursing home. Jalisa and JaTrina never went to visit her. Knowing that the truth would hurt her, Jules told his mother that Jalisa and JaTrina moved out of the state, got good jobs, and got married.)

"So what are we doing today, womb-mate?" Trina asks unenthusiastically.

"Let's clean up your filthy apartment and get you dressed. Then we can get something to eat and relax on the boat. I made reservations for us," Jalisa anxiously says.

Jokingly, Trina says, "You and this spiritual shit. I don't want to hear the waves and sit there and watch you read a book about the art of dancing."

Feeling unbothered by Trina's comments, Jalisa says, "Too late! Now come on!"

They both begin horse playing while cleaning up. Trina shuffles a playlist of Hip-Hop and R&B music that they grew up listening to. Jalisa goes into Trina's closet and picks out something less revealing for her to wear. When she grabs something for Trina to wear, she goes and shows it to her. Trina gives her a look of disgust and happily goes to her closet to pull out something more revealing.

Black Pain't, Vol. I

Trina showers while Jalisa continues to clean her room. Once Trina gets out of the shower, she turns on some raunchy music. Jalisa can't stand that type of music, so she changes the music while Trina is in her room getting dressed. "HEY! What are you doing?" Trina yells from her room.

"NOBODY WANTS TO LISTEN TO THAT NON-SENSE RIGHT NOW!" Jalisa shouts.

Once Trina is dressed, they leave. They get into Jalisa's luxury car and Jalisa drives them to the pier, catching one another up on their work lives, conversations about their financial ventures and financial gains, and they even talk about their future and maybe one day moving away.

They go to a sea-food restaurant near the pier to eat. Trina gets her favorite fried catfish, crinkle fries, and a water. Jalisa gets grilled fish with a Caesar salad and a water. While they eat, they engage in conversations about one day getting married, the type of men that try to talk to them, family ties, and the good childhood memories.

During their brunch, Trina remembers the event that Darryl and Alvin were telling her about. She says, "Jalisa, we should go to this event next month."

"Okay, what's the event called?" Jalisa wondrously asks because Trina never goes anywhere or does anything. She's either at home or at work. Jalisa is the one that exposes Trina to different occasions around the city.

Trina tries to remember the name of the event but cannot. She says, "I forgot the name, but I guess it's this guy that travels throughout the world teaching people about self-love, relationships, following your dreams, and all that other shit that people be arguing about on social media."

"Sounds good to me, sis. We could most definitely go. Just get all the information for me so I can add it to my calendar," Jalisa says animatedly. She is happy that her sister is wanting to do something that is out of her comfort zone.

Anthony Crawford, Jr.

After their brunch, they drive to the dock where Jalisa made reservations to float on a boat for two hours. Once they get there, the owners of the dock realize that they made a mistake on the reservations and accidently double-book them with someone else.

"I'm sorry, Miss Williams. You two can either schedule a different time or share the boat with the gentleman that was scheduled the same time as you," the owner says.

Trina angrily awaits while Jalisa says, "Look sir, that's not fair. We do this every third Sunday of the month. This is unprofessional."

Trina jumps in and says, "Muthafucka, give my sister her money back. This is bullshit. We don't have to be here."

As Jalisa pulls Trina to the side, she says, "JaTrina, calm down."

"Don't fuckin' call me that," Trina rapidly strains.

"Why you always gotta act so ghetto everywhere we go!?"

"You wasn't saying that when I beat that parent up for you..."

"Ahh, is this what this about? You always wanna mention how you took boxing lessons and was oh so ready to show off your lil' moves by beating up that parent. I didn't ask you to fight her."

"I'm just supposed to let someone beat up on my sister? You wasn't gon' hit her back, I saw it in yo eyes..."

Jalisa snappishly says, "The bottom line, Trina, there are no refunds when you make reservations. We put money into this. Let's just see what kind of person this 'gentleman' is before we decide to call my lawyer."

Several minutes later, the gentleman walks in the main office wearing a black t-shirt, black jean shorts, and a pair of black sneakers. Trina internally judges the types of clothes he has on, but his energy does not match her judgment. To her, he exemplifies a man with nice, mature demeanor and an attractive appeal with a vibrant smile. Jalisa and Trina watch him as he talks to the owner about the scheduling mix up.

Black Pain't, Vol. I

"I'm Tony Givens, I had reservations for the two o'clock float," he says naturally. While the owner is scanning the reservation book, Tony peacefully glares out the large windows to see the water.

Then the owner waves to Trina and Jalisa and says, "Ahh yes, Madams. This is the gentleman that would be joining you if you're still willing to get on the boat." While the owner is talking, Tony walks by the window to await the decision.

Trina immediately says, "I'm down, if you down, sis."

Jalisa surprisingly looks at Trina, sarcastically wondering why she had a change of heart. Seeing Trina's calm spirit after she was just angry allowed Jalisa to collect herself. She becomes cooperative and walks to the counter to sign the document.

The owner says, "Right this way, ladies. Sir? Are we ready to board?" He guides them to the boat while telling a brief story on the history of the boat, the dock, and the ocean. Once they walk out to the dock, he begins telling them about the rules and regulations they must follow during their short cruise. He points and tells them the name of the captain that will be navigating. As they walk on to the boat, the owner stays on the dock to untie the rope that was holding the boat. "You three have a good time on the boat."

The three individuals find places to sit as the boat sails away from the dock. Tony sits at a table that was across from the beach chairs to complete his assignments for Dr. Carson's class. Jalisa and Trina sit on the beach chairs to bathe in the sun. Jalisa slightly meditates while sitting upright on the beach chair. Before she sits down, she pulls a book out of her purse and begins reading.

Trina takes out her cellphone from her purse and begins to take pictures. She gazes into the sky and takes pictures of the sun and the clouds. She stands up to take pictures of the boat. She goes to take pictures of the water and sees two ducks floating together. She's filled with a different kind of joy and takes photographs of the two ducks. She begins to take pictures of herself and catches Tony smiling at her. She walks towards him and asks, "Hey, what are you doing?"

Anthony Crawford, Jr.

He looks up and notices the suns reflection bouncing off her rich-chocolate skin. He replies, "Grad school work. They're normally due on Wednesdays and Fridays, but I like to get mine completed early."

Impressed, she says, "That's good. What are you in grad-school for?"

"African American Studies."

"Why African American Studies?"

"I wanna learn more about my people?"

"Your people?" Trina asks sardonically. "Where is your people from?"

"West Africa..."

"How do you know?"

"What you mean how do I know?" He laughs. "We all from Africa."

"Negroid, you ain't from Africa......"

"Where am I from then?"

"You're from here...... your ancestors didn't come here on any ship........ there weren't any slave ships, pimpin'......" Trina says comically. Then she switches her voice to try to sound like Malcolm X and says, "We didn't land on Plymouth Rock, Plymouth Rock landed on us!"

They boy laugh in harmony, feeling a connection and a moment they did not want to end. "I have never heard anyone say that. I'll have to look into it."

"Let me know what you find......"

Chuckling, he replies, "Will do...."

"So why are you getting your masters?"

He puts his pen in the crest of the book, closes it, and says, "My mentors were telling me I should go ahead and get my masters. They told me that if I didn't have a goal or plan after college then go back and get your Master's. So I listened."

"Are you going to get your Doctorate's too?"

He scoffs and says, "No, I am not. I am done with school."

Black Pain't, Vol. I

Instantly, she puzzlingly asks, "Why you say it like school is bad?"

"I'm not saying it as if it was bad, I just have a dream now. I don't need school to do live that dream."

She looks out unto the waters and looks back at him to ask, "Most successful and rich people don't have degrees, and they live better than the ones who do."

"That's true," he says while nodding his head. "Plus, school takes us away from our imagination, school didn't teach us what we really should have been learning; it's just a daycare now."

Intriguingly, she asks, "What do you think we should be learning in school?"

"Well, one, we need to be teaching our youth sex education. Our children need to learn how to appreciate and understand sex so they will learn not to abuse their bodies or their energies. We need to teach our youth about true happiness and to not get caught up in materialism. We need to teach our youth how to truly accept and love themselves. We need to teach them how to make a conscious decision. Schools need to teach our youth how to use their God-given abilities and their minds. Let's teach them how to support one another, how to forgive and accept one another, and how to resolves conflicts," he says passionately.

She promptly asks, "What about taxes, loans, and interest rates? What about stocks and bonds or how to build and run a business?"

"We need to teach them those things too."

She peeps that he's still sort of stuck in the system of the American dream but admires that he's trying to figure it out for himself. She sits in the chair close to him and says, "That's interesting that you say those things though. I have always felt that way about school. That's why I didn't go to college. It just wasn't for me."

"College is not for everyone, but for some of us, college is the only way out," he says while staring out into the water. "Aaron James once said that 'Love is our only true nature; it's our true essence.' What happens to a child that grows up not knowing that?"

"Is that why the world is the way it is?"

Anthony Crawford, Jr.

Instantaneously, he asks, "How is the world?"

"Cruel, evil, wicked, and mean," she says sharply. "We live in a fucked-up world with fucked up people."

He waters the fire within her by saying, "Our words have creative power. What do you think you just created based off what you just said?"

Trina hesitantly replies, "A fucked up world, but that doesn't change the fact that fucked up shit happens."

"What would be the purpose of our existence if we didn't have challenges, tests, and 'fucked up' occurrences that did not guide us to our purpose?" He asks. "Have you ever read *Conversations with God* by Neale Donald Walsch?"

She thinks for a second and says, "Nope, I never heard of it before. I've read *Pimp* and *Trick Baby* by Iceberg Slim..."

They both laugh as Tony says, "That's hilarious..."

"Why did you mention his book though?"

"That book put life in a different perspective for me. It taught me that we're not living through life, but life is living through us. I learned that everything that happens in our lives are results of our thoughts, words, and actions. Our every thought, word, and action have creative power."

"So why does a young girl, who knows nothing about molestation, get molested? Did she think or say it? Why does a young teen, who never wants to be raped, get raped? Did she speak that into existence? A woman doesn't go in a relationship thinking that she'll never get beat on, but then he abuses her. What did she do to deserve the *pain*?"

Patiently, he tenderly says, "I can't answer that for them. I can't tell you why another person had to go through the *pain* that they went through. I can only tell you why I went through the pain I had to go through. What I have learned from reading the book is that our *pain* gives us a strong sense of our purpose. That pain gives us just the right strength we need to continue on with the life that our soul desires."

Black Pain't, Vol. I

She soaks in his words and asks, "What else did the book teach you?"

"It also taught me so much about God."

"Like what?"

"That we are all Gods. I know this sounds like blasphemy; it's why Christ was crucified. Christ even declares this. You can read it in the Holy Bible," he says as his strong compassion induces her with an uncomfortable but opening feeling.

She asks, "Where at in the bible?"

"John 10:34," he says instantly.

They pause for a moment staring in each other's eyes. She squints into his eyes trying to understand her blank feeling and his soothing mystery. He closes his eyes to receive her resisting energy. They embrace the space that they are in as the wind softly whistles and the smell of sea water touches the air.

She observes him. She picks up her phone, takes her left thumb, and begins slightly pressing it on the power button. She swipes, taps, and begins to type. She locks her screen, lays it on the table, and stares back at him. "Who are you?" She says inquisitively.

He chuckles and says, "I am scripture and consciousness mixed. I am a messenger from the far and beyond, and I am here to remove the veil from this false perception of love. I'm...."

She interjects and irritably asks, "Nigga, you think you're some type of savior or something?"

"Jesus is my brother."

"Jesus is not your brother."

"Do you consider yourself to be God's daughter?"

She hesitantly says, "Yes, but...."

"Then Christ is your brother too," he says as she begins to genuinely laugh. Her smile clinches his heart. As their eyes lock, he confidently says, "I'm just saying."

She pauses for a moment to evaluate his statement. She looks over her shoulder to see Jalisa peeking over her book. Her energy shifts as she asks Tony, "What else did the book teach you?"

Anthony Crawford, Jr.

"It taught me why it's important to forgive and how to see love in everything and in everyone."

She contritely asks, "How do you forgive?"

"By remembering that *forgiveness is the only way to heal*."

Trina ponders on his statement observing his dreaded hair and thick beard. She tries to find the truth in his puffy, brown eyes.

He continues to stare in her eyes and asks, "How's your heart?"

"It's still piecing back together," she unapologetically replies as he writes his number on a corner piece of paper.

He says, "I left my phone in my car, so I won't be on it while I am on the boat, so here. We gon' do it the old school way." They both laugh as he hands her the piece of paper. "Hit me up some time."

"I'll think about it baby boy." She finds the will to ask, "So you spend over a hundred dollars just to do your work on a boat?"

He meekly answers, "Well, even though it's very costly, it's very peaceful. We live in a big city; there's never really any peace and quiet. I'm always hearing police sirens, ambulances, and helicopters. So, I save up and do this at least once a month. It's refreshing and I get rejuvenated. Other than writing, this is my therapy."

"So you like silence?"

"That's one of the most effective ways to hear God."

"Oh, naw! You're better than me because I need the lights on, the T.V., or my music playing. I can't do the silence," she says unashamedly. "You're interesting. I'm about to go back over there to my sister and let you finish your work. It was nice meeting you, Tony."

"I appreciate you, Love. It was meeting you as well," he says charmingly. As she walks back to her beach chair, he observes her compelling aura. She's gorgeous and he appreciates her outspoken nature.

Jalisa, with her face in the book, says, "Be careful, you know how men are."

As Trina sits down in the chair, she becomes aware of Jalisa's overprotectiveness, rolls her eyes, and says, "You have nothing to worry about, Jalisa. I know how men are."

Black Pain't, Vol. I

Jalisa suppresses Trina's demeanor. She thinks that Trina is stubborn and hardheaded. She hates that she always has to play the "big sister role" because she's been doing it throughout their life....

(One thundery night, the twins were having trouble sleeping. An uncomforting silence entered their room. They were scared and many disturbing thoughts traced minds. JaTrina said, "Jalisa! I'm scared. Is outside going to get us?"

Jalisa sprang in JaTrina's bed to lie down and hold. JaTrina. She said, "It's okay, JaTrina. I will protect you from the outside."

While they lied in Trina's bed, they heard slow and heavy footsteps heading to their bedroom. Trina whispered, "Jalisa, is that daddy?"

Scared, Jalisa said, "Don't worry, JaTrina. I will always protect you." As the door slowly opened, she quickly jumped out of JaTrina's bed and dove into hers. She was seen by Jules Sr. He silently walked into the room and closed the door.

He sat on JaTrina's bed and slowly pulled the covers down away from JaTrina. Jalisa raised up from her bed and said, "Daddy, it's my turn tonight." Jules Sr. smiled and walked slowly towards Jalisa's bed.)

"Jalisa!" Trina yells as Jalisa winces up from her sleep on the beach chair. "Come on, sis. We're back at the dock."

Jalisa gets up and asks, "How long was I asleep?"

"Well, I don't know. Probably like half the boat ride," Trina cynically says as they both grab their purses. They walk off the boat and onto the dock. While walking to the parking lot, Trina watches Tony as he walks to his car. She admires his mysteriousness and thinks about their stimulating conversation. Once they got in the car and drive off, Trina texts Tony while blushing.

Observing Trina's smile, Jalisa asks, "What are you smiling about?"

"I texted the guy anyway. He was cool."

"Oh, really? Saying what?"

"It was very nice meeting you."

"That made you smile?" Jalisa sarcastically asks.

Irritably, Trina says, "Don't start, Jalisa."

"I mean you just met the guy. You're already liking him? I mean get real, JaTrina."

"Don't fuckin' call me that!" Trina aggressively requests. Getting more aggravated, Trina asks, "So I can't be happy?"

"You can be happy. I want you to, but how are you going to be happy when you aren't even happy?"

Trina's feels internal anger creeping up her spine. She heavily sighs to release it and tries to say, "Jalisa…look……."

Jalisa interposes and asks, "Did you see what he had on? He looks like a thug."

"Okay Jalisa."

"Trina, you deserve better."

"Okay Jalisa."

"Don't you believe that?"

"Stop it, Jalisa. Please just stop it," Trina says as she pulls her seat back and lifts her feet onto the dashboard.

"I'm just saying be careful. You don't know that man. I think you just need to…"

Before Jalisa gets the chance to finish her statement, Trina interrupts and says, "WHAT, Jalisa? Get my life together? Get my ducks in a row? Focus on me? I'm tired of just focusing on me, Jalisa! I'm lonely. I want someone around that understands me and loves me for me."

"How do you want that when all the last man that came into your life did you wrong?" Jalisa disconcertedly asks.

"Okay Jalisa."

"I remember ol' Quincy…."

"Why even bring Quincy up?"

"I remember you being all depressed about this idiot."

"He wasn't an idiot… just a lil' wet behind the ears."

Black Pain't, Vol. I

"All I'm saying is that men cannot be trusted. You can disregard what I am saying but remember daddy used to………"

Objectively, Trina yells, "Daddy's gone, Jalisa! He doesn't have to be the example for all men! He's dead and gone! We're good now. We can move the fuck on!"

In disbelief, Jalisa calmly says, "Yes, Trina. We have to move on but that doesn't mean we can trust these niggas! They're all the same."

"Okay, Jalisa, but let me find that out! Let me have that experience! You can't keep 'protecting' me!" Trina yells sarcastically.

Heatedly, Jalisa painfully yells, "Who was there to 'protect' you when we were little? Who took most of Daddy's fucked up actions? Who? Or did you forget that, too?"

"How long are you going to be holding that against me, Jalisa? We are grown now!" Trina yells. "FUCK! Grow the fuck UP!"

"Oh, I need to grow up, Trina?" Jalisa angrily asks. "I know you're getting paid enough money from 'bar tending,' but is that all that you want for the rest of your life? You need to stop the smoking weed, quit the drinking, and get a real job. If you want to talk about being grown. Then you'll have time to see and bring a real man into your life."

Trina looks at Jalisa in despair and calmly says, "You're not my mama!"

While trying to keep her eyes on the road, Jalisa immediately asks, "Then who is? Mary Ann? What has she done for you other than allow daddy to do what he did to us? What has she done for you since you left the house at 18?"

Trina yells, "Stop, Jalisa! I'm tired of hearing this shit! I can figure this shit out on my own!"

An awkward stillness roams around in the car on the way to Trina's apartment. As they pull up, Trina takes a deep sigh, unbuckles her seat belt, and begins to furiously grab her purse and bags from the back seat. Jalisa says, "Look, Trina. I'm sorry. You're all I got. I just don't want to see you making any mistakes that will hurt you in the long run. You have to start thinking about the ramifications of your decisions because they affect me, too. Internally, just so you know, I hate that my sister is out here living like this. It is hurtful."

"It is okay, Jalisa. I am learning. I'm finding myself. One of the biggest lessons I've learned thus far is how to truly love and accept myself. I think it's very okay to have someone around me that will love and accept me too," she humbly says while watching her sister's watery eyes. "Jalisa, I respect and love you so much because you're all I got, but I know it's more out there for me. Lately, I've been wanting to hang out with my lil' brother. I've been wanting to visit mama."

Jalisa interrupts and says, "Visit mama? How come she can't visit you?"

"After all that I've just said, that's all you've heard? Jules told me that mama thinks we're in another state, that we're married with good jobs and that she has grandchildren." Trina says haughty.

"Let her have that lie. She kept what had happened to us a secret."

"Forgiveness comes a long way, 'Lisa. Though she allowed our daddy to do what he did to us, after he died, she did all she could to make up for it. I think she never said anything about it because it was too much of a burden. We're hating our mother. I don't think we should hate anyone," she says effectively.

She takes heed to what Trina's words and says, "I'll think on it. I'll have to think it through. You can go see her if you want. I'm not ready."

Trina extends her arms to give Jalisa a strong hug. As Jalisa smiles and embraces Trina's arms, Trina says, "I love you, womb-mate. Take a chance for once. In your life."

"I love you more, womb-mate," Jalisa says as Trina gets out the car. She patiently watches as Trina walks into the house. She says, "I will take a chance," under her breath and drives off.

~

Black Pain't, Vol. I

That evening, Jalisa goes to an art museum that is approximately ten minutes away from her dance studio. While at the museum, she walks around slowly glazing at the *paintings* and sculptures. She loves the way they make her feel as a dance artist. She imagines an artist *painting* her while she's motionless in a unique dance position.

She feels like her experience at the museum deserves a selfie. For a few minutes, she has been trying to find the right angle to take the picture of herself. She snaps a few, views them, and feels disgusted at what she sees. A gentleman from across the hall is witnessing this entire moment of Jalisa trying to take a selfie.

As soon as she finds a good angle to take her selfie, she snaps pictures of herself. The man walks towards her and firmly says, "Excuse me, ma'am." Jalisa flinches as she drops her phone. "No taking pictures of the artwork."

While steadfastly picking up her phone, she modestly says, "You scared me, and I was taking a picture of myself." She examines her phone to see if it has any cracks on the screen.

The man confidently says, "I know." He winks his left eye and walks off while continuing to look at the *paintings*.

She evaluates his warm smile and senses his consoling energy. As he walks, she glances at his navy blue fitted t-shirt down to his black-fitted jeans with a pair of navy-blue oxfords on his feet. She's taken by his pecan skin tone, his poise, and refreshing compliment. She thinks to say something before he got too far away from her. She keeps thinking about what Trina said earlier.

She decides to take a chance and says, "Excuse me, sir, do you work here?"

He glares at her beauty and replies, "No, ma'am. I just appreciate and love art. You look like art to me."

Intrigued by his response, she asks, "What other kind of art do you like?"

He contemplates for a moment and says, "Poetry, of course; dancing, music, singing, and I love singing. I think good conversation is an artistic expression when two individuals are optimistic. Sex is a form of art."

Revoltingly, she asks, "Sex? How is sex an art?"

Noticing her discomfort, he gently says, "Sex is like dancing on the dance floor with the one you love. Rather it's slow dancing or the DJ has decided to play some Juvenile and the woman decides to back it up on her man, it's all art. When two individuals truly love each other, they make music, when I say music, I mean they make love; making love is passionate sex."

She sarcastically says, "So I guess passionate sex is your favorite form of art."

"Actually, my favorite form of art is singing," he says promptly. "I make music."

She interrupts, "You gave the analogy of passionate sex being like making music, so do you 'make love' a lot?"

He chuckles and says, "No, ma'am, I don't in that sense. I see what you tried to do there."

"Are you celibate?"

"No, I'm definitely not celibate. I just refuse to open a woman's legs if I don't have any intentions of opening her heart."

"I can respect any individual who can do that," she says as she extends her hand to him. "I am Jalisa Williams."

He gently clasps her hand, slowly shakes it, and says, "Jalisa Williams, nice to meet you, Terrance Robins. So what do you do?"

She sneers and says, "I'm a dance instructor. I have my own dance studio and auditorium. I also have a dance program called DYSO, *Dance Your Soul Out*."

Notably, he says, "That's amazing and, judging from your beautiful smile, dancing is your passion, your own personal form of art."

As they start walking around the museum, she says, "Yes, indeed. I've been dancing since I was nine. What about you? What's your occupation? Any kids? Wife? Girlfriend? Mistress? Hoes?"

Black Pain't, Vol. I

He recognizes her ridicule and says, "I'm a freelance writer. I also get paid for writing songs and verses for other artists. I don't have any kids. I don't have a wife, I don't have girlfriend, I don't have a mistress, or any hoes."

"Hmmm. I wish it was that easy to believe you. A guy that likes art seems hard to come by. Are you gay?" Jalisa asks hoping not to offend him.

He rapidly says, "No, I am not gay."

"I'm just asking. Did I struck a nerve? Are you homophobic?"

"I am not homophobic. I respect people's sexual preferences as long as they respect mine. Plus, I love women, specifically Black women," he says as the PSA system comes on to tell the visitors that the museum will be closing in the next ten minutes.

"That's nice to hear. Why do you think people have a problem with the LGBTQ+ Community?" She asks inquisitively.

As they walk into the lobby area of the museum, he passionately says, "I don't think it's just the LGBTQ+ Community that people have a problem with. Our people have a problem with acceptance. Most of them have a hard time accepting themselves; when you haven't accepted yourself, then you won't be able to accept yourself."

"So is it just acceptance?"

"No, it's not just acceptance…..." he says confidently. "But without acceptance, it will be hard for anyone to understand others. We must see past our differences for the greater good."

She takes a moment to taste his words. As they walk out the main entrance, she says, "It was a pleasure meeting you, Terrance." She opens her billfold and pulls a card out. "Here's my card. It has my personal contact information on there."

"Nice meeting you too, Jalisa," he says while taking her card. He stands next to Jalisa's car to add her number in his phone and texts her. "I just text you. Store me in your phone."

"Okay, I will."

"So do you have a man?"

Anthony Crawford, Jr.

"Yes sir, I do. The only sad thing about him is that he doesn't like coming to museums with me. He thinks that they're a tad bit boring," she says while shaking her head. She feels his consoling energy shift.

With his hopes up, he smiles and says, "Oh, lucky guy. Well, okay Jalisa. Have a safe and good evening."

While she gets in her car and starts the engine, she says "You too, Terrance. Bye."

As she drives away, he walks slowly to his 2017 Red Mustang. Once he gets in, he takes a moment to think of Jalisa and how time seemed to have stopped while he was with her. He shakes his head to avoid more thoughts. He starts his car and drives home.

~

Once he gets home, he sits on his sofa and pulls his phone out to check his text messages. He sees one from Jalisa. He taps on the message icon and the text read, "Sorry for lying. I don't have a man ☺."

He leans back against the sofa, puts his head on top of the couch, and happily laughs for a quick moment. He texts her back saying, "GLORY HALLELUJAH!"

She responds, "Good night, Mr. Robins. Let's do lunch soon."

Terrance, full of joy, texts back, "Fasho."

He leaps up and does an abnormal dance. He laughs at himself and enjoys this upsurge of butterflies flying through his stomach. He slides across his living room floor and grabs a writing utensil and a small notepad from off his bookshelf. He two steps his way back to the living room while beat boxing.

He sits down to think about his encounter with Jalisa. He does not remember when he just clicked with someone like that. It is like he could have been at that museum for hours. He wants to continue messaging her but does not want to come off too desperate.

"*Her beauty and her conversation was very musing,*" he says internally. Realizing he does not have anything to write with, he jumps

Black Pain't, Vol. I

up to find one in one of his bookbags. With his thoughts and heart still on Jalisa and her divine feminine, he breathes to clear his mind of all the clutter. He takes thirteen deep breaths, in and out, to allow his creativity to flow within him.

He takes out his phone to play lofi instrumentals on YouTube. With his mind and heart aligned, while the atmosphere's vibration is grooving, and his chakras start turning, the words come to him like a message from the Divine. He begins to write:

I caught her at a museum taking selfies, being bored;
I walked up to her and said,
"Excuse me ma'am, no taking pictures of the art works;"
She apologized and said,
"I was taking pictures of myself;"
I winked and said, "I know."
She was impressed,
because no one ever flirts with her there;
she laughed when she found out that I didn't work there.
we walked around the museum, acting a fool;
she's full of conversation,
got her own business and didn't finish school.
she comes here because she finds a peace of mind.
the same reason why I go, so I wanted to give her a piece of mine.
she gave me her number so that we can be museum buddies,
I asked, "Where your man at?"
She says, "At home," and I didn't understand that.
we connected so well; I thought I had a chance;
that night she texted me that she lied about having a man,
girl, why you play too much?
Guess, I'll laugh and play it off because I don't want to say too much.

Anthony Crawford, Jr.

Chapter 5:
Tiffany's

It's Monday afternoon in W.E. Dubois Middle School's library. School is about to be let out in the next hour and a half. Patricia, the school's librarian, is putting books on shelves. One of the teachers comes in to get the assigned books for her classes. She assigns 30 books for the teacher's class, grabs the book wagon from out of the storage room, and helps put the books on the wagon. She escorts the teacher to their classroom.

While they are walking, the teacher asks, "Are you going to the training at the district building after school?"

Black Pain't, Vol. I

"Umm I believe so. As the school's librarian, I think it's mandatory that I go."

"I was chosen to go by our principal, so I'll be there too. Thank God, I don't have to be there alone," the teacher says while walking into the classroom, moving desks out of the way for the wagon to roll through.

"Where do you want these books, Ms. Freeman?" Patricia asks.

Ms. Freeman points and says, "Right on that bookshelf over there."

Patricia pulls the wagon near the bookshelf and starts to place the classroom books on the shelf. She says, "Yeah, I'm usually the only one that's there by myself from this school."

Ms. Freeman starts to help put the books on the shelf and says, "You're not the only one today. I'm wondering why the district does these trainings every month."

Patricia sarcastically whispers, "It's the Department of Education. They want to micromanage what our schools in the district are teaching. It's their way of making sure that we follow their white-washed curriculums."

Ms. Freeman mutters, asking, "Why would they want to do that?"

"To keep us in line. They don't want to really liberate and teach our children. Do you know what that does for society?" Patricia passionately whispers while putting the last book in the wagon on the shelf.

"It sounds like a revolution," Ms. Freeman murmurs. "Can we stop whispering now? I don't think it is inappropriate for us to be having this conversation."

Patricia giggles and whispers, "Ssssshhh, the government might be listening in on our conversation." Patricia goes back to her normal tone and asks, "A revolution of what?"

"A revolution of truth, infinite possibilities, freedom, and a whole different way of living."

Anthony Crawford, Jr.

"Exactly," Patricia energetically says. "Corporations want to keep the people 'in order' to keep us mentally enslaved, to keep us spending, and to keep us in a limited environment with the lack of resources. They're teaching our youth to be slaves through the education system."

"How so?"

"They're teaching our youth how to confirm to society. As soon as one of our school's state test scores begin to rise as a whole, they'll wonder what's going on and intervene. This system isn't meant to work for us, especially our young Black kids," Patricia says while pulling the wagon back outside the classroom.

Ms. Freeman thinks and asks, "You really don't believe that do you?"

"Yes, why don't you?"

"I don't believe in that because we are society. We make up this society. We can change, solve, and cure any and everything if we learn to understand to work in unity and in peace."

Patricia calmly asks, "What is peace when you have the police killing us, white supremacy killings; hell, we're killing us!? What's equality when white privilege exists?"

"Police kill people, not just Black people. White privilege exists because we say it exist. We gave them the power to have privilege."

"So you're saying that four hundred plus years of slavery, Jim Crow, the Ku Klux Klan, Regan bringing drugs into Black communities; Joe Biden and Bill Clinton's mass incarceration platform did not have an effect on our people?"

"I'm not saying that, but…"

Patricia interpolates and says, "Our people are traumatized by the effects of this inhumane society where we slave, fight, and die over greed and power. This is the system that was built to keep people mentally and physically enslaved. The change we seek is not going to happen overnight."

"Maybe the change we seek starts within us first," Ms. Freeman replies. "We can't keep using the same excuses as to why Black on

Black Pain't, Vol. I

Black Crime happens, why our communities are the way they are, and why we're so mentally enslaved. Everyone is claiming to be 'woke' but what are they actually 'woke' to?"

"Good question......," Patricia impressively says. "We shall continue this dialogue later, was there anymore books that you may need for this semester?"

"No, I'm good for now. Thank you so much, Patricia," she says. "I don't know what this school would do without you."

"No problem at all, Tiffany. I'll see you at the training," Patricia responds as she walks down the hallway while pulling the book wagon.

"Hey, we're you off to now?" Tiffany shouts.

Patricia comes to a halt and yells, "To my mentee's classroom."

"Can I come with?"

"Sure. It's just right around this corner here."

Tiffany catches up to Patricia and they walk towards the science classroom to check on Patricia's mentee's progress. When They get there, Patricia knocks on the door a couple of times, and the science teacher opens the door seconds later.

"Hey, Ms. Skinner and Ms. Freeman. What do I owe the pleasure?" The science teacher says while widening the door for them to walk in. As they walk in, Patricia's mentee, Abbyielle, sees Patricia, smiles hard, and continues her work.

"I'm here to check on Abbyielle Johnson. How has she been doing?" Patricia asks.

The science teacher turns around and see Abbyielle working on the class assignment. As she turns back to face Patricia, she answers, "She's doing so much better. I met with her auntie last week and I told her about her high academic advancement."

Happily, Patricia softly says, "That's good. I'm so proud of her. Well, let me get out of here. Thank you so much."

As Patricia rushes to give Abbyielle a quick hug, Tiffany observes and absorbs Patricia's nurturing and loving energy. As they exit, Tiffany says, "I'm going to go back to my room to finish cleaning and packing before the bell rings so I can beat after school traffic."

Anthony Crawford, Jr.

"That's smart, girl! I'm going to do the same!" Patricia strolls off pulling the wagon as Tiffany strides the opposite way.

Once Tiffany gets back to the classroom, she cleans and organizes her desks before she leaves for the district training. To beat the after-school traffic, Tiffany grabs her purse, her school's keychain, and leaves her classroom and right out of the building.

As she walks outside, she sees students dressed in uniforms, pulling down the United States flag from a flagpole. She sees hundreds of parents parked outside the school, waiting on their children to find them. There is a hand full of school buses lined up ready for students to get on. There is security walking around, making sure all the children are safe.

Tiffany gets to her car in the staff parking lot, unlocks the door and gets in. She places her purse on the passenger side of the car, puts her key into the ignition, starts her car, and drives off to the training while listening to the radio.

When she gets to the training, she signs the attendance form and notices that there were so many people there with more walking in. She sits closer to the door and saves Patricia a seat right next to her.

While waiting for the training to start, she pulls out *Peace from Broken Pieces: How to Get Through What You're Going Through* by Iyanla Vanzant and begins to read.

Five minutes into her reading, Patricia walks in, saying, "Thank you for saving my seat; everybody and they mama was trying to talk to me while I was leaving the school..."

Tiffany says notices a fine gentleman walking towards them. She looks up, thinking that he is coming to speak to her, but he enthusiastically says, "Patricia!"

Tiffany looks at Patricia as Patricia sees it's the guy that she met at the bookstore the other night. She shakes her head and impatiently says, "Wow."

"Well, would you look at what the serendipities and the coincidences and the random turn of events have done to bring us two together again? What was that word you used?" He comically and sardonically asks.

"Synchronicities......" she firmly says.

Unconquered, he scans the room in search for an empty chair, finds an empty chair, and carries it to the table where they are sitting. He sits right next to Patricia, and animatedly says, "Well well well, we meet again. How have you been since I saw you at the bookstore?"

Tiffany pulls out her phone, pretending to mind her business but is listening very intently on their conversation.

Patricia collectively says, "I've been well."

"How was your weekend? What do you do on your days off?" He asks with such interest.

"It was nice. Thank you for asking," She exasperatingly says trying to keep the conversation short.

He recognizes her insolence and says, "That's good. I read and went site-seeing downtown."

She abruptly asks, "Who did you go with? One of your hoes?"

"I don't have any of those. Would be nice to, though," he says mordantly.

"Look, Mr. Darryl, I don't know who you take me for but I......"

Before Patricia gets the chance to finish her statement, one of them members from the school board announces, "We're having some technical difficulties, we'll just need five more minutes."

Darryl notices the person sitting next to Patricia and pleasantly says, "Hi, I'm Mr. Jones; Darryl Jones...."

Tiffany holds her hand out and says, "Yes, I'm Ms. Freeman. Where do you teach Darryl Jones?"

"I'm a middle school history teacher at George Washington Carver Middle School. I'm Patricia's boyfriend," he replies as he gently grabs her hand and shakes it.

Patricia's face erupted after Darryl's claim and Tiffany teasingly says, "I didn't know you had a boyfriend, Patricia."

Anthony Crawford, Jr.

"Don't you entertain him, Tiffany. He is not my boyfriend," Patricia says.

Darryl jokingly says, "Always denying me."

Patricia intolerantly says, "Darryl, sit down, and stop it."

"Patricia, I will walk all around this room and announce myself as your boyfriend if you don't stop being mean to me," he says.

Patricia instantly says, "You wouldn't!"

Tiffany giggles as she perplexedly discerns them. She notices Darryl's charm and attractive mannerisms. She views his nice haircut, his smooth goatee, and his dark skin. She likes his tailor-made suit and his vibrant smile.

"Watch me," he says as he gets up and begins to yell, "HEY, EVERYONE! I'M DARRYL AND I'M…..."

Before he gets to finish, Patricia grabs him, pulls him down in the chair, and furiously whispers, "Okay, okay. What do you want from me, Darryl?"

He looks into her eyes and keenly says, "I want a chance. I want you to keep your word. We had a connection that evening when we saw each other, and you know it. Now, it doesn't take a genius to see that you've been hurt before, Patricia. I can only imagine what you've been through. Hell, I'm scared to even ask. Now the synchro-sancrhon-syndo…."

"Synchronicities," Patricia says while cracking a smile.

"Yes, Synchronicities. Wait…. Was that a smile?" He asks triumphantly. "Please tell me that was a smile and that I am not trippin'."

"No, definitely not a smile."

"Yes, Patricia that was definitely a smile. I know a smile when I see one, and that definitely was a smile."

"That definitely was a small grin. Not even a half of smile," Patricia whispers while trying to keep their conversation as quiet as possible.

He looks at Tiffany and says, "Ms. Freeman, wasn't that a smile?"

Black Pain't, Vol. I

Tiffany looks at Patricia, then back at Darryl, and hesitantly says, "Yes, that definitely was a smile, Patricia."

"Whose side are you on?" Patricia asks Tiffany.

Tiffany instantly says, "I am on the truth's side. That was definitely a smile, Patricia."

Patricia gives Tiffany a surprising and embarrassing look as jaw drops. Darryl says, "You see! And I can tell you haven't genuinely smiled in a while."

The program starts and all the district employees sit down. The host of the training welcomes everyone and introduces the superintendent. The superintendent starts her presentation. During the superintendent's presentation, Darryl writes a note on a small piece of paper that reads, "*Let me treat you to dinner*," and passes it to Patricia.

She reads it, writes, "*No*", and passes it back to him.

He chuckles, writes, "*Come on, love! You got me writing on a small piece of paper like we're in elementary school. I think that deserves some of your time,*" on the piece of paper and passes it back to Patricia.

Patricia reads it, starts blushing, writes, "I don't even know you, sir," and passes it back to him.

He writes, "I saw you blushing," and passes it back to her.

She writes, "That definitely was not a blush," and passes the paper back to him.

Tiffany witnesses this exchange of 'love notes' going back and forth between them. She grabs the paper after she sees Patricia passing it to Darryl. Patricia and Tiffany start silently horse-playing with the piece of paper as Tiffany is reading it.

They stop and Tiffany writes, "Give him a chance. He seems like a good guy," and passes it back to Patricia.

Patricia reads it and looks at Tiffany with a straight face. She then looks over to see Darryl with a huge smile on his face and crumbles up the paper.

During the superintendent's question and answer period of her presentation, a teacher from a high school raises his left hand and asks,

Anthony Crawford, Jr.

"Discipline is one of the many issues in our classes. These kids are out of control and it's happening all over this district. We can give these policies, procedures, and these consequences, but these kids are still out of control. How can we get better control of our classrooms? What will the district implement to ensure that we are in an environment in which we can effectively do our job?"

The superintendent hesitates to answer. She sees Darryl raising his hand, and acknowledges him by saying, "Yes, sir?"

Everyone in the room stares at Darryl. Darryl looks around cautiously. He stands up, takes a deep breath, and says, "I may have some negative reactions for this statement, but a lot of teachers have disciplinary issues, especially Caucasians, because of the underlining misunderstanding of our young Black boys and girls. Remember that we all work for a high-risk population in a high-risk area. Look at the environment that they are living in. Most of our students live in a single parent household. It's always the mother or the grandmother taking care of them. Some go to school just for breakfast and lunch because they're not getting fed at home. Then they come to school to sit in classes where we teach lies through these false doctrines from the history books.

"So of course you are going to have discipline issues, you're not teaching them anything that will liberate their minds. Of course you will have trouble managing your class...... you don't and can't relate to them. Most of you teachers talk down on our students but expect them to respect you........... You are not showing them that you care for their well-being and their advancement into this world, so they fight back! We focus on discipline and control because you're molding them to be slaves, to fit into this dying society; a society that takes away their natural, God-like abilities. We're teaching them how to confirm to society when society pushes them to poverty, gang affiliations, drugs, alcohol, and crime. And, instead of teaching them how to survive in this society, our district's only interest is teaching them how to pass these biased state test."

Black Pain't, Vol. I

Uncomfortable tension entices the people in the room. Darryl feels the rigidity and continues to say, "My mentor once told me that standardized testing was one of the worst things to happen to Black children in education. We are just teaching them how to pass state test and not life's tests. We are NOT teaching them what they need to know on a financial level, an academic level, and on a social level. This is an epidemic to all inner-city schools from all across America.

He pauses for a moment to scan the room. He takes another deep breath and says, "I think the most scandalize part about these disciplinary issues thing is that, since you all can't control your students, you complain and write dramatic referrals. Then doctors diagnosed our students with some form of learning disorder or ADHD like symptoms that pushes their mind into a belief system that will be difficult for them to break once they are older. They are not the problem, WE ARE PROBLEM."

The people in the room stays silent. The superintendent begins to prickly look around the people. Patricia stares at Darryl as he sits down. Darryl quietly sits noticing his hands trembling. The superintendent looks around the room scarcely and sympathetically says, "Meeting adjourned."

While people are leaving, a few teachers commend Darryl on his passionate response. He spots Patricia and Tiffany walking in the parking lot conversing. He quickly says, "So, what you think? You think now you'll let me take you out to eat, Patricia?"

Patricia courageously says, "Maybe. You got scared after your little spill back there."

"That's because he knows that type of attitude towards the educational system isn't welcomed," Tiffany says.

"Yeah, but if we don't have the conversation, then the problem will continue. This education system doesn't want to help our kids. That's why a lot of public schools are being closed, charter schools are at a rise, and free education is among us. We live in a dying society," Darryl says mutually. "Have you two ever heard of Aaron James?"

Anthony Crawford, Jr.

Patricia and Tiffany think about the name for a moment. Patricia says, "I don't have a clue."

"Neither do I," Tiffany declares.

He says, "He's an inspirational speaker that's speaking at 18th St. Missionary Baptist Church next month. He speaks about societal issues along with dream fulfilling, self-love, and many other topics. You two should go. The brotha is cold."

Tiffany types the information about the event in her phone's calendar. She looks at Patricia and says, "Hey, girl, I'll see you tomorrow. I am about to head out," while giving her a hug. "It was a pleasure meeting you Mr. Jones."

"The pleasure is all mine," he says smoothly.

Tiffany walks away as Darryl and Patricia continues their conversation. She walks to her car, gets in, starts it, and minutes later she drives off.

While driving, she decides to stop at a clothing store to shop, which is about five to six minutes away from where she lives. She loves to shop just as much as she loves to exercise. In the store, she moves slowly between aisles searching through clothes. She grabs an all-black blouse and finds some grey slacks to match it.

As she heads to the check-out line, she notices a young, handsome man with an interesting demeanor at the counter working hard. He looks very familiar to her as she continues to observe his aura. When it is her turn to pay for her clothes, she reads his name tag, and figures out who he is. "Working hard this evening, Mr. Givens?" She asks him while observing his beard and dreaded hair.

He smiles and says, "Very hard. I thought when I got promoted, I was going to be done with this aspect, but I'm all over the place. I forgot whose world I was living in."

Confused by his comment, she asks, "Whose world, is it?"

"It's ours," he says mysteriously.

Curiously, she asks, "What do you mean by that?"

Black Pain't, Vol. I

"Within our big world, within all these possibilities, and within all these inventions, we chose to make our people give their precious time to work and school. We work our lives away for minimum wage."

"Well, that's why we go to school, get degrees, and have a higher chance of making more money."

"I see what you're saying, but then most of our luxurious time goes toward hours of class, studying, and working minimum wage so we can pay for tuition. Then we basically pay for school put me in debt," he chuckles and says, "Life is much more than school and work. Life is much more than what has been presented to us by society. Again, I ask you, do you enjoy the world that we've created?"

Mind in awe by his question and captured by his energy, she says "That's an interesting question," while handing him cash. "So with that perspective of society, why are you working here? Why are you in school?"

He humbly says, "I didn't know what I wanted to do with life until last year."

"What happened last year?"

"I started having revelations and premonitions."

"Of what?"

"Happiness, of freedom; I was getting visions of me with great wealth, good health, and just all-around joy," he says gratefully. "It was if God was trying to show me my purpose or something."

Favorably, she asks, "What's your purpose?"

"I don't know it fully but for sure I know that part of my purpose is to show people the lack of love that we endure upon ourselves and upon others. I am here to remove this false perception of love that we get from television and through my writings and words," he says passionately. "I see myself getting paid for doing what I love."

While he counts her change, she asks, "So what about your degrees? What about moving up in the ranks here at your job? You're just going to give these up?"

"Most millionaires don't even have degrees. Moving up in the ranks at a job is like a slave moving up as an overseer," he says while pausing and allowing her to soak in his opinions. "And the only thing I'm giving up is fear. Fear holds us back from our dreams."

While he hands her the bags, she says, "I respect your reality, Mr. Givens." As she walks a few steps away from the counter, she intriguingly asks, "What are you getting your Master's in?"

"African-American Studies," he says while scanning another customer's items.

"Why did you choose African-American studies?"

"I had some influencers that encouraged me to. I guess they saw a lifestyle for me that they assumed suited me."

"What lifestyle is that?"

"A professor, a teacher, or a counselor. They want me to work a job that requires me to reach the youth and adults my age."

"You don't want to do that?" she asks inquiringly.

He hands the customer their bags and says to Tiffany, "Yes I do," while shrugging his shoulders. "I just want to reach them differently. I want to build on my own platform and my own message."

Impressively, she says, "That's wonderful. I pray that you are successful throughout your endeavors. You seem focused."

"That's love. Thank you so much," he says while she is walking away.

She walks out the store full of inspiration. She thinks to call her mentee to tell her who she ran into at the store but decides to wait to inform her. She gets in her car analyzing the receipt. She then puts her bag and purse in the passenger seat and drives out the parking lot to her apartment complex.

When she pulls up to her apartment, she notices one of her neighbor's cars outside and instantly sighs. Her neighbor plays her music loud every night while disturbing her peace. She parks her car, gets out with her purse and bag in hand, and walks to her apartment.

She oddly does not hear any music from her neighbor's apartment as she walks into her apartment. She turns on the light in the living room and walks to her room. She turns on the light in her room, takes off her shoes, places her purse, hangs up her new clothes, and walks back in the living room.

She sits comfortably on her couch for a moment to view her phone, turns on the television, and watches *The Vixens of Hip Hop*. She then gets up, goes into the kitchen, opens the refrigerator, and grabs a pot of left-over chicken Alfredo. She grabs a spoon and a plate out of the dishwasher, scoops a decent amount of food onto the plate, and places it into the microwave for two minutes.

After the food is ready, she goes back into the living room. She starts eating while watching television. She cynically observes the women on the television show and gets disgusted by what she sees. She mutes the television for a moment to listen to the silence. She wonders why her neighbor is so quiet. Suddenly, her cellphone rings loudly scaring her.

She answers the phone and says, "Hey, girl. What you doing?"

"Nothing at all, girl. What you doing?"

"Eating and watching *The Vixens of Hip Hop*," Tiffany says disgustingly.

Her friend excitedly says, "Ooh girl, that's my show! Did you see Destiny messy ass try to go behind her friend's back for Brady cheatin' ass?"

Feeling a sense of uneasiness after her friend's question, Tiffany asks, "You think this stuff is real?"

"Yes! I like it. It's entertaining. Plus, I love me some Alyia! She's a baddie and she can sing her ass off!" Her friend says avidly.

Blankly, Tiffany asks, "You think a fake ass, clown make up, wearing fake hair, and a boob job considers someone to be a baddie?"

Her friend hesitantly says, "I mean, she's confident in what she has and who she is. She has the money to do it. Hell, you wear weave!"

Tiffany calmly says, "I think, if she truly loved herself then she wouldn't have done any of that to herself. To me, it's all staged. It's all fake. Like why would television networks and corporations want to *paint* this ugly, ratchet, disgusting, and ignorant picture of Black women and Black men? And we praise them."

Anthony Crawford, Jr.

"I don't praise them" her friends defensively say.

"Yeah, but you laugh at it. You watch it every week. You're condoning it. What do you think our daughters and those young girls are thinking when they watch things like that? Especially when we naturally imitate what we repeatedly see. Is that really okay to you?" Tiffany says as a slight and uncomfortable pause covers their conversation. "If we're 'God made' and truly believe that we were all made in God's image, then why demoralize and shift what God has crafted with fake boobs, birth-control, fake asses, fake hair, and a lot of make up? Why are we hiding from our true selves? We have to think and hold each other accountable."

"Girl, you trippin'. You watch it. Plus, if a girl doesn't like her real hair or her natural look then she has a right to wear weave and make up. Let her get money and play these niggas the same way they do us." Her friend says. "You don't even know what a woman may be hiding under her make up, so you definitely shouldn't judge."

Tiffany reflects on her statement. She thinks about the women that she knows that were victims of domestic violence that wore a lot of make-up. The thoughts of the many cuts and bruises that she saw on Patricia's face a few years back flashes through her mind.

Her friend says, "Yes so let that shit ride, Tiff! Ooh let me tell you about this nigga, Brian!"

Not wanting to gossip, Tiffany interrupts her friend's rant, and says, "Hey, let me call you back; my mama is calling."

"Oh okay, tell your mama I said hi, and don't for get to call me back! I got to tell you this shit!"

"Okay, I got you," she says as they both end the call. She examines the television show for a second and turns it off while feeling perturb. She reflects heavily on the life lessons that she received today.

She then gets on her phone to check her social media pages. She scrolls up and down on her timeline looking at friends and family members' pictures. She sees that most of her friends are getting married and having kids. She's internally happy for them, but she feels like she deserves that type of love and happiness.

Black Pain't, Vol. I

She comes across a picture of her ex-boyfriend and his son. She says, "Awwww that's so precious," to herself and continues to scroll through the timeline. She gets up and walks in her room to put her phone on her charger. While putting her phone on the charger, she stares a poster of her favorite actress on her wall. It was a gift from Charles that he had gotten her on her birthday a few years ago. She sits down on the edge of the bed admiring the poster and starts to ruminate over her past relationships................

(Three years ago, Tiffany was in a relationship with Charles "Sir Charles" Mason. Though Charles was a talented singing and rap artist, he was also eight years older, but Tiffany loved dating older men who had a lot going on for themselves. She loved how he supported her throughout her endeavors, motivated her during her last years of college, took her out on dates, invited her to his shows, bought her nice clothing and accessories, and treated her to a few trips out of the country.

Charles worked in the Department of Mental Health. He was an artist and Tiffany loved his sense of fashion. She respected the way he expressed himself through his music. His greenish blue eyes held her hostage. She wanted to dive in his command every time he stared into her eyes. She treasured his childhood stories and what it was like for him to grow up in a household with a Black father and a White mother.

She fell in love with him throughout his persistence and consistency. She trusted him more than she ever trusted anyone else. Their sex was passionate, their bond was unbreakable, and their love for each other grew more and more over the years.

As time went by in their relationship, he had the opportunity to tour the world, opening for a popular, global artist. However, he declined the offer. He loved Tiffany too much to leave, knowing how it is on the road, he didn't want to lose the person he come to love. He also stayed thinking that, when Tiffany graduated, they would have more time together to build a future and a family.

Anthony Crawford, Jr.

Everything was everything until one summer, Charles took it a step further. He got her ring size and put money away for a ring. He talked with Tiffany's stepdad to get his approval. With the help of Tiffany's birthday celebration, he was able to bring Tiffany's family and friends in on his proposal. However, that late night after Tiffany's birthday party, she told Charles that she decided to study abroad in Korea for a semester. Charles was not too fond of her decision, because he didn't go on that tour. He respected her impulsive decision, and they both made a pact to remain emotionally strong while they were apart.

Times were challenging for Charles. He was still enacting as a local artist, getting paid for performing, ghostwriting, and giving vocal lessons, but something was missing from his life. It felt like how it feels when one has been wearing a sweater for so long that, when you finally take it off, it still feels like you have it on.

The time difference conflicted with their work schedules. Sexy, gorgeous women were shooting their shots at his shows and through social media. Temptation taunted his heart, body, and mind. After the first couple of months of Tiffany's absence, and two to go, Charles cheated with a woman who used to come to his performances back when he was younger. She expressed that she was also in a relationship, but the man she was with was cuckolder.

Even though he gladly beat her pussy up like a meat tenderizer, the guilt followed him like a shadow. It would creep in his thoughts and alluded them to ways to get away without telling her. He promised himself to take it to the grave. To defeat the guilt, he would tirelessly and shamelessly contact Tiffany just to display his continued pursue for her heart.

November rolled around; Charles had one more month and a few days to go before Tiffany's return home. It has been three weeks since his deceit. The same woman popped up at his show dressed down to perfection. He had already been sipping, feeling her eyes every step he made. While she drank, she made sure he kept eye contact on her when he sang his song about the carnal desires.

Black Pain't, Vol. I

 After the show, she texted him, asking for his address. He sent it to her and met her at his place. Once they got in the house, he found himself kissing her wildly against the door, forgetting to lock it after he closed it. They got lost in the touching and he had her pinned up against his refrigerator. He swung her onto his kitchen counter and masticated on her pussy. The feeling was too enticing, she gave him just the right amount of passion he needed. She allowed him to blow off some frustration and steam by taking trips to pound town.
 Knowing that Tiffany would be home soon, Charles had to find a cutting off point with his affair. He didn't communicate with her, and what was even better was that she stopped coming to his shows. Weeks went by and Charles felt like he was in the clear. The guilt had worn off and stopped making him feel unscrupulous about his actions.
 One evening, when he got home from recording sessions, the woman that he had cheated with told him that she was pregnant. While in fright, Charles denied that the baby was his, because he knew about the woman's boyfriend. She proclaimed that her and her boyfriend wasn't having sex since she found out that he cheated and caught a STD. He didn't want to believe her and called her a liar for saying it. He was more fearful of losing and hurting Tiffany than anything else. He blocked all contact he had with the woman, hoping that she would see him for who he really is and leave him be.
 It was a cold December when Tiffany returned from Korea. Charles picked her up from the airport and they embraced each other with strong hugs and deep, sweet kisses. Though their reuniting was pleasant, he recognized that her mind and aura was different. His circumstances would not allow him to truly enjoy their proximity.
 After a few days after getting her mind and schedule back to mainstream America, she taught him so much from her trip. She began to notice Charles's strange acts and the heavy energy that he would carry. She couldn't quite put her finger on it, but she felt uneasy around him.

Anthony Crawford, Jr.

One day, while they were driving home from the movie theater, she asked him, "Charlie, are you okay? You haven't been seeming like yourself."

Sorrowfully, he replies, "I'm good. I've just been tired from working a lot. Things can get overwhelmed at times. Plus, things weren't easy when you went away. I didn't have you around to put me at peace during rough times."

Inconspicuously, she said, "Sorry to hear that boo. Is there anything that I can do now?"

"I think you already do enough, Love," he said.

She pauses for a moment and desperately says, "You know you can talk to me about anything. We can go do something that you really want to do and talk. I know I've been gone for four months but we can go somewhere and just share our hard nights."

"Oh, naw, we're good Tiff. I'm just happy that you're back," he innocently said.

The next weekend, Charles took her out to eat. When they walked into the restaurant, Tiffany saw a lot of her friends and family members sitting in different sections. She asked, "Charlie, why is there a lot of people we know here?" She didn't get a response and when she turned around, Charles was gone. She spotted her mother and walked toward her. Suddenly, the room got dark. A light appeared on the stage where a live band started playing. Charles walked on the small stage with a microphone in his hand.

He said, "I call this poem, Tiffany's." He recites:

"It's been a while,
but there's this girl named Tiffany.
I like her mind,
she be looking good in them blue Tiffany's.
I like her style,
so I took Tiffany to Tiffany's and got her ring-size,
because I truly like our chemistry. I took a chance with her,
I envisioned me on a rooftop, dancing with her.

Black Pain't, Vol. I

I just want to romance with her, change her last name and make some
plans with her. She keeps my mind flowing,
she's my Ms. Bonita Applebaum in them Apple Bottoms
and she got it going on. I know you're right for me, ain't the type to be
wrong. You made me call my mama because she's the type you take
home. Reminiscing on nights when we would read alone,
those nights when we would sing some songs;
most night you'd be in different color heels and thongs,
that would be all that you would have on before we did the grown.
My Queen, you had been the one. To lose you is scary to me,
I just love our tales, you're a fairy to me.
Tiffany, I want your love to continue to carry me.
So I'm asking you, "Will you marry me, Tiffany?"

When Charles finished, he hopped off the stage and walked up to Tiffany. The stage's spotlight shined on the two. He pulled out a small box from out of his pocket. He got on one knee and slowly opened the small box. As she gazed at the beautiful ring, he asked, "Will you, Tiffany? Marry me? Will you marry me, Tiffany?"

She began to cry and said, "Yes." The crowd of their family and friends cheered them on. There were a lot of videos and pictures taken of the proposal that their loved ones posted on their social media pages.

Since Charles rented the building for the night, he, Tiffany, and all of their family and friends finished the night drinking, dancing, and celebrating their engagement.

Ten months passed and everything seemed to get better between Tiffany and Charles. There were a lot of wedding planning and wild nights of them partying out their stress and fucking away their frustrations. They decided to push the wedding to a further date just so Tiffany can graduate, so Charles can finish his E.P.; they were enjoying life on a much happier scale than before so it wouldn't hurt anything, and it gave their family and friends more time to prepare.

After Tiffany graduated from college, she landed a job as a teacher. They both went on a road trip to several states around the *country to celebrate Tiffany's accomplishment and his upcoming release date for his E.P. through parasailing on beaches, snorkeling at waterfalls, skydiving in country sides, and dancing at different clubs. Life was good in all aspects for them both.*

    When they returned home, they decided to start saving money for their marriage and get on the same page about how they wanted it to go. They chose a new date, decided to hire a wedding planner, and worked extra shifts just to pay for everything.

    One evening, when Tiffany arrived home, she received a picture text message of a baby. The caption said, "Who does this baby look like?"

    Confusedly, Tiffany stared at the picture and disbelief. She saw the baby's greenish blue eyes and her heart dropped. She trembled while she called the anonymous number. Once they answered, Tiffany scarcely asked, "Hey, I'm sorry, but who is this?"

    "I'm Ella," she said dastardly. After a painful pause, she proceeded to say, "I am Charles's baby mother."

    "Charles who?" Tiffany said instantly praying and wishing that she wasn't talking about her Charles.

    Ella wrathfully said, "The 'Fuck Boy' that you're engaged to sweetheart. Don't play. That baby looks just like him. He blocked my number, and he blocked me on his social media, so I got your number from one of my friend's friends and reached out to you."

    "Who... who are you talking about?" Tiffany slowly fell to the floor.

    "I don't know if you know Jazmine, but her friend Rayven gave it to me. Sir Charles just so happen to come up in our conversation and I told them what happened between me and him. Rayven pulled up a picture of him and knew that was your man, because she was supposed to be a maid of honor for your wedding. Woman to woman, I thought I'd let you know who you're marrying."

    She started shaking as if someone grabbed her heart right out of her chest, pierced through it a hundred times, and placed it back into

Black Pain't, Vol. I

her chest for her to live with. She built enough courage to cautiously asked, "How…… When? Are you sure?"

"We had sex last year around the end of October. I called and told him that I was pregnant around mid-November. He got mad and accused me of trying to put the baby on him because I had a boyfriend at the time. But me and him wasn't fuckin' so I knew it had to be Charles. Then he tried to convince me to abort it. I told him that we could just take a DNA test after I have the baby to be sure. But I knew from the moment this baby was born that it was his," she said. "The moment I seen those eyes; I just knew."

"I just thought you should know the type of nigga you're marrying. I'm sorry, but he's sorrier and just another 'Fuck Boy' that preys on women younger than him. Tell him that I do plan on putting him on child support real soon, but I will grant him visitation because no child should have to grow up without their father," Ella said while hanging up the phone.

Tiffany sat on the floor in total distress. She cried for an hour and a half until Charles came home. When he walked through the door, he noticed her on the floor with her shirt drenched in tears, her eyes bloodshot red, and the outside of her eyes swollen. He crouched to the floor and fearfully asked, "What's wrong?"

She looked at him downheartedly and began to heavily cry again. She had a silent cry for a moment and breathed as if she was having a panic attack.

"What's wrong? Who did it?" He desperately asked while his heart pumped super-fast.

She pointed at her cellphone that was thrown against the wall in front of her. Charles looked to her cellphone and said, "What? Did you break your phone?" He grabbed it and handed it to her. She unlocked her phone and showed him the picture of his son.

"That's you! That you! THAT'S YOU! LOOK AT THOSE EYES! LOOK AT THOSE EYES, CHARLIE! THAT IS YOU CHARLIE! THAT'S YOU!" She said in an intense way as she continued to cry her heart out.

Anthony Crawford, Jr.

Stressed and panicked, Charles covered his mouth staring at the picture. He looked at Tiffany crying her eyeballs out on the floor. He hopelessly said, "Baby... I'm..."

She instantly rushed from the floor, swinging her fists. He dodged a couple of her thrown fists of fury until he got hit by one. He then grabbed her arms, held her, and yells, "TIFFANY! CALM DOWN!"

"CALM DOWN? YOU WANT ME TO CALM DOWN? This is fucked up! Why now? We're getting married! Why would you do this shit to me? While I was in Korea? OH MY GOD! NO! Charlie! Why? Why would you do this to me?" She said as he slowly and gently released her.

He stood up, gathered himself, looked around for a moment to hold back his tears, and cautiously said, "I'm sorry, Tiff. It was a drunk night. I was with my fraternity brothers. It wasn't anything special baby, but what I have with you is special. I'm sorry."

She repeatedly shook her head and said, "We can't do this, Charlie. You have a whole child; a whole new life."

"We can work this out, Tiff. Give me a chance to fix things, baby," he said while gently grabbing her. He wiped her eyes and repeatedly kissed her around her neck. He said, "I'm sorry, baby. I don't want to lose you. I love you. Say you love me back!"

"I love you, Charlie!" She said while allowing him to take her clothes off. "You promise she didn't mean anything to you? I'm the love of your life?" She said while he picked her up and took her to their bedroom.

He laid her on the bed, took off his shirt, and said, "You're the only thing that means the world to me, Tiff. I love you. You're the one I want to marry and be with for the rest of my life."

He began to slowly lick and suck the pearl of her privacy. He grabbed her buttocks with her legs wrapped around his neck. He then takes off his pants and underwear and smoothly inserted himself within her.

Black Pain't, Vol. I

She moaned and grasped for air as she stared at the ceiling. She slightly began to cry, trying to enjoy the sexual sensations of his manhood exploring her womanhood. He repeatedly whispered in her ear, "Baby, I'm yours. I'm sorry. We can make this work. Say we will make it work!" He got more aggressive as he went deeper within her.

She gradually said, "We will make it work. We will work it out baby." They both encountered a climax like no other. To her, it felt like the turning point of their relationship. However, to him, it was a chance to make things right.

Tiffany never slept well after that experience. She lost a lot of weight due to stress. She wondered what her family and friends were going to think and say about Charles's child. She told her family and some of her friends and they wanted her to leave him. Some of her family and friends were supportive with whatever decision she decided to make, while most couldn't believe the news and stopped talking to Tiffany because they felt she was making a huge mistake. Tiffany's mother opts out of paying for the wedding and hated Charles for what he did to her daughter.

She wasn't able to be an effective teacher in her classroom because the pain rushed through her body and mind. It cringed her heart to think that Charles had a baby by another woman and the fact that he had unprotected sex with her.

Charles tried all he could to make it up to Tiffany. He bought her things, took her out every weekend, and participated in some of her favorite activities, however, Tiffany wasn't happy at all. It was like he was fighting an uphill battle. She was bitter toward their relationship and felt as if their engagement was a fraud. She hated herself for trying to make it work with him. She isolated herself from her friends and family. She felt that if she wouldn't have never left for Korea, then none of it would have happened.

Tiffany canceled their wedding. Family and friends of Tiffany and Charles were worried about the two of them. She wanted to wait until she recovered from her heart break to see if she'll be able to trust and love Charles again. She moved out to live with her mother. Charles stayed in their apartment.

She worked and came home every night for two years in sadness. She spent some of her time at her sisters with her nieces and nephews. She picked up a habit of shopping because it made her feel good. She was slowly but surely letting go of what happened but felt a great sense of hope when Charles would call. They would converse about life, his child, and reminisce about old times between them. He would try everything in his power to see her or take her out for dinner, but he didn't seem sincere to her.

They spent a few times together. They would have a good time, too. They ate, played games, conversed about getting back together, talked about getting married, and would have incredible sex.

Charles started living with one of his fraternity brothers. He paid child support. He and his baby's mother would switch off every two weeks. He accepted and took care of his responsibilities while trying to get back with Tiffany.

Their communication slowly began to fade. Tiffany stopped blaming herself for Charles's actions. Charles got impatient with fighting to spend time with her and stopped trying to make things work between them.)

Tiffany puts her phone down on her lampstand and puts on her pajamas. She goes into the kitchen to put the dishes in the sink. She turns off the kitchen light, turns off the living room light, and walks back in her room.

To herself, she says, "As I lay myself down to sleep, I pray to the Lord, my soul to keep; if I should die before I wake, I pray to the Lord my soul to take. Amen." She then slides under her cover and looks at her phone to see the time. Tiffany turns the lamp off and goes to sleep.

Chapter 6: The Cycle

He clocks out of work and heads out of the store to his car that was parked in the employees' parking lot. He checks his cellphone as he unlocks the car and gets in. It's a text from Trina that reads, "Hey Tony! What are you doing?"

He starts his car and texts back saying, "Just getting off work. What about yourself?"

She texts back saying, "Just at home, reading. What are you about to do now?"

While he is driving, he gets to a red stop light, looks at his cellphone, reads Trina's text message, and texts back saying, "I'm about to head home. I don't have to be up in the morning, so I probably just relax and get ahead on some of my work."

Trina texts back saying, "Come hang out with me. You can do your work while I'm reading."

He responds by texting, "Okay. I got you. Text me your address." He drives for a bit as he waits for her to text him the address. She texts it to him, he activates his GPS, and realizes he must go in the opposite direction. He makes a U-Turn at a light and, on the way to her place, he stops by a nearby gas station to get some snacks.

When he gets to her door, he knocks. Seconds later, Trina opens the door, wearing red and yellow boy shorts and a white tank-top that outlined her nipple piercings. He immediately tries his best not to take a bite of her rich, dark, and chocolate skin. He increases his self-control while he walks in and says, "Hey, Love." He gives her a hug and gets taken by the touch of her oily skin. He fights the temptation.

Wittily, she says, "Was there traffic or something?"

He lays his backpack on the side of the hall and says, "I stopped to get us some snacks," he says while closing the door behind him. He looks around her living room noticing the weed tray under one of the couches. He scans the photos of *Bob Marley*, *Erykah Badu*, *Rihanna*, and *Lauryn Hill* on the walls. He dazzles at the pictures of her and her twin sister. He sees a 52-inch television sitting on the wall near the entertainment system that has surround sound. He sees a red incent burning from an incent holder and some heels sitting in the corner of the living room.

He says, "You have a nice place. I didn't know you smoke weed."

"Thank you. How did you know I smoke weed?" She thoughtfully asks while feeling as though he's going to be judgmental.

"Other than the weed tray under your couch, the room has an 'I smoke weed' feeling. Plus, I smoke too," he says as her aura brightens, she develops sparks in her eyes.

Enthusiastically, she says, "That's wassup! You want me to roll up?" She walks to the couch and grabs the weed tray from under it.

Black Pain't, Vol. I

"I'll roll up," he says while gently grabbing the ash tray from her hands. "One thing that many people don't know about me is that I'm from the hood."

She gives a confused face and asks, "You? You're from the hood? Hecks naw! Negro, I'm from the hood." She laughs to herself. "You had a silver spoon, boy, don't play."

He chortles and says, "Not at all. More like a plastic spoon." They both laugh. While breaking down the wildflower and slowly admiring its stickiness, he says, "I was blessed to have my mother and father in my life. They taught me all they knew. They nurtured and loved me and my siblings with all the love and wisdom that they had received. They both worked their asses off to make sure that we had all that we needed in life. Even though we lived in a city of mixed gangs and problematic poverty, we had each other; we had family. I learned the importance of family values early."

She sympathetically stares at him. She wonders as to why his energy feels so comforting and gentle. His nappy hair, full beard, and adventurer-style of dressing made sense to her. It's relaxing to her to know that he came from an environment that she can relate to. It turns her on to see a man that she admires rolling up weed. "You think you'd ever go back home?"

"Of course. My family is there," he says as he splits the swisher down the middle to dump the tobacco into the ashtray. He slowly licks the sides and the tips of the swisher while she observes, wishing it was her. She foresees his pinks lips on her as he gradually spreads the weed into the swisher. "I feel like I had to do what Simba did. Leave his prideful land and went back to be King." He rolls up the swisher making it into a blunt. He then lights the blunt with a lighter, takes a few puffs, and inhaling. He hands it the blunt to her. "Hit it. Don't mess up the rotation." She closes her eyes, takes a few puffs, and begins to cough. "Virgin lungs! I thought you smoked?"

While coughing hard, she is able to say, "I'm usually on point with it."

Anthony Crawford, Jr.

"You ain't never smoked with a real one before either," he says confidently as she passes the blunt back to him. He taps the blunt over the ashtray, takes a few more puffs, and asks, "Why do you smoke?"

She heavily smokes and says, "It's a spiritual thing for me. I'm something like a gypsy." They both laugh as she passes him the blunt. The atmosphere shifts when she says, "Plus, life can seem fucked up at times. I smoke to take away the *pain* that shows up when I'm trying to be happy."

He put the blunt to his lips and inhales to ponder on her statement. As he exhales, he asks, "How long does the *pain* usually last?" He gives her the blunt and gets up to wash his hands in her kitchen sink.

She discerns his suave mannerisms as he dries his hands off with a paper towel. She looks when he goes to the refrigerator and says, "I don't keep track of the time. *Painful* thoughts come and it go. They always seem to come when I'm alone."

"If we create with our words, what do you think you just created?" He asks while penetrating her mind with his thought-provoking question.

She hesitantly replies, "I guess I just created more *pain* to come when I'm alone."

"*Pain* will definitely do that to you though; it sneaks up on you at times of the day when you're most vulnerable," he says empathetically as he opens the freezer door and discovers a large bottle of Jack Daniels. "You're not an alcoholic, are you?"

"There you go judging me again."

He comes back into the living room to sit down and kindly says, "No judgment. I try not to judge anyone or anything."

"Why is that?"

"I realized a long time ago that when I judge another, I am judging me; when I judge anything else, then I am taking away from its true purpose. If I do find myself judging, I realize that it's just an interesting to me, and I ask questions."

"What's interesting about me?"

Black Pain't, Vol. I

Rapidly, he says, "You're not afraid to be yourself."

She's chained by his response. She asks, "Why is that such a big deal to you?"

"If you're not yourself then who are you? Who are you pretending to be? What is this lie that you're telling yourself? What's wrong with the person that God designed you to be?" He asks as an intense wave of tension circles the room. "A lot of people are trying to be someone they're not and hiding behind masks. Not you though. You don't have masks. You show yourself fully in every moment."

"Yeah, whatever nigga. I won't call myself no alcoholic, but it does help me sleep at night. Jack Daniels is like my boyfriend," she says while passing the blunt.

He grabs it out of her hand, takes a few more puffs, and says, "I see. What's your relationship like with him?"

While he hands her the blunt, she giggles and says, "Well, he doesn't judge me. He's a smooth, hard, and dark man that touches me on the inside. I don't have to worry about him leaving me or hurting me even though I know that he's bad for me. Me and Jack cool. He doesn't say much, and he would rather chill in the freezer than in my bed, so it's like he gives me my space."

"Sounds like a good guy."

She gets up and heavily hits the blunt again. She passes it to him and walks into the kitchen to grab two shot glasses and the liquor from out of the freezer. She asks, "You want to meet him?"

"Naw, I'm good. I don't swing that way," he says modestly.

She walks back into the living room and hops on the couch by Tony. She sits up, puts the shot glasses on the coffee table and opens the Jack Daniels. She pours the liquor into the two shot glasses, and says, "You don't have to be up in the morning. You can take one."

He looks deep into her eyes searching for some truth to this situation and says, "I am not trying to get drunk with you love."

"Why is that?"

"Because the more I drink, the less I think," he says prophetically.

Anthony Crawford, Jr.

Wanting to open Pandora's Box, she says, "Okay, just take one and I'll leave you alone."

"Just one?"

"Just one, I promise," she affirms innocently.

He hesitates and says, "Aight, let's go."

They both grab their shot glass and drink. He makes a sour face and she looks like she just drank a little glass of water. He makes sound effects one would make after they taste something nasty. She laughs and says, "You cool as fuck. I thought you were a square or very weird."

They both laugh and he says, "I'm more of a circle."

"Why a circle?" She asks.

Promptly, he says, "Because I'm well rounded."

"Nigga you drunk already," she uncontrollably laughs while falling on him. "After a shot or two and smoking, I usually put on my dance music and dance around the house, but naw. I don't want to have you in here hypnotized."

"It's all love," he says while trying to avoid the strong sexual energy coming from Trina. He looks to her movie shelf and asks, "What movies do you have?" He stands up and goes through her movie collection. He lifts a movie and analyzes it. "Have you ever seen *Hidden Colors*?"

"What's *Hidden Colors*?"

"It's like a series of documentary films. They all have African American doctors, philosophers, intellectuals, conscious, and pro-black men and women who talks about Black history, our culture; they inform us about undocumented truths. They expose us to some of America's hidden agendas," he understandingly says while placing the movie back in its previous position. "It's all fishy to me though."

"Why?"

"There were two things that caught my attention about the documentaries. One, how can you have a two-hour documentary about White Supremacy and don't mention *Neely Fully Jr.*?"

"Who's he?"

Black Pain't, Vol. I

"He wrote the book on White Supremacy. It's like he broke through their system's codes and wrote a book about it back in the early '70s. They didn't even mention the brother. They began falsifying terms and definitions of words that's associated within White Supremacy."

"What is White Supremacy?"

He chortles and says, "You have a lot to learn, love. White Supremacy is the reign that we're living under, the current rulers of the world. We are in their cycle." He allows her to fathom his words and proceeds to say, "They run this system. They wipe out all that oppose and all that speak against their system. *2pac* tried to speak against it, *Pimp C* spoke out against it, *Huey P. Newton* spoke out against it; *John F. Kennedy*, *Gaddafi*, *Malcolm X*, and *Dr. Martin Luther King, Jr.* spoke out against them. They all were assassinated. You try to 'wake' the people to the system then *they* will take you out."

He pauses for a moment noticing the atmosphere shift in the room. He squints his eyes while staring into her red eyes. "What do you think happened to Jesus Christ?"

"What happened to Jesus Christ?" she asks while breaking free from the intense friction in the room.

He grins and says, "He tried to wake God's people and the Roman Empire took him out."

"Nigga, what cycle?" She says irritably.

"This system, love," he softly says calming her inner beast. "This system is the cycle. It has just been ruled by different empires. Right now, White Supremacy rules this cycle. Christ was around during the cycle of the Roman Empire. Moses was around during the cycle of Egyptian Empire."

"So what can break this cycle?"

"By breaking our own cycles."

She waits for a second and asks, "Can you stop speaking in parables?"

He smiles and remorsefully says, "Oh, my apologies. In order to break this cycle we must break our own life's cycles, because we can't change anything if we're not willing to change. Some people are afraid of change while some resist it. We aren't taught that change is inevitable. We aren't taught that everything and everyone change all the time, every day, in every way. Change is good."

"So if I change then the cycle changes?"

"Yes."

She considers his logic; however, it is not making any sense to her. She asks, "How does that work?"

"We have to understand our cycles. Our cycles are the situations that continuously occur in the same format but with different characters or settings throughout the year. If you don't like the situations that keeps occurring, then make a new decision. Change your mind and develop a new way to do things. I'll use my cycle for an example." He pauses, allowing her to take heed, and says, "I struggle with lust. Any time I lust after a woman, things never work out. That's one of my cycles. That's why I always try to be a good friend to a woman before I tried being a good lover, because if I sex a woman early then it ruins things between me and that woman."

"So early sex can ruin a relationship…"

He interjects and says, "Having sex early ruins the friendship and then relationship."

"How? There are plenty of couples who had sex early that are married, or in a relationship. Some even have families."

He instantly says, "That sounds like a situationship." She smacks her lips as he asks, "Are they happy? Are they living together or dying together? Why is the divorce rate so high in this country? Why do people continue to cheat on their spouses?" He waits an instant allowing the flow of questions to massage her mind. "When we have sex early, what experiences or opportunities are taken away?"

While he continues to look through her movies, she's in awe from their active conversation. She watches him as he walks to grab his backpack and back to her living room to sit down. As he begins going over his work, she grabs her book and lies against him. She openly says, "You can take off your shoes if you want. Unless your feet stink. Then leave them mutha fuckas on."

Black Pain't, Vol. I

"My feet don't stink, punk," he says while taking his shoes off and placing them on the side of the couch that they were sitting on.

She laughs and asks, "Who are you calling a punk, chump?" She playfully shoves him. "I'm from the hood, too!"

"You're the only one in the room, right?" He asks sarcastically.

She wrestles with him in a sexual manner, hoping that he gives her some type of sexual attention. He starts tickling her and causes her to uncontrollably laugh. She falls off the couch and Tony, remorsefully asks, "Are you okay?" He tries to help her up and she wrestles with him again.

He lifts her up and she kisses him on the lips. The embrace of his succulent lips against her fine, full lips fill them both with enchantment. She looks at his beard to remember the way it felt against her face. As he slowly brings her down, she can feel his third leg rubbing against her legs stopping at her stomach. He look deep within her eyes to find her intentions. Her dark, smooth, and oily skin lures into his thoughts as they continue to stare into one another for a soft moment.

She puts her head down shamefully, says, "I'm sorry. I didn't mean…" and he passionately starts French kissing her on her lips.

They fall back onto the couch with Trina on top of Tony. She starts unbuckling his belt while kissing him on his neck. He grabs a hold of her neck while kissing her cleavage. She pulls his hands to the back of the couch, takes off his shirt, and starts kissing his chest.

She begins to take off his pants and his underwear. As she gets on her knees, she grabs his penis with her left hand, puts her right index finger into his mouth, and begins to suck his shaft. She touches herself with her right index finger using the saliva she got from Tony's mouth.

She repeatedly slurps, chokes, sucks, and spits on his shaft. He puts his left hand on her head, and she removes it saying, "Don't touch my hair."

She gets up from off her knees, pulls her panties off, and slowly sits on Tony's penis. She smoothly puts it inside her. She says, "Oh My God! I'm cuming already."

Anthony Crawford, Jr.

Tony can feel her legs quaking as she continues to ride him. He lifts her while still being inside her. He rhythmically begins to pull her up and down while standing up. After a minute or so, he lays her on the couch and starts bouncing on her while she screams. She grabs his left butt cheek. Then he turns her over in the doggy-style position. She has her right hand holding onto the arm of the couch and her left arm touching the left side of his abs.

She screams, "I'M CUMING!" He continues to sex her while feeling her legs vibrate against his thighs. He pulls out of her, picks her up, and walks her into her bedroom. He sits on the edge of her bed as she gets into the missionary position. She bounces up and down on him while moaning and groaning. She turns around facing him with his penis still inside her. They pause for a moment to stare into each other's eyes. She lies on his chest slowly grinding on him. They lie there, holding each other.

They use the next several minutes to catch their breath. There is a great calm that enters in the room. Tony feels foul from his sexual encounter with Trina because he did not want it to happen so quickly. He watches as she falls asleep into his arms. He thinks to himself, "What if my theories about the cycle are wrong? What if I have been wrong all this time about early sex?" His thoughts drain the remaining of his energy and he gradually falls asleep.

It is morning and someone is repeatedly knocking on Trina's door.

"Trina," he says lightly while waking up. "There's someone at your door."

Irritably, she grouches and says, "OH SHIT!"

"Who is that?" He asks anxiously.

Slowly waking up, she softly asks, "Who is who? Wait, who are you?"

"Stop playin' JaTrina," Jalisa teasingly says.

"Don't call me that!" Trina demands as she gets up out her bed.

Black Pain't, Vol. I

As she walks into her living room, he slightly yells, "Is that your boyfriend? Husband?"

"Nigga, I'm single," she yells while throwing his clothes into her room. She opens the door and her sister, Jalisa, slowly walks in.

"Weed smell? Check. Alcohol on the coffee table? Check. Well, everything seems to be the same. But who were you talking to?" Jalisa asks while walking closer to her bedroom.

Trina playfully runs in front of her to stop her and says, "I was talking to Tony."

Conspicuously, Jalisa shoves Trina out of her path, runs to the bedroom, sees Tony putting on his shirt, and says, "Oh so you're Tony?"

He turns to face her, smiles, and humbly says, "Yes, ma'am. And you're Jal...."

She interrupts him and says, "I'm Jalisa. The evil twin sister. Well, that's what Trina thinks I am."

As Trina walks in putting on her shirt and some sweatpants, she brusquely says, "Don't worry about her, Tony. She be acting like she never had any dick before."

"TRINA! Don't tell no stranger my business!" Jalisa angrily says instantly.

Trina sarcastically says, "Yeah, yeah. Jalisa this is Tony, Tony this is Jalisa. The nigga from the boat? Yeah, the one you told me to be careful. Guess I wasn't careful."

He says, "You're the one from the boat. I couldn't tell that you two were twins at first because your hairstyles are different. Plus, you two had different sunglasses on."

Trina jokingly says, "Yes, the one that's always, in all ways, giving everyone a hard time for no apparent reason every day, all day. This is the one and only Jalisa Williams."

"Nice to meet you, Tony. My sister tells me a lot about you," Jalisa says while everyone is walking into the living room. Trina sits down, grabs the blunt and the lighter from off the weed tray, and lights it.

Anthony Crawford, Jr.

Tony modestly says, "Well, based off how she just introduced you to me, I hope she's been saying some good things about me."

"Of course I told her good things. How you're a schoolboy and an uptight ass square. Had him smoking and drinking last night though. So you're not all that square," Trina says while laughing and smoking. "He from the hood too."

While straightening up her living room, Jalisa asks, "So you're in a gang?"

"No ma'am," he says respectfully.

Jalisa absorbs him for a moment and asks, "Good because I don't see a purpose for it."

"I do," he says.

"What do you think is the purpose of gang banging other than killing each other?" Jalisa asks satirically.

Instantaneously, he says, "I think the purpose of gang banging should be to protect, to serve, and to build up our communities. That was their original purpose."

Jalisa begins to ask, "So do you think……"

Trina interjects and impatiently says, "Damn Jalisa, enough with the interview."

"It's all love Trina. She's just being a good sister. This is what sisters and brothers are supposed to do."

Jalisa smiles and animatedly shouts, "Finally someone who understands!"

"He's a good dude. You don't have to worry about him," Trina says cynically.

Tony feels the friction in the room and says, "I have to go. It was nice meeting you, Jalisa."

While he leans down to give Trina a forehead kiss, she whispers, "Hit me up later when you get out of class." Tony walks out of Trina's apartment closing the door gently while Jalisa is angrily staring at Trina.

Tony slowly walks to his car and sees a lady struggling to get a box into her car. He runs over there to help her and says, "Let me help you with that." He grabs the box from the bottom while she lifts the trunk open.

She looks at him closely and says, "Hey, it's you. Mr. Givens! You're not following me around, are you?"

He laughs while repositioning the box into the trunk of her car, and says, "Naw, I just left a friend's home that lives in these apartment complexes."

Suspiciously, she moderately says, "You were at apartment number 43 last night?"

"Yes, I was," he says hesitantly, but proudly. "How'd you know?"

Unbelieving, she says, "Oh, wow. That girl who lives in there is always extra loud and plays her music almost every night! Very annoying. Oddly she didn't do that last night. And I was so diligently wondering why it was so quiet last night. You must be a good man, sir."

Closing her trunk, He says, "Thank you. That means a lot, Miss?"

"Oh, please. You can call me Tiffany, Mr. Givens."

"And you can call me Tony, Tiffany. Were there any more gigantic boxes that you need help with?" He asks comically.

She grins and says, "No, sir. Thank you so much! I appreciate it." She makes a mental note to tell Rayven about Tony and her next-door neighbor.

"No problem at all, have a good day. Thanks for allowing me to serve you," he respectively says as he slowly walks to his car. He unlocks the doors with a button on his car key. He gets in and puts the key into the ignition, starts the car, and plugs his phone up to the car charger and the auxiliary cord. He finds a playlist to play on his phone and he turns his music loud. He puts on his seat belt and drives off heading to his apartment.

On the way home, he's rapping and is very animated while driving and listening to the music. He pulls up to his apartment and feels an ounce of joy. He couldn't help but to think about the night he had with Trina.

Anthony Crawford, Jr.

He gets out of his car, pushes a button on his key to lock it, and slowly walks to his apartment. Once he gets to his door, he unlocks the door, walks in, and goes to his kitchen table that has his course books, his school supplies, and notebooks sitting on it. He sits down in a chair to look at the syllabus to see what work is due next week.

During his reading, an unbearable truth swam through him, *"I have not known Trina that long and we had sex last night."*

He shakes his head to avoid the verity while he grabs his notebook and a pen. The truth boomerangs back to his heart and he begins to question his feelings towards Trina.

He gets inspired to write a poem. He closes his eyes for a moment and begins to take slow, deep breaths. Flashbacks of last night keeps running through his mind. He thinks about his ex-girlfriend and wonders what she would have thought if she had seen someone as beautiful as Trina with him? He even thinks about buying Trina another bottle of Jack Daniels. He opens his eyes and begins to write:

She had a boyfriend when I met her, his name was Jack.
She said, "When all her friends left me, he stayed to have my back."
Her ex-boyfriend cheated on her; He was there to pick up the slack.
He was there when she was feeling sad.
Jack's last name is Daniels, and he is a strong and dark brother,
but she didn't tell her family and friends about him,
not even her beloved sister.
She enjoyed his words, a taste that numbed her pain;
he healed the scars from when she cut herself time and time again.
He there for her, she was just so happy to have someone around.
Jack cared for her.
Although Jack was too strong for her and would watch her as she cried out her make up; she got used to him and never needed a chaser.
she never needed to chase him.
She found herself through those moments; and, at her lowest,
she took Jack to the road and poured his soul on the tracks.
So as he hit the road, Jack was to never come back.

Black Pain't, Vol. I

His cellphone rings in the midst of his writing. He immediately puts his pencil down and rushes to his cellphone. He answers and delightfully greets, "Wassup, Big Bro?"

"How have you been young king?"

"I'm still learning. What about you?

The man says, "I hear you, brother, and I'm good. Real good actually. Aaron James is coming to the city soon. He'll be speaking at 18th St. Missionary Baptist Church."

"Ahh man, Mr. Jones is going to be at a church?" Tony asks comically.

He says, "The brother speaks about some real stuff man. He just makes a lot of references from the bible. He reminds me of you sometimes. Come soak in some wisdom and some knowledge. It'll help you with what you want to do after graduation."

"Most definitely big bro! Dr. Carson was just telling us about that. I'm there this year. And I'm going to bring a friend."

He suspiciously says, "Oh snap! Who's this friend of yours?"

"Her name is Trina. She's fun, beautiful, has a twin sister, and is just looking for her way in life," Tony says fervently. "It feels good that I can fully be myself around her."

Darryl ponders on the name for a second as if he knew her. He lets it go and says, "That's beautiful brother. Sounds like you really feeling her. All I'm going to say is to just be cautious and take your time. If it's meant, it will be. If not, then let it be. Don't let sex blind you two from your journeys."

"I will most definitely keep that in mind, and I'll be at the event."

"Okay, cool. How's Dr. Carson's class? Are you being receptive of the truth yet?" He asks firmly.

Tony pauses for a second to caution himself before he speaks. He says, "He speaks about this 'truth' all the time. I can't be receptive of tainted truth. The Ancient Egyptians may have invented everything in

Anthony Crawford, Jr.

the world but why did they have slaves? Why did God send Moses to free His people?"

"Still questioning the truth, huh?" Darryl asks shamefully. "You'll understand soon young grasshopper. I'll see you soon."

"Okay." As Tony ends his call, he thinks about the first time he met Darryl…...

(A few years ago, Darryl did a presentation called, "Curing from the Disease of Post Traumatic Slave Syndrome," at Newton University, a Historically Black College & University named after the legendary revolutionary, Huey P. Newton.

At the end of his presentation, Darryl gave the students the opportunity to ask questions about the presentation. A young woman asked him about relationships and how black men and women can better be prepared for relationships. Darryl said, "Black men and black women need to value and love themselves first before getting into a relationship. They both need to focus on their goals, dreams, and the following of their purpose before they get into a relationship. A Black man needs to be able to look deep within his woman and deep within himself to see if he'll be able to be committed to loving her; forever.

"Take time to get to know one another inside and out. Too many times we start on the outside, like their physical attributes, and then we look within just to realize that the person, who they've been messing around with and knowing for a while, isn't the person they thought he or she was. Love is patient, love is kind. Love keeps no records of wrong. Love is truth; it knows no lies. Love is careful. Love forgives all the time, not sometimes, but ALL THE TIME. Understand that and you and whoever you get with will be forever on the path of love. Aaron James claims that there's only one type of Love and that's unconditional."

Young Tony Givens was sitting in that crowd listening in as the crowd stood up to give Darryl a standing ovation. After the event was over, Tony waited in line to personally meet Darryl along with other students. Once he got the opportunity to meet with Darryl, Darryl gave

Black Pain't, Vol. I

him a curious look and said, "Brother, I see it all in you. What's your major?"

Not knowing what Darryl meant by his statement, Tony said, "My major is African-American History, sir."

He absorbed Tony's energy and asked, "They finally made a major for African-American History, instead of having it as an elective?"

"Yes, sir," Tony said self-effacingly.

"That's powerful. I'm happy for you, King. What's the program like?"

"It's meaningful. I'm learning a lot about my origins. I grew up thinking that our history started with slavery, but in the book, <u>What They Never Told You in History Class</u> by Indus Khamit Kush, it went deeper into our history," Tony says enthusiastically. "I just hate that there are a few foreigners that aren't African or African-American teaching a couple of the courses."

"But that's because there aren't enough brothers and sisters willing to take on the burden to liberate our people. But you, King. You? You're a part of Asar's army! You will begin a deep ripple effect that will change worlds, brother," Darryl said vehemently as they shook hands.

He gave Tony a brief history lesson about the origins of Christianity, Islam; about Heru, Asset, Asar, the Ankh, and many other Ancient Egyptians' beliefs. Tony being very intrigued by Darryl's knowledge and passion, curiously asked him, "The Ancient Egyptians had slaves, right?"

"No. They had prisoners that committed unlawful crime."

Tony hesitantly asked, "How can you say that the Ancient Egyptians were such great rulers if their people were committing crime?"

"I don't know what you're inquiring."

"What would make an individual want to commit a crime? Is he starving? Does he have to make ends meet? What does society do to a man that instills that type of desire? If the Pharaohs, Kings, and Queens

of Egypt were so great then why didn't they have the power or resources to truly help those prisoners to a better lifestyle?" Tony asked rhetorically.

Darryl analyzed his questions and did not have an answer for him. While Tony awaited an answer, he said, "Yup. It's all in you."

Tony confusedly asked, "Why do you say, 'I see it all in you'?"

Darryl scoffed and said, "You see this system for what it is. You question things that many don't question. When you receive the overall truth, which stems from the Ancient Egyptians, then you'll be able to see it too."

"How do you know it's the truth?"

"Brother, I graduated at SCU! Stokely Carmichael University and I majored in African American History, but I did grad-school out here at Turner University. Dr. Carson, who you'll meet if you choose to go to grad-school out here, which I strongly recommend you do, was my professor and my mentor. He saw it in me as well when I attended his presentation. I walked up to him afterwards with the same shine in my eyes wanting to know more."

"That doesn't tell me anything, Bro. Jones."

Darryl absorbed his energy once again and said, "Trust me, King. It's like an aura that follows us around. You're a walking light. You have power. That melanin in your skin is made up with the same matter that's in the Universe. You, me, us, them, they, we are all God in the flesh."

Before they departed ways, Darryl gave Tony his cell number promising him that he would take him under his wing and continue to guide him on his journey. Tony was so inspired that he couldn't wait to go to his dorm room to call his ex-girlfriend and tell her what had happened. They would usually call one another at least once a month to keep one another updated on all their successes throughout their college journey.

Tony and his ex-girlfriend were high school sweethearts. They broke up because they both were going to separate colleges. However, they promised one another to keep in contact to share their accomplishments and to keep one another in the know about their whereabouts with hope of one day reuniting.

Semesters passed and Tony and his ex-girlfriend grew apart. As Tony got very involved in college opportunities and active in many campus organizations, he found himself sleeping with many women once his popularity status grew. He was living the college life to the fullest with cognizant thoughts of his ex-girlfriend and her whereabouts.

His ex-girlfriend found herself in two terrible, but meaningful relationships. They were terrible because she was in an abusive relationship and, after that one, she was in a relationship where the guy would consistently cheat on her. They were meaningful because she learned that her energy, solitude, and well-being were valuable. She stopped allowing men to use her. While Tony was suffering from the idea of never finding true love, she wasn't happy with herself for a long period of time.

They rarely shared their sexual experiences with each other about the partners they've had since they lost their virginity to each other, but, when they did, they would try to encourage one another to be patient and make better decisions. Her stories left Tony's feelings hurt, because he couldn't fathom the idea that the woman he once loved was in a relationship and having sex with another man. She felt the same way but would never tell Tony her feelings because of her pride. Plus, she wanted him to live his life.

When Tony got to his dorm that evening, excited to tell his ex-girlfriend the news about his meeting with Darryl. He called her from his room phone. She answered and said, "Hello?"

"Wassup, Rayven! What are you doing?" He enthusiastically asked her.

It was a slight pause over the phone before Rayven said anything, "Hey, Tony. I'm just chillin' before I get on this homework. It's been a long day. What are you doing?"

Observing the slight pause that she gave him, he replied, "I'm just reflecting on the conversation I had with this speaker that came to our school today."

Anthony Crawford, Jr.

"What did you two talk about?" She asked dully.

He passionately said, "We talked about world issues. I tried to bring up the notion of the Ancient Egyptians having slaves in comparison to today. It's all a cycle to me with different empires and rich emperors ruling the people."

"Oh, Tony. So caught up in the worldly cycles that you can't even see your own. I'm about to start my homework. I'll talk to you another time," she said irritably.

"Okay Ray, I'll holla at you later," he said as they hang up the phone. He felt like she flipped his mood, but she was right. He thought about the last conversation that he had with her and how he told her about the situations that he had been involved in.

Inspired, he grabbed his book bag, pulled out a pencil and one of his notebooks. He flipped through a few pages until he got to a blank page. He closed his eyes and took a few deep breaths. He then opened his eyes and began to write:

I called her, "Hey, Queen. You busy?"
Within three tenths of a second,
she thought of a way to let me down easily.
Lately, she's been dealing with men who expect her to be their savior,
pushing their sexual agenda on her and asking for favor.
She has a good heart, she's very supportive;
taking on other people's issues left her with tissues and now her
thoughts are distorted. To get away is one of her fantasies.
If she doesn't, she feels like she'll lose her sanity, which builds her
meekness, learning to deal with those that takes her kindness for
weakness. She knows her worth, and she knows she's royalty;
her loyalty on a high level and doesn't care about idolatry.
It confuses her when others take advantage.
She breaks the habit of allowing the world to use her for her status.
She says, "Yeah, I'm tied up at the moment."
When I know she's at home feeling lonely.
We hang up.........

Black Pain't, Vol. I

They haven't spoken since that night. They grew apart. Even though they both had their share of lovers since their separation, their distance was what disturbed their dynamic friendship. Tony was more hurt with hope of one day reuniting and getting back with Rayven.

Darryl's words, "If it's meant, will be. If it's not, let it be," always replayed itself in the back of his mind. Tony prepared for the day that a beautiful, Black woman would one day sweep him off his feet. To get prepared he took himself out to eat, to the movies, and to certain places that couples would go. He would watch romantic love movies and would get the butterflies with the faith of experiencing life with someone that he genuine loves.

The school year was coming to an end and Tony's quest for love left him in unpleasant situations with women that he was not too proud of. There were times when he was sexing multiple women while knowing he did not have any intentions on being in a relationship with them.

He began feeling certain types of energies roam through his body. He learned about the energies that transfer during sex. He understood the blindness from logical thinking that sex causes.

Not enjoying what he was experiencing, he decided to not look for love. He realized that looking for love blocked him from finding love. He realized that he is the love. The more he loved himself the better his life got. Not communicating with Rayven did not bother him as much and he began to move on.

On a Friday night, weeks before his graduation, Tony took himself to a restaurant and sat at the bar to reflect on his decision of going straight to grad-school after graduation. His recent conversations with Darryl encouraged him to pursue his Master's in African American Studies. He thought about how he had to enter the real-world single with no one to build a life with. He felt urges of contacting some women in his phone but resisted and reminded himself about his goals in life.

Suddenly, he noticed a woman walking in the restaurant. She was alone. He saw that she had on a one-piece dark blue dress that complimented her smooth shiny legs. She had on black heels and a nice

Anthony Crawford, Jr.

inexpensive purse. He admired her from a far. She brought a different feeling into the atmosphere. He watched her as she smiled at the waiter and ordered a water with lemons. He watched her as she observed the room.

The woman's long, dark hair waved as she looked from left to right. She looked at the ceiling for a moment and back at the menu. Tony was praying and hoping that she could telepathically hear him telling her to look his way so they could catch eye contact. The waiter brought her the water with lemons and handed her a straw.

Tony began to build the courage to go say something since she wasn't looking his way. She ordered her food, gave the waiter the menu, and sipped more of the water. Tony stood up from the bar and she looked over to him. He pretended that he didn't see her looking his way and sat back down. "Damn," he said to himself. "Get up and go over there!"

He got up and saw that her head was down as she kept tapping her cellphone. He slowly walked her way. She lifted her head as if she felt a presence heading towards her. She smiled and he smiled back. She got up from the table and he stuttered stepped. His heart started beating fast and he began to sweat. She opened her arms as a gentleman quickly walked past him with his arms opened. Tony walked pass them as they kissed and hugged. Tony caught eyes with her for a half a second as he passed by. Tony walked straight to the bathroom to look in the mirror feeling inferior to his ideas of love.)

Snapping out of his trance, Tony gets up from the kitchen table to get ready for class.

Black Pain't, Vol. I

Chapter 7
The Note

"Good evening, ladies, gentlemen, special guest, parents, friends, family, and alumni participants. Welcome to the dance recitals of all recitals," she says as the crowd claps and cheers. "My name is Jalisa Williams, and I will be your mistress of ceremony for tonight's event. Who did you all come to see?" The audience begins to scream names, nicknames, and chant.

As the audience gradually stop their applauses, Jalisa proceeds to say, "These young ladies have been working very diligently on putting on a show for you all this evening. Please give the people around you high fives for coming out on a Wednesday night." The people in the audience take a minute to intermingle, laugh, and high five each other.

Anthony Crawford, Jr.

"I know half of you could have been at Bible Study while the rest of you could have been at home in your warm beds watching *Empire*. However, this was one of the only nights the auditorium was available this week. Tonight you will see stories and fables told through dance. Pay attention to the skills, poise, elegance, fun, love, and intensity from our dancers. Get lost in the moment and visualize the scenes. Please turn your cellphones off, or on silent. Without further a due, please put your hands together for Dancing Your Soul Out!"

Jalisa walks to the side of the stage next to Terrance. He rubs her shoulders and says, "Good job, Lisa."

She does a haughty smile and innocently says, "Thank you. I hope the family and friends of my girls like the show." She looks around and recognizes some familiar faces in the audience. She spots Trina and Tony sitting in the middle of the auditorium. She sees Tabitha and her son sitting in the front by the stage recording the show with a tablet. Jalisa gives a signal to the sound tech guy. The sound tech guy plays the music as the lights in the auditorium dim and the stage lights brighten.

Three acts performed and there are three more to go. Jalisa walks on stage and announces, "There will be a brief intermission before we continue with the last three acts. There are concession stands in the foyer and restrooms, as well. We will proceed with the show in 20 minutes."

Crowds of people got up from their seats and hastily walk to the lobby area and the foyers for food, interactions, and to use the restroom. Tabitha steps outside to call David Sr. on her cellphone but did not get an answer from him. She throws a short and silent temper tantrum while texting David Sr. She closes her eyes and takes deep breaths. "Something doesn't feel right, but nothing ever feels right," she whispers to herself. She thinks about Phillip. She wants to see him again just to have a pure conversation. She collects herself and walks back inside the building to watch the rest of the recital.

At the end of the recital, Jalisa is humbly mingling with the parents and other attendees about how proficient the recital was.

Black Pain't, Vol. I

Tabitha, Talitha, and David Jr. approach her. She embraces them with a smile and says, "Great job, Talitha! You were magnificent! Mrs. Thomas, thank you for all that you do with her. She's a natural."

"Oh no, Thank ya! Yar doing such a wonderful job with these girls. I know it's not an easy job."

"Thank you so much Mrs. Thomas, I appreciate that," she says. Discretely, she asks, "Where's Mr. Thomas?"

Tabitha and Talitha both feel uncomfortable and embarrassed from Jalisa's question. Jalisa sees it all over their faces as Tabitha says, "He had ta work late dis evenin'. He would have made it if he could."

"I understand. It was nice talking with you again, Mrs. Thomas," she remorsefully says. "See you next week at practice, Talitha."

"Yes, ma'am," Talitha says while walking away with her mother and little brother.

Jalisa and Terrance watch as they walk out the auditorium feeling shameful for asking the question about David Sr.'s absence. He walks up behind her rubbing her shoulders and asks, "Ready to lock up, so we can go get something to eat?"

"Yes, let's do it. You're always trying to feed me. You're trying to fatten me up," Jalisa says as she turns to the seats in the auditorium to see Tony and Trina horse playing. "HEY, YOU TWO STOP PLAYING! Y'all always playing around everywhere y'all go."

As Tony pushes Trina away to stop playing, Trina gives Jalisa a distraught look, and comically says, "Aight, Mary Ann -Ethel..."

Tony greets Terrance, saying, "Nice car out there Terrance! Is that the 2017 model?"

Terrance replies, "Yessir, the GT!"

"Y'all so blinded by the glitter, you forget it's not gold..." Jalisa says to Tony.

"Trina, get your sister...." Tony says to Trina.

Trina says, "Terrance, get your girl."

"Hey, hey, way now...... Don't bring me into this," Terrance says innocently.

Anthony Crawford, Jr.

Tony laughs and says, "Naw, you're in this, brother. You know these two argue all the time." He shakes Terrance's hand and then hugs Jalisa. "Good job, tonight, Jalisa."

"Thanks Tony," Jalisa responds joyfully.

"Haha, true. They're like Sister/Sister," Terrance says jokily as everyone laughs. "What are we eating tonight, family?"

Jalisa asks, "I thought you were cooking, Trina?"

"Too late for all that shit. Let's grab something and head to Jalisa's," Trina suggests as Jalisa's turning off the lights in the auditorium.

"Sounds good to me," Jalisa says as they walk out the auditorium, heading to the parking lot.

As Tony and Trina are getting in Tony's car, he yells out, "Terrance! Your car may look better than mine, but my girl looks better than yours!"

Terrance laughs and yells, "Hecks naw! Trina looks like a gremlin. Look at this Goddess getting into my car!"

"Terrance, I know you ain't talking with that big ass head you got...... your head don't even fit your body, you shaped like a bobble head," Trina says, watching Terrance hurrying to get in his car, knowing Trina is a real-life comedian.

~

There is a displeasing silence during the ride home between Tabitha, Talitha, and David Jr. Talitha is upset about her father not coming to the dance recital. At every stop light, Tabitha looks through the rearview mirror at Talitha's facial expressions, noticing the hurt in her demeanor.

"Ya hungry babygirl? How about we stop by ya favorit' restaurant?" Tabitha asks.

David Jr. rises in excitement and loudly whispers, "Yes."

Still looking outside the window, Talitha sorrowfully says, "No, I'm fine. I just want to go home. Imma lil' tired Mama."

Black Pain't, Vol. I

"Talitha!" David Jr. says dramatically.

"Okay sweety. We have some leftovers in the 'frigerator just in case ya geta lil' hungry," Tabitha says while David Jr. pouts and mumbles under his breath.

Once they get home, Tabitha told David, Jr. to take a bath because he smelt like outside. Talitha storms to her room, slams the door, and locked. Tabitha hears the door shut and the locking and feels terrible. She sits in the living room to watch television to take her mind off what's going on in her life, her kids' life, and her marriage.

An hour or so later, David Sr. comes home. He sees Tabitha sitting on the couch but stops in the kitchen before making his way towards her. After noticing that there isn't any food on the table, he walks in the living room and inconsiderably asks, "Hey, honey, where's the food?"

Tabitha ignores him as he walks through the kitchen to check the refrigerator. He then checks microwave and the oven in an orderly fashion. He walks back in the living room and asks, "Tabitha, did you not hear me? Did you cook?"

Rarely acknowledging his presence, she calmly says, "Ya missed ya daughter's recital today, Davy. She's pretty upset about that" in her countryfied voice.

He took a deep sigh, rubs his head, and dreadfully says, "Oh my God. That was this evening. I'm sorry. How did she do?"

"I know the world is gonna hurt her somehow, someway, but it shouldn't be you hurting her, Davy," Tabitha sensitively says.

He sits down on the couch attempting to rub her feet. She moves her feet out of the way and continues to watch television. He takes another deep sigh and says, "Look, Tabitha…"

She interjects and firmly says, "David now! I don't know what's been up witchu dese past months…… hell, years, but ya love, and, and, and and ya position in our chillern's lives is not the same."

He stares at her and angrily whispers, "I don't want to hear this right now. I've always been a good father to my kids and a good husband to you. I work and pay the bills. The bible says that a man is the hea...."

She quietly interjects again and furiously whispers, "Da church pays the bills, David! You don't think I don't know that?" She takes a quick moment to gather herself as she closes her eyes and leans her head backwards to keep from punching David's eye in.

"Now, honey, the good Lord says that in............."

Strong tension enters the room as she picks her head up and interjects, saying, "Stop it, David, just.... stop it! Stop using da bible as an excuse for ya absence and lack of comfort towards our family. Stop using that bible as a way to justify ya unrighteous actions towards me and our family. I don't know what or 'who' it is that ya doing, but just know I feel it. I always felt it. I see it in ya. I don't expect ya to tell me. Ya ain't man enough to tell me. Ya be..."

David resentfully interrupts her and says, "Waait, wait, woman. What did you say to me?"

Tabitha calmly but angrily states, "Davy boy, don't act like you 'bout sum action church boy, I really lay hands on ya boy...... Walkin' around the church like ya some godly man, but behind close doughs ya foul fuck.... I have allowed ya to lie like ya always have because I thought that was what a godly woman does........"

Before she finishes her statement, he suddenly feels his son's presence and turns away as David Jr. says, "Are y'all okay?"

Tabitha unpleasantly stares at David Sr. She says, "There goes ya son, Davy. Go ahead, spend some time with him. Tell him about where ya been. Tell him...... since ya can't tell me."

"Stop! Not in front of them...."

"Ya don't think they know? Ya think ya children 'er stupid or somethin'?"

David, Sr. walks off, guiding David Jr. back to his room, trying to avoid Tabitha's rant. He never seen this side of Tabitha. He's been to her hometown and seen where she grew up, but he did not know that she could fight.

Black Pain't, Vol. I

While in David Jr.'s room, David Jr. asks, "Daddy, why is everybody mad at you?"

David pauses for a moment and thought about his father.........

(When David Sr. was a child, his father was an active member of a church. His father took him to church every Sunday and Wednesday. His father would read the bible to him and explain to him the importance of believing in Jesus Christ as their Lord and Personal Savior. At a young age, David admired his father's persistence and ability to have the faith that he had.

One year, his father was laid off work due to a recession. To save money, during the summer of that year, David stayed home with his father while his mother was at work. His father stayed home to "search for jobs."

Months of unemployment with no luck of finding work, his father began acting odd. His mother sensed it, but she was too restless from work to put the puzzle pieces together. On certain days throughout the month, David would hear odd noises coming from his parent's bedroom. Instead of exploring what he was hearing, he secluded himself to his imagination.

One day, while playing with his toys by his bedroom's window, David saw a man walking up to the front door. Several minutes later, those same strange noises captured him. He walked out of his room to discover what those weird sounds were. As he approached his parent's bedroom, the sounds got louder. He slowly opened the door and saw his father on top of somebody.

His father instinctively saw him by the door and hastily gets out of the bed in shock. He hurriedly put on his sweatpants, picked up David, carried him out the door, and back to his room. When he got to his room, he sat David down and said, "Stay in here and finish watching cartoons."

David looked confused and said, "Okay, daddy."

That evening, his mother came home from work feeling exhausted as usual. David's father prepared dinner. While they ate at

Anthony Crawford, Jr.

the dinner table, the tension in the kitchen was intense. David's silence worried his mother and internally panicked his father. His mother sensed that his energy was uncomfortable and asked, "What's the matter David?"

David unsuspectingly looked at his father while not having a clue as to what he saw. He felt a strong wave of anger fly from his father's eyes. He had no idea of the words he could use to say what he wanted to say. His mother continued to conspicuously observe him, feeling like something's wrong.

Due to financial hardships, despondency, and stress, David's parents decided that splitting up was best for them and David. His father moved to a different state claiming that he had found an opportunity for a great paying job. His mother was left with bills, a son to raise by herself, a full-time job, and $300 in child support every month. She didn't have any help from her friends and family.

David's mother cried throughout the weeks, especially when the stress would overwhelm her. She would look at David and find the courage to continue making a way for them. She used to take him to church in hopes that tithes and worship would turn all her circumstances around. They eventually got active in the church and the church members became their support system. The church helped her find a higher paying job and allowed David to attend their K-12 Bible School.

While David was transitioning into the ninth grade, he got in trouble at school. One of the Bishops informed his mother that the other kids were teasing him about not having a dad at home and David fought them. The bishop detected that David's mother had no idea on how to influence David's behavior, he decided to take David under his wing to please David's mother.

That evening, David's mother was elated about the bishop becoming his mentor. David was not too pleased but felt like it was worth a try since he had respect for the bishop. However, he was still confused and hurt as to why his father was not in his life and his mother noticed it. As they ate dinner at the dinner table, David asked her, "Mama, why don't I have my dad around?"

Internally indignant by her child's hurt, his mother walked to her bedroom to grab a note that his dad left him. She calmly said, "Son I am sorry. I cannot answer that because till this day I still don't understand what happened between your father and me. I would not even know where to begin to tell you." As she watched the tears fall from his face, she said, "He left you this note. I hope it helps you. I pray it helps you understand that before you have kids to really understand that no woman can truly raise a man on their own without the wisdom and love from a father. It may not seem fair son, but God has a purpose for everything that may not seem or feel right."

As she returned to her room to relax, he began reading the note. He read that note over 30 times that night to make sense of his father's logic. He ripped it up in anger. He walked to his mother's room with tears running down his face. He lied down by her as she rubbed his head. She said, "Son, don't ever become who hurt you."

"How do I do that?" He asked.

She smiled and said, "By forgiving." A sore silence entered the room and she asked, "Do you know why we named you David?"

"No, why?"

Softly, his mother said, "We named you after King David from the Bible. He was the one who beat Goliath with a stone. You will have a few Goliaths in your life, son. The odds may appear like they are stacked against you but, in all actuality, they are stacked in your favor."

David heeded her proclamation, and it inspired him to be a better person.)

"She's mad at my actions son."

"What did you do?"

He pauses for a second to think how deeply transparent he wants to be with David Jr. He says, "I've been an unfit father, son. Not being there for you, your sister, and your mother."

"Why are you doing that?"

Anthony Crawford, Jr.

Guilt wraps around David Sr.'s heart while he humbly says, "I'm still learning and growing myself son. I make mistakes; I am not perfect. There was only one perfect person and that was Jesus Christ. Be more like him son, not like me."

After David Sr. puts his son to bed, he walks to his bedroom to see Tabitha sleeping on her side of the bed. While leaning against the bedroom door, he stares at her admiring her beauty as if he has not looked at her in years. He instantly feels ashamed of his actions, thinking about his affair with the ravishing and the beautiful Rayven Little.

While he walks towards their closest, he accidently steps on Tabitha's jacket that is lying on the floor. He picks it up and a business card falls out of the pocket gracefully hovering to the floor. He acknowledges the card, picks it up, and reads its information. He confusedly mumbles the title and the name on the card. He ponders for a moment because the energy he felt from reading the card did not feel decent.

"Why was she there? Why did she talk to him specifically?" He thinks to himself. He then hangs up the jacket and inserts the card in his wallet. He stares at Tabitha thinking, "Could she be….no, not her, but…. I don't know." He turns off his lamp, lies down on the bed, and falls asleep.

~

Meanwhile, on the other side of town, it is almost mid-night and Tony is driving Trina to her apartment. She is infuriated, so she mopes throughout the drive. Once he pulls up to her apartment complex, he confidently says, "Trina, stop it."

She stares at him in despair while he parks the car. She shrugs her shoulders and says, "It's cool. I'm not trippin'. This ain't the first time you left me alone at night."

Black Pain't, Vol. I

    He leans across and gently grabs her by her head, kisses her on her forehead, and sympathetically says, "Good night love. I'll call you right after my meeting in the morning."
    She sighs while shaking her head and says, "Those forehead kisses." She opens the door and, before getting out, she says, "Let me find out that there's another bitch, Tony. I'm going to beat her ass and imma beat yours." After she slams his passenger door, he watches vigilantly as she walks in her apartment. Once he sees her walk in, he drives home.
    Five minutes into his drive home, his cellphone rings. He answers and says, "Wassup, Rayven."
    "How are you?" She asks softly.
    Feeling excited to tell her some good news, he says, "I'm good. Real good actually. Working, taking care of school stuff. You know? Same ol' same ol'. I got something to tell you."
    "That's good, Tony. I'm happy for you. What is it that you have to tell me?" She asks sadly.
    Noticing the tone in her voice, he asks, "What's the matter with you? Why do you sound like that?"
    "Nothing's wrong, Tony," she says gloomily.
    "Don't lie to me, Rayven. I've been knowing you for far too long for you to be acting like this."
    She grouches and says, "TONY! JUST TALK TO ME! I need your positivity. Please, Tony." She sniffs. "What is it that you have to tell me?"
    "I've found someone, Rayven. I really like her."
    Feeling hurt by the news, she says, "That's good. I'm happy for you, Tony."
    "Thank you, now can you tell me what's up with you?" He hears her heavily cry and empathetically says, "Rayven, don't do this love. What's wrong? You can talk to me."
    She says, "Tony, I need your help."
    Worryingly, he asks, "What's the matter? What do you need?"

Anthony Crawford, Jr.

"Tony, I'm...." she says while struggling to get out her statement. She painfully cries over his car speakers.

"It is okay, Rayven. Everything is okay. What's the matter? You're what? Rayven, you're what?"

She repeatedly sniffs while huffing and puffing. She tries to catch her breath and barely says, "I'm..." She cannot confess to her confession. Tears stream down her cheek as she takes deep breaths and pronounces, "I'm pregnant, Tony. I'm pregnant Tony."

Chapter 8:
"...the Truth shall set you free."

It's Wednesday evening, and Jules gets a call from Jazmine saying that his mom had a stroke. She informs him that the nursing home rushed her to the hospital, however. She is in better condition. Jules leaves his job to attend to his mother.

Once he arrives, he sees Jazmine sitting next to her bed, holding her hand. "How is she?" He asks while giving her a soft and firm hug.

"She's alright. The doctors say she should be okay."

Anthony Crawford, Jr.

"What happened?"

She tenderly replies, "During lunch time, I walked into her room, and she was on the floor. I yelled for help and one of my co-workers called 911. The ambulances came and got her in the nick of time."

While she is talking, he notices her anxiety, and asks, "Was that the first time you had to do something like that?"

"Yes," she says as her eyes get watery.

"Thank you so much, Jazmine. My heart dropped when you called. Didn't think I'd be able to talk to my mama again," he says. He stares at his mother for a moment, holds her hand, and says a silent prayer.

Jazmine rubs his back gently. She witnesses a display of love that he has for his mother and says, "She's a strong woman."

"Yes, she is," he says as he releases her hand and walks around the bed to sit. Jazmine follows him and sits next to him. He looks around the room and says, "I just hate hospitals."

Her eyebrows frown and lift as she curiously asks, "How can you say that after they just saved her life?"

"It's a billion-dollar industry. This industry gets paid billions of dollars all around the country benefitting from people being sick. There's a cure for every disease."

"If there is a cure for every disease then why are there people sick and dying from them?"

"Why would a government want to cure you if they can make money from your death?"

She says, "Yes but, at the same time, look at how we eat, look at what we put in our bodies, look at how we live. We need hospitals to help those people right?"

"I hear you, but why should we live that way? Why would you eat something that can kill you? Why would you consume things that destroys your bodily functions? Why would you want to go through that and pay thousands to have a hospital give you more drugs that ruins your bodily functions? Dr. Sebi once said that *'there is only one disease, and that's mucus. If we get rid of the mucus, we get rid of the disease.'* Talk to these nurses, they'll tell you the same."

"Who is Dr. Sebi?" she perplexedly asks.

"Dr. Sebi rediscovered the cure for all diseases back in 1984," he says while noticing the tight look in her eyes. "Once he began healing people, the government came to arrest him and tried to sue him for 'illegal practices.' All Dr. Sebi had to do was prove that his medicines work, so Dr. Sebi brought over one-hundred and thirty-something patients that he had healed using herbs and spices, drinking good water, and eating good fruits and vegetables."

She assesses his speech and asks, "Why would our government keep cures from us?"

He shrugs his shoulders, saying, "Corporations profit from us being sick. That's why it's a billion-dollar industry." An uncomfortable silence filled the room as he continues to say, "It all just seem like a game, and we're getting played because we're not knowing that we have always had life's controller in our hands."

"Damn," she says as she marinates from his information.

"How many people do you know that had died from these so-called natural causes?"

"Millions."

"The bible says that *'people are destroyed from the lack of knowledge.'* Maybe we need a different way of doing things," he says passionately.

As the evening continues, Jazmine's supervisor allows her to be at the hospital with Mary-Ann for the last two hours of her shift. She spends those two hours conversing with Jules, laughing the time away, sharing their childhood stories, reminiscing on their most embarrassing moments. He asks her questions that make her smile. He repeatedly reminds her on how nice and sweet she is.

She deeply connects with him during their brief moment under the dark clouds in the hospital. She feels a feeling that she had never felt before. She feels safe, secure, and comfortable around him. As she gets up to leave, he inconspicuously says, "For some reason I get this sense

Anthony Crawford, Jr.

that you've been hurt before. I see it all in your eyes. The *pain* is deep within you to the point you can seem a bit guarded. Whenever you feel comfortable enough to share your past with me, please let me know."

She pauses for a moment and her eyes become watery again. She looks away so he does not see the tears. Jules smoothly grabs her hand and says, "We've all been hurt somehow in some kind of way, but we always find some way to move on and be happy again. You're a survivor, Jazmine. Those tears don't show that you're weak. They show how strong you really are and how long you've been enduring your *pain*. I salute you, Queen."

"Thank you, Jules," she cautiously says while feeling an intense uproar between her mind and her heart. She cognitively says, "It's just so hard to go through life wanting love but not trusting anyone. Plus, who would want a woman with a child, you know?" She looks away holding her tears. She quickly turns back to Jules noticing his precarious expression. "My ex just did me so wrong. He was someone I trusted. When I got pregnant, he got ghost, and I had to make it out here with just my mother's help. I have a beautiful, smart daughter. She's my pride and joy. Every time that I look at her, I see me. I didn't know that something so good could come out of a bad situation, but she came from me."

Jules slowly grabs a box of tissue from off a counter in the room. He hands it to her, and suspiciously asks, "Where's her father? Do you two keep in touch? Is he paying child support?"

"He lives here in the city. He texts me every now and then being petty; always disrespecting me, and he leaves threatening voicemails. I get scared that one day I might see him, and all hell will break loose," she says while wiping her eyes with the tissue. He stares while evaluating the fallacies between her story and energy. "I never told anyone else. Only my mama knows. I feel like such a failure some days, but that's why. Once I get my masters, I'm out of here! That's why I can't wait to go to this event in a couple of weeks. Maybe the speaker will help make a few other things clear for me."

He instinctively asks, "What event?"

Black Pain't, Vol. I

"It's an event that my professor told me and some colleagues. Some man name Aaron James is going to teach people about why we're so lost and hurt in this society."

"That sounds interesting."

"Yeah? You should come. Be my date or something," she says as they both share a smile.

Smiling, he sardonically says, "Normally, first dates are at restaurants or somewhere where two people can kind of get to know one another."

Instantly, she asks, "That's what society says is normal right?"

"Righ......" he hesitantly says before being interrupted.

"Relationships shouldn't be based off of money, materialism, and expectations. A relationship grows from time and understanding." She says as he gazes into her eyes with his impressive expression. "Plus I've already told you too much about me. I'll text you the information and you can pick me up that day," Jazmine scarcely says. "Time for me to go. I have to get Miracle and drop her off to her grandmother's before I head to class. Thanks for listening, Jules."

As she gets up from the chair, he says, "Have a good evening." He watches her as she leaves the room and slowly closes the door. He sits in the hospital room until visiting hours are over. While he is leaving, he calls Jalisa, but gets no answer. He calls Trina and she answers saying, "Hey, lil' bro!"

"Wassup Tri, where are you? I have to talk to you."

She questionably says, "I'm at home. Is everything alright?"

"Okay, I'm on my way. I'll tell you everything when I get there," he says while getting in his car.

It takes him approximately twenty minutes to get to Trina's apartment. When he gets there, he knocks on the door. Trina opens the door for him, and he slowly walks in. He spots a man sitting on the couch.

Trina, in courtesy, says, "Jules, this is Tony. Tony this is Jules; my lil' brother that I've told you all about."

Anthony Crawford, Jr.

Tony rises and respectfully says, "It's a pleasure to meet you, King! Your sister has told me a lot about you. Do I need to step out while the two of you talk?"

"Yes, please," Jules vigorously says as Tony walks to Trina's bedroom. "Who is that?"

Trina looks at Jules and offensively says, "DANG! Business – Get some!" She sits up on the couch and comically asks, "Are you still telling woman that you are a virgin just to get them to want to have sex with you?"

Instantly, he says, "I was young when I use to do that!"

"Whatever nigga."

"Anyway, Mama is in the hospital. She had a stroke," he says ardently.

She looks at him with despair and bluntly says, "Oh, how is she?"

"She's okay for now. You and Jalisa need to go see her," he says steadfastly.

"For what?" She asks rudely.

He walks around one couch to sit down on the other couch. He looks Trina in her eyes and says, "Trina, she's our mother. Look, I don't know what happened in the past, but it's in the past. You need to go see your mother."

"I don't know if I'm ready right now, Jay-Jay. I'll think about it. Where is she," she asks unintentionally.

He shakes his head and boldly says, "She'll probably be dead by the time you're finished thinking about going to see her."

She loosely shrugs her shoulders, looks up at the television, and says, "Not my problem, bro."

He gets up to turn off the television and asks, "What happened, Trina? Why are you so hateful towards our mother?"

"You don't want to know the truth, Jay-Jay. Just let me be," she says calmly.

He shakes his head again and shouts, "I must know! This has been going on for far too long! What the fuck is it?"

Black Pain't, Vol. I

"Man! Okay, I'll go see her tomorrow, bro. There, I said it. Are you happy now?"

He screeches, "TRINA! What the fuck? What happened?"

Trina stares at Jules in exasperation, takes a deep breath, and sympathetically asks, "Do you really want to know, Jules? Are you positive that you want to know?"

Jules yells, "YES! Trina, FUCK! Just tell me."

"Our father molested me and Jalisa, Jules! There, I've told you! The mutha fucka used to molest us. For almost two years straight! And you know what? One of those nights when that filthy mutha fucka came in there in the middle of the night to put his filthy fucking hands on me and Jalisa, I saw mama. Yup, at the mutha fucking door, watching the entire time. She was looking on as our daddy molested us!" Trina devastatingly says while shakenly breathing.

"Oh my God," he disgracefully says while sluggishly sitting on the couch.

She takes a few deep sighs. She swiftly wipes her eyes and says, "Look. I'll go visit the lady, but I can't promise you that Jalisa's will. You will have to go and talk to her yourself."

"Why do you say that?" He wonders as tears began to gradually fall down his face.

Trina sensitively says, "Because during those two years when daddy was molesting us, she would take most of the *pain* to protect me. Her hatred for mama is unbelievable." As she gets up and sits by Jules, she says, "I love you, bro. I will never stop loving you. Maybe one day we'll all be able to sit around, get drunk, smoke some weed, and laugh at all this bullshit. For now, it's going to take us some time baby bro. There are too many dark shadows that we must face before we get to the light. I'm almost there though."

He ponders on her declaration as a silence of relief enters the room. He wipes the tears that fell from his eyes, gets up, and says, "Aight, Tri, I'll holla at you." He gives her a resilient hug and walks out of her apartment.

Anthony Crawford, Jr.

Tony strolls back into the living to see tears slowly streaking down Trina's face. He sits next to her and puts his arms around her. She narrowly asks, "If I go see my mama, can you go with me? I'm not trying to bring you into my life's problems, but I just would truly appreciate you there."

He has never seen Trina hurt. He kisses her on her forehead and sensually says, "Of course, just let me know when you're trying to go and I got you, Love." He watches her as she grabs the remote from the arm of the couch. She then lies across his lap and turns the television on. They fall asleep watching television.

The next morning, Trina decides to go to the hospital. They take Tony's car. Pulling up to the hospital's visitor parking lot, he parks the car closest to the outside entrance. While in the car, Trina's hands begin to quiver. He kindly asks, "Trina, are you okay?"

"Tony, I haven't seen this woman since high school. What am I going to say to her?"

"Start with a '*Hi*' and see where it goes from there. You're a strong woman, Love. This is just another fear for you to face," he says sensually. They both get out of the car. He grabs her hand as they walk into the building.

When they get to room, Mary Ann was sitting up being fed by one of the nurses. Trina slightly knocks on the room door as the nurse and her mother look up to see them standing by the door. Mary Ann stares at Trina in amusement.

The nurse notices the uncomfortable friction in the room and says, "I'll give you guys a moment alone."

As the nurse exits the room, Trina hardly says, "Hey, Mary Ann. How have you been?"

Mary Ann starts smiling and says, "I've been here, baby. Are you Trina or Jalisa?"

"I'm Trina," she says while rolling her eyes.

She deeply smiles and says, "Aww, baby. Hey! I've miss you. Is this your husband? Where are my grandbabies?"

Black Pain't, Vol. I

"Naw, Mary. This is my good friend, Tony. I don't have any kids," she affectionately says while walking in and sitting on one of the chairs by the bed.

She frowns for an instant, looks at Tony, looks back at Trina, and says, "That's not what your brother told me."

"He lied, Mary. He lied just so you wouldn't think we abandoned you," she snappishly says while crossing her legs and folding her arms.

Perplexedly, Mary Ann says, "Well, how are you? What are you doing with your life these days? Are you in school? Where are you living?"

Instant irritation boils up inside Trina as she brusquely says, "Look, Mary – I came to see you; you're fine. I'm out."

As Trina gets up to head towards the door, Mary Ann decisively says, "You want to know what happened to your father?"

She stops by the door, looks at Tony in frustration, turns around, and emphatically says, "I have no father; I already know how my sperm donor died."

"How did he die, Trina?" She softly asks.

She walks closer to her bed, stands over her, and says, "He passed out one day because his sugar-level got too high."

"How do you think his sugar level got high?" Mary Ann asks intensely.

Trina ponders on her question for a moment and tersely asks, "What?"

"I could tell by the way we had sex that neither one of us were ever being satisfied, but we continued to try. The only thing that was fulfilling was our friendship; he was my best friend. I cared for him, and he cared for me." Mary Ann says while noticing that she has Trina's undivided attention. "I never really trusted any man because I saw my father beat my mother for years. I trusted your father, honey. We got married. We both wanted a family, so we were successful in creating that. When we found out we were having twins he was so ecstatic. I remember when he held you two in his arms. I felt like I was in heaven," she says as tears began to steadily fall from her face.

Tony leans against the door with his arms folded listening in on Mary Ann's Story. He watches as Trina's demeanor change. Mary Ann proceeds to say, "I watched my soul mate hold my two most precious gifts that life had ever given me. Then Jules, Jr. was born years later. We were a happy family, so I thought. Then he started acting strange. We had completely stop trying to satisfy one another."

She shifts and says, "One night, I had a dream that I was falling. I immediately woke up hearing a slight scream." Trina sits down closer to her mother while actively listening to the story. "I reached over, and your father was not lying next to me. I got up thinking that he was checking on wherever that scream came from. You and Jalisa's room door was cracked open. I peeped inside and saw him fingering either you or Jalisa. He was bent over and touching himself. My heart shattered from watching. I didn't know what to do. I just didn't know to do," she says as her voice cracks.

Trina grabs some tissue and hands them to her. Mary Ann wipes her eyes with the tissue and Trina says, "Continue."

"He would go on for months and I hated myself for it because I was so scared. I never knew what to say or do. I couldn't believe what was going on. During that time we found out that he had a high cholesterol. The doctors gave me a menu of foods to feed him, but I never used it. I just kept feeding him collard greens, spinach, and asparagus knowing that it would raise his cholesterol levels. He was taking blood thinners that kept his levels borderline high. He was taking Coumadin or Warfarin at least twice a day, but he would still experience chest pains or shortness of breath."

Mary Ann clenches the back of her silent cry and continues to say, "One day, after taking his scheduled medicine, he had realized that he took his last pill. He asked me to pick up his medicine from the pharmacy. I told him that I would get it after I pick up your brother from day care and pick up you and your sister from school. After I got you three, we went to the pharmacy to get his medicine. While we were at

Black Pain't, Vol. I

the pharmacy, I seen a small box of placebo pills and bought them. When we got to the car, I emptied his bottle off medicine into a Ziploc bag and put the placebo pills in his medicine bottle."

"When we got home, I handed him the medicine just in time for his schedule time. His head got dizzy, and he lied down to sleep. While he was sleep, I flushed the placebo pills down the toilet and refilled his medicine bottle with the pills inside the Ziploc bag. I disconnected our phone line, and we left the house. I drove us to a restaurant, and we ate. Then I took you all over to a friend's house and asked her if she could watch y'all for an hour or so. I went home and I found him lying down on the bottom of the staircase. I connected the phone line and called the police."

In tremor, Trina begins to cry. She gently rested her head on her mother's chest. Mary Ann holds her head and shoulders as if Trina is a newborn baby. Tony is witnessing their encounter with tears in his eyes and says, "Trina, stay here with your mother. I have to go."

Mary Ann humbly says, "No, no, no, baby. She's going with you. I finally got the chance to see and hold her. I'm fulfilled for the day. Please go. Let mama get some rest."

Trina looks at her mother, closes her eyes, and kisses her on her cheek. She then gets up, wipes her eyes, and grabs Tony's hand as they walk out the room together. When they got to the elevator, Trina jokingly says, "I hate that you had to see me cry. You know I'm a G." They both laugh while getting on the elevator.

Meanwhile, Jazmine is out shopping at the All-Purpose store. She sees Tony speed-walking to the back room to clock in and yells, "Tony!"

He stops, acknowledges her, and says, "Hey Jaz."

"You still got me on that discount?"

He eagerly says, "You already know! I'll be in the back putting up some stock. Just have one of the associates come and get me whenever you're ready to check out."

Anthony Crawford, Jr.

"Okay, cool. Thanks Tony," she says as she continues to shop. For the next 30 minutes, she walks from aisle to aisle, grabbing items and clothes. She has a cart full of groceries and some clothes for Miracle. She asks one of the associates to go and get Tony from the back while she is waiting in line. Tony comes out as soon as the cashier gets finished ringing up all of her items. The cashier bags all of the items and puts them in the cart.

Tony types in a discount code on the register and says, "There you go, Jaz!"

"Thanks, Tony! You don't know how much I appreciate this," she says thankfully.

"Oh you know it's all love. Let me know when you're wanting to come back," he smiles as he gets his things and tries to head back to the storage room but is stopped by a customer.

While leaving the store, Jazmine's senses heighten, and an ounce of fear troubles her from within. When she gets closer to her car, she sees someone from a far that throws her energy off even more.

She pushes the button on her car keys that lifts the trunk open. The guy's not even paying attention to her but eventually recognizes her walking in the opposite direction. Jazmine tries to rapidly push the cart to her car while he hurries her way.

He roughly grabs her by her arm, and tries to calmly ask, "Wait, ... wait.................... I just want to talk................ I just want to talk, can we please talk?"

"Let me go!" She scarcely yells while trying to yank her arm away. "HEEELLLPPPPP"

He accidently pushes her cart against her parked car trying to get around from getting hit by her cart. As Jazmine swings on him, he pushes her arm almost making her fall, but she catches her balance. "Let's not do this shit here. Just grant me my visitation, so I can see my daughter and I'll leave you the fuck alone. I don't want to deal........." before he got the chance to finish his rant, Tony suddenly struck him in his face.

Black Pain't, Vol. I

As they both fall to the ground, Tony quickly hops up and comforts Jazmine. He worriedly asks her, "Are you okay, Jazmine? Did he hurt you?"

"I'm fine," she says innocently as she swiftly throws her bags in the trunk.

Tony helps put a few bags in her trunk and says, "Get your things and go. I'll handle this." He turns around to see the guy sluggishly getting up from the stiff punch. "Alvin? What the fuck are you doing to her?" He asks frantically.

"What you mean nigga?" Alvin says disrespectfully while watching her get into the car. "You don't know what the fuck is going on. I wasn't trying to harm her ass."

Tony balls his fist and says, "Bruh, you're Darryl's patna. How do you think he would feel to know you're doing this stupid shit? Especially, to a girl like Jazmine. What the fuck is wrong with you?"

He stares at Tony bewilderedly and angrily says, "Nigga, you don't know her like I know her. She's playing you and everyone else who thinks she's so innocent. All I want to do is to see my daughter. I don't want or need to be in Jazmine's life."

"Why would she allow you to see her daughter when you're acting crazy? You're smarter than this. Society is already fucked up for you to be doing this to our women. Don't you understand? Do you?" He asks as they watch as Jazmine speeds out of the parking lot.

"We need to stand up, bruh; be kings again! Stop acting immature and learn to be men again." Tony squares up with Alvin, thinking that he was going to attack him. He turns around and sees the store manager, co-workers, and some customers looking on in glee. Some people are recording it.

Alvin frowns as he walks back to his car, not even getting the chance to get the groceries that he came to get. And as Tony walks back into the store, the store manager says, "I need to see you in my office real quick, son."

Anthony Crawford, Jr.

While Jazmine is at home scarcely putting up groceries, she calls Jules on her cellphone.

"Hey, Wassup, Jazzy?" He flirtatiously says while answering the phone.

Full of anxiety, she says, "Jules, I'm scared!"

"What's the matter?" He asks impatiently.

As her voice trembles, she says, "I ran into with Alvin today. You think you can grab Miracle from daycare and come over when you get off?"

"Okay, I got you, just calm down. Lock the doors, get your gun from out of your closet, and stay calm," he says collectively.

For the next two and a half hours, Jazmine spends her time peeping out the window every ten minutes or so. She thinks to call her mom, but she does not want her mom to call the police. She does not want to bring the court system into the situation, which might grant him visitation rights. She lies down on her bed to take a short nap with the gun under the pillow.

While asleep, she lucidly dreams of Alvin appearing in her apartment. While in the dream, He is holding Miracle in one hand and the gun in the other. He forces her to put Miracle's clothes into a suitcase. He makes her walk the case to his car and tells her to put it in his trunk. He puts the gun to her face and says, "I told you I was going to get you, bitch!" By the time he pulls the trigger, knock at her door wakes her up from the dream.

She gets up sweating and shakenly breathing. She hops out of the bed with the gun in her hand. She silently runs to the door, looks through the peephole, and sees Jules holding Miracle.

She opens the door and says, "Thank you so much, Jules." Jules walks in behind her to close and lock the door. She grabs Miracle out of his arms and carries her to Miracle's bedroom.

"So what happened?" He asks as he follows Jazmine to Miracle's room.

"Hold on, let me put her to bed. Did you guys eat?"

Black Pain't, Vol. I

"Yes, we grabbed something on the way here. I tried to call you to see if you were hungry, but you didn't answer your cellphone."

"I apologize, I was sleep," she whispers while almost awakening Miracle.

He regards the way Jazmine is staring at Miracle. He wonders, "What I could do to make you feel better?" Jazmine quietly explains what had happened earlier. Jules gets internally frustrated. They walk into the living room because Jules is having a hard time whispering his comments. "Jazmine, I hate that you have to go through this."

She grabs his hand and says, "I just appreciate you for being here. You have been a great person to me and Miracle. I feel safe when I'm around you. That means more to me than you will ever know."

He smiles as their eyes connect. A wave of carnal energy flows through them. She leans close to kiss him, and he dreamily meets her halfway. They begin slowly kissing by the couch. Then they gradually start to use their tongues as she says, "Mmmm." Their strong attraction encourages her to get on top of him as she sucks her teeth. She throws her head back and forcefully grabs his head. She forces him to tongue kiss her neck and says, "Mmmm."

While she is moaning from his neck kisses, he finds himself in a familiar situation. He stops and hesitantly whispers in her ear, "I've never had sex before."

She tries to catch her breath in wonder. She analytically stares into his eyes and directly asks, "You're a virgin? I mean how? Why?"

"Yes," he shamefully says while putting his head down. "I spent my life in school, working, and taking care of my mother. I never really had the time to talk or to be with a woman."

She gently grabs his chin, lifts it up, and says, "I'll take my time."

As they begin to slowly kiss again, he cannot resist to think, "I thought she didn't get down like this. Could she be lying about what happened between her and her baby's father?" He blacks out to the taste of her lips because they are a little more delectable than before. He outlines her body with his hands.

Anthony Crawford, Jr.

While sexually staring at him, Jazmine stands to slowly take off her pants and panties. She sits on the other sofa and spreads her legs across the couch. She sucks her right index and middle finger to soak them. She takes the two fingers and erotically open the gates to her hidden treasures. She sexually says, "Come tongue kiss it."

Dumbfounded by her actions, he gets up willingly. He sedately gets on his knees as he glares at her pear shaped-physique and soft-caramel skin. He starts tongue kissing it. He slowly kisses around the lips while slithering his tongue. His gliding tongue finds its way toward her pearl. "Mmmm," she says as she roughly grabs his head to hold his location.

Her legs vibrate as he begins to taste a moist substance dripping from her. With her eyes closed, she says, "Mmmm." She suddenly forces him to his feet. Hastily removing his belt buckle and pulls down his pants. She sees his manhood hood dying to escape and gently grabs it. She then takes off his boxers and examines his endowment.

She grabs it and spits a great amount of saliva on the top of it. She spreads it all over it to make it slippery. She slowly and repeatedly begins pulling the skin up and down with her mouth on it. "Mmmm," she says.

"Who is this girl?" He thinks to himself. As she continues to enjoy her oral skills, he internally asks himself, "What the fuck?"

As he stares in disbelief, she stops and says, "Grab my hair." He swiftly grabs her hair as she continues sucking his penis and rubbing his testicles with her other hand. With her lips glistening from all the saliva, she lies back down on the couch in the doggy-style position and says, "I want it. I want it from the back." While he stands behind her, she gently grabs his penis and slowly slides it inside of her. "Mmmm……. start off slow and deep."

He obeys. While he strokes, she says, "Mmmm." She grips the edge of the couch. She sensually looks back at him while biting her bottom lip. His eyes are fixed on the visual of his pipe going in and out of her. He's mesmerized by the way her butt jiggles. He sees a tattoo of a Scorpio on her lower back. As he looks closer, he can sort of see an outline of a name that appears to be covered up by the Scorpio.

"Mmmm……harder!" She says which snaps him out of his thoughts. He begins to speed up, grabbing her hips, and roughly going strong. "Yes, Jules. Give it to me, baby. Yes." She quietly yells.

"Right there?" He asks confidently.

"Oooh yes, baby! Right there! Don't stop! I'm about to cum!" She says as he finds his rhythm.

She is silently screaming with her hand over her mouth. Her legs begin to vibrate again. It sounds like someone is repeatedly and slightly clapping. She looks back at Jules biting her bottom lip and says, "Oooh yes! Just like that daddy. Give it to me!" He gets more into the motion and the rhythm. He goes harder and deeper. She says, "You're in my stomach!"

She pushes him from her as she climaxes. She lies there for a moment and commands that he take her to the bedroom. He conforms and, when they arrive in the bedroom, he lays her down. He then lies down next to her, and she maneuvers to lie down on his chest with her eyes closed. A few minutes pass and they progressively catch their breaths. While lying in the bliss, she suddenly thinks to herself, "He was not fucking me like a virgin." He rubs on her lower back as she peacefully falls asleep analyzing his sexual talents.

She scarily wakes up around three o'clock in the morning. While heavily breathing she shoves Jules a couple of times to wake him up.

Tiringly, he asks, "What's wrong love?" as he wraps his arms around her.

"You stopped rubbing my back and I couldn't sleep," she says as she embraces his arms.

"Having those dreams again?"

"No, and for some reason, I feel a lot safer than ever. This is the first time Miracle ever slept in her own room," she happily says.

Anthony Crawford, Jr.

Pondering on the sex that they had, Jules says, "Jazmine, now I know you've been hurt and scarred from your previous encounter with the Alvin guy. But where did you learn to have sex like that?"

A painful silence entered the room while she thinks of an answer. She quickly thinks to herself, "Can I trust him with my darkest secrets? Will this scare him away?"

Jazmine's procrastination heartens him to critically think to himself, "Damn, she's hesitating."

She says, "I watch a lot of porn."

"Why?"

Confidently, she says, "Every woman has needs. So whenever I want some satisfaction, I explore my own body. Sometimes I need porn to help me out with my imagination."

"So you watch the rough and aggressive videos?" He thoughtfully asks.

She laughs and says, "Those are my favorites."

He thinks of a question and asks, "Do you think that porn blinds us from a false perception of sex?"

She evaluates his question and replies, "No, I don't think that porn blinds us. To me, there are two types of sex: Fucking and Making Love."

"Which one did we just do?"

"I…." she halts herself. She unapologetically says, "We fucked."

He contemplates her answer and asks, "Why didn't we make love?"

While smiling, she says, "I'm sorry, I just go with the mood. Plus, everyone remembers their 'first time,' I want you to say something good about me when you're telling your 'first-time' story."

While giggling, he asks, "What or who inspires you?"

"My daughter inspires me. I try to be the best example for her as possible."

While he begins to rub her back again, their moment fades, and they both fall into a deeper sleep. Jules awakens knowing he has to be at

Black Pain't, Vol. I

work in a few hours. He shoves Jazmine to get her off of him and she turns over. He gets out the bed to put his clothes on and grabs the rest of his things.

He then kisses Jazmine on the forehead and informs her to call him whenever she needs anything. He leaves the apartment, walks down the stairway, and gets in his car. Before starting the car, he sits and reflects. He takes his phone out of his pocket to type some words in his notepad. He types:

*She's been hiding who she is for years
behind that mask and her fears;
when I removed what was not of her,
all I found was tears;
I was saddened by what I saw,
she covered up her true essence;
she does not know that she's a blessing,
and chooses deep depression;
she said,
"I dreamed of a prince to save me into a bliss; but
no man was allowed in my castle, I don't even accept gifts;
I have had dreams of getting cheated on or getting beat on,
but still held my vision;
of one day finding true love,
not the one we see on television."
When she cries,
I can tell it's her form of letting out what's inside;
pain became a drug to her, and she has been overdosing;
smoked all of her rolled up emotions,
Regardless of the scars her main cause was to keep on going;
When she cries.
she's just hurt from the thought of never finding what she always
dreamed of,
she says, "life ain't what reality TV makes it seem of."*

Anthony Crawford, Jr.

He then locks his phone, starts his car, and drives off. On the way home, he can't help but to brood over Jazmine's sexual actions. He couldn't believe the type of sex that he had with her.

When he gets home, he looks around at the house his father's insurance paid for. Mary-Ann made sure that Jules put the monies into something that he could have as an asset. He feels gratitude around the home. He then internally wishes that he could have stayed with Jazmine even though he has to get ready for work soon.

Chapter 9:
Just Friends

"Do you know where your pigment comes from?" He asks.
She satirically says, "No, but I'm pretty sure you're going to tell me."
He snickers and says, "If I'm talking too much or always trying to have deep conversations then let me know. I don't want to be a burden."
"No, it's fine. Trust me, this is just how I talk like... this is how I engage in conversation. I really want to hear about where the pigment of my skin comes from."

Anthony Crawford, Jr.

He chuckles and notices that someone is trying to call him on the other line. He says "Patricia, I'm going to call you back. One of my mentees is calling me."

Understandingly, she replies, "Okay."

While he answers the call, he energetically says, "Tony-Too-Tone, talk to me, King."

"Wassup Darryl, you good?" Tony respectfully says.

"Yes sir, I'm more than good. Are you good?"

"I'm excellent. I don't know if you had heard already, but I got into a fight with Alvin."

"My best friend Alvin?"

"Yes."

"How did that happen?"

"I saw him outside about to fight my homegirl, Jazmine."

Jazmine's name triggers Darryl's memories, but he cannot remember who she is. "Who is Jazmine?" He confoundedly asks.

"She's a friend of mine. We're in grad-school together."

"Did anyone see y'all?"

"Everyone seen and heard that scene," he humbly responds. "Customers, co-workers, and manager all seen me. I got written up. I'm just glad they understood that I can't just sit there and allow man to hit on a woman. Plus, I would have never guessed that one of your friends would be acting like that. He's a reflection of you, and they say you are who you hang with."

"You' right, Tony. I'm going to holla at him. Thank you for letting me know. I'm going to talk to you later."

"Peace and blissing," Tony says.

"Hotep," Darryl says as they both hang up the phone. He sits on his lounger and ponders about the situation. He thinks about the dinner that he scheduled with his mentor. After looking at his watch, he grabs his pee-coat, his keys, and hurries out the door. He locks the door and walks to his car. While in his car, he tries to call Alvin, but he didn't answer. He drives in silence.

Black Pain't, Vol. I

As he pulls up to the restaurant, he sees his mentor's car parked and hurries into the restaurant. The greeter greets him, and he spots his mentor from a far, sitting and looking down on the menu. He powerwalks to him and says, "What's up, Doc. How are you?" He then takes off his coat to put it on the back of the chair and sits down.

"After all these years, you still can't show up on time, huh?" He says with eyes still fixed on the menu.

Picking up his menu, Darryl says, "Come on, Dr. Carson. I just had to handle a few things before I came."

Dr. Carson examines him, grins, and asks, "So, who is she?"

Darryl titters and asks, "What? What are you talking about?"

"I know you, Darryl. Now who is she?" He asks confidently as if he just pieced a thousand pieces of a puzzle together.

Skimming through the menu and he says, "Her name is Patricia."

"Patricia! Oh okay, so tell me about this Patricia," he says comically as he sips his water.

Darryl smiles and says, "Well, she's a school librarian. She's very optimistic in learning about culture and who she truly is. She's beautiful, oh my God, like stunning. She's a natural haired woman; a strong feminist and she reads a lot. I can tell she's been through a lot in life based off the bits and pieces of her stories that she chooses to share with me; she's very different. She loves exploring and experiencing new things. She loves kids, mentors a kid from her school. The kids at her school view her as a mother. She is just an all-around good woman."

"Is she a nun?" Dr. Carson asks as they both laugh.

The waiter comes. They order their food and Darryl modestly says to Dr. Carson, "She's no nun. She just has a high level of respect for herself. She's amazing, Doc."

"Are you ready for such a commitment?"

Darryl envisions on Dr. Carson's question……..

(Several years ago, Darryl tried to get with a woman named Brittany. She was very beautiful with her light brown eyes and expresso

Anthony Crawford, Jr.

skin. She was very opinionated and courageous about what she believed in. She was very sexual and unapologetic about it. She loved hanging out with friends. She enjoyed drinking, smoking weed, and going out dancing.

They started off just as friends until, one evening, they got drunk and had unbelievable sex. They felt obligated to one another. To save their friendship, they would cook for each other, drink, and smoke a lot. They had a lot of fun together. They would do erotic things to one another when they had sex. Sex is what kept them together. They were friends with benefits.

He would always teach her history and about white supremacy. She loved hearing him speak; it stimulated her mind. Nevertheless, she was very religious and hated when he would bring up Christianity.

One night during the Christmas season, he asked her, "When you were a kid, you believed in Santa Claus right?"

She irritably said, "Yes, I did. Why?"

"At what age did you find out that he wasn't real?"

She thought over his question and said, "I don't know. Um, around eleven, I think. Why?"

"It broke my heart thinking of all the years and the billions of dollars that our people spend on Christmas."

"Christmas is Jesus's Birthday. It's not about the gifts, the money, or the fat white guy in the red suit. It's about Christ."

He uncomprehendingly asked, "Okay, so why do we have to do all this extra stuff?"

"It's an American tradition that many love to celebrate."

"It's psychological warfare, Brittany. It's like we're living through materialism by telling this lie to ourselves and passing it on to our children. Look at the subliminal messages that are molding our youth into idiocrasy. It takes away their way to critically think by telling them that there is a fat white man in red suit that travels around the world with nine reindeer going down chimneys, and delivering gifts," he said keenly. "I never had a chimney growing up."

Black Pain't, Vol. I

She impatiently said, "It's for kids' imagination. Damn, don't take that away from them."

"But imagine how that effects them mentally as they grow up. How will they be able to distinguish between a truth and a lie? Watch how people are going to feel when they find out that there is no Jesus. It indoctrinates our people. Most believe in this fictional character because of what our parents have fed them. From Santa Clause to Jesus Christ. There's no Santa Claus and there's no Jesus the Christ. No one is coming to save us from white supremacy; we have to save ourselves," he said brazenly.

She furiously said, "I hate when you say that knowing I believe in Jesus. Stop bringing that up around me."

"Okay, last thing," he said enthusiastically.

She took a deep breath and said, "What, Darryl?"

"Have you noticed that since white supremacy can't find a great white hope in real life that they make them up? Rocky Balboa, Santa Claus, Superman, Batman, Jesus Christ?"

"Yeah, I hear you. Anyways. Let's talk about something else. You're fucking up my high."

"Okay, how do you feel about relationships?"

Doubtfully, she asked, "Which kind of relationship are you talking about?"

"Like that intimate, we're together, courting, and working on marriage relationship," he said poetically.

Prosaically, she said "They're overrated. We don't even know ourselves fully to even be in those relationships. Then once you give someone a title of a boyfriend or girlfriend, they change. Their true colors come out. That's why I just don't want to be in one right now. I'm living, learning, and trying to find more of me."

Internally miffed by her answer, he asked "So am I wasting my time?"

"Are you?"

Anthony Crawford, Jr.

He looked her deep in the eyes and said, "I really like you, Brittany. Like I want to be with you type of like you. So am I wasting my time since you're not wanting to be in a relationship?"

"I mean...." she hesitated. "No. Of course not. I love what we have going. No rules and no hard feelings. We have fun, good conversation, and good sex. Plus, I learn a lot from you. Well, when you're not talking about my Lord and personal savior."

As the night faded, Darryl could not sleep. He truly liked Brittany. After that late night conversation, Brittany began to get distant from him because she didn't want him emotionally fall for her. Darryl would text her and wouldn't get a reply. He would call her, and she wouldn't even answer or return his phone calls. She would only contact him whenever she wanted some good food, good weed, and for good sex. He would get upset when she posted on social media, but not respond to his messages. He would go to her place, they would smoke, eat, take a couple of shots of liquor, and have meaningless, but good sex.

They stopped cuddling and stopped having those late-night conversations after their "fun" was over. He never could sleep by her side knowing that she didn't feel the same way that he felt about her.

One night, he got tired of the distress he was feeling internally. He called Brittany and auspiciously, she answered. He said, "Hey, Love, I bought a bottle. You trying to po'up and chill?"

She said, "You already know! Come through."

When he got there, she was already half naked walking around her house listening and dancing to music. They laughed, cracked jokes, and talked mess to one another about who can drink the most. They were dancing on each other and getting very sexual.

After about five shots each, she relentlessly sucked the soul out of his manhood. He stared at her knowing that he just doesn't want to be friends with benefits. He ate her out, making her squirt multiple times while knowing this would be the last time. He sexed her like he never sexed her before and put her to sleep.

Black Pain't, Vol. I

He knew that it was the last time. He walked into her living room, getting ready to leave. Before leaving, he decided to write a poem on a napkin that he got from the kitchen. He wrote:

She lays there,
I can literally feel the emotions that she's about to give me.
She needs someone to leave and let go, so
I guess that person is me.
I was watering dead flowers that I should have let die and left alone months ago,
thinking about what you put me through and wondering where those tears would go.
I believe that whatever comes out of you is born,
so there's a broken man running around with his feelings on his arm.
I broke my rules for you,
now my heart needs mending.
We were going through the same movie,
praying for a different ending.
She lays there,
I already know what she's going to say.
I'll just get my things and get on my way.
Postscript, it's over, I just can't do this anymore.
I loved you but can't approve of this shit anymore.

He left her apartment that night to never talk to her again. He blocked her number, he blocked her on his social media pages, and he didn't show up to the events that she attended. He deleted her off his social media and blocked her so she couldn't see what he was up to.)

"Yeah, I'm a sucka for love. What about you, Doc? You're getting a little up and age to still be single, right?"

Dr. Carson laughs and says, "You know I'm very transparent, Darryl. I've met a married woman with kids."

"WHAT? STOP IT! Don't do that!" He says appallingly.

Anthony Crawford, Jr.

Dr. Carson instantaneously says, "I know that's not morally right, brother. I can feel the discomfort that's deep down inside her. It's a hurt that I've felt before. It's a hurt that I've experienced. Her *pain* attracted me to her. Besides, she's not going to give me the permission to love on her that way. She's too faithful and virtuous."

"That doesn't justify intervening with her life and her kids. You can't save all our sisters from their turmoil. Some are just going to have to learn and suffer."

"I hear you. Maybe it's the superhero in me talking."

"Most women don't want to be saved, superman. I think it's the loneliness in you talking. How's Tony doing in your classroom?" Darryl asks as the waiter brings them their food.

Dr. Carson takes a sip of his water and grabs the knife and the fork that was on the right side of his plate. He starts to cut his meat into pieces and says, "That young boy, Tony, is just as analytical, unusual, and gifted as you were when you first stepped into my classroom. He's not receptive to the truth."

They both laugh as they proceed to eat and converse about life, deities, love, and current events that are plaguing the country. A man at a nearby table overhears their conversation. Just as Dr. Carson pays their bill, he gets up from his seat and asks them, "How can you assume that the Ankh is the key to Black people's salvation when the Ancient Egyptians had slaves? You two also spoke about there being no Jesus……. help me understand your logic."

Darryl looks at him in desolation. Dr. Carson side-eyes Darryl while wondering what he is going to say. Darryl says, "You see, brother, the way this conversation is going to go is that I'm going to educate you with cold hearted facts and truth. You're not going to be open of it because you believe that Black people are the cause of Black people's problems. Then I will counteract with more cold-hearted facts and truth. What you fail to realize and accept are those that put us in these types of conditions. Then I will tell you why we are the way we are spiritually, mentally, physically, and socially.

Black Pain't, Vol. I

"Then this conversation becomes an argument, then it becomes a 'battle of egos,' and then it becomes hate between two men. That's what white supremacy wants us to do. See, you think that America is fair and you probably think that we're free. You think that all Blacks have equal opportunities as all other races in this world. You make your judgements without considering slavery, the reconstruction era, injustice, inequality, integration, the KKK, police brutality, the 'War on Drugs,' share cropping, and Jim Crow.

"I look at you and see that Willie Lynch Syndrome that's scattered through millions of Africans, African Americans, Black folks or whatever label we have accepted by the white supremacist. Be like Harriet Tubman: Free your mind, free yourself, and come back to free your people. I love you, brother. Two men in a burning building have no time to argue. Have a blessed evening." He then looks at Dr. Carson and asks, "Are you ready to go, sir?"

Dr. Carson nods his head as they both get up. They both drop a tip on the table and walk out the door leaving the man speechless and internally upset. While Darryl is walking Dr. Carson to the car, he says, "I dislike House Niggas!"

"Two men in a burning building do not have time to argue. That's an African Proverb that I love to live by whenever I find myself in heated debates and arguments with our brothers and sisters, especially on social media. We have to be patient with our people, brother. We have over 400 years of hate, envy, distrust, and fear within us that we must drain out of us. It's going to take more than social media posts and arguments to set us free from the mental bondage that we have always had the key to," Dr. Carson says as they stop by his car.

"I hear you, Doc. Are you ready for *Remove that Ribbon* next weekend?"

"Come on now, Mr. Jones. You know that I will be the first one there," he says as he gets into his car. "Keep up the good work, brother. I know the kids love you at the school. Oh and understand that your search for love is actually what's blocking you from finding it, Ase."

Anthony Crawford, Jr.

"Alright, Doc. I'll holla at you!" He says as Dr. Carson drives off. He shakes his head and begins walking to his car. Once he got into his car, he calls Patricia on his cell phone.

"Dang! It took you like forever to call me back?" Patricia says while answering the phone.

He chortles and says, "I love it when you show me that you care."

"Boy, please. You're my friend. Plus, we have interesting conversations," she feverishly says. "Don't get it twisted, sir."

"I take that as flirting."

"But I wasn't flirting! I was….."

He interrupts her and asks, "Can I ask you a question?"

She smacks her lips and says, "Oh, dear Lord. What's your question, Mr. Darryl Jones, sir?"

"If you were a man, theoretically speaking of course, and you had a friend that told you that one of your friends raped a woman. Then you find out the woman had a baby by him after being raped. Now, your friend is going around acting crazy without you knowing, trying to be the father of his child. How would you handle it?"

She thinks and says, "Wow. That's crazy. I mean, you can confront him about it. Especially, being the type of friend you are. Like you always say, 'Iron sharpens Iron.' If someone you consider a friend is doing things like that then you should confront them. It's not morally or ethically right."

"You're right, Patricia," he says as he's driving home.

"You're a good friend, Darryl. Only you can help someone like that. When is the next time you will see this friend?"

"Tomorrow night. We always get together on Friday nights at Kemet and have a few drinks. Guess I'll confront him then," he says.

She says, "Good. If it's one thing I agree with is the notion that Black people need to start holding one another accountable. My name is Patricia Skinner and I approve this message. Good night, Darryl. You know we both have to be up to change the world in the morning. Sleep tight, King."

Black Pain't, Vol. I

"Good night, Queen! Sleep well. I'll talk to you tomorrow," he says as they both hang up.

He parks his car, turns it off, and sits for a brief moment to think. He eventually gets out and locks his car doors. He walks to his apartment, unlocks the door, and walks in gracefully. He rhythmically breathes as he sluggishly walks to his room's closet.

He takes off his pea coat and hangs it on a hanger by the rest of his coats. He removes his tie and tosses it in the tie case on the floor. He takes off his dress shoes and places them next to the rest of his shoes. He unbuttons his shirt and takes off his slacks to hang them up.

After hanging up his clothes he walks back into his room to get his pajama pants out of his dresser drawer and puts them on. He lies down in his bed realizing that he is not sleepy. He picks up the book, *The United Independent Compensatory Code/System/Concept* by Neely Fuller Jr. and starts reading until he falls asleep.

~

The next day, after school, Mr. Jones stops David Jr. while he is walking out of his class and asks, "DJ, are you okay? You've seemed kind of down during class."

Sorrowfully, David Jr. says, "Yes, I'm okay."

"Are you sure? You didn't seem too eager to learn and be energized today in my class," Mr. Jones inconspicuously says. "If something's bothering you, let me know."

"My dad made my mom angry about something. They really haven't been speaking to each other around the house. I just hope they don't hate each other."

Noticing the hurt in his tone, Mr. Jones cheerfully says, "It's all love. Adults are humans, too. We all go through ups and downs. If you need anything, don't hesitate to ask. I got you."

"I hear what you're saying. It's just a lot of my friends don't even have their dads. Most don't even know their dad. I don't want to not know mine," he says discouragingly with his head down.

Anthony Crawford, Jr.

Mr. Jones firmly says, "Head up, King. You have nothing to worry about. They'll work it out. This is another lesson of love."

He felt a sense of hopefulness after Mr. Jones's comment and says, "I understand. Thanks, Mr. Jones!"

As David Jr. walks out the classroom, Darryl takes a deep breath and starts cleaning his classroom. He neatly straightens the classroom's desks. He shuffles through his students' classwork and homework while putting them in the class trays. He grabs his lap top bag and puts his laptop computer and notebooks inside of it.

As he's grabbing his things to leave, Ms. Hall slowly enters into his classroom unexpectedly. After startling him, she gently asks, "Now what's a conscious brother like yourself leaving so early for?"

Stutteringly, he says, "Just preparing myself for a relaxed weekend, that's all."

As she walks around his classroom staring at the pictures on the wall, she sardonically asks, "Why do you seem so tense? Calm down, I'm not going to hurt you; like you hurt me. So what have you been teaching your kids lately?"

He gives her a look of suspicion and says, "I've been teaching them how to get directly to the point when answering questions. I'm also teaching them how to explain their answers by being very specific."

"That's interesting," she enchantingly says while she reads quotes that are posted around his room.

"What's going on, Luna?" He asks while putting his laptop bag on his shoulder.

She gives him a haughty look and says, "Oh, nothing. Just thought I'd stop by and destroy this unnecessary tension between us, since you're too prideful to do it yourself. I'm not here for an apology, because that is way past due. I'm not even here to show you any resentment. I just want to show you how to let go, forgive, and move forward for the better."

"I respect that and I...."

Interrupting, she says, "Save it, Mr. Jones. Instead of always speaking about Black liberation, Black love, and Black consciousness,

Black Pain't, Vol. I

how about you live it. *Paint* the picture of Blackness with your life, not just your words. Be the example of the change that you wish to see. Have a good weekend." She walks to the door. She stops and says, "Oh and by the way, thank you. You taught me something very vital about who we are as a people."

"What's that?"

She folds her arms and collectively says, "Black men are scared. They're either used to running away or standing behind the Black woman. Black men are cowards that need to stand up and be men, our warriors, our protectors, our leaders. So stop walking around here being a keyboard activist. We have enough of those."

Ms. Hall does an about face and walks out of his classroom. He stares at the door for a moment and considers her words. She comes back in and takes an Angela Davis poster off of his wall. She says, "Thank you. I think this would look better in my room." She struts out.

He then admires her bravery and her words. He walks out while closing the door and locks it.

~

Meanwhile, Alvin is at home thinking and internally analyzing his situation. He knows that Darryl knows about it. He thinks twice about meeting up with him tonight.

He goes to the kitchen to get some potato chips from off the counter and sees his phone on the counter. He picks up his phone to check the call log and notices a few missed calls from Darryl and a couple from his mother.

He walks back into the living room to wonder if he should call them back. He tosses his phone on the couch and stares at his high school graduation.

(Alvin was not always accepted amongst his peers as a teenager. Other kids used to bully him around school and girls would talk down to him. He sat in the front of his classes so no one will bother

Anthony Crawford, Jr.

him. During lunch, he would stay inside his teachers' classrooms because he didn't have any friends.

One day, when he was in the 11th grade, a gorgeous girl approached him before their last afternoon class and asked him, "Hey, could you hold my books. They're a bit heavy." He looked around confusedly and grabbed the girl's books. One of the students from the school's varsity football team came behind him and knocked the books out of his hands. Alvin and the books went flying to the ground. While Alvin and the girl were picking the books up, other students were hysterically laughing. His anger emerged as he got up and charged at the varsity football player. Another football player tackled him before reaching his teammate and three other football players jumped in kicking him.

Another student came out of nowhere and blindsided one of the football players with a punch to his jaw and he continued to fight off the football players. The girl that told Alvin to hold her books was swinging and pushing the football players off of Alvin. As Alvin lied down by the lockers, the student and the girl continued fighting. The school's police officer ran down the hallway breaking up the fight and making all seven students go to the office for suspension.

A half an hour had passed while they waited in the office with the football players in another office, Alvin said, "Ahh, man, thank you. No one ever stands up for me before."

While holding an ice pack to his hand, the student said, "It's all love my brother. I hate bullying with a passion. You really should be thanking Sistah Souljah right there. She jumped in to help you, too."

"Thank you so much," Alvin said to the girl.

"No problem. I was just fighting because they knocked my books to the floor," she said comically.

They all laughed as the student asked him, "What's your name, man?"

"Alvin."

"Oh, like the chipmunk?"

Black Pain't, Vol. I

"Ahh, man, yeah, the ghetto version," Alvin said while they all shared another laugh.

"I'm Darryl, fam. Nice to meet you."

"Why do you hate bullying so much to the point you'd jump in to risk your own life?"

He replied, "When I was in the seventh grade, I had an eighth-grade elective class. Till this day I don't know why I was in that class because they only had me in there for a semester. The eighth graders used to pick on me and this other dude that was in the class. They talked about our clothes, our shoes; plus we were small and fragile. So it was like we had a target on our heads every class. The other dude had enough though. He was already dealing with some things at home, so he wasn't going to take any shit from anyone this one day. While we were in class, the eighth graders started throwing around jokes on us as usual and dude said, 'Man, fuck all y'all.' Everybody went crazy in class; the teacher didn't know what to do!"

"He stood up for himself, huh?" Alvin said while switching his position in the chair.

"Surprised the entire class, bro. Then they started threatening him, calling him dirty, and all kinds of names. Then after class they saw him walking, they ran behind him, pushed him to the ground, and started stumping him out. Instead of jumping in to help him, I ran. I ran like Forrest Gump, boy! That night, he found his big brother's gun in their closet and shot himself."

"Wow," the girl said sorrowfully.

"Yeah, I told myself to never ever run again unless I'm runnin' up. I told myself that if I see someone getting bullied that, no matter who it is, I'm jumping in. Bullying is wrong. That haunts me till this day," Darryl said regretfully.

Alvin and Darryl became good friends after the incident. Darryl was a year older than Alvin and very popular around the school. He brought Alvin around his friends that eventually became Alvin's friends. Darryl protected Alvin and would invite him to high school functions.

Anthony Crawford, Jr.

Alvin looked up to Darryl and viewed him as the big brother he never had.)

"Darryl! Wassup, King? Where's Alvin? It's unlikely for you to beat him here on Friday," she asks heartily.

He takes his jacket off, lays it on the back of the chair, sits down, and says, "Wassup Trina, I don't know where he is. This is unlike him."

"Oh, well. What are we having tonight, dark or light?"

"Dark."

She feels an unusual vibe roaring from Darryl. She quickly tries to analyze his energy. As she starts to prepare his drink, she says, "What? The pro is trying to go to the hall of fame tonight? You must have been really going through it lately."

"Yeah, something like that," he says depressingly. "What's up with you, tonight? Why do you seem all cheerful?"

While handing him the drink, she surely says, "I am in a happy place."

He internalizes her answer and impressively asks, "How did you get there?"

She poses to think about her answer and blissfully says, "I'm learning to let go. I'm learning to accept my position in life. I know that I am here for a purpose. I am finally at peace with my past. That was the biggest thing for me."

"That's great to hear Trina," he replies while taking a sip of his drink. He evaluates her as she moves back and forth behind the bar. He notices her vibrant smile. He thinks to himself, "She's been hanging around a man."

As the night passes by, Darryl continues drinking while watching a basketball game. Trina is too busy serving other customers to converse with him and it is too late for him to remain waiting on Alvin. He looks at his watch and realizes that the bookstore is closed. He pulls money from out of his wallet, tosses it on the counter, and gets up from his chair. "Alright, Trina! I'll catch you next Friday," he slightly yells as she is taking an order from someone at the bar.

On his way home, he calls Patricia to see if she can meet up with him at a 24-hour coffee shop. She is skeptical because she knows that Darryl is a little intoxicated and she does not want him to get the wrong impression about their friendship. However, she agreed to meet up with him anyway.

As he pulls up to the coffee shop, he gets out his car, shuts the door, and leans against the car. He gazes at the city lights and at the moon in search for a sign. He slowly begins walking to the building and sees Patricia pulling up into the parking lot. He shifts towards her while she parks.

Seeing her getting out of the car, he says, "Good evening, Queen, thanks for meeting up with me." He embraces her with a strong sensual hug.

Awkwardly, she manages to say, "No problem, Darryl. What are friends for?"

On the way to the store's main entrance, he politely opens the door for her and asks, "How was your day?"

As they walk inside, she says, "It was good and very productive, yours?"

"That's good to hear and I can say the same," he says smoothly. They sit down at a booth, and he orders two cups of hot cocoa. Courageously, he pronounces, "You know, Patricia. I really enjoy our time together. I really appreciate you taking your time to come, hang out with me, and listen to my shenanigans."

"No problem. I think you're a good friend, Darryl. I don't mind. Thank you for the hot cocoa."

He interestingly asks, "How are things at your job?"

"I'm glad you just asked that," she says pleasantly. "Okay, why is it that the African American sections in most libraries and bookstores have depressing content? Why isn't there anything positive to read about us? Our people did not just struggle throughout humanity. It is as if they want us to continue to accept these labels that they have for us. It's propaganda."

Instantly, he zealously says, "Schools across this country are eradicating slavery out of the history books, if our authors don't document our past for us to read, then we will be doomed to repeat it."

"Yeah but…"

He interposes and says, "America has committed heinous and inhumane acts against us. They are the root cause for mental and physical behaviors. If we don't learn to see through the lies, then we will continue to perish. Even with the truth dead in our eyes we continue to fund our own genocide. Television is one of America's biggest murder weapons. It's a weapon because it destroys people's perceptions, their moral character; it causes division."

"Okay, so why do we have to be left with reading about struggle and oppression? Why not read about happiness and unity? It all seems traumatizing and gloomy."

"As long as our people are filled with knowledge and truth, we will never go back to slavery."

"You don't think that we're in slavery now?" She firmly asks.

"No, I think that…."

She intrudes and asks, "What about mass incarceration and the shackles that are on our people's mind? What about how we work these nine to five jobs for less than what our time and energy is truly worth? We're not free. We're just in a different caste system."

He's speechless. He thinks to himself, "Damn, she's right." Her attitude entices him.

As they're walking towards the register, she catches him staring at her and looking away as if he wasn't. She playfully says, "Stop! Why are you staring at me and looking away. Boy, what's wrong with you?"

"I can stare at you!" He jokingly says.

"Okay, but it has to be a reason as to why you're looking over here."

He licks his lips and softly says, "You're beautiful. I wonder if you see what I be see."

Black Pain't, Vol. I

"Oh, whatever. You're always building my head up," she says while blushing.

Darryl professes his feelings and says, "No, really, Patricia. I think you're a beautiful, intellectual woman. I love our conversations and our bond. We can talk to each other about any and everything. We share our past and we have a good time when we're around each other."

"I'm flattered. So, what are you really saying?"

"I'm saying that I like you. Like, really, really like you. I hope that one day we can take it further," he bravely says. The awkward silence humiliates him. He begins to feel shameful for sharing his feelings. He modestly says, "Sorry, if I've overstepped my boundaries. I just thought I'd let my intentions be clearer."

"No need to apologize. You didn't overstep any boundaries. I appreciate your honesty. I'm just not looking for whatever you're looking for right now, Darryl. I think you're a good guy. A real good guy. And I do like our friendship, but that's all I can emotionally afford right now."

He can feel his heart tremble as he says, "Oh, I understand. And excuse me for my words. I just couldn't help but to let you know about my intentions. I respect your honesty as well. I would love for us to continue to build on our friendship."

"Are you sure?" She asks eagerly.

"Yeah, yeah, of course. You don't know this, but you help make me into a better man. I can't help but to at least have you in my life as a friend, even if you don't want me for more than that," he says.

As they both rise and walk to the counter, she confusedly asks, "How do I make you into a better person?"

He pays for the hot cocoa and says, "You don't allow me to get away with anything and you're very shielded. I realized a long time ago that in order for me to get in your heart, I must be willing to be patient and very understanding. Even if I don't make it in your heart as a potential mate, at least I'll be in there as a friend." They walk outside to the parking lot.

Anthony Crawford, Jr.

They walk towards Patricia's car, and she says, "I'm glad that we have an understanding." She opens the door and gives him a church hug. "You have a good night, sir."

"You too, Queen," he says as he watches her get into her car. He walks away as she drives out of the parking lot.

He calls Alvin to see if he'd answer, but no luck. He gets in his car, takes a deep breathe before turning on his car, and sits in silence. He then turns the car on, reverses it and drives out the lot heading home.

When he gets home, he does his nightly routines. Once he puts on his pajamas, he gets in his bed and lies in the dark room. He grabs his phone off the nightstand, scrolls through to find his notepad in his phone, and his creativity inspires him to write a poem.

Patricia's rejection made him want her even more. When he feels rejection, he gets really competitive and determined to get what it is that he wants. He ponders on how he wants this poem to be and begins to type:

Is this the price you pay for pursuing a Queen?
I've learned that they don't sexually reveal themselves,
and they say what they mean.
They are outspoken, most have been broken,
and they rather for you to touch their minds before you try to get their legs opened.
I know this could be a very hard path to her heart
most brothers couldn't last, some even failed at the start.
"What are your intentions with me?" she asks,
the overwhelming commission to answer that is a very hard task.
Honestly and ironically, Queen, I want to see you walking down the aisle with her dad,
or on a honeymoon thinking that these are some of the best times that we've ever had,
we can have some babies and begin our own family.
I professed my feelings to her,
I took a chance,

Black Pain't, Vol. I

I just had to express them.
She denied me.
The resilience that follows the rejection is a blessing,
and I guess wanting to love someone is considered to be aggressive,
especially if they're not ready.

His phone rings in the middle of his typing. He hesitates to answer because he does not recognize the number. Something told him to answer, and he says, "Hello?"

"Hey, this is Dionte Anderson from The People's Hospital. I was calling to inform you that Alvin Johnson is in the hospital," he says caringly. "He's okay."

"Thank God," Darryl says. "What happened?"

"He overdosed on some pills and tried to drive, but he didn't get far. One of his neighbors found him lying motionless on the stirring wheel and called the police. You were listed as one of his emergency contacts so I'm just calling to let you know that he's okay," he says.

"Which room is he in?"

"743."

Darryl felt a sense of relief and says, "Okay, thank you so much, brother."

"No problem," Dionte says as they both hang up the phone.

Darryl quickly puts on some clothes and shoes. He hastily grabs his phone, his wallet, and his keys. He rushes out the door and locks it. He gets into his car and drives to the hospital. When he arrives, he parks, and hurriedly walks into the building. While walking fast to the elevators, he sees someone inside a closing elevator and yells, "Hold the elevator please." He walks in quickly examine the man appearing to be in his early 20s holding the doors open for him.

"Thank you, my brother."

"Which floor?" He asks modestly.

"Seven, thank you."

"You're welcome," he says as he pushes two buttons on the right side in the elevator.

Anthony Crawford, Jr.

He notices the navy-blue scrubs that the man has on and a name tag with the name Jules carved in it. He curiously asks, "You work here?"

"No sir, I work at a nursing home on the other side of town."

"That explains the scrubs..."

"Yeah," Jules says as the elevator raises.

Darryl cannot help but to feel connected to the brother in some strange way. He asks, "What brings you here?"

Jules stubbornly, but courteously answers, "I came to check on a loved one."

"I respect that, and I'll pray for you both."

"Thanks," he replies. A slight silence creeps through the crack of the elevator. He dubiously asks, "What about you? What brings you here?"

Darryl falters, "A good friend of mine got into a wreck. I came to check on them to see if they are okay."

As the elevator stops and the door slides open, Darryl walks out saying, "Peace and light king."

Jules responds, "Peace" as the door closes.

Darryl then powerwalks to Alvin's hospital room. Once he gets to his room he knocks and slowly walks through the door.

Alvin appallingly lifts while watching Darryl walk towards him. He rapidly and angrily says, "Ahh, man, before you say anything, please understand that I am happy to be alive. It was just a dumb decision. I had time to think about what I have done. I am good and I do not need a lecture from you."

"I am happy that you're still alive too, brother," Darryl says while sitting down in one of the chairs next to the bed. "How are you feeling?"

"Ahh, man, I'm feeling better. The doctor said that I can leave in the morning."

"What made you want to do that?"

He irritably says, "I don't know. It seemed like the better option at the moment."

Black Pain't, Vol. I

"Is it because of Jazmine?" Darryl vacillates.

He stares at Darryl in anguish and asks, "Do you remember us going to RED'S a few years ago? I think you were invited by one some girl you were messing around with at the time...."

(From Alvin's perspective, a few years ago, Darryl invited him and a couple of other men to a night club called RED'S to party with some beautiful women. Once they arrived, Darryl spotted his "friend" in the V.I.P. section of the club. He walked towards her noticing the short black dress with the light green pumps that she had on. She saw him approaching her and embraced him with a sensual hug. He greeted her, "Hey Ella, you all have room for four more?"

She excitingly said, "We do."

He then waved to his group of friends, and they all joined the ladies in the section. The gentlemen sat and mingled with the ladies, but Alvin distanced himself. Darryl noticed Alvin standing off to the side, strolled near him, and asked, "You good fam?"

"Ahh, man, yes, I am good. I'm just enjoying the moment," he replied while he continued to drink, and people watch.

Ella suddenly strode to Alvin, pulled him to the side, and said, "My girlfriend thinks you're cute," in his ear. He looked up at Ella's friend and she swiftly turned her head away hoping he didn't see her watching.

"What's her name?"

"Her name is Jazmine."

He analyzed the situation, walked up to her, and said, "Jazmine.... is it?"

She noticed him wearing a white button up, black pants, black casual dress shoes, and a black blazer. She was enthralled by his tall, athletic physique, and dark skin. She friendly said, "Yes that's me."

"I'm Alvin. I'm one of Darryl's friends."

"Nice to meet you, Alvin."

"Congratulations on obtaining your degree. What are your plans after graduation?"

Anthony Crawford, Jr.

"I'm going to get my Master's in Higher Ed."

"Why?"

"I love college. I had an awesome undergrad experience. I always kept good grades; I pledged a sorority, and I was very active in Student Government. I see myself working at a Historically Black College or University. I want to be a professor one day, too," she said enthusiastically.

"What is it that you want to teach?"

"Either Feminism or African American History."

"I think that's amazing!" He said smiling and eyeing her lustfully.

While everyone else danced, drank, and socialized they got to know each other's passions, goals, strengths, weaknesses, and hobbies. A few times, they danced but stopped every time their friends would hype them. Alvin thought that she was shy and didn't like attention.

When the club was closing, Darryl and Ella's friends all gathered. They started walking outside acting vulgar and obnoxious. Alvin walked Jazmine to her car while letting her know how much he enjoyed celebrating her endeavors. Out of fun, their friends were yelling out embarrassing comments about them and causing them to blush.

"What are you about to do?" He asked.

She sensually replied, "Go home and get in the bed. I have church in the morning."

"Which church do you go to?"

"18th St. Missionary Baptist Church."

"Oh, that's good. Church girl that knows how to have fun! What a perfect combination."

"Thanks, Alvin. It was nice meeting you," she said while getting in the car.

"It was nice meeting you too, Jazmine," Alvin walked away from her car looking for Darryl and the rest of his friends. He instantly thought to ask her for her number, hesitated for a moment, and ran back to her car as she was backing up.

Black Pain't, Vol. I

Jazmine quickly noticed someone running and stopped the car. As he walked to her window, she sighed in relief to know that it was Alvin. She let down the window, and calmly asked, "Are you forgetting something?"

"Your number."

She blushed as she pulled her phone out of her purse. Alvin said his number aloud while she typed. She texted his phone and said, "Store me in."

"Aight, cool. You know I will."

After that night, Alvin would call and text her consistently during her last couple of months of college. They would always talk about their goals and aspirations. They had conversations about sex, relationships, and Jazmine's plans after graduation. They would send each other naked pictures to one another, indulging in phone sex whenever Jazmine was not busy around campus.

He surprised her by driving out to her school to attend her graduation. He cheered her on when they announced her name. After the ceremony, she went off strolling and chanting with her sorority sisters and fraternity brothers. He watched her strange and odd demeanor while she socialized, especially with one of her fraternity brothers.

Her actions made him feel irrelevant while she treated him like a regular friend during his entire stay. He stayed in a nearby hotel suite. He expected Jazmine to spend the night with him after her night of fun with her sorority sisters and fraternity brothers, but she never showed up.

That morning before his departure, he tried calling her a few times, but he did not get an answer. During his ride back home, she called him while she was leaving a frat house. She told him, "I am so sorry! I got extra drunk last night and one of my sisters had to bring me home."

He distrustfully said, "It's all good," while turning down the radio. "I'm glad you enjoyed yourself."

Anthony Crawford, Jr.

"I promise I'll make it up to you when I move back," she said sexually.

They conversed for about an hour during his trip back home. She had to finish packing, so they ended their call. He reflected on his time at Jazmine's school. Something did not quite feel right, but he didn't give any attention to his intuition.

When she moved back home, their proximity developed. They would go out to eat, to the movies and to the gun range. They went swimming, to the fair, and Alvin even went to church with her on a few Sundays to hear her sing. Their sex was incredible. Jazmine's sex was like a wild fantasy for him. She was experienced.

Alvin would always tell Jazmine about his childhood and his anger issues. He informed her about his past relationships and what caused the separations. She would tell him about her childhood but was very doubtful to inform him about her past relationships, especially the ones in college. He detected her reluctance but ignored his intuitive feeling.

One evening, after Alvin had dinner with Jazmine, her mother, and her stepfather. Alvin sensed that her mother didn't like him. Later, when they drove to Jazmine's apartment, he expressed his hurtful feelings towards Jazmine's mother not liking him. Jazmine did what she could to relieve his sensitivity.

When they get to her apartment, they both begin to remove their clothing and put on something more comfortable. Jazmine decided to take a shower and inserted her phone onto a charger by her bed. A rush flowed through Alvin as he thought to go through her phone. He fought the feeling while watching her get naked.

As she got in the shower, the strong desire tempted Alvin. He hurriedly unlocks her phone and scrolled through her text messages from "Terry-Bear." He had gotten angry towards the texts he was reading. He went through her social media pages' inboxes and direct messages to discover more deception. He thought to himself, "All this time she has been entertaining another man?"

Black Pain't, Vol. I

As she hopped out the shower, she saw him on her phone, and furiously asked, "Why are you going through my phone?"

Angrily, he asked, "Who is Terry-Bear?" as she grabbed her phone from out of his hand. She walked back into the bathroom to ignore his question and he followed right behind her. "Jazmine, who is Terry-Bear?"

Irately, she said, "Get the fuck out my bathroom, Alvin."

He took his crippled heart and walked out of the bathroom. He went to her bedroom to put on his clothes and gather his things to leave. While walking towards the door to leave, she aggressively snatched him from behind and said "The fuck is wrong with you, where you goin'."

He kept walking while dragging her along with him. He gets to the door, unlocked it, and said, "Get off of me Jazmine." They wrestled while he attempted to get her off of him. "Jazmine, just stop!"

"You're trying to leave, and I didn't even do anything!"

He tried to stop wrestling with her and petulantly asked, "Okay, so who is Terry-Bear?" While she dilly-dallied to answer and not release her strong grip on him, he said, "I'm out."

She yelled, "No!" and sprang on his back causing him to run into the door, accidently knocking over a living room lamp. While he collected himself with her on his back, he managed to stand up. She wrapped her legs around his waist with her arms wrapped around his neck. He sat her down on the top of her couch. She still had a strong grip on him, saying, "Don't go!"

He maneuvered his way out of her submission hold, turned around to face her, and confidently said, "Jazmine...... I'm out."

She aggressively started kissing him. When he turned his head, she would grab it and proceeded to kiss him. He stood up with her arms wrapped around his neck and her legs wrapped around his waist from the front of him this time.

He lifted his head to keep her from kissing him, so she began tongue kissing his neck. He walked backwards and stopped at a wall with her seducing him with neck kisses. He lost himself in the erotic pleasures as she brought her legs down and pushed him against the

Anthony Crawford, Jr.

door. She locked the door and removed his belt buckle. She pulled down his pants and instantly pulled down his drawers. She grabbed his erection and began sucking it. She gulped it down her throat while making sexual sound effects. She slowly dragged it out of her mouth, spat on it, and repeatedly jerked it while moaning. While he was being captivated from the stimulating sensations, she continued to tongue kiss it and suck it some more.

She stood up to kiss him. He lifted her up and sat her on a bar stool. He aggressively removed the towel that she had wrapped herself in. She spread her legs more as she sucked on a couple of her fingers and spread the saliva over her clit. He completely came out of his clothes and inserted himself in her.

He got deep inside her as she graphically groaned and strongly sighed. He slowly began to thrust in and out of her. Once he found his tempo, she closed her eyes to get ready to receive all his anger.

"Oh fuck!" She screamed while he began going harder and faster. He stopped and lifted her up by her buttocks. He belligerently propelled himself in and out of her while standing up. "Yes daddy!"

He walked her into her room while still being inside of her. He laid her on the edge of her bed and proceeded to rhythmically go in and out of her. She constantly gripped the sheets enjoying the pleasure. Suddenly, she slapped him and yelled, "Make me cum, yes!"

He continued with a rattled brain. When she raised her hand to hit him again, but he hit a spot in her that made her motionless. She silently yelled. Her eyes rolled to the back of her head as she grabbed a pillow and bit it. He stopped and pulled out of her watching her legs quiver.

She frozenly lied in the corner of her bed. He pleasurably watched her and walked to her living room. While in the living room, he got dressed. He collected his possessions and left.)

"We did not talk for a while after that. A year and some months had passed, and I tried to purchase something online, but my bank account information wasn't working.

Black Pain't, Vol. I

"Ahh, man, I called my bank to find out what was wrong and found out that I was put on child support. Came to find out that Jazmine got pregnant and claimed me as the father. She told the court that I was denying the baby, that I wasn't doing anything to support my child, and a whole lot of other shit. I just wanted a DNA test and an opportunity to be around my child, if that's my child," Alvin states.

Darryl internally evaluates Alvin's story. He tries to remember who Jazmine is but cannot recall. He asks, "Why does she have a restraining order against you?"

"She wants me to stay away from her and the child, so she brought up excuse to keep me from her. So not only am I paying child support, but I can't even see my own child."

"What happened at the All-Purpose Store between you two and Tony?"

He remembers the situation, hisses, and says, "I was on my way to the store, and I saw her leaving. I tried to talk to her, and she made a scene. I grabbed her to keep from hitting me, and that's when Tony came out of nowhere and hit me."

He tries to believe Alvin's story, but the details are not making sense to him. He asks, "Something is not adding up bro."

He grins and replies, "That's because Jazmine is smart. I saw her in action when I went to her graduation. It's like she plays this game with everyone. She has everyone fooled and thinking that she's all holy and sanctified. She's so innocent and sweet, but she plays victim. Regardless of what I say about our situation, she's going to win at this game every time."

Darryl then notices the nurse walk in and says, "Excuse me sir, visiting hours are almost over."

Darryl says to the nurse, "Thanks."

Alvin says, "Ahh, man, thanks for coming to check on me brother."

"Alright brother. I'm praying for you. Call me if you need anything," Darryl says as he exits with so much running through his mind.

Anthony Crawford, Jr.

Chapter 10:
Moving Forward

"Good morning and Happy Birthday, wombmate!" Jalisa enthusiastically says while brushing her teeth over the phone.

Yawning heavily, Trina tirelessly says, "Good morning, wombmate. Happy Birthday to you, too."

After spitting into the sink, she asks, "Sounds like you're just now waking up. What did you do last night?"

Black Pain't, Vol. I

Taking her time, Trina bluntly says, "Shiiit, once I got off work, Tony's ass got me super high and damn near fucked my brains out." They both laugh hysterically. "What are your plans for the day?"

"I don't know. Terrance wants to surprise me with a few things today, so I'm going to spend it with him," she says deservingly as she rinses her mouth out with mouthwash.

"Ohhh shit! Jalisa gon' finally get some dick!"

She embarrassingly laughs and says, "Oh my God! Quit it, Trina! You play too much. It's not even like that between Terrance and me."

Mockingly, Trina replies, "It's not even like that between Terrance and me. Whaaaat? Y'all been dating how long, and you've haven't given him any?"

She stutters and says, "No, we haven't even spent the night with each other. I'm not ready for all that, yet, and he respects it."

"Damn, Jalisa! He must be a good guy for him to be waiting this long, or he got some side pussy," she aggressively says. "I would have been cheated on your ass."

She humbly says, "Trina, you know why I'm making him wait. I don't want sex to clog our perception of love and friendship. I don't want us to lose sight of what we're building as our foundation. Too many of us have made the mistake of having sex early and too many of us have ended up in situationships because of it. There are too many relationships that don't last because of it."

"Damn," she says cautiously. "That sounds like a lonely and horny life."

"Trina!"

"I'm just saying," Trina says as they laugh. "What do you think about, Tony? I already gave him the ass."

She giggles and says, "I like Tony. He is a good man. He knows what he wants in life. He knows where he's going. He's almost done with school; he's a gentleman. He's polite, strong, and modest. Plus, he understands and accepts your crazy self for you. Can't ask for anything better than that."

Anthony Crawford, Jr.

"Thanks, Sis. Your views mean a lot to me," she says appreciatively. "Well, I'm about to shower and shop for a birthday outfit for tonight. Tony and I are hitting up downtown. I'll call you to see how your evening goes with Terrance. I love you, sis."

"I love you more, Trina. Have a good day and be safe," she says as they both hang up the phone.

Jalisa, at that moment, looks deep into the mirror. She stares at herself searching for a part of her that is ready to trust and love another soul like she's never done before. She leaves the bathroom and goes into her room singing. She puts her clothes on and straightens up her room. Suddenly, she hears someone outside repeatedly honking their loud horn.

She looks out her window and sees Terrance standing outside of his car honking his horn and yelling her name. She grabs her sweater, purse, and keys as she walks out of her apartment. She shouts, "Stop, Terrance!"

"Happy Birthday, Beautiful!" He hollers as Jalisa locks her door and walks downstairs to him.

"OH MY GOD, TERRANCE! You're so crazy!" She says as he opens the passenger door for her. As she is getting in she notices some flowers and a card in the passenger seat. She picks them up and lays them on her lap while smiling hard.

"Happy Birthday!" He shouts as he gets in the car turning the music up. "We're about to get lit!"

Embarrassed and giggling, she calmly asks, "Are you done?"

"Hap-py Birthday to you, Happy Birthday! Hap-py Birthday to you, Happy Birthday!" He continues singing while he is driving.

She smiles while shaking her head and asks, "Are you done?" He ignores her and continues singing. She mutes the radio and stares at him.

"What? Girl, you better turn up! It's your birthday!"

She laughs and says, "Thank you, Terrance, for the flowers and the card. No one has ever bought me flowers before."

He looks at her and says, "Bought? I didn't buy those!"

Black Pain't, Vol. I

"Oh," she says in a dissatisfied tone.

"I actually picked them from this garden and wrapped them myself," he romantically says. "I thought that it would have meant more to you."

She blushes and gets teary eyed. To stop herself from crying tears of joy, she curiously asks, "So, where are we going?"

"Well, first, I thought I'd take you to get a manicure and a pedicure, a full body massage, then we'll have lunch, after that I can take you back home so you can take a nap. You know how you love your naps. And, after that, I'll pick you up for dinner! How does that sound?" He heartily asks while driving and keeping his eyes on the road.

She beams and gladly says, "Sounds perfect, Terrance. Thank you so much. This really means a lot to me."

"Oh, no problem, Love! You deserve it. You're always doing so much for others, especially those young girls in your dance program. This is nothing, really," he says while driving. "All you have to do is kick back, relax, and enjoy your day."

She is speechless. She's really appreciative but questions herself about his acts. She turns on his radio to block her thoughts and begins singing one of the songs that's playing on the station. Terrance frequently would see her passionately singing and smiling.

Once they pull up to the shopping center, she notices the nail salon where she's getting her pedicure and manicure. Right next door to the nail salon is the spa where she thinks is the place that she's getting her massage. He parks, hurriedly gets out, and opens the door for her. He helps her out the car and escorts her to the salon.

While walking to the salon, they begin horse playing. They get to the entrance, walk in, and, to the greeter, Terrance says, "Hi, I made an appointment for the beautiful, Miss Jalisa Williams."

The store clerk checks the schedule and says, "Right this way, ma'am." Jalisa follows the clerk and Terrance follows behind Jalisa. "Here you are, ma'am," the clerk says while pulling up a chair for Jalisa to sit in. Terrance pulls up a chair and sits beside her.

Anthony Crawford, Jr.

Throughout Jalisa's pedicure and manicure, Terrance is conversing with her. They are laughing, joking, and giving one another sweet comments and gestures. He is enjoying her continuous smiles, her graceful gratitude, and heartwarming conversations. For the first time in a long time, Jalisa is glowing. When the technician finishes, Terrance pays for the services and walks Jalisa to the spa next door for her massage.

While walking in, the clerk greets, "Hello, how may I help you?"

"I made an appointment for the gorgeous, Miss Jalisa Williams."

The clerk checks the reservation booklet and says, "Yes, here she is." The clerk writes a checkmark by Jalisa's name on the list. "You're about ten minutes early, but you're the only one that showed up this morning for their appointment so the masseuse can take you now." Jalisa walks to the room for her massage and Terrance waits in the waiting room on his phone.

While waiting, he notices an old couple getting their feet rubbed across the room. He watches closely at their beautiful interaction and how the man is looking deep into his woman's eyes as if he's falling in love with her all over again. He feels the butterflies throughout his stomach while he wonders.

After 15 minutes or so, Jalisa walks out from one of the back rooms. Terrance stares at her as he pays for the massage. In his mind, for a fleeting moment, everything is moving in slow motion as she's smiling and walking towards him. It was as if for the first time he is watching an angel glide across the room. He develops a sweet tooth for her Hersey skin.

"Terrance," she says while noticing that he's daydreaming. "Terrance!"

He snaps out of it and says, "My bad. I was stuck."

"Stuck on what? Are you okay?"

Black Pain't, Vol. I

"Yes, I was taken over by your beauty. I'm sorry," he sweetly says as he gently grabs her hand. They walk out the spa and he open the passenger side door for her.

He is driving her to get lunch with the goal to get her back to her studio apartment so she can take a nap. She sits quietly in deep thought. He notices her energy and asks, "You good?"

"Terrance, I have something to tell you," she hurtfully says.

He looks at her momentary, put his eyes back on the road, and says, "You know you can tell me anything. Wassup, Love?"

"I'm scared to get hurt, again."

Confusedly, he asks, "What do you mean? Do you think I'm going to intentionally hurt you?"

"I don't know. I just have a hard time with men," she says sorrowfully.

He gathers himself and says, "I'm not in this to hurt you, Jalisa. I'm not in the heartbreaking business."

"Yeah, that's what they all say until they slip up and cheat or get tired of the woman, they're with and leave, or even just get the booty and don't call her anymore," she says inconsiderably. "I just don't want to feel any more pain. Don't open my heart or lead me on if you don't plan on staying. A woman can get easily attached to a guy like you. So, if you do decide to leave, please take the memories with you. Those things last forever."

As he pulls up to the drive-thru line, he's internalizing her statements. He thinks for a moment............

(While Terrance was an undergraduate student, he was in a relationship with one of his sorority sisters. They promised each other marriage and a family. While in college, they supported one another throughout their college experiences and made each other happy.

They were known as the campus's "Greek Couple." They were always busy with schoolwork, fraternity or sorority business, and extracurricular activities around campus, but they would always find time to hang out and do something special for each other.

Anthony Crawford, Jr.

One night, at the school's welcome back party, she was drunk with her sorority sisters. They were encouraging her to twerk on other guys. While Terrance and his fraternity brothers were strolling into the party, he saw her slow grinding on some guy.

Terrance instantly got upset and charged at her. He pulled her off of him and pushed him away almost causing a rumble between the guy's friends and his fraternity.

"What the fuck is wrong with you, Jazmine?" He furiously asked as they walk away from the scene.

She removed his hand from off her arms and said, "It's just dancing! Dang! Stop tripping." She walked back to her sorority sisters strutting and feeling unbothered.

One of Terrance's frat brothers placed his arm over Terrance shoulder, and said, "Bro, that's Dennis who works in the café, don't worry about that nigga mane!"

Terrance removed his brother's arm as he caught eyes with "Dennis." Dennis grinned at him while Terrance mean mugged him.

That week, there were rumors going around campus about Jazmine coming out of the boys' dormitory the night after the school's party. One of Terrance's fraternity brothers tried to tell him, but Terrance didn't believe him, because he talked to Jazmine that night after party.

That following week, Terrance and Jazmine went out to eat dinner. They conversed, horse played, and being affectionate. During their dinner, Terrance thought about what his fraternity brother told him and asked her, "Where did you go after the party last weekend?"

Conspicuously, Jazmine said, "I went to my prophyte Rayven's house. I was too drunk to drive home, so I went to her house to spend the night. I told you that when I talked to you."

Terrance looked deep within her eyes in search for the truth and said, "Just wondering."

After dinner, they drove to his frat house that was a couple of minutes off campus. They ended their night cuddling and watching movies.

Black Pain't, Vol. I

A couple of weeks went by. Terrance and one of his fraternity brothers, Jacob, his prophyte, were eating in the school's cafeteria. Jacob was talking to him about being the fraternity's president during his senior year of college. One of their sorority sisters walks in and sits next to Jacob. "Terrance, this is Rayven. Rayven, this is Terrance," he modestly said and continued eating.

Terrance pondered on her name and said, "Hey, nice to meet you,"

"Nice to meet you as well, Terrance. Why do I feel like I know you?" She dubiously asked.

"He's Jazmine's boyfriend," Jacob said.

She astonishingly said, "Oh, that's right. Duh! She's told me so much about you."

Terrance paused for a second to gather his thoughts. He then asked her, "So you're the one that Jazmine was telling me about."

"What do you mean?" She asked.

He said, "I guess she spent the night over your house after the welcome back party."

"No, I was out of town for an interview for this internship that I need in order to graduate," Rayven innocently said.

Terrance felt as if someone started stabbing him in his chest. He tried to pretend as if the news was not bothering him while he ate. Jacob could tell that something was wrong with him but didn't shine light on it.

Throughout that day, Terrance was not in his right mind. He was hurt and in a frantic. He went to the frat house and sat there for hours contemplating on how he was going to handle the situation. A lot of people called him and text him during that time, but he didn't answer, nor did he respond to any of them. He went to sleep.

Later that evening, while Terrance was sleep, Jazmine came banging on his room door. He gets up and, once he opened the door, he saw Jazmine pouting while a couple of his fraternity brothers stood behind her.

Terrance exasperatedly says, "I got this, bros, thanks."

Anthony Crawford, Jr.

Jazmine barged in, closed the door behind her, and yelled, "WHAT THE FUCK, TERRANCE? YOU GOT EVERYONE WORRIED ABOUT YOU! WHAT'S WRONG WITH YOUR PHONE?" She looked around his room as if someone was in there.

"Nothing," he said unapologetically as he closed the door and leaned against his closet. "Wassup?"

She irritably asked, "Wassup? What the fuck is 'Wassup?' And when did you start talking to me like that and ignoring my calls and texts? People are worri...."

"I'm good, Jazzy," he said interrupting her while she was talking.

"You're not good, Terry-Bear. You never act this way. I mean Wassup? Let me know something," she wrathfully said.

He stared at her in disgust. He looked down for a moment, back up at her, and said, "I met Rayven today."

In a high-pitched tone, she inquisitively asked, "My prophyte?"

"Yes, your 'prophyte,'" he said mimicking her high-pitched tone. "I asked her if she was the one whose house you were over after the welcome back party. You know? The one you claimed you spent the night with. She said that she was out of town for an interview. So let me ask you again, where were you, Jazmine?" He watched as her eyes began to water. She was distraught and felt that he deserved the truth. "Look at me, Jazmine!" He yelled. She lifted her head as tears began to fall. "Did you fuck him?"

Softly, with a tear falling down her cheek, she said, "Terry-..."

"DID YOU FUCK HIM?" He heatedly yelled as he stood up over her, waiting for her answer.

She covered her face and quietly said, "Yes."

He exploded. He threw a temper tantrum around the room. He picked up some pictures, books, and papers that were around his desk and threw them across the floor. He then punched a hole in his wall by the door. As his fist bled, he said, "Get the fuck out, Jazmine."

In search for forgiveness, she scarcely said, "Terrance."

Black Pain't, Vol. I

"DID YOU NOT HEAR ME? GET THE FUCK OUT JAZMINE!" He irately yelled while opening the door. She walked towards the door, he shoved her out, and slammed the door behind her.)

"I understand, Jalisa," he compassionately says.

While he was driving, Jalisa keeps observing his poised presence. When she looks into his eyes, she always felt that he is sincere. She observes him carefully.

He catches her staring at him as she looks away. He places his hand on her thigh. "I know what's it's like to feel pain. To have your heart ripped apart by someone you love. I don't want to ever inflict that *pain* on anyone else, especially you, Jalisa."

Jalisa feels a sexual sensation crawl up her legs. It runs spirals around her hips and caresses her shoulder blades. It is a feeling that she has never felt before. She quickly removes his hand to keep herself from exploding.

He looks at her perplexedly and apologetically asks, "Are you okay?"

"I'm fine," she dishonestly says as he pulls up to her apartment.

He confusedly stares at her as they sit still. She stares straight out the window while he looks around wondering what is wrong with her.

"You want to come in?" Jalisa melodiously asks.

He gives her a puzzling expression and says, "I thought we agreed on me dropping you off and coming to get you later."

"I know, but I don't want to be alone."

He slowly nods his head and says, "Okay, cool."

He parks his car next to her car. He rushes out of the car to open the door for her. Once she is out of the car, he closes her door, and locks his car with the button on his keys. They start walking.

As they both enter her studio apartment, he astoundingly gazes around as she walks into the back closet to put her belongings away. There is a piano that sits in the middle of the apartment. He sees her king-sized bed lying next to the tall, wide window. He notices a large

Anthony Crawford, Jr.

kitchen on the other side of the apartment that has a bar and stools a few feet away from her balcony. Between the bed set and the large kitchen is an entertainment center with a wide screen television that is mounted on the wall. There were three large, comfy-appearing couches that surrounds the entertainment center. There are pictures of herself, her sister, and her brother around the entertainment center.

He glowers at the photos of some famous Black dancers on the walls and admires the African sculptures that surround the apartment. He spots a bookshelf near her closet and walks towards it. He skims through the many books. He picks up a few books to see her expressive taste in reading. There is an incense holder on top of the bookshelf, and he notices more on the kitchen counter and on the coffee table.

Coming from out of her closet, she says, "This may seem like a random question, but do you like being a part of a Black-Greek Letter Organization?"

"I enjoyed the experiences. It had its ups and downs."

"What are some of the downs?"

He cogitates his answer and steadily replies, "It separates Black people even more than we already are. We fight over letters, colors, or bumping into one another while we stroll at parties. We fight over whose fraternity or sorority was the best and we fight over who run the yard.

"It's just one big competition. A lot of friendships are lost, relationships are broken, and people forget who they are in the Greek-life. So many of us were so ready to go Greek, but barely even knew what it meant to be African American.

"Another notion of Greek Life is the hazing. We don't want to admit nor talk about it, I even fought the truth of it, but hazing is not the way to go. I don't need to beat you to call you my brother or my sister.

"Your finances should not have to lessen, and your GPA should not have to drop for you to join an organization. The torture and the suffering that we put each other through needs to stop. We have to find a better way for brothers and sisters from all walks of life to come together," Terrance completes his opinions.

Black Pain't, Vol. I

"I have never heard a Greek member speak about Greek life like that," she says. "What are the ups?"

"You meet some awesome people. You gain a support group. You experience what it is like to grow with strangers through fellowship, business settings, step shows, road trips, and a lot more. You learn how to work with people. You eventually learn how to forgive and make amends with those that you used to battle with," he says as he yields to recollect some learned lessons. "You eventually realize how stupid those altercations were and how dumb division is. We are all stronger together than we are apart."

"I respect that." She walks to the kitchen and says, "Follow me."

As they walk by the couches, he expresses his fascination and the vibe of her home by saying, "You have a beautiful home."

She watches as he sits on her couch and good-humoredly asks, "Who said that you can sit down on my couch?" He hastily gets up as she laughs. "I'm just playing. You want something to drink?"

"No, thank you," he says as he sits on the arm of the couch staring at her while she looks into her refrigerator and grabs a bottle of wine. He absorbs her graceful presence and admires her dark beauty. "I didn't know you drank wine or any alcoholic beverages."

"Don't pass any judgement. Jesus drank wine. Plus, my sister bought me this for me a few months ago. She says that I'm too uptight and need to relax. I thought this was a good occasion. You sure you don't want a glass?"

"Sure. I'd take some."

"I thought you didn't drink?" She asks mockingly as she pulls two glasses out of the cabinet above the stove.

He laughs and asks, "Is that how I sound?" He walks and stands by the kitchen counter.

"Sometimes," she says while pouring wine into one of the glasses. "Here you go," she says as she hands him the glass. She pours wine into her glass and makes her way to the living room section of the apartment. She holds her glass up in the air and says, "Cheers."

Anthony Crawford, Jr.

As they take a sip of the wine, he stares at her in amusement while she makes dramatic gestures. "It's not even that strong," he says entertainingly.

"I don't drink, Terrance. I never knew how to even drink it. My sip was like a gulp," she says then taking another huge gulp. While enduring the pain with a sour-face expression, she says, "Bet I finish before you."

He barely takes a huge gulp and cautiously asks, "What are we betting?"

"Well, if I win, you have to massage my shoulders and wash these dishes that are in my sink."

"You want me to be your lil' slave I see. And if I win?" He asks then taking another huge gulp.

She innocently gazes at him and says, "I don't know. What do you want?"

"You," he romantically says while finishing his wine before her and making a refreshing sound effect with his mouth.

She smiles and happily says, "Welp, it looks like you got me. So what will you be doing now that you have me?"

"Hmm," he confidently mumbles as he slowly walks up to her grabbing her by her waist. "You're looking mighty delectable."

She slowly closes her eyes enjoying the sweet words flow from his mouth. It is as if his words are swimming through her body leaving cold spots and causing her to shiver. Goose bumps begin to appear all over her skin as her body responds to his touch. He sits the wine glasses on the coffee table and guides her close to her closet.

Her eyes close as he pins her against the wall like a painting. Her heart begins to beat fast. She feels his right hand gripping her waist as he moves down to her arms.

He lifts them up against the wall. She feels his tongue flickering across her neck as she stands there into a bliss. She feels her clothes being taken off and she stands naked.

He stares at her chocolate, toned and petite body. Her perky breast and round nipples excite him as he pulls her left leg onto his right shoulder. She simultaneously puts her right leg upon his left shoulder while he lifts her in the air. Her arms fall to his head as he proceeds to lick the privacy between her thighs like ice cream.

She grasps for air while his tongue touches the essence of her being, the creation of all life; the eternal organ from which everything comes from. The wetness from his tongue became the wave of her ocean. She bites her bottom lip as an unusual substance starts to flow from her. The substance drips down to his lips and streams to his chin.

Her eyes are still closed while he brings her down to his waist. She feels this large, endowed, thick pole rubbing against her womanhood while he carries her to the couch. Her heart is beating faster than ever before as she anticipates him entering her private business. He gently grabs her hips spreading her legs like a flower blooming in the spring.

She says, "Please take your time."

He slowly allows his pipe to slide inside her. He felt like an Olympic swimmer who just dives in a pool. She grasps for more air as he whispers in her ear, "Breathe." He slowly and gently penetrates her insides.

Her eyes are strongly closed, and her body begins vibrating at an abnormal rate. While he thrusts, she to moans. Her legs are tightly wrapped around his waist. Her arms are tightly tied around his neck, and she moves her left arms to his back scratching him as he penetrates.

She opens her eyes while quickly grabbing his face. They sensually stare at one another as he proceeds to infiltrate his penis into her world of pain and passion. She throws her head back and stares at the piano. She feels like an explosion is getting ready to erupt from within her volcano.

She says, "I'm about to cum." He goes deeper while kissing and sucking her neck.

Then, a slight, motionless pause comes from Jalisa. She slowly closes her eyes expecting an unfamiliar outburst. She screams as she pushes him out of her gripping the armchair and repeatedly rubbing her legs against the couch.

Anthony Crawford, Jr.

Witnessing her climax, he lies on the side of her holding her while she's moving into another dimension. She lies there with her eyes closed. He gently rubs his fingers against her stomach, down to her legs, and back up to her stomach. Her breath mirrored his slight hand movements. When he moved his fingers up her body, she inhaled. When he moved his fingers down her body, she exhaled.

As time escapes them, Jalisa's eyes finally open. She sees Terrance on the side of her asleep. She moves to wake him.

Caringly, he asks, "Are you good?"

She lifts and kindly says, "Yeah, I think so."

"How was it?"

She looks at him, says, "It felt amazing. I don't know why I want to thank you and take you out to eat or something."

They both laugh. "Do you know how to play that thing?" Terrance asks while pointing at her piano.

She confidently says, "Yes, I do. I love dancing to the sound of a piano. It allows my moves to be limitless."

While appreciating her passion, he thinks of a bright idea. He says, "Why don't you play something, and I'll recite a poem to it?"

"I didn't know you did poetry, Terrance," she says shockingly.

He blushes and says, "I haven't done it in a long time, though, so I don't know how it will come out."

"Why haven't you done it in a long time?" She wonders painstakingly.

He lifts and says, "My poetry stems from my feelings. I guess I just haven't felt anything in a long time."

"Why haven't you felt anything in a long time?" She asks curiously.

He considers her question and humbly says, "Life can be painful at times. Sometimes you can become immune to that pain and not know you're in pain. Then you can get numb to that pain and like totally get used to it.

"There are millions of Black folk livings with that indescribable pain. It's to the point that we're walking around here like zombies; dead to the world. Dead to a society that doesn't give a damn about who we are. We have forgotten how to feel.

"We forget how to feel for each other, feel for our future, and feel for ourselves. We all have forgotten the purpose of pain. Pain leads us to our purpose; it's supposed to give us understanding and wisdom of what we're supposed to do with our gifts. Our pain is supposed to teach us the most valuable lessons that life throws at us.

"When we don't allow pain to do what it supposed to do, then we miss the lessons. When we miss the lessons, we tend to find ourselves in the same situations over and over again. Lessons will always continue to repeat themselves until we learn and grow from them; until we elevate from them," Terrance concludes.

"I love hearing you talk; it's so refreshing to hear a man think the way you do," she says as she cascades into his arms. "Do you feel for me?"

Instantly, he says, "That's why I pursued you. You gave me something to feel. I haven't felt this feeling in a long time. I want to see where this feeling may take us."

She's taken by his response, she asks, "Where do you want to go?"

"Is this one of those 'what are your intentions?' type of questions?" Terrance jokingly asks.

"Sure...... if you want to view it that way."

"A relationship."

"That's odd coming from a man. I didn't think men wanted relationship these days."

"I wanna say that I'm a real man, but I'm pretty sure that you've heard that before."

"Hundreds," Jalisa says. "It's a red flag for me."

"I didn't say it! I was going to say it, but I held back because I rather show you!" Terrance keenly says, trying to prove his point.

She laughs and says, "I know... it's okay. Calm down. You still want me to play the piano for you?"

Anthony Crawford, Jr.

"Of course. I would love to recite a poem that I wrote about you," he says. "Let me go get my phone!"

He runs to grab his phone from out of his pocket. He searches for the poem about her in his notes. While walking back to her, he stops to watch her stand to her feet. Her dark, shiny nakedness and natural hair polishes the room. She sits down on the bench of her piano and begins to play.

He admires her free spirit. He begins to recite:

> She was my favorite melody,
> her beauty told me everything.
> She's all I want to know, thinking
> of overseas and places we can go;
> let's sow seed so we can grow.
> She was my favorite love song;
> that "my mind's telling me NO
> but your body's telling me YES" song;
> She gave me that "all my life" feeling;
> she was a "I prayed for someone like you" woman;
> she made me want to "thank God that I finally found you" type of
> woman; she was my favorite late-night jam
> that comes on, on your way home with bae,
> watching her as she sings along;
> the way her fingers played that piano;
> had me imagining things
> Miss Dirty Diana, I'll be your Dirty Daniel;
> butt naked, her hair's natural;
> my melanin angel,
> you know what to instru- to get my -mental moving.
> My love song,
> Here, take this love poem.

Chapter 11:
Land of the burnt faces

David Sr. is in his office at the church thinking heavily. He's wondering if he should call the card that he found in Tabitha's coat pocket. He has not been able to sleep because this card has been heavily weighing on his mind. He repeatedly asks himself, "Who is Dr. Phillip Carson?" He searches the name on Turner University's main website. He tries to search the name on social media but is unable to find any profiles.

He thoroughly thinks of the situation. He thinks of the possible outcomes of confronting Tabitha. He thinks that if he does ask her about the card, she may lie. He thinks that all this time he has been cheating, she has been cheating, too. He internally gets angry with the thoughts of his wife having sex with another man. He thinks that maybe she is trying to get some information from him, so she can go back to school. The card just brings an unknown energy.

He calls Dr. Carson's office phone, but Dr. Carson does not answer the phone. He ponders on if he's not answering because of the unknown number or because he's just not in his office. He thinks, "Unknown numbers call him all the time, he's a professor."

Suddenly, Dr. Carson's voicemail comes on. In a deep, sophisticated voice, the answer machine says, "You have reached Dr. Phillip Carson. If I haven't picked up by now, it's merely because I'm teaching or that you called on a weekend. My office hours and emails are posted on the school's website. If this is an emergency, contact the school's operator and they'll be able to assist you in any way possible. If you just want to leave a message, go right ahead after the beep."

David feels insecure. He creates this image of Dr. Carson in his head and instantly imagines why his wife wants him. He thinks, "He must be taller, more masculine with a deep voice; very educated, and is a doctor." He feels as though he'll have to fight to get his woman back. Then he realizes that he never hung up the phone after the beep, so Dr. Carson's answering machine was still recording.

Stuttering, David Sr. says, "Ummm this is Paul Wagner. I was wanting to get more information on your graduate program. Please, let's set up an appointment, so I can meet with you during your office hours." He leaves his contact information before hanging up.

Once he hung up, he thinks to call his wife to let her know how much he appreciates her for all that she does. As soon as he picks up his cellphone to call his wife, he notices that Rayven sent him a text. Even though he has not spoken to Rayven since their last sexual encounter, he feels something in his spirit that something is not right.

He opens the text message and reads, "We need to talk, it's important."

Black Pain't, Vol. I

Strange, negative thoughts and emotions surrounds him. His heart begins to beat fast. He wants to know the important news is now. He replies, "When and where can we meet?"

Moments later, Rayven texts, "At my place. I don't get off work until 4:30pm. I won't be home until 5:00pm or so."

David Sr. replies by texting, "Okay, I will call you when I'm on my way."

Rayven is at work scared because she does not know what to expect from David Sr. She is feeling nauseous. She thinks about calling her mentor to tell her that she is right about her being pregnant. At the time, she is scared because of her affair with David Sr. and her carnal encounter with Tony. She thinks to herself, "What would happen if I kept the baby? Is Tony or David the father? Do I want to be someone's baby mama?" She swiftly shifts her thought process. She thinks about when Jazmine found out about Rayven's affair with David…….

(A couple of years ago, after choir rehearsal, the choir members were all leaving one by one. A few of the choir members were waiting on rides, some left immediately after they had adjourned, and the others stayed to converse and seek guidance from Deacon Thomas. Throughout the night, Rayven kept giving David lustful stares and smirks. Jazmine would notice their exchanges while she was on her phone that was plugged into the charger on the side of the pulpit.

Jazmine, Rayven, and David Sr. were the last people there. David Sr. was in his office getting ready for church service on Sunday while Jazmine and Rayven were in the sanctuary reminiscing on their college days. They walked outside and into the parking lot. They said their goodbyes and they both got in their cars. Rayven waited until Jazmine drove off to get back out of the car and walks back into the church.

After a few minutes of driving, Jazmine realized that she left her phone plugged in on its charger. She made a U-turn at the stop light and drove back to the church. As she gets closer to the church's parking lot, she noticed that Rayven's car was still there.

Anthony Crawford, Jr.

She parked her car in deep thought. She turns the car off and slowly gets out. She walked inside the church surveying the sanctuary. She grabbed her phone and unplugged the charger from out of the outlet. She tried to hear any floating sounds but didn't. She quietly walked towards the offices and started to hear moans and grunts echoing in the hallway. She gets to Deacon Thomas's office and could clearly hear where the sexual sounds were coming from.

She leaned her head against the door to listen. Suddenly, her phone fell out of her hand. The noise stopped the sexual sounds that were coming from the office. There was an awkward silence as Jazmine slowly picked up her phone and hurriedly ran out of the building. While she got into her car to drive off, she saw David Sr. starring and standing outside of the entrance on top of the stairwell.

David Sr. walked back into his office while Rayven was putting on her clothes. She asked him, "Who was it?"

He stressfully sighed and said, "It was Jazmine."

Relieved, she said, "Jazmine is my sorority sister. She's not going to say anything."

"Yes, but she knows," he firmly said while shaking his head. "You may have to talk to her and stay away from the church to see how everything plays out."

Though she was not pleased with his suggestion, she managed to say, "Okay." She kissed him and rubbed his torso.

After that night Jazmine and Rayven removed themselves from out of the choir, however, Jazmine continued to attend the church. Rayven stopped attending and the affair sustained.)

During her lunch break, Rayven calls her mentor, knowing that she's taking her lunch break as well. The phone rings a couple of times, and her mentor sincerely answers, "Hey Rayven!"

"Hey, Tiffany. How are you?" She asks in a wrenching tone.

"Oh I am well; I am here teaching these bad ass kids so everything's awesome. How are you? How's work?" Tiffany asks sympathetically while leaving the school building to get lunch.

Black Pain't, Vol. I

Trying to find the right words to say, she replies, "I'm okay. I guess. Could be better," as she walks into the lunchroom.

Tiffany Thoughtfully asks, "What's the matter? Did you take those pregnancy tests?"

Shamefully, she answers, "Yes, I did, and I am pregnant." She holds back her tears because of her co-workers that are in the lunchroom. "I am so confused and scared. I don't know what to do."

"Calm down, sweetie. Everything's going to be fine. Let's start off with who's the father?" Tiffany asks while trying to stay collective about the matter.

She sniffles a few times and says, "I don't know. It's between two men."

Tiffany's driving and is anxious to know about Rayven's sexual encounters and why she's in this position now. She intriguingly asks, "Who?"

"David and........." she says while checking on her food in the microwave.

Tiffany interrupts her and instantly asks, "Wait, is this the same David that......?"

Rayven disappointedly says, "Yes, the deacon from that church where I used to sing."

"The one who's married with the two kids, right?"

"Yes."

"Damn, niggas ain't shit! Especially them church going folks! They're the worse ones! He took a vow before God and still cheated on his wife. That's crazy."

"I know! It's all my fault, Tiffany," she says remorsefully as she gets up to take her food out the microwave.

Tiffany gets angry and says, "It is not entirely your fault, Rayven. You're younger than he is. He should have had more respect for his wife, his kids, you, and himself. He could have prevented this whole thing! And the funny thing is, I wondered why you stop going to that church too. You didn't want to destroy his image, right? You really care for him?"

Anthony Crawford, Jr.

"Yes," she probingly says as she uses her fork to move around the food.

"So who is this other guy that could possibly be the father of your child?"

"Tony," she says softly while she eats.

Astonishingly, Tiffany asks, "Your ex-boyfriend, Tony?"

"Yes."

Tiffany pulls up to the restaurant's drive thru window and says, "How and when did you two get it in?"

"A couple of weeks ago…..."

(Tony was at work. He had about thirty more minutes until he was off. Rayven came into the store not knowing that Tony works there. She spotted him when she walked in. It's been a minute since she had seen him. She observed his thick beard and nappy, dreaded hair. He felt different to her, and she was curious to find out.

As she walked towards him, he saw her walking his way and he comically said, "Well, if you look at what the cat, and the dog, dragged in." They both hysterically laughed while he continues to work. "It's been a long time Rayven, what can I do for you?"

She smiled and kindly said, "I need a few things. I didn't know you worked here. You think you can give me a discount?"

"That's fine. You better hurry up, though. I get off in about 24 minutes. I can't do discount when I'm off the clock," he said good-naturedly.

She hurriedly went through three specific aisles to get the items she needed and came back to Tony's line within eighteen minutes.

"Find everything okay?" He playfully asked while she puts her items on the conveyer belt.

She teasingly looked at him and said, "Stop it, Tony. You of all people know that you don't want these problems man."

Black Pain't, Vol. I

"I already had those problems," he said while scanning her items and bagging them. "That'll be 64 dollars and 32 cents, but with the discount, it brings you all the way down to 42 dollars and 10 cents."

She took out her debit card, swiped it onto the machine, punched in some numbers, and awaited as he gave her the receipt. "Thanks, Tony. I really appreciate you."

"It's all love, I'm pretty sure you would do the same for me," he said while he cleans his area.

"I would," she said sensually. She lustfully examined him as he gathered his things to go to the back and clock out. She said, "What are you about to do now?"

"I'm about to clock out and go home! I'm tired!" He said fervently while moving away from his area. "Hold on, let me run and take these things back there and clock out. I could at least walk you to your car."

She agreed and waited by the exit door for him to return. He rapidly came from the back and met up with her. "Dang, it took you long enough," she wittily said as they both exit out the automatic doors.

While they walked to her car, he asked, "What are your plans on this fabulous Friday?"

"Nothing at all. Go home, rest, and catch up on my shows. What about you? Going out partying like you still got it?" She asked teasingly.

He helped her put her items in the trunk and gently said, "Naw, I don't do the things I used to; I had to grow up."

Spontaneously, she mockingly asked, "Why did you want to break up with me again? Oh, yeah, because we were going to separate colleges."

He softly said, "We both agreed on the separation."

Snappishly, she asked, "Why did you want to still keep in contact? Were you going to have me waiting on you while you were living and hittin' hoes left, and right?"

He nodded his head and said, "I wanted us both to live. Why are you acting like we didn't agree to it?" As he squinted his eyes at

Anthony Crawford, Jr.

her, "Keeping communication was for us to make sure that, no matter what shenanigans that we had going on, that we were going to always be there for one another and to always be friends. It hurt when you used to tell me all your stories about the guys you were involved with when you were out there, but I was happy that you were living. That's all that mattered to me when it came to you. Is she happy? Is she okay? Does she need some encouragement? That's all that I was thinking about every time you would cross my mind."

She felt his sincerity. She had not been in his presence to feel his loving energy in a long time. She internally craved for more. She unpretentiously said, "You want to come chill at my house? You know, so we can talk more."

Firmly, he replies, "I don't think that's a good idea. I'm going to have to pass."

His answer shocked her on the inside. While keeping her innocent composure, she said, "Damn, I thought we were friends, Tony. You can't spend an hour of your time to attend to a friend?"

Her words gripped his heart with guilt and lured him into her ruse. He modestly said, "Okay, I'll come. I'm sweaty and dirty from work. I hope you don't mind me walking through your house like this."

She smirked and confidently said, "I still have a few of your old underwear, shirts, and basketball shorts at my house. You can just take a shower and wear those."

"Aight, I'll follow you," he said before smoothly walking to his car. She got in her car and watched him walk to his. She didn't like that he was feeling uneasy about coming over.

On the way to Rayven's, Tony kept thinking about Trina and how she would feel if she knew that he was going to spend time with his ex-girlfriend. He thought about how he would feel if Trina would do him the same. "As long as I don't fuck, I'm good," he said to himself.

Meanwhile, in Rayven's car, Rayven kept looking in her rearview mirror to make sure Tony was following close behind her. She was still feeling butterflies float through her stomach from his energy.

Black Pain't, Vol. I

They pulled up to her apartment complex and parked right next to each other. She got out the car and he followed her seconds later. As they walked, they both kept thinking about what to expect being around one another privately again. They walked upstairs and he said, "How much is rent?"

"About eight hundred a month," she said while she unlocked the door. "The only utility bill that I have is the electric bill."

As they walked in, he glanced around the beautiful apartment and breathed in the compelling smell of cherry blossom. He said, "Wow, you'd always knew how to decorate greatly."

"Thanks Tony," she replied appreciatively.

"When was the last time you did something fun?"

While they both take a seat on her sofa, she said, "It's been a minute."

"Why?"

"What do you mean why?

"Life is supposed to be fun," he calmly said.

She considered his comment and asked, "What about problems, challenges, or struggles?"

Instantly, he said, "Those are blessings in disguise."

"How are those blessings in disguise, Tony?"

He expressively said, "Those are blessings in disguise because, when those 'problems' appear, they come with lessons and understandings that push us further in life. To move further in life is a blessing. Once you grasp those lessons and understandings then you'll see the blessing."

"What do you think holds us back from seeing these blessings?"

Sympathetically, he said, "Fear keeps us from seeing them. We fear to view our 'problems' as more than just problems, so we overlook them. Most people block their blessings because they don't feel like they deserve them; you cannot keep what you feel like you don't deserve."

His soft, raspy tone massaged her mind. She said, "Let me get you what you need to shower." She goes to her hallway closet to get

Anthony Crawford, Jr.

him a face towel and a big towel. She walked back to the living room and tossed them to him. "I'll have your clothes out waiting for you. I have to go deep in my drawers to find them."

He sighed and said, "Okay, cool." He got up and went into the bathroom.

While he was in the shower, Rayven checked her phone to see if David Sr. had texted her back. She hated that David Sr. would only communicate with her whenever he wanted to.

Fifteen minutes later, she heard the water getting turned off. Tony strode out the bathroom and asked, "Do you have any lotion? And where did you put the clothes?"

"It's all in my bedroom. The lotion is on top of my dresser and your clothes are on my bed."

"Thank you," he said while walking to her bedroom. The large towel was wrapped around his lower body covering him from the waist down. He grabbed the lotion from the top of her dresser and removed the towel from his waist to lotion himself.

She observed him from where she was sitting in the living room. She always loved his bronzed skin. She saw the beauty of his hair that looked like it was flowering all around his head. She remembered how she used to wrap her arms around his broad shoulders. She thought about how he used to kiss her with his full, succulent lips.

"DANG, I'VE BEEN LOOKING FOR THESE EVERYWHERE!" He yelled while putting on his underwear and basketball shorts. His statement made her snap out of the past.

He picked up the towel, folded it, and threw it in a dirty clothes hamper in Rayven's room. He walked back into the bathroom to pick his clothes up from off of the floor. He then walked into the living room to fold his clothes and to lay them in a pile by her door.

"You want some liquor?" She asked.

He innocently grinned and said, "I stopped drinking a long time ago."

"Why?"

Black Pain't, Vol. I

"I didn't like who I would transform into after a drink or two," he said timidly. "Plus, Jesus turned water into wine, not water into liquor."

After they laughed, she said, "I have some wine too." She got up and boogied towards the kitchen. She grabbed two wine glasses from the cabinet and the wine bottle from out of the refrigerator. Speed walking back into the living room, she sat the two glasses and bottle on the coffee table. She removed the corkscrew that was midway in the bottle. She poured their glasses to the brim, emptying out the bottle.

"Oh you're trying to get lit?"

She vivaciously said, "It's Friday! We're young, single, and working hard throughout the week. Why not get lit?"

The evening faded as they drank and conversed about their high school days. They told one another stories about their college experiences and laughed at each other's most embarrassing moments. He thought about a conversation that he had with Jazmine a while ago and asked, "How has church been going?"

Many thoughts and questions flooded through her mind, and she hesitantly said, "Church is always good."

"You still singing?"

"Yes, I am still singing. We actually have a gospel fest coming up."

He smirked to hide what he truly wanted to say and looked at the clock on her wall. He said, "It's time for me to leave. It's getting too late."

As he got up to gather his belongings, she sadly said, "That sucks, but it was great hanging out with you." She got up to meet him at the door.

"No problem at all," he said as an awkward silence filled their space.

He tried to give her a hug with his clothes in his arms and she said, "Nope! Put your stuff down and give me a real hug." As he put his clothes down, he turned to her with open arms. She curdled up into his arms embracing his soothing touch. She listens to his rapid heartbeat

Anthony Crawford, Jr.

while her head was up against his chest. They stood still. "I can be in your arms forever."

He tried to let her go but she wrapped her arms around him. He let his arms fall to his side while she held him. "I have to go Ray," he said tenderly.

"What if I don't want you to leave?"

He politely said, "Then that's too bad."

Whiningly, she smacked her lips and vulnerably said, "Why are you treating me so mean?"

Her declaration made him feel remorseful. He thought about Trina, but the sexual urge that they once shared gripped his hormones. He looked at the door motionless as she began rubbing her hands between his thighs. He closed his eyes to fight the temptation, but her touch defeated him.

As she rubbed between his thighs, she felt his manhood rise. Then she reached down into his basketball shorts to hold and caress his shaft. She grabbed his hand and guided it into her panties. She whispered, "I'm wet." He gently slithered his finger in her. She tightly grabbed his arm and spread her legs while his finger circled inside of her. While licking his ear, she whispered, "Is it wet enough for you daddy?"

He smoothly pulled away his hand and turned her around. He pulled her close to him, so her butt was grinding on his manhood. He grabbed her neck and put his wet finger into her mouth. She sexually sucked and licked his finger dry. He lifted her up and she immediately wrapped her legs around his waist. He sat her on her kitchen table taking off her shirt and then her panties. He took off his basketball shorts and his drawers at the same time.

He smoothly slid inside of her as she falls back on the table, gasping for air. He held her legs in the air and proceeded to thrust in and out of her. Her legs shook, the table rocked, and a chair fell to the floor. She leaned up and wrapped her arms around his neck.

"Fuck me daddy," she said erotically. He pulled and pushed her buttocks back and forth while he repeatedly plunged in and out of

Black Pain't, Vol. I

her. "Yes, daddy, yes. Right there. Right there. Don't stop, I'm about to cum." She climaxed and he instantly pulled out noticing the fluids that was dripping out of her. He grabbed the towel that he washed up with and cleaned himself. She was stuck, lying on the table.

Instantly feeling the guilt, he helped her down from the table. They put their clothes on allowing themselves to be comforted by the silence. She went to the couch and sat down while watching him grab his work clothes from off the couch. She asked him, "So what does this mean?"

"What do you mean?"

"You know what I mean, Tony. Where do we go from here? What does this mean to you?"

He internally battled between his truth and the lie that he wanted to tell. He then said, "Nothing."

Instantly and irritably, she confusedly said, "Nothing?"

He firmly replied, "Yes, nothing." Her face lit up. "I know you, Rayven. I know your body and your behavior. I don't want to get caught in another cycle with you. Good night, love." He grabbed the rest of his belongings and walked out the door.)

"And that's how it all happened," Rayven says.

Tiffany asks, "You've told Tony, right?"

"Yes, I did," she says. "But I have yet to tell David."

"Why haven't you told David?"

"I don't know."

Tiffany thoroughly wonders and says, "Because he's married with kids. So, in a sense, you're hoping the father is Tony?"

"Yes, because I know Tony is a good man, he's single, and he has his head on straight," she says desperately.

Something dawns on Tiffany and she says, "We're going to have to go somewhere to eat and talk, because I'm hungry and I have something to tell you."

Rayven curiously asks, "What is it that you have to tell me?"

Anthony Crawford, Jr.

"I'll tell you later. I have to handle some business real quick. Let's meet at Kemet later this evening. Is seven o'clock cool?"
"Yes, that's fine."
"Okay, see you later."

~

Meanwhile, Dr. Carson is announcing, "Reminder, Aaron James will be here this Saturday at six o'clock p.m. at 18th St. Missionary Baptist Church. I will be there with a roll sheet for those who would like to attend for extra credit. I suggest you come and get the extra credit because I never give extra credit." The class laughs. "Class dismissed."
As the class rapidly exit the classroom, Tony waits for Jazmine in the hallway. As she walks toward him, she gratefully says, "Tony, thank you so much for what you did for me the other day. I really appreciate you for that."
"It's all good, Jazz," he says as he observes her demeanor. "How are you and Miracle holding up?"
She blushes and happily says, "We're good and we're safe. I technically have someone around now so we're safe."
"Oh snap! My dog Jazzy?" He humorously yells. "That's beautiful, I'm very happy for you. What's his name?"
She modestly says, "Thanks, Tony. His name is Jules. He's such a sweet guy. Very pure and kindhearted."
The name sounds too familiar to Tony. He can't think of who Jules could be. It troubles his thought process, but he manages to say, "Well, Jules is a lucky guy."
"Aaww, Thanks Tony. And what about you?" She asks as they walk outside the building side by side.
He hesitates to tell her about Trina. He remembers that he still didn't tell her about his encounters with Rayven. He says, "You know me, just staying low key. Are you bringing Jules to the event tomorrow?"

Black Pain't, Vol. I

"Yes, I am. He'll be there," she says amenably. "Welp, I got to go get Miracle from day care. See you tomorrow, Tony."

He lifts his index and middle finger from his right hand, smiles, and says, "Peace, Goddess." As they both depart ways, he can't help but to continue to think about who this Jules person is.

~

While Dr. Carson is in his office, he notices that someone left a voicemail on his answering machine. It is very odd to him because people know that he's very hard to contact, so people rarely leave voicemails.

He checks the voicemail. The first fifteen seconds of the message is silence. Suddenly, "Ummm this is Paul Wagner. I was wanting to get more information on your graduate school. Please let's set up an appointment so I can meet with you during your office hours," is said by the anonymous gentleman. Paul Wagner even left his number on the voicemail as well.

Dr. Carson calls Paul. The phone keeps ringing and the voicemail came on. The answer machine said, "Hello, you have reached David Thomas, Sr., Deacon of 18th St. Missionary Baptist Church. I'm not in at the moment. Please leave your name, number, organization, or church in which you're calling from. Thank you. Have a blessed day."

He hangs up before the sound of the beep. The name sounds so familiar. He knows about the church. He says to himself, "This is not Paul Wagner. Who is David Thomas?"

He calls Darryl. Darryl answers, "What's up, Doc?"

"Did I call you at a bad time, sir?" Dr. Carson self-effacingly asks while packing his bags and getting his paperwork in order.

Darryl says, "No, sir. School just let out a few hours ago. I'm just up here talking to coaches that are trying to keep their kids on the eligibility list for sports. What's up, OG?"

"I need to talk with you about something. What are your plans for this evening?"

Anthony Crawford, Jr.

"I'll be at Kemet this evening."

"Perfect! I'll come. What time will you be there?"

Darryl hesitantly says, "Around seven o'clock-ish."

"Solid, I'll see you then."

"Gotta go, Doc. One of my most intelligent students just walked in."

Mr. Jones notices that David Jr. is crying and asks, "What's the matter, King?"

"My dad was supposed to come pick me up an hour ago," David Jr. hopelessly says hoping that Darryl had an answer for him. "He's always doing things this!"

He unreservedly says, "Life's too short to be thinking negative. Maybe something happened on the way here. Cut the man some slack."

"Can you take me home?" David Jr. enquires while looking up to him praying for a yes to his request.

He hesitates and says, "Yes, I'll take you, young brother. Let's get out of here." As they both walk to his door, he looks around the room to make sure he has everything. He turns off the lights, closes the door, and locks it. "Ready, King?"

"Yes, sir."

"Well let's get this show on the road," he says as they both walk down the hall and down the stairs to the main entrance.

As soon as they get outside to the parking lot, David Sr. pulls up. He sees his son walking to some man's car and pulls up to the side of them. David Jr. says, "There goes my dad. Thanks anyway, Mr. Jones."

While David Jr. walks to the passenger side of his dad's car, Mr. Jones walks to the driver side of the car to greet his dad. He says, "Wassup brother, I'm Mr. Darryl Jones. I'm David's history teacher."

"I'm David Thomas Sr., sir. I am one of the Deacons at 18th St. Missionary Baptist Church," he says while they shake hands. "It was nice meeting you, keep up with the good work."

Darryl watches as they drive off the school's parking lot, wondering about David Sr., and worrying about David Jr. He then walks to his car, puts his belongings in the back seat as he gets in the driver's seat, closes the door, and starts his car.

"What's up, DJ! Sorry I'm late. You hungry?"

David Jr. desolately says, "Naw, I'm okay."

"You sure about that, son? Your mama may not have cooked."

"Mama, always cooks."

Confusedly, he asks, "When?"

"All the time. You just don't eat with us," David Jr. says as his father takes at quick glance at him in sadness. "Mama is like my hero."

"Yeah, well, son. As you grow older, you'll figure out that all women have superhuman powers," he says while driving.

As they pull up to the house, David Jr. runs out of the car as David Sr. is yelling, "Slow down, DJ!" Once David Sr. is able to get out the car, he walks into his home and sees his wife in the kitchen cooking. He watches as David Jr. is eager to see her, hug her, and kiss her on the right cheek of her face.

"I told you mama be cooking, dad."

"I see," David Sr. says while he walks up to Tabitha and says, "Hey, beautiful. How are you?"

She cantankerously replies, "I'm good, David. How'r ya?"

"I'm good, and I was thinking maybe we...."

She interpolates him by asking, "Are ya still picking Talitha up from dance rehearsal?"

He wavers because he really had something nice to say to Tabitha. He then says, "Yes, of course. I'm picking up my daughter."

"I hope so. Yar late picking up your son," she says complainingly. "Ya know she gets out in twenty minutes right?"

He swiftly looks at his watch, rushes out the house, unlocks his car door, gets in, starts the car, and drives off. It took him fifteen minutes to get to the dance studio.

He parks the car in the parking lot. He gets out noticing how parents were already at the building waiting to pick up their kids. He

Anthony Crawford, Jr.

walks in to see the dance instructor talking with a few parents as the kids were running around playing.

Talitha spots him. With a confused look on her face, she runs to him and says, "Hey, daddy! Where's mom?"

"This was my week to pick up you and your brother, honey," he says while patiently waiting to talk with the dance instructor. "You got all your things?"

Talitha says, "They're over there." She runs to get them.

While he approaches the dance instructor, she says, "Deacon Thomas, good seeing you again, sir. We missed you at the recital."

"Good seeing you too, Jalisa. I have been kind of busy at the church," he says as Talitha runs up to them. "How come I haven't seen you and your sister there lately?"

She warmly hugs Talitha and says, "We've both just been busy working and paying bills."

"You can't be too busy for God," he says feverishly. "Will you be at the service tomorrow night? We're having an anointed speaker that's coming to bless us with his unique style of fellowship with God."

She nods her head and says, "Yes, my sister invited me to attend it with her. I'll be there."

"Amen, amen. Well, I will see you tomorrow."

"Okay, please tell Tabitha I said, 'hello'."

"Will do, Sister Williams," he says while he and Talitha are walking out of the building. He then whispers to himself, "That's Mrs. Thomas to you, Sister Williams."

Talitha, who's listening in on her father's personal conversation, interestingly asks, "Dad, are you talking to yourself about Instructor Williams?"

"No, no, no. I was not," he claims. "I was complimenting her on a job well done."

Talitha courageously says, "Dad, I'm getting older. Which means that my understanding is evolving. You said, 'That's Mrs. Thomas to you, Sister Williams' because you didn't like the fact that she called mom by her first name instead of her married name."

Black Pain't, Vol. I

He is in awe about his daughter's intelligence. He cannot hide the truth on how that comment by Jalisa made him upset. He then says, "That was unrighteous of me." They get in the car, shut their doors, and put on their seat belts.

As he starts the car and drives off, Talitha encouragingly says, "It's okay, dad. We all make mistakes. That's why we're human. I learned that, when I'm out there performing, if I mess up, I don't get mad or down on myself. You have to get up and keep dancing. That's what Instructor Williams always say."

"Thank you, Princess. I appreciate that reminder. Are you hungry? Do you want to stop somewhere and get something to eat?"

Talitha looks at him with a look of despair while he's driving and responsibly says, "Dad, you really have to start being home more. Mom cooks on Fridays. We watch good movies, too."

"Oh, really?" he says aloud. The hew whispers to himself, "DJ left out the movie part."

Once they got back to the house, David Jr. and Tabitha are in the living room watching a cartoon movie while eating fried chicken and fries that are on the coffee table. "Hey, Mom! Hey Brother!" Talitha says while throwing her things to the floor.

"Uh huh, ya betta pick ya stuff up and take it to yar room," Tabitha commandingly says to Talitha. "Ya know betta."

As Talitha picks up her belongings and runs to go put them in her room, David Sr. sits down in her spot on the couch. David Jr. says, "Dad, that's Talitha's spot."

"Boy, I paid for these dog-on couches. I can sit where I want," David Sr. says sturdily as he picks up a few fries and eats them.

Tabitha notices his rude comment to David, Jr. and peacefully says, "David, that's Talitha's seat. She sits there every Friday."

Talitha walks back into the living room. "Dad! You're in my seat," she says brutishly as David Sr. stands up. "Thank you, daddy."

David Sr. then checks his watch and asks Tabitha, "What time does the game come on?"

Anthony Crawford, Jr.

Tabitha says, "It comes on at seven-thirty."

"I'm about to head to Kemet to watch the game. I got a lot of things on my mind," David Sr. says dreadfully as he grabs his coat and walks out the door. He notices how his family barely even care that he's leaving.

Black Pain't, Vol. I

Chapter 12:
Situationships

It's approximately six-thirty and, for the first time in months, Trina beats everyone to Kemet. She even got there before some of her co-workers. She cleans the bar, washes the glasses, and she puts more ice into the ice trays. She checks the fountains to make sure they were filled and then awaits the arrival of customers to barge in.

As customers are coming in, she's working and moving around the bar swiftly serving customers. Suddenly, she notices the Deacon of the church she used to attend with her sister walk in alone. He spots her and paces to the bar saying, "Jalisa? I didn't know you worked here, too."

While pouring beer into two long glasses, she laughs and says, "I'm her twin sister, Trina."

"That's right. That's right. How have you been? Why don't I see you at church anymore?"

"I'm good and I just had to take a break on religion for a minute. Most of the time, I feel like it isn't for me. Not to knock those that are religious, but it's just not for me," she deferentially says watching him sit at the bar counter. She confusedly looks around the bar. Then she suspiciously observes him and asks, "Don't you think that this is an unusual setting for a Deacon?"

"Why do you ask that?"

"You're at a bar."

He scoffs and says, "Let he who is without sin cast the first stone."

"That still doesn't make the sin okay."

"Well, then don't judge a book by its cover."

"What do you mean by that?"

He hisses and confidently says, "Just because I'm at a bar does not mean that I am consuming any of the alcoholic beverages at the bar or doing any sinful behavior. Jesus went to the bars, to the clubs; to dangerous areas in the cities. He wasn't always in those temples."

She nods her head in agreement and modestly asks, "What can I get you to drink?"

He kindly says, "Oh no, I don't drink. I'm just here for the wings and the basketball game. I hate that you've had some bad experiences with religion, especially when the bible says that Jesus Christ is the truth, the way, and the light. That, without him, we don't see Heaven."

"Jesus did say that we will do greater things than he, right?"

"Yes, but I believe you're interpreting that wrong. What that verse truly means is that…"

Black Pain't, Vol. I

She interposes and instantly asks, "Who's to say your interpretation is the only right interpretation?"

He annoyingly says, "I'm not saying that my interpretation is the only right interpretation. There are thousands of different interpretations, but you hav...."

She interrupts him again by asking, "So out of those thousands, who's right? Who's wrong? It all sounds like confusion. There are so many different interpretations of the bible and people's perspectives of the bible that we miss what the point of the bible."

Irritably, he clears his throat and says, "No matter which interpretation, the commonality of our interpretations is that Christ is the truth, the light, and the way."

Noticing his energy shift, she favorably says, "Yeah, okay. I'll be sure to put in the order of wings for you. They should take about ten to fifteen minutes," she says while walking to the other side of the bar noticing Darryl sitting down. "Hey, Darryl. You haven't been around these parts here lately. You forgot about a sistah huh?"

As he is taking off his coat, he smiles, and says, "Of course not, Trina. I've just been taking care of some business."

"Or taking care of some beautiful, black woman! I've heard about her," she says knowingly as she begins to make his drink.

He unpretentiously says, "Yeah, yeah; I'm just trying to prove to myself that I can be a good man to a good woman."

"Oh, I understand," she says while mixing his drink. "It's kind of been the same for me, you know?"

As she hands him his drink, he confusedly asks, "What do you mean by its kind of been the same for you? Who's the knight and shining armor in your life?"

"You'll see him later. He's coming up here once he gets off work," she says favorably. "He was a square when I met him. He's an OG now."

They both laugh and he unexpectedly says, "I went to go visit Alvin in the hospital."

Shockingly, she asks, "Why is he in the hospital?"

Anthony Crawford, Jr.

"He tried to kill himself."

Frantically, she says, "Wow, is that why I haven't seen Alvin in weeks? That's crazy."

Phillip walks in and sits next to Darryl. "What's up, Doc!" Darryl enthusiastically says as he high fives him. "Trina, this is my mentor, my good friend, Dr. Phillip Carson. Doc, this is my lovely friend, Trina."

"You can call me Phil. Darryl just over exaggerates with the whole doctor thing. Nice to meet you, Queen," he says while gently shaking her hand.

She smiles and says, "Nice meeting you as well. What can I get for you?"

"I'll take some of that Tennessee Honey on the rocks. Thanks sweetie," he says charmingly as he faces towards Darryl to tell him the story of the strange voicemail. "So someone left a voicemail on my office answering machine and left a number."

Wondrously, Darryl asks, "So, who was it?"

"They said their name was Paul Wagner, but, when I called back, no one picked up. So when their answer machine came on, the person on the recording said his name is Deacon David Thomas Sr. of 18th St. Missionary Baptist Church," he says as Trina hands him his drink.

Darryl's mind instantaneously goes into deep thought about the name. He says, "Hmmm. One of my student's names is David Thomas Jr. I actually met his dad today. His dad was taking too long to come and get him and as I was getting ready to take him home, he pulled up."

Hesitantly, Phillip asks, "Wow, well ummm, do you remember the married lady that I've been flirting with?"

Darryl puts all the puzzle pieces together and asks, "Is she the wife of David Thomas Sr.?"

"Yes, I believe so. I'm just curious as to how he got my office number," he says as he sips his drink. "Do you remember what the guy looks like?"

"Yes, I do."

Black Pain't, Vol. I

Meanwhile, on the other side of the bar......

David Sr. notices his son's teacher, sitting on the other side of the bar. He vigilantly observes him and the guy next to him.

Trina comes back with his order of wings, and she politely asks, "Was there anything else I can get you, sir?"

He cringes to the sound of her voice and says, "No, thank you Sister." He discretely points over to Phillip and Darryl and says, "Who are those guys over there that you were just serving?"

She looks across the bar at the two gentlemen that he is pointing to. She awkwardly says, "That's Darryl and his mentor. I forgot his name, but I remember Darryl saying that the guy was a doctor or something. Why you ask?"

"I was just wondering. They just look familiar." As Trina walks away, he has so many thoughts going through his mind. He develops a strong feeling that the guy just might be the doctor that gave his wife the business card. "But why?" he thought to himself eating his chicken wings.

He looks around the facility admiring the progress. He sees afro-centric paintings hanging on the walls. He gazes at the hieroglyphic writings and pictures around the room. While looking at the entrance, he unexpectedly sees Rayven entering the building with another woman. His heart begins pounding like someone playing the base drum in his chest. He watches as the waitress escorts them to their table.

~

Meanwhile, after the waitress takes their orders and walks away, Rayven says, "Thanks for inviting me here, Tiffany. I have never been to this place before. What's it called again?"

"It's called Kemet. Their wings are great and even their vegan specials are scrumptious." Tiffany says vividly. "It's black owned, too."

"What does Kemet mean?"

Anthony Crawford, Jr.

"Kemet means the Land of the Black faces. That's what the Ancient Egyptians called Egypt long before it was called Egypt."

Rayven looks around the facility and at the customers to get a vibe of the good energy in the atmosphere. "So what is it that you wanted to tell me? And why couldn't this be told over the phone?"

"I didn't want to tell you this over the phone, because I was afraid of how you were going to react. So it was best that I sat down with you so we can plan your next move, because you're not going to like what I have to say," Tiffany says cautiously.

She suspiciously says, "Alright. Wassup?"

"Remember your ex-boyfriend that you were telling me could be a possibility of being your baby's father?" Tiffany asks while watching Rayven nodding her head in agreement. "Well, he's just been popping up everywhere I go. One evening, I talked to him at the store that he works. He helped me put some things in my car one morning."

She interjects and asks, "How or why was he helping you put some things in your car in the morning? He doesn't even live near you."

"That's the thing! Do you remember that loud and obnoxious neighbor that I used to tell you about? The one that blasts her music all freakin' night?" Tiffany asks vigorously.

"Yes, I remember."

"Well, that's whose house he's been visiting."

Rayven's torn on the inside because she doesn't want to feel like she's ruining a happy home. She asks, "What does she look like?"

Tentatively, she says, "She's dark skinned, short. Umm......" Tiffany stops during her description because she surprisingly sees Trina at the bar. "Matter of fact, there she goes right there. The bartender serving drinks."

Rayven looks Trina's way and discerns her. She observes her beautiful, dark skin and vibrant smile. She notices her height and petite shape. She asks, "You think I should go over there and tell her?"

"NO! Don't do that. You don't know what Tony has told her about your pregnancy," Tiffany replies candidly. As they capture each other's eyes, Tiffany can see her hurt.

Black Pain't, Vol. I

She desperately asks, "What should I do? I know Tony had to tell her something. Tony is honest. He's not going to hide anything from anyone, especially if he's involved with them."

"You may be right, but you don't know how that woman over there is taking it in or if he actually has even told her," Tiffany says maturely.

She looks around to avoid crying and angrily says, "Is that why you brought me to this specific restaurant. To show me her?"

Tiffany holds her composure and says, "No, I didn't even know she worked here."

Rayven spots someone and slightly says, "Ahh shit!" She puts her hands on her head with her elbows on the table.

Tiffany perplexedly asks, "What? It's the truth! I would never do anything petty like that."

She says, "NO! Tiffany! NO! I'm not worried about that. David is here sitting on the other far left end of the bar." Tiffany tries to look and Rayven yells, "NO! Don't look. He might catch us staring."

"Does he know you're pregnant?"

"No, he does not. He doesn't know."

~

Meanwhile, back at the bar, Phillip and Darryl are still trying to discover David Sr.'s motives as Tony finally arrives.

He energetically walks up to Dr. Carson and Darryl. He energetically says, "Luke and Obi Wun Kinobe! What's the deal my brothers?"

Dr. Carson kindly asks, "Mr. Tony Givens, how are you, sir?"

"Good now that the semester is almost up. Darryl never mentioned all the work you give while taking your class."

Darryl laughs and says, "That's usually what makes us turn around and not go to grad-school. What brings you around these parts, youngsta?"

Anthony Crawford, Jr.

"I came to visit my girl," Tony warmheartedly says acknowledging Trina with a smile and a head nod.

Phillip and Darryl meet eyes for a moment. Darryl confusedly asks, "Trina is your girlfriend?"

"Yes," Tony says graciously.

After sipping his drink, Darryl says, "You're the good man that she's always talking about. That's wonderful, brother."

"Thanks, big bro. I'm just happy about the blessing, you know what I'm sayin'?" Tony says while taking a seat on the bar stool.

Trina comes over to them and says, "Hey, Baby! Thanks for coming."

"No problem, Love," Tony says smoothly. "How's work going?"

She grabs change from one of the customers and says, "Crowded as usual. What you want to drink?"

"I'll take some water for right now. I already know how you get later. You ain't about to have me dazed out," Tony comically says.

She laughs while Tony admires her beautiful smile. She says, "Oh stop. I don't do anything," then walks off to get Tony's water.

~

Meanwhile, Rayven turns around and sees Tony conversing with the two other gentlemen. "There goes Tony," she says heartlessly.

Tiffany turns around to see Tony with the two gentlemen. She notices Darryl and says, "One of the men that he's with talks to one of my co-workers."

Rayven looks at Tiffany and gets out her seat saying, "I have to talk to Tony." She starts walking towards Tony and, suddenly, David Sr. unexpectedly runs into her. They both bounced off one another as Rayven tries to hold on to a chair to keep from falling.

"Rayven, what are you doing here?" He asks. "Are you following me?"

Black Pain't, Vol. I

Staggering Rayven looks over to the bar at Tony while David Sr. is talking. Tony notices her. They meet eyes for a brief second. Tony quickly looks over to Trina hoping she isn't paying attention towards what is going on. He pretends that he doesn't see her. Rayven recognizes his avoidance and starts walking towards him.

David Sr. grabs her arm, turns her back around to face him, and says, "Where are you going while I'm trying to talk to you?"

She angrily stares at him wondering why he grabbed her arm. She quickly glares at Tony and recognizes him looking their way. She looks back at David Sr. and says, "David, I'm pregnant."

~

Meanwhile, back at the bar, Darryl witnesses Tony looking across the restaurant while trying to stay engaged into their conversation. He gawks towards the area where Tony's eyes are aiming towards. He sees David Sr. talking with some woman and says, "Say, Doc. There goes David Thomas, Sr. right there." He nods his head in the direction that he should look. "That's the brother that picked up his son today after school."

Phillip looks in the direction of Darryl's head nod and sees David Sr. with some other woman other than Tabitha. He says, "And that ain't Tabitha."

"Then who is that?" Darryl says inquisitively. "And why are they here?"

Tony smoothly says, "That's Rayven."

"Who's Rayven?" Darryl and Phillip ask at the same time.

Tony shakes his head, looks down, and says, "She's either my future baby mama or she's his future baby mama."

Trina walks to them noticing the change in atmosphere between Phillip, Darryl, and Tony. She disconcertedly asks, "Are y'all good?"

Snapping out of the reverie, Tony hesitantly says, "Nothin'," then he snaps Phillip and Darryl out of their train of thoughts. "We good, baby. Just looking out at life."

Anthony Crawford, Jr.

Trina gives him a haughty look, rolls her eyes, and proceeds to work. Once Tony gets the opportunity to turn around to witness David Sr. and Rayven's scene. He sees Rayven and another woman storming out of the building while David Sr. is nowhere in sight.

Chapter 13:
Detachment

On the way home from Kemet, Tiffany is on the phone informing Patricia about Darryl and his "Little Playa Clique." Patricia asks, "So your mentee is pregnant by who?"

"It's either Tony or the Deacon," Tiffany says promptly. "Tony is Rayven's ex-boyfriend, but now Tony is in a relationship with my neighbor."

"And the Deacon is having an affair with your mentee?"

"Yes, and I think the older guy that Darryl and Tony were with is trying to get at the deacon's wife. I wouldn't be surprised if the deacon's wife allowed him to trespass all on her property," she says animatedly.

"What does any of that have to do with Darryl?"

Tiffany, while driving, firmly says, "You are the company you keep. If the people he hangs around are dogs, then what do you think he is? I just want you to be cautious."

Patricia is getting internally angry. She's allowing Tiffany to bother her and the feelings that she gained for Darryl.

~

Meanwhile, back in the parking lot of Kemet, Phillip, Darryl, and Tony are still talking about the incident that has just taken place. Phillip and Darryl are questioning Tony about Rayven's pregnancy and what they think Tony should do.

Darryl asks, "So, you're going to wait until the baby is born to start taking responsibilities as the father?"

"I just feel like I should not have to commit myself to something that's a possibility of not being mine. Rayven has been in and out of sexual relationships with guys for a long time. What, I'm supposed to just give her what she wants at the time that she wants it?" Tony asks.

Darryl says, "You're still going to have to be a man for her. If you wait to tell Trina and the baby turns out to be yours, then you're not only breaking Trina's heart, but you're digging yourself a grave that only honesty can fill. Her wrath will bury you. Then you're going to have to play catch up with Rayven, which will be a continuous uphill battle. You're going to have to do all that you can to make sure baby-mom's is happy or you'll feel the fury from her scorns."

"But what if it's not mine, I'll still lose Trina from telling her about the possibility of the baby being mine. It sounds like I'm in lose-lose situation," Tony says heartlessly.

Phillip says, "Yes but you should want to go into any relationship with honesty. Who wants to live a lie?"

"I see where you're coming from. If I'm the father then I will take responsibility," Tony meekly says. "But if it's not my child, then I'll pray and wish Rayven the best."

Phillip asks, "So are you going to tell Trina? She's going to be broken-hearted no matter what, but I know you don't want to keep her in the dark."

Tony contemplates on Phillip's question. He frankly says, "I don't know yet."

Darryl says, "Tony, listen…"

Interposing on Darryl's statement, Tony asks, "What would you two do? Have any of you ever been in this position? If not, then how can you tell me what's right and what's wrong? I know this shit ain't morale, I know it ain't cool. I just want to put myself in a win-win situation."

As soon as he tries to finish speaking, Trina comes walking around corner of the parking lot. "Hey, gentleman," she says as she stops right next to Tony. "Hey baby, thanks for coming again."

Tony swiftly changes his demeanor and says, "It's all love. Anything for you."

"Boy, please. Stop trying to game me up. Darryl, I didn't know that you knew Tony," she says probingly.

Darryl smiles politely and humbly says, "Yeah, that's my protégé right there."

"Oh, trust me. He tells me all the time," Trina says as Tony puts his arms over her shoulders.

Phillip notices the youthful bond between Tony and Trina. He says, "So how did you two meet?"

Tony and Trina happily look at each other and Tony confidently says, "We met on a boat ride."

"Yeah, the nigga was reading, and I was like… niggas don't read. Let me holla at this square," she says comically.

Tony laughs and says, "She's been sprung on this square ever since."

Anthony Crawford, Jr.

"I'm just trying to turn him into a solid circle. So he can be well rounded," she says as Tony roughhouses with her.

Phillip and Darryl laugh in amusement. Phillip then says, "Young love is always beautiful."

Trina and Tony stop playing around to continue their conversation with Darryl and Phillip. Tony says, "It's getting late. We have to go. I'll see you Gods tomorrow," as he daps Darryl.

"Alright, King. Keep doing what you do mane! Proud of you," Darryl says culturally then gives Trina a hug. "I'll see you next week, Tri."

She grins and says, "You'll see me tomorrow too."

"So you're going to hear Aaron James's speech?" Darryl asks.

"Yes, I am," she says proudly.

Tony daps Phillip and Phillip says, "Aight youngster, keep chasing the dream." He then shakes Trina's hand and says, "Good night, Queen. It was nice meeting you."

Darryl and Phillip watch Tony and Trina walk to Tony's car. Once they saw them get in, Phillip says, "That won't last long."

"Damn! Why do you say that?" Darryl asks curiously.

"Because Tony isn't walking in truth. You can only withhold something from a woman for so long before she figures it out. It's this feeling that they get when they know that their significant other is up to something or is guilty of something. Then the woman would question you in ways that you will surely slip up.

An intuitive woman finds ways that will make you feel bad about the crimes that you've committed, especially when she doesn't have a clue about her intuition. Women pays attention to her man's demeanor; it's like they can read men. If something is off about their man, then they would feel it. Women know everything, they're always two to ten steps ahead. They just want the truth. No matter how much it will hurt," Phillip says wisely.

Darryl closely listens to Phillip while taking heed to his words. He then says, "You're absolutely right, Doc."

Black Pain't, Vol. I

"Yeah, bro. The power of a woman's intuition," he says while getting ready to walk to his car. "I'll see you tomorrow, Brother J. I have some things to do to prepare for tomorrow's event.

Darryl walks him to his car and says, "Okay, O-G. I'll see you tomorrow." He walks to his car as Phillip gets in his car and drives off. He checks his watch and notices that it was too late for him to go to the bookstore to get a book. He gets in his car and drives home. On the way home, he thinks about Patricia and decides to call her.

The phone rings, she answers, and says, "Hello."

"Hey, Queen! How are you?" he asks excitingly.

She irritably says, "I'm good. Wassup?"

Darryl notices the tone of her voice and says, "That's good that you're good. How was your day?"

"My day was good. Wassup?"

Before allowing her attitude to upset him, he asks, "What's the matter with you?"

She cantankerously takes a deep breath and says, "I told you when we first started talking that I have a hard time trusting men. I told you that I didn't like hearing things about the person I'm talking to from someone else I told……"

He interposes and asks, "Did I miss something? What have you heard?"

"You know what I'm talking about!"

He effortlessly says, "Patricia, I don't know what it is that you're talking about. If I did, I promise you that I wouldn't be acting like I didn't. Let's be mature adults about this and talk it out."

Quickly, she asks, "Did you see Tiffany tonight?"

He thinks for a moment on why she mentions Tiffany. He truly does not understand why Tiffany has anything to do with their current situation. Then he says, "I didn't see Tiffany. Did Tiffany see me?"

"Yes, she saw you. She saw you with your 'Little Playa Clique.' She told me everything," she says snappishly.

In dismay, he confusedly asks, "What did Tiffany tell you?"

"It does not matter," she says inconsiderably.

Anthony Crawford, Jr.

"It does matter, Patricia."

"Why Darryl?"

"Because you matter to me."

She's slightly speechless. She is able to say, "All I'm saying is that you could have told me about your circle of friends."

He begins to put some of her puzzle pieces together from this puzzling situation. He takes time to breathe and to stay calm. He thinks about his mentor and his mentee. He says, "You're talking about Phillip and Tony? What about my 'circle of friends,' Patricia? What exactly did Tiffany say to you because your accusations aren't adding up? Whatever problem this is can easily be solved if we communicate with one another."

"She told me about Phillip and how he's talking to some deacon's wife. She told me that Tony got her mentee pregnant while messing around with another woman. Why haven't you told me about the type of friends that you have? What else are you hiding? They say that you are the company you keep! So if they're that way then you must be that way too," Patricia says sharply. "You tell me all the time that we attract who we are! You know I'm guarded, Darryl! You know I've been hurt. I don't have time for whatever game that you're trying to play with me."

He listens attentively. As her voice screeches, he feels for her. He softly says, "Patricia, you're right. My inner circle is making damaging decisions that are, not only effecting their lives, but everyone around them. Including mine. It's hard knowing that the man I look up to is pursuing a married woman even though her husband isn't treating her like the Queen she is. It weighs on me knowing that my protégé might have some girl pregnant while he's involved with another woman. I'm not debating with you on that, but I am not them. I don't' want to hurt you or add any more pain to your hurt."

"Come on now, Darryl. You're always talking about holding each other accountable and liberation and a whole bunch of other things that you don't mean because, if you did, then they wouldn't be your friends," she says immediately.

Black Pain't, Vol. I

He instantaneously says, "If that was the case then we wouldn't have any friends. We're all flawed in our own ways. We all deal with at least one; we all make mistakes. We all make decisions that most wouldn't consider righteous, but who are we to judge? Who are we to condemn? Who are we to throw the stones? We can't just give up on people because they're making unconscious decisions. We're operating from post-traumatic slave syndrome and fear. Most don't know who they really are, and those same people don't even know where we come from. The spiritual system that we once had was taken away from us when our Ancestors were shackled on them ships and brought to this dying society. They gave us this self-refueling and self-generating system that allows us to kill each other, pull each other down, and hold us back from advancing in life."

"What does that have to do with who you hang with and the things that they do?" She asks upsettingly. "You have to be the example. It sounds to me like you're trying to justify people's actions and why they do the things they do. We know right from wrong. We know not to talk to a married woman; we know to wrap it up when we're having sex. We know not to beat on women! Slavery, this society, and our spirituality does not exclude the actions of others."

"But we must also be forgiving. We must have compassion for our people! They're hurting and dying on the inside because majority just don't know why they're hurting or have not accepted their past. Most are too dependent on the system to truly want change. Whenever someone tries to enlighten them, they get defensive and begin to convert back to the same religion, the same system, and the same pain that has been killing us for centuries."

"Well, what's the best thing that we can do, Darryl? Because if people are too messed up then why don't we all just……... I don't know," she hopelessly says.

He collectively says, "We must do as you say and that's to live by example. We must promote self-love, unity, truth, and equality! We have to figure out better ways to live in peace and in love together with purpose and understanding."

Anthony Crawford, Jr.

"Sometimes I feel like it's too late. The world just seems too crazy and evil. Is pain and sorrow all that we have to offer to each other?" She asks forlornly.

Sagaciously, he says, "That's one of life's biggest challenge. That's part of this illusion that exist on this planet. We're just not seeing the bigger picture behind that pain and sorrow."

"What's the bigger picture?"

"That everything begins and ends with us. Nothing changes if nothing changes. In order to make any change in the world, everything must start with the person you see in the mirror every day. Noticing our own actions and embracing our own truth, can lead us to our collective purpose, but we must start within ourselves first," he says compassionately.

Taking heed to his words, she says, "That's why I remain to myself and do everything and anything alone because you can't trust no one in this world. Sometimes you can't even trust your own family. I'm sorry, Darryl, but I can't do this anymore. I'm done with the drama, and I'm done trying with love. Hope you can understand."

His fast-beating heart causes his body to tremor as he hurtfully says, "But you're made out of love, but I completely understand where you're coming from."

"I just need some time to myself," she says guardedly. "You know, to think things through."

As he pulls into his apartment complex's parking lot, he parks his car in his usual parking spot and says, "Okay, I guess there isn't anything left to say at this point. I'm sorry for making you feel the way you feel."

"No hard feelings, right?" She inoffensively asks.

"None whatsoever, Queen. Nothing but love," he humbly says as they both hang up their phones.

Darryl sits in his car for a moment in deep thought. He feels hurt from the thought of never finding love or someone that he actually likes. The illusion of loneliness corrupts his emotions. The idea of living

Black Pain't, Vol. I

alone for the rest of his life enters his train of thought and rides down to his heart's station where a whole lot of love is being captive.

He gets out of his car and walks to his apartment. He reflects on the incidences that have recently taken place. Once inside, he showers to happy thoughts of Patricia. He lotions himself to the most memorable moments that they had.

Meanwhile, Patricia is at home feeling betrayed, but, at the same time, feeling like she is saved from Darryl. She cannot believe that she made herself vulnerable to him in various ways. She feels stupid. She comes to a temporary conclusion that she just needs to completely leave men along and focus on her.

While at home, she bathes in her tub of emotions. The water makes her feel like she's washing away any detachments she has with Darryl. The bath feels like an extended baptism. She gently cleans herself and meditatively soaks in the water. She then drains the water and gets out the tub to dry.

She stares at herself in the mirror, accepting her flaws, and forgiving herself. She oils her body to the way Darryl hugged her. She thought about the event that Darryl invited her to. She really wants to go but is unsure now because of her feelings towards him has changed.

During the duration of Patricia and Darryl's farewell, David Sr. is pulling up to his driveway anxiously waiting to discuss Tabitha's motives with Dr. Phillip Carson.

When he got out of his car, he slams the door, and locks it with the button on his keychain. He storms in the house to see Talitha, David Jr., and Tabitha lounging on the couch and watching television.

"Kids, go to your room! Mommy and daddy have to talk," David Sr. firmly says while Tabitha's looking at him disgustedly. As Talitha is gathering her things to take to her room, David Sr. says, "DJ, you too!" David Jr. heavily sighs and walks to his room.

Tabitha complaints deeply and asks, "Ya interrupt our Family Friday so we can talk about what?"

Anthony Crawford, Jr.

"Who is Dr. Phillip Carson?"

She scoffs and calmly asks, "Is that what this is about? Phillip?"

"Yes! You've been caught! This is adultery," David Sr. says intensely pacing around the living room. "I can't believe this! I truly trusted you!"

She gives him a repulsive look while he has his outburst. She says, "David, ya have yar nerves! Ya don't know that ya'r here makin' accusations that ya have no clue about! Yes, Phillip wants me, but I deny him every time. I have no interest in him. While ya'r treating me and ou' kids like we don't have feelin's, I'm still being loyal and faithful to such a deceitful man! Ya don't spend time with me or the kids; ya don't show me any kind of love and affection. Ya don't go to ya'r daughter recitals and ya'r always late pickin' up DJ! But ya find the audacity and ya dare to come in here to talk crazy to me about somethin' that not even true?"

He stands dumbfounded. He calmly says, "I found his card in your jacket and I just thought maybe you were...."

She cuts him off and asks, "So a card means that I'm cheatin'?"

"Yes! Well, no. I mean I just think that...."

She interrupts his statement by saying, "Ya don't think at all! What's the matter, David? Ya guilt has ya thinkin' that I'm doin' the things that ya'r doing?"

He explodes and deceitfully asks "What are you talking about? You think that I'm cheating?"

She pauses for a moment to gather herself from his foolishness. "David, ya haven't attended any of those 'conferences' ya claim that ya attend. When I asked other members at church about their experiences at these 'conference,' they're clueless as to what I am talking about. I can't put my finger on it, but I know ya been livin' foul. I know because I feel it. I feel an unknown hurt all the time.

"I feel like I've been betrayed by the man that I fell in love with at a pivotal moment in my life. We have two kids together, David! I feel more like a 'single mom' than anythin' and ya know I don't like that phrase. Ya took advantage of my love and of my commitment towards ou' marriage; ou' family. And ya just feel like ya could get away with the things that ya doin' because ya'r involved in church?"

He's speechless as he continues to stand motionless. He remorsefully says, "I'm sorry, Tabitha. I know…."

She interjects him again and says, "I don't have time for ya apologies. We've put too much time and energy into this marriage for ya to disrespect me and ou' kids. I have gotten so complacent in this pain that I've been feelin' that I forgot that I have a life of my own to live. I deserve to be happy."

"So what are you trying to tell me?" He asks repentantly.

She puts her hands over her eyes and says, "I want a divorce, David. I can't keep doin' this to myself and to ou' kids. I can't keep pretendin' to be happy just so I can protect ya'r reputation with the church."

"A divorce?"

As tears begins to fall from her eyes, she stands up from the couch, and says, "Please don't act surprised, David. I'm not asking ya to admit to anythin' that ya done. I don't want to know about ya whereabouts. I'm not leaving ya for anyone and I'm not wantin' anythin' from you. I do plan on goin' back to school to get my master's. I hope ya can understand."

As she exits the room, he stays stagnant while staring at the couch that Tabitha just got up from. He falls to his knees in anguish. He feels like his heart has been pulled right out his chest leaving a hole in his rib cage that kept his heart safely kept. The woman who truly has his back just demanded a divorce. He's dreadfully starts crying on the floor of the living room. He's holding his stomach as if he had food poisoning.

David Jr. walks in to see his dad on the floor cripplingly crying. He sees his dad's nose running with his eyes blurry from tears. "What's the matter, dad?" He asks.

In a strenuous voice, David Sr. says, "DJ, go back in your room. Go back your room DJ!"

"Why dad?"

Anthony Crawford, Jr.

Still struggling to speak, David Sr. says, "You shouldn't be seeing me like this. Go to your room, Son!" David Jr. slowly walks to his room while David Sr. puts his face in the living room's carpet to cry. He gets up and sits on the couch with so many thoughts running races in his mind. He thinks about Rayven's pregnancy. He questions himself on rather he will still be able to be deacon of the church. He wonders about his children and how they will react to the divorce. He falls asleep on the couch.

Meanwhile, Tony and Trina are walking into Trina's apartment. Trina's intuition is very alarming. As they walk in Trina's room to put their possessions down and put something more comfortable on to wear, she suspiciously asks, "Is everything okay with you?"

Taking off his shirt, he hesitantly says, "Of course, why'd you asked?"

"I don't know," she says while shrugging her shoulders. As they walk in the living room, she proceeds to say, "I just got this strange feeling. Usually when I get this strange feeling, something is up with the ones that I love. I text my sister on the way here and she said that her and Terrance are real good. Jules and his little girlfriend are good, so that leaves you."

She sits on the couch and Tony sits next to her thinking that she knows about his situation with Rayven. He thinks about what his mentors told him about the situation. He feels like he's in a tight dilemma. It's as if one side of him wants to tell the truth, while another side of him wants to wait until the baby is born to see if the baby is his or not.

"I'm good, Queen. Just kind of been thinking about finals, that's all," he says ashamedly. He looks at her and feels so horrible for keeping his problem from her. He wonders if he'd be able to go months withholding information from her. As he sits and watches Trina crumble the marijuana, he says, "I do have something to tell you."

Black Pain't, Vol. I

She confidently and calmly says, "I know. I was just waiting for you to tell me. I was going to let you ride, but I also was going to keep account of how I'm going to fuck you up. So go ahead."

"How did you know?"

"Stop stalling and tell me........."

He takes a deep sigh. He asks, "Do you remember my ex, Rayven?"

"Yeah, what about her?" She asks instantaneously while grabbing the blunt to split it, so she can dump the tobacco out in the trash bag next to her couch.

He apologetically says, "Well, she's pregnant. It's a fifty-fifty chance that the baby is mine."

"How is it a fifty-fifty chance that it's yours?" She asks bewilderedly while licking the sides and tips of the blunt.

"Because she was fuckin' some married man long before I fucked her."

"Did you do it before or after you started fuckin' me?" She asks indignantly as she rolls the weed into a blunt.

"After," he says narrowly while picking up the lighter from the coffee table and handing it to her.

She smoothly hisses and says, "Hmm. So you expect me to stay around if it's yours?"

"I don't expect you to do anything you don't want to do, Trina," he says instantaneously. "You know how I feel about you, and it runs deep. But if that child is mine then I'm going to take responsibility as a man and raise it."

She takes heed as she lights the blunt and begins to smoke. She takes a few puffs and says, "Yes or no, Tony? Stop beating around the bush. You usually don't do that, so I don't know why you're doing that now." She hands him the blunt.

He puffs and says, "I'm not beating aroun..."

She angrily interpolates and yells, "YES, YOU ARE!" She watches him turn his face away. She stares at the side of his face as he passes her the blunt. "You are beating around the bush. You're not being honest with me and you're always honest with me."

Tony's motionless, observing her taking puffs to the pain that he just handed her. It seems as if physical agony is meeting up with mental hurt. Her energy is heavy. He knows that she opened her heart to him and allowed him to experience a love that she never got the opportunity to tap into, because of her battered and bruise heart. He calmly says, "I don't expect you to stay around, Trina, but I want you to be around."

She's really suffering from Tony's news. As she passes the blunt to Tony, she stares at him while he inhales and exhales. Suddenly, she throws her right fist in the form of a hook. Her fists collide with the left side of his face. He is able to grab her right wrist immediately after the collision. He then grabs her left wrist when she tried to swing with her left fist. He roughly picks her up and slams her on the couch saying, "TRINA! WHAT THE FUCK! CALM DOWN!"

She screams while she tries to kick her legs up. With her eyes closed, she covers her head thinking he is about to hit her. She says, "DON'T HIT ME! I'm sorry, I'm sorry!"

He lies on top of her crisscrossing her arms. He's angrily staring at her as she cries silently. She ducks her head into his chest. Tony, breathing rigidly and stridently, looks around her room. He feels her tears soaking his shirt. He lets her go and moves about five feet away from her.

She's lies on the couch to cry more heavily. She turns over to hide her waterworks. He stands by the other couch to catch his breath. He gently touches the left side of his face trying to caress the pain. While sniffing and crying, she regretfully says, "I'm sorry, Tony. I didn't really mean to hit you."

He remorsefully and unworthily says, "It is okay, Trina. It's just how your heart felt at that moment. I understand. I'm sorry about all of this, I was foul." He goes into her bedroom to gather his possessions. He comes back into the living room and to the door. "I got to go, Trina. I hope you find it in your soul to forgive me one day. I love you."

Black Pain't, Vol. I

She watches as he opens the door and walks out while gradually closing it. She continues her agonizing weep. After several minutes, she stands to walk and get the Jack Daniels bottle out of the refrigerator. She unspins the top from off the bottle and starts drinking it as if it was Kool-Aid. She quickly and roughly closes the refrigerator door and walks back into the living room. She stumbles on the couch not spilling a drop of the Jack Daniels.

Meanwhile, Tony is driving home while still feeling the effects of Trina's hurtful energy. Regret fills his mind and the will to fix everything pinches his heart. He hates that he hurts Trina. A cloud of wicked thoughts covers his discernments. He does not know what to do, so he calls Rayven. While the phone rings he thinks that he's repeating his life-long pattern. "It's the cycle," he whispers to himself.

She answers, "Hello?"

"I told her."

Confusedly and reactively, she asks, "What are you talking about Tony? You told who what?"

"I told my girl about the pregnancy."

Unaffectedly, she asks, "Oh, how did she take it?"

"She swung on me," he says as they both laugh. "Got me on the side of my face. She can hit too."

"Ouch, a woman's wrath isn't anything to play with."

"That shit hurt."

Rayven begins to internally weep while trying to remain calm over the phone. She says, "I can tell that you really like her."

As he make out her sniffling, he says, "I do really like her; for the first time in a long time I was feeling a type of feeling that I once felt while I was with you." His statement causes a penitent silence as he parks his car. He does not like that she's pregnant, however, he knows that he must take accountability for his actions.

She thinks about her situation with Tony and David Sr. She sorrowfully says, "I used to feel like a good person, Tony. What's wrong with me?" Another uncomfortable silence fills their void. "What did I do? Is it Karma? Why is God doing this to me?"

He listens attentively as he walks inside his home and begins to unwind. He says, "One thing that I've learned from life is that lessons will continue to repeat themselves until they are learned. Even then you'll have to stay aware of your decisions because everything in life is a cycle. I'm learning that love lets go, so there are many things and people that I must let go. I'm learning that sex ruins things if a friendship isn't the foundation. I'm learning about this false perception of love while understanding the true purpose and meaning of love."

"How are you doing that?"

Passionately, he says, "By loving myself first. It's through self-love where we meet our true selves. Self-love is the best love. When I love myself properly, I know how to love others properly. Once we understand that our true nature is love then we won't have to go outside of ourselves to find it."

She takes heed to his words and melts into his understanding. Then she remembers a quote that he used to tell her. She says, "It's just like what you used to tell me: trying to find love is blocking us from receiving it."

Impressively, he says, "That's right."

She respectfully says, "I appreciate how you're handling our situation. It truly means a lot."

"I'm just trying to be a man about the situation," he says humbly.

Reminiscently, she says, "I always think about those times when we were so in love. We used to talk about having kids and a family. I thought I could be happy forever as long as I was with you. You were my best friend."

As he thoroughly listens, her statement inspires him and he says, "I used to feel the same way, Ray. It was crazy coming home after college just to see everyone and everything had changed. I saw how gentrification had begun in areas of the city, friends weren't the same friends, and a lot of people were dying. Family wasn't the same."

Black Pain't, Vol. I

"Everything and everyone changes. Change is the only thing that's constant, right?"

"You're right."

She yawns and says, "Okay, Tony, it was good talking to you. I'm about to go to sleep."

"Okay, Rayven."

"Good night, Tony, and don't worry about your little girlfriend. True love always returns, right?" She asks rhetorically. "You see I came back. That's why we're in this predicament that we're in."

They both laugh and he says, "Good night, Rayven." As they hang up the phone, he sits on his bed in deep thought. He keeps asking himself what he would be like if that baby was his. He wonders about the type of father he can be. Then his train of thought travels down to Trina Williams. He ponders if she would still be around if the baby is not his. "Only time will tell," he whispers to himself.

Cannot stop thinking about Trina and all the pain he cause. He grabs his phone from off the bed, unlocks it, scrolls to the memo pad application, and begins to type:

Abandoned,
well at least she felt so.
It seems as if everyone she ever loved left and left her speechless like strep throat.
She doesn't allow outsiders to get close;
never allow anyone to see her nakedness and not just any man can deep stroke.
She comes home to turn her favorite songs on;
dance naked around her room with her favorite thong on.
Her strength is strong, but it seems as if she's always getting done wrong.
She keeps her window open to let the sun or the moon in;
another channel for God to work through, so she stays tuned in.
She loves being alone with no one to disappoint her nor hurt her.
She keeps her name clean, so no one can dirt her.

Anthony Crawford, Jr.

She curves a lot of men, so she don't go out on dates.
She wakes up early, but goes to sleep late.
For her goodness is sake and she hates acting fake.
She reads and meditates as she cries out lakes.
She smokes weed and drowns in some liquor.
She coughs up her tears, thinking it'll make time go by quicker.
She's anti-social, but can be very social, fun, and cool, if you ever get to know her.
She dreams of love and a family, because she feels like she's getting older.
While her world feels colder, she wishes for a man that's not afraid to hold her.
I just miss her already.

Chapter 14: **Remove that Ribbon**

It's the evening of Aaron James' speech. Alvin is sitting and waiting outside of the church in his car. As people pull into park, he observes how big the church is and internally disapproves of its huge facility. The church resembles a dome. He sees four reserved parking spaces that are near the building for the pastor's four luxury cars and reserved parking for the deacons.

He sits to devise a plan and decides to sit as far away from the pulpit as possible. He knows that Darryl, Tony, and Dr. Carson are all going to be there. As people are walking in the building, he waits on a

Anthony Crawford, Jr.

cue to enter. He checks his watch and realizes that the program will begin in fifteen minutes. He gets out of his car and walks in the church incognito. While inside the lobby he notices how incredibly vast the lobby is. People were crowding around the entrance that leads to the sanctuary.

He looks around for a sign that will direct him towards the balcony, he sees elevator doors to the far-left side of the lobby area. He takes the elevator up to the balcony. While finding a seat on the balcony, he scans the huge church. He looks at the unique pulpit and at the large crowd filling up the seats. He sees Tony, Darryl, and Dr. Carson sitting next to one another near the stage. As he looks towards the center aisle of the sanctuary, he sees Jazmine walking and holding Miracle's hand with a man following close behind them.

Meanwhile, sitting on the far-right side of the balcony, Patricia whispers to Tiffany, "I don't know why I let you even talk me into coming here knowing that Darryl is going to be here."

Tiffany looks around the balcony and notices a tall, dark, and handsome man sitting down on the far-left side of the balcony. She then scans the crowd for Darryl and asks, "You see him anywhere?" Patricia means mugs her. She recognizes Patricia's attitude and says, "My bad. I'm sorry. I heard these the speaker's speeches are legit. He just might be able to help us lonely sistahs out before we convert to white men."

Smiling, she firmly says, "Darryl would have probably tackled you if he would have heard you say that."

"Damn Patricia, you really like Darryl."

"Why do you say that?"

"You glow every time his name comes up."

"No I do not!" She says defensively.

Amusingly, Tiffany asks, "Does he call you Queen like it's your first name?"

"Girl, whatever."

In her Shakespearian voice, Tiffany poetically says, "Oh, Queen, how do I love thee? Let me count the many ways you make me feel and how much you make me horny." They both laugh.

Black Pain't, Vol. I

In the meantime, Tony turns around to the entrance and sees Trina, Jalisa, and Terrance enter the sanctuary. He takes a big sigh and says to Darryl, "I'm not goin' to lie, big bro, not talkin' to Trina hurts."

"Ahh man, you'll be alright. You know what they say, 'if it's meant to be then it'll be. If not, then leave it be.' So don't sweat it," he says wisely while looking out into the crowd.

Tony watches Trina, Jalisa, and Terrance as they take their seats. He stuck admiring Trina's beauty as he remembers her taste. He thinks to himself, "Wow, she's so beautiful." Her energy gives him the chills. He grabs his notebook and pencil from out of his backpack and opens the notebook to a blank page.

Meanwhile, Jazmine spots Dr. Carson and hurriedly walks up to him to sign in. Dr. Carson mordantly says, "Ms. Knight, I see you care about your grade." They both laugh. "I'm glad you were able to make it."

"I could use the knowledge, wisdom, and some extra credit," she says humorously. "Hey Tony, how are you?"

Tony smiles vibrantly and says, "I'm good, Jazz, what about you?"

"I'm good," she says innocently while feeling an uncomfortable glare from Darryl.

Darryl analytically asks her, "You're Ella's friend, right?"

"Yes, I guess you can say that" she replies critically as she holds her hand out to him. "My name is Jazmine Knight, sir."

While he shakes her hand, he politely says, "My name is Darryl Jones. It's a pleasure meeting you."

"The pleasure's all mine. You gentlemen enjoy the program," she says as she walks back to her seat.

The lights dim and the program begins. One of the church members walks onto the stage wearing a navy blue, tailor-made suit with a burgundy tie. He sensitively says, "Please close your eyes and bow your head for a word of prayer." As the crowd follows his command, he waits for complete silence to give him the cue to begin. "Dear Most Gracious and Heavenly Father, we enter into Your presence

Anthony Crawford, Jr.

in thanksgiving and in gratitude. We want to thank You for the many blessings that You have bestowed upon us. Thank You for safe travels and guiding all of us here for this special occasion. Father, please send Your angels to guide our speaker's words and allow Your will to be done on Earth as it is in Heaven. For those struggling with love, this prayer is for you. For those struggling with forgiveness, this prayer is for you. And for those struggling with accepting who they are, this prayer is for you. In Jesus Christ name, we pray…."

The audience says, "Amen," and the church member exits the stage during their applause.

The pastor of the church walks on the stage wearing a three-piece, black suit with white stripes. He walks up to the microphone and pleasantly says, "The Lord is my Shephard, I shall not want. He makes me lie down in green pastures; He leads me besides the still waters. He restores my soul, and leads me down to the path righteousness, for His name's sake. Yea, though I walk through the valley of the shadow of death, I will fear no evil, for though are with me. Your rod, your staff shall comfort me. You prepare a table before me in the presence of my enemies. You anoint my head with oil, my cup runs over. Surely, goodness, and mercy shall follow me in all the days of my life, and I shall dwell in the House of the Lord forever." He allows a cold silent to maneuver through the sanctuary.

"Welcome to 18th Street Missionary Baptist Church; I am Pastor Washington." The audience claps. As they gradually stop clapping, he says, "We have a heavenly treat for you all this evening in which Brother Thomas will be introducing in here shortly. Before we get to the real reason why we're here, I would like to take this time to welcome our faithful church members. Thank you to our stake holders that continue to bless us with their resources. I would like to give a huge shout out to our youth that are here this evening, Amen? Amen. We have college students in attendance along with some teachers."

"Without further a due, I will deliver the occasion for this evening: When we view society and the wickedness that it entails, somehow, and some way, we find that our problems will not suffice as long as we have the blood of Jesus covering us. We have been given the signs of the end of time and we have to be prepared. That's why I am so glad and happy that tonight's speaker is here to help us in the preparation."

"God's people without further a due, here to introduce our speaker for this evening is a very good friend of mine. He's a God-fearing man who loves God, his family, and his community. Please help me welcome to the stage, Brother Deacon David Thomas, Sr."

As David walks on stage, the audience applause. In the course of his stroll to the podium, he sees Tabitha, Talitha, and David, Jr. entering into the sanctuary and sitting in their usual seats. He humbly says, "Good evening, congregation, friends, family, and guest. I have the honor and distinct privilege in introducing tonight's speaker. He really does not need an introduction, because his works speak for themselves. He's a profound speaker, an author, a spoken word artist, and a visionary. He has many accolades that he didn't want us to mention because we'll be here all day." People in the audience laugh.

"Though he didn't want us mentioning all the great things he had accomplished in his lifetime, he did want us to mention his involvement with the youth throughout his years because, he believes, that they are our future. Ladies and gentlemen, please stand to your feet, if you're physically able, and help me welcome.... Mr. Aaron James."

The audience cheers and claps as Aaron James casually walks onto the pulpit. David observes his black-fitted jeans and the white t-shirt he is wearing. He notices the black hat that he has on and looks down to view his black and white shoes. He notices the tattoos on his arms and absorbs his robust aura. He sees his dreads hanging from the side and back of his hat as he approaches him. He shakes his hand and exits the stage.

Aaron walks up to the microphone and closes his eyes to feel the vibes from the audience. He appreciatively says, "Thank you, thank you. I appreciate each and every last one of you for coming on a Saturday." As the audience takes their seats, energetically proceeds to say, "Peace and love, family. I am so happy and grateful to be here. You

Anthony Crawford, Jr.

all may want to strap in to your seats and put on your invisible seat belts because this will be a bumpy ride. Pastor Washington, thank you for bringing me here to deliver this message from the Heavens. This message is for God's people and, before I get started, I would love to give you all a poem."

He turns his head away from the microphone to clear his throat and begins to recite:

Babies being born in the sin of poverty, forced to grow in this field of propriety; They seek guidance, hearts become infected with silence,
Until all they're left with is a hate that breeds violence.
Propaganda causes riots as we fight through the crisis.
We try to find the answer through false politicians, false pastors, and false prophets; We cry to undermine the process.
They inject you with diseases and fill you with ignorance.
They make a natural plant illegal but puts cancer in a cigarette.
It's like we're living in flashbacks.
When we don't see this matrix, we're the ones that they laugh at.
We're the ones being drafted.
We're the ones being divided into classes and, at the end of the day, we're the one being put in those caskets.
We're the ones being poisoned.
We can't even hear God because we're too distracted from the noises and being fed drama, my people....
This is trauma.

The audience gives Aaron a round of applause once he finishes. As they steadily stop applauding, he smiles and modestly says, "Thank you, I appreciate you. Let me go ahead and apologize early for my cynical and optimistic views on life, society, and religion. They may make most of you uncomfortable, but they may guide you to the true meanings of life and why we're all here on this earth.

"Five years ago, I found myself at the lowest point of my life. I felt like I lost everything. I was not in my right mind spiritually, emotionally, and mentally. I even blamed our Creator for all my problems. What hurt the most was being fresh out of college and could not find a job. So, there I was, lost, with a college degree, working for minimum wage, and just going through internal resentment. I wanted to kill myself.

"I remember reflecting on my life at that time; I thought I deserved everything that was happening to me. I thought, 'Maybe, I should take everything with a grain and salt.' I felt like I was broke because of the many times I had stolen. I felt like I was losing friends because of my unfaithfulness towards past friends. I felt like my relationships with women were horrible, because of my player attitude and the domestic violent situations that I participated in." After his statements, he stops to feel the audience's disapproving vitality. "Before you judge me and discredit everything that I have to say, I like to remind you of John 8:7 - *Let he who is without sin cast the first stone.*

"Every savior in the bible struggled with some type of "sin." Noah was viewed as a drunkard, Jacob was viewed as a liar, Rehab was look down upon as a prostitute, Moses was considered a murderer, King David took his best friend's wife and sent him away to die in battle; even Jesus drank the wine - and the good Lord still used them all! So whatever it is that you're enduring or fighting with, just know that God can still use you!

"So, after embracing my own flaws and imperfections, I began observing our society and the systematic oppression that usually leads people to destructive behavior. I noticed this matrix that we're living in that is operated through *fear*, which is cultivates indulgence, self-hate, suicide, separation, and crime. I saw the many aspects of this society that we pursue that contribute to our depressions, our sadness, and our lack of compassion for one another. I saw how we feed our egos and abuse others in the midst.

"Within those trying moments of my life, I turned to the bible for answers. Here's where things get too apocryphal. I interpreted everything that I read totally different from most pastors and those that always force their teachings into people's throats and minds. Can I share some of those interpretations?" The audience remains silent and he comically says, "Y'all can talk back to me."

The people in the audience laughs and gives Aaron consent with head nods and "Amens." Aaron smiles from hearing someone yell, "Let Him use ya."

"The first interpretation that I discovered was that herbs is mentioned throughout the bible. Everyone knows what herbs are, right?" He stops to allow the audience to suppress his question. "Yes, family, I am talking about marijuana." The audience laughs and he continues to say, "It just made sense to me, so I researched information about marijuana and its effects. What was revealed to me was that marijuana is a plant that naturally grows from the Earth. Marijuana cures cancer, depression, arthritis, blindness, and many other commonly known diseases. Why would our government make something illegal that cures us?" He waits as the silence and tension fills the sanctuary.

"I'm not telling you all this to get you all to smoke marijuana, I'm telling you all this because corporations put diseases in our foods and sells us the medicine that makes the diseases even more badly. These same corporations push the tobacco industry, which brings you nothing but cancer. You thinking you're being relaxed when you're actually slowly dying. How many of us have lost someone to cancer?"

After seeing the many people in the audience raise their hands, he proceeds to say, "I'm telling you this because society will push things on you that will slowly kill you while herbs heal. Even Moses met the burning bush." People laugh. "Speaking of Moses, the book of Exodus talks about how Moses was sent to free God's people from the Kings, Queens, and Pharaohs of Egypt. However, God did not send Moses alone; he was accompanied by his brother, *Aaron*. Moses had a stuttering problem and God used Aaron to deliver the message of freedom while Moses performed the miracles. That's why I became a speaker because I knew, at the time, that I am here to deliver God's message. Are you ready for God's message?" The audience members cheer as he removes the microphone from the microphone stand and walks to the front of the stage.

Black Pain't, Vol. I

"The bible says that God is Love. Since we were made in the image and the likeness of God then that makes us Love; that makes us God. This is the unspoken truth that many have a hard time accepting. How can we claim to be God's children, but not Gods? We are all God. This is the *'blasphemy'* that Christ was crucified for. In John 10, Christ was talking to the Pharisees about him considering himself to be a God. After they interrogated Christ, John 10:34 says that Jesus answered them and said, 'Is it not written in your laws that you are Gods?' He was referring to Psalms 82:6 which says that *'ye are Gods, and all of you are children of the Most High.'* This is your true and only identity. This is who we all are. To do deny this truth is to deny who you are, and when you deny who you are, you deny God.

"We Are Love! Love is Life and Life is Love. Love celebrates; Love is so jazzed that you exist; that you are you. Love celebrates your birthday every day! Love uplifts: It raises you higher; It elevates you. Love heals; It's nutrients for the soul; It's healing energy. Love gives. Love is a giving energy, It has a giving presence. Love knows no wrong. With Love, you never do or have done anything wrong in your life. Love forgives; It's always forgiving. Love wants you to be happy. Love has given you full permission to follow your joy.

"You also have permission to stop what doesn't make you happy. Love wants you to have what you really want; that's why the bible says that God gives us the desires of our hearts. Always remember that you are a Divine Spark of God, so by you not asking for what it is that you want is irresponsible; that's the biggest and only sin. Love does not judge you; Love appreciates you; Love accepts you. Love does not judge or label you; It does not attack you, It does not condemn you. There is only one type of Love and that's unconditional. Love is unconditional. Love does not need you to do or be anything different than you already are. That's Love. That's God. That's Us.

"When it comes to our relationships with potential spouses, we need to understand what Love is. Love is built from friendship and trust, not sex. Sex should always come after the friendship. Sex should come after the trust. Sex takes away your energy when you're abuse the energy. When you Love someone, you accept them for who they are. You allow time to develop the two of you. But, when two individuals have sex early, they can cause emotions that they have not learned how to control which leads to destruction. Love is patient and love is kind. Love keeps no record of wrongs. Love is forgiving. These are the things that must be the agreement in every relationship." He pauses for a second to ask, "What would life be life if they taught these things to our youth in school?

"This truth is hidden from you. The illusions of life keeps us from seeing this truth. Society keeps you from this truth. You're not going to learn this in school, church won't even teach you. The powers that be will kill you for speaking this into people. This is the 'system' that we're living in; this is the matrix. Once you begin to see these illusions, this system, then that's when you're able to maneuver through life choosing the things that you want to experience and choosing the things that you want to have in your life. It does not matter where you come from, you can choose where you want to go. It does not matter what you've been through, you can choose fun and loving experiences.

"One thing that I try to get God's people to understand is that we are all slaves to this society, and we must be feeble towards that. When we were born, we were all giving social security numbers which is our barcodes. We were giving birth certificates, so they labeled you the moment you were born. We are all property of the United States Corporation. That's why police officers can get away with murder, because it's a way to keep us in line just like they did when they tar and feathered our ancestors. That's why we work jobs that funds our own genocide. That is why this system poisons our air, inject chemicals in our foods, put hate in our music, and uses propaganda to disrupt our subconscious thinking patterns. This is why the FDA approves food that slowly kills you. The powers that be know that we are God's people, they know what we're capable of. They know our astrology. They know their time is up, so they will do anything and everything to destroy your mind and body for they perish, but they can't destroy your soul.

Black Pain't, Vol. I

Passionately, he says, "Freedom is your birthright. Freedom should be your political views! You are not anyone's property! You don't have to kill yourself to be somebody because you were born somebody! Without society, we have Earth! God is so intelligent that he put the medicines in the earth and called them fruits, herbs, and vegetables. Earth is all that we need.

"One thing about our soul is that it knows that it is limitless while living inside a limited body. The soul knows that there is more to life than just tainted schooling and working a nine to five. The soul knows when something isn't right; it knows that you are meant for boundless experiences! But we have allowed this system to have control over our minds and beliefs to the point that we don't seek nothing higher or greater than what's been presented to us.

"Five years ago, God gave me a vision of our future in the form of a dream. While in this dream, I remember walking outside of my home and was lifted to the sky. As I looked down, I saw the destruction of peace. I heard war; I heard mothers crying from watching their babies being dead onto the streets. I saw nothing but fire and smoke surrounding our air. I tried to warn people about this dream that we're all living in by exposing them to the lies that our government tells us. I tried to warn people about this dream that we're all living in by exposing them to the propaganda and mind-control that we watch on television. I became argumentative and pessimistic. I hated people and became impatient. Though my critical analyses and controversial attitude towards life brought me success and admiration, I still was not happy; it was not as fulfilling as I would have liked it to be. I was really doing what everyone else was doing when it came to 'waking up' my people.

"A couple of years ago, something happened to me that started this journey to teach people about *Love*. God gave me another vision of our future. It's called the New Birth. It's like a new covenant or something that seemed beyond farfetched than anything I have ever imagined. It was absolute and unconditional Love. It was absolute truth. It was total peace. It was nothing but happiness. It was so beautiful. Our

Anthony Crawford, Jr.

Creator displayed to me our youth together as One. They were burning weapons and getting rid of the evil that remained on the Earth."

"The message that He gave me was so clear to me. It was the message of Love. I have to be the example of Love and, in order to be that example, I have to Love myself first. I have to understand the concept of change. Change is inevitable. Change is the only thing that's constant. Change is very okay. Besides, nothing changes if nothing changes. So in order for us to make that change in the world, we must make that change within ourselves first.

"Other than self-love and change, there are two other things that can bring us to happiness and world peace. The first thing, in which I will speak on shortly, is to follow that gift that God gave you. The second one is unity. We must bring people together for a common goal regardless of their backgrounds, regardless of their skin tones, and regardless of their views on life. We are stronger together than we are separate! Unity is what's going to dismantle this system. We must understand that we are God's people so that automatically makes us the majority! This system wants us to be separate in order to keep control, because they know if you can divide people, they can conquer them. This system wants us fighting and killing each other. This system does not want us united!

"This system killed many of our leaders for trying to teach people about love and for trying to unite people. Our leaders were given the same visions that God gave me; they saw a better future for our children to live. In the *Autobiography of Malcolm X*, there was a chapter about how Malcolm went to the Mecca for the Hajj. A Hajj is a trip that Muslims take in order to fulfill their calling as a Muslim. A Hajj is the fifth and final pillar of Islam. So during Malcolm's Hajj, he observed Muslims from different ethnic backgrounds with different shades of skin. He had a spiritual revelation. During the Hajj, he was taught the true meanings and teachings of Muhammad. He learned that Muhammad was a Messenger of Love.

"When he returned to the states, his mind was different. He stopped believing in the teachings that was taught to him by the Nation of Islam. Malcolm had a new mind set. He became more interested in unity and in love. Trouble emerged for Malcolm because the system needed him be radical. The system needed him to keep people angry and unwilling to come together for common goals. That speech that Malcolm was going to give on the day of his assassination was about equality, unity, and love. He wanted to bring people together by exposing them to the truth. That's why the system assassinated him. That's why the system assassinated Dr. Martin Luther King, Jr. and other well-known leaders such as Gaddafi, Huey P. Newton, Tupac Shakur, Dr. Sebi, and John Lennon, just to name a few. And the system killed them for the public to see – just how this same system sent Christ down Calvary Road for the public to see.

Rhetorically, he asks, "Does that scare you? Does it scare you to take a stand against the upheaval of evil that spreads across our world? Love is the answer. Love has always been the answer. Love is you and you are Love. Once you begin loving yourself, it will be easy for you to love others. Once you begin loving yourself, it will be impossible to hate anything or anyone. Self-Love is the key to your salvation.

He walks toward the podium, stands in front of it, and humbly says, "I'm glad Pastor Washington recited Psalms 23. When it comes to overcoming the things that you fear, Psalms 23 is one of the greatest references to use as you walk through the shallow of death. Fear is the opposite of Love. Fear holds you back. Fear does not allow you to let go. Fear keeps you stuck and stagnant. Fear keeps you from taking risks. Fear keeps you from living! Fear is a disease. We cannot fear this system! This system fears us more than we fear them. They know who we are! They know Who we have on our side!

"Going back to the first thing that I mentioned that will dismantle this system and these illusions that we endure, which is to follow that gift that God put in you. Everyone has a gift. It's your duty to find out what that gift is and learn how to use it. Your gifts are your powers. That's why we say that *'we are powerful beyond measure.'* When all of our powers combine then we can see this system disable.

Anthony Crawford, Jr.

Matthew 18:20 says, '*For when two or three gather in His name, He will be in the midst.*' What could we all create together?

"Your gift is also the key to your freedom. Proverbs 18:16 says, '*A man's gift shall make room for him on Earth.*' So if you want your 40 acres and your mule then follow your gift because this country is not giving us reparations. Face it and understand that your gift is essential to the life that you came to live. Your gift shall lead you to happiness. Your gift is a part of your soul's contract. Another huge 'sin' is to live a life without utilizing the gift that God gave you!

"We all have gifts but most never open their gift. Most don't even know what their gifts are. You can figure out what your gift is by removing any ribbons that you have wrapped around it. Ribbons are those fears that you have allowed your subconscious mind to accept. Ribbons are those excuses that you use. Ribbons are any past traumas, doubts, heartaches, hurt, mistakes, false realities, and pain that causes you to not open your gifts.

"There are a few ways to removing these ribbons. One of the most effective and quickest ways of removing those ribbons is through Self-Love. Once again, *Self-Love is the key to your salvation.* Loving yourself is a constant remembrance that you are Love, knowing that you are an aspect of Divinity, and accepting all of aspects of yourself throughout your process. Once you start loving yourself then expect your dreams to come true. Once you begin loving yourself then expect your relationships to get better. *Self-Love is the key to your salvation.* How can you not Love the way God made you? You are perfect in every being of your existence. You are loving, lovable, loved. You are worthy, enough, and always deserving. You have to love yourself if you want to see those ribbons removed from your extraordinary gifts.

"Self-Love is total acceptance. You have to accept yourself. You have to accept everything about you. How can you love yourself and not accept yourself? How can you not accept the life that God has blessed you with? How can you not accept your calling? When you look in the mirror, do you accept everything that you see? If not, then why?

Black Pain't, Vol. I

"Self-Love is total forgiveness. When Christ hung on that cross, he said, '*Forgive them, for they not know what they do.*' Forgiveness is the only way to heal. A lot of us are walking this earth holding grudges and extra baggage because we refuse to forgive. Why would you want to hold onto such pain? Why would you want to hate someone for something that they did to help you? We must forgive in order to move forward.

"Self-Love provides you with vision. That vision is your gateway to freedom. That's why the bible says, '*Without a vision, the people will perish.*' How many people do you see perishing? How many people do you see dying with unlived dreams and unaccomplished goals? Don't you think that's torture? It's torture to live an unfulfilled life. You automatically put your body in a dis-ease when you're not utilizing what God has put in you. Your heart yearns for happiness, for peace, and for love. You owe it to yourself to do whatever it is that you are called to do. Your purpose is an important piece to God's puzzle.

"Christ knew his purpose. He knew it at a young age. When his father, Joseph, asked him why he roamed off to the temples, Christ would reply, '*I was doing my Father's work.*' He was following his heart. He knew that the people needed saving. He began his ministry at 30. He traveled city to city to teach people about Love and who they are to God. He gave people eyes to see this illusion, this matrix. He helped people believe that they can be healed and healed them. He sacrificed his life for others to know and understand their powers. He didn't allow his life to be consumed with ribbons because he knew they didn't serve his purpose.

"Remove those ribbons, family. Understand that you have a purpose in this life. I appreciate every last one of you for taking the time out to come and hear me speak. I pray that your dreams are fulfilled. I hope that you ask God to show you the truth of you are, no matter how beautiful it may be. Peace and Love, family, until next time. I love you."

He holds up the peace sign as the audience stands to give him a standing ovation. As the audience gradually stop cheering, Deacon Thomas walks to the podium and says, "Brother Aaron James, thank you for blessing us this evening with that powerful speech." He makes a few announcements and dismisses the program.

While the audience begins to exit the sanctuary, Darryl sees Alvin walking out the building. He runs after him while yelling his name to get his attention. Tony didn't see Darryl take off running, but he sees Trina, Jalisa, and Terrance heading out the building and starts walking towards them.

Outside in the parking lot, Darryl catches up to Alvin and yells, "Alvin!"

While Alvin gets near his car, he stops and slowly turns around. "Wassup, Darryl?" he shamefully asks.

"Good to see that you have made it brother. When did you get release?"

"Ahh, man, feels good to be out. I was released this morning and I caught a cab home."

"What did you get out of his speech?" Darryl asks while folding his arms to listen attentively.

Alvin thinks for a second and says, "There's some things that I need to work on within myself. I need to let go of some of baggage and past hurt. I need to start being honest with myself."

"I respect that, family."

"What about you? What did you get out of his speech? I'm surprised that you even came to a church," he says comically.

Darryl chuckles and meekly says, "There are many things that I have to accept and love about myself. I can't keep lying to myself and others about who I am and what I do. I guess I need to be more transparent as well."

"It's just what the bible says, '*The truth*......"

"...*shall set you free*," Darryl says to finish Alvin's statement. "I'll holla at you later bro bro. We'll have to catch up."

As they shake hands, Alvin says, "Alright, brother."

Meanwhile, in the lobby, Jules, Jazmine, and Miracle are walking towards Trina, Jalisa, and Terrance. Terrance sees Jazmine for the first time in years and feels a sense of uneasiness. Jazmine sees Terrance awkwardly.

Jules feels so delighted to see his sisters that he did not notice the tension in Jazmine's face, neither did Jalisa observe Terrance's facial expression once he seen Jazmine. Trina and Jalisa are happy to see their brother.

"Who told you about this presentation? You don't go to stuff like this, lil' nigga," Trina says to Jules.

He laughs and says, "I came with this gorgeous Queen right here," as he gently pulls in Jazmine while Jazmine is holding Miracle. "Trina and Jalisa, this is Jazmine and her beautiful daughter, Miracle. Jazmine and Miracle, these are my twin sisters, Trina and Jalisa. And I believe this is Jalisa's boyfriend...?"

"Terrance," he says disturbingly while shaking Jazmine's hand.

"Jazmine," Jazmine says uncomfortably.

"That's right, Terrance," Jules says pleasantly.

"Nice to meet you all. He's told me a lot about you," Jazmine says gracefully.

Trina comically says, "What has he said about me? That I was the mean sister and Jalisa was the control freak?"

Jazmine laughs and says, "No, most of the time he's talking about how much he misses you two and how he wishes he could spend more time with you. He really loves you."

"Aww, well ain't that sweet of you," Jalisa says while holding onto Terrance's hand. "Where are you three headed to now?"

Jules smiles and says, "We're about to grab some to-go-food and head to the house. What about y'all? What are you young whipper snappers about to do?"

Before Trina begins to speak, Tony walks up on her. "Trina," he says watching her turn around quickly.

"Yes, sir? Can I help you?" Trina asks him sarcastically.

Tony humbly and remorsefully says, "I'm sorry for what happened last night. I just felt like you needed some space to get your thoughts right."

Anthony Crawford, Jr.

"Yeah, well my thoughts are alright," Trina says impolitely while getting enticed by his aura. "I'm sorry for swingin' on you, kid."

"It's okay, really. At least I know who to call on in case of fights," he says as a Trina's lifeless silence wraps around him. "Well, I just wanted to acknowledge you before you left. I'm glad you came, and I hope you learned something."

"Well, thank you, sir," Trina says derisively. Before they depart away from Tony, she says, "Goodbye," as he stands there looking like he just lost his best friend. He hides his hurt with a side smile.

While they're walking away, Jalisa asks Trina, "Dang, what happened between you two?" while walking outside onto the parking lot.

"He got another girl pregnant. Well, it's like a fifty-fifty chance it's his and he expects me to want to stay around. Not I said the cat," Trina says snappishly.

Jules accidently intervenes on their conversation and says, "Jalisa, have you been to the hospital to see mom?"

"No, I haven't. Don't really plan to either," Jalisa says firmly. "Besides, Trina didn't go, so why are you telling me that I should go."

Trina instantly feels some kindheartedness taking over her and says, "Mama, told me everything, Jalisa."

Jalisa confusedly asks, "Everything about what?"

"About our sperm donor."

Angrily, Jalisa says, "There's nothing that she can say or do to make up for those times she allowed dad to put his filthy hands on us."

"You heard what the speaker said, Jalisa. *Forgiveness is the only way to heal*," she says as she walks close to Jalisa to embrace her stubbornness. She whispers in her ear, "She killed him."

Jalisa's face goes into complete shock. While putting her hands over her mouth, she asks, "Are you serious?"

"Yes, Jalisa. That's why you need to go to mama and get the full story. I swear it'll be like a load is lifted off your heart," Trina says meekly.

Black Pain't, Vol. I

Jalisa ponders on the news and says, "I just might do that."

Meanwhile, Darryl is walking back into the building to go converse with Phillip. Once he gets midway into the lobby, Patricia and Tiffany runs into him. He smoothly says, "Patricia, I'm so glad you came."

"I'm glad I came too," she says indecently. "You were right about this lil' event. It was a unique experience."

Darryl adores her lips as she speaks. He looks at Tiffany and asks, "What did you think of it?"

"It was good. Real good. I typed some of his quotes down in my notepad on my phone. I enjoyed it," Tiffany says as Tony walks up to them.

Darryl knows that Tiffany badmouths him to Patricia, so he asks Tiffany, "What was the biggest lesson that you learned from his speech?"

"That's an interesting question," she says. "I think the biggest lesson that I learned from his speech is to put myself first. There have been too many times when I put others' happiness before mines. I guess when you put others first, you teach them that you come second."

"That's real," Tony says optimistically as Tiffany admires his essence.

"Wassup, kid! Glad that you can join in on the conversation," Darryl says to Tony. "What about you, Patricia? What did you learn?"

She innocently says, "He gave me a different perspective of Love. I never thought of myself or life as Love. What about you, Darryl?"

He stares at her sensually and says, "Forgiveness is the only way to heal."

"Do you feel like there are some people that you need to forgive?" Tiffany asks.

"I have forgiven everyone. I just think that there are people that I would want to forgive me," he says apologetically. He observes Tony's vibe and asks, "Is everything okay?"

Anthony Crawford, Jr.

Tony dreadfully says, "Yes," and Tiffany absorbs his pain, but is trying to stay inconsiderate of his feelings because of what he has done to her mentee, Rayven.

"Alright cool. We're about to go holla at Dr. Carson."

Tiffany asks, "Are you ready, Patricia?"

"Yes," Patricia replies while looking into Darryl's eyes. She says to him, "I guess I'll see you another time."

Darryl amiably says, "Hopefully. We'll just have to let the synchronicities of life bring us together again."

Patricia smiles and cheerfully says, "HEY! You got the word right this time. Good job," as they high five each other. "Stay out of trouble, King."

"Keep being who you are, Queen," Darryl says while watching Patricia exit the building with Tiffany. As Darryl and Tony searches for Dr. Carson, they spot him talking with Tabitha.

Phillip sees Tony and Darryl walking towards them and says to Tabitha, "Come to my office on Monday and we can take care of all your paperwork for the summer and the fall."

"Okay, I will. Thank ya, Phillip," Tabitha says while walking back into the sanctuary to see David Sr. with Talitha and David Jr. "Talitha and DJ, are yall ready to go?"

David Sr. sadly observes Tabitha careless attitude and says, "Thanks for coming, Tabitha."

As Talitha and David Jr. walks away from David Sr., Tabitha says, "No problem."

David Sr. watches as his family exits the sanctuary as Pastor Washington walks up to him with Aaron James. Pastor Washington says, "Good job this evening, gentlemen. Bro. James, I appreciate you for coming and sharing your message."

"To God be the Glory. I appreciate you for allowing me to come," Aaron says prophetically. Humbly, he says, "I hope I wasn't too provocative."

Black Pain't, Vol. I

Understandingly, Pastor Washington says, "Oh, no, my brother. You gave the people what they needed to hear. You gave them the truth."

"Your interpretation of the bible is quite intriguing, Bro. James." David says.

Aaron says, "Thanks brother, it's all Love."

"Do you think people are receptive of your message?" David Sr. asks interestingly.

Prophetically, Aaron says, "I always pray and hope so. Even if they don't take heed towards what I say, I pray they start believing in the visions and dreams that God gives them. I pray that they begin understanding and utilizing their gifts. I always pray that God heals our hearts and minds from any pain and scars that we receive. I pray that we all are able to see this cycle and the illusions that feed our egos and cultivate our fears. I pray that we choose to change this cycle and learn to feed our souls. I pray that Love continues to cover us all, that peace and prosperity is the foundation of humanity, and happiness is the only lifestyle we choose. I pray that our pain leads us to our purposes in life."

Pastor Washington says, "Amen, brother. Amen."

"Thank you for everything Pastor Washington," he says while he shakes his hand. He shakes David's hand. "I hope that you bring me again next year. It will be an honor and a privilege to continue spreading God's message to His people."

"We can make that happen. I'll have our church's financial advisor set aside the budget for you next year," Pastor Washington opportunely says while walking Aaron to the door.

Aaron smiles and says, "Peace and Love, Pastor. Deacon Thomas, it was a pleasure meeting you, brother. Until next time." He walks out of the building.

Anthony Crawford, Jr.

Character and Glossary List

Black – nickname given to aboriginals who were already in "America" (Turtle Island) before the Europeans came.

Pain't – a triple entendre of how artists (singers, poets, rappers, painters, dancers, etc.) all present their pain amid their creative expressions; it's also a contraction for "pain not," which is a metaphor for pain not actually being pain, but an artistic expression of life; lastly, it serves as an allusion for how the original people of America (Turtle Island) history of economic pain, mental pain, physical pain, and social pain has always been used as profit – my book included.

Kemet – made up Black owned bar named after Egypt's original name; it means the land of burnt faces.

RED's – made up Black owned club/bar

Turner University – made up HBCU, named after fictional character, Nat Turner

Stokely Carmichael University – made up HBCU, named after Stokely Carmichael

George Washington Carver Middle School – made up middle school, named after George Washington Carver

W.E.B Dubois Middle School – made up middle school, named after W.E.B. Dubois

Newton University – made up HBCU, named after Huey P. Newton

Dance Your Soul Out – made up dance team owned by Jalisa Williams

Black Pain't, Vol. I

Darryl Jones – *the intellectual-playboy* - in his late-20s, charming, suave, groomed, handsome, corporate powerhouse style of stylist; he has a strong presence and is very social. He's a womanizer. He graduated from Stokely Carmichael University and got his Master's; he's a middle school history teacher at George Washington Carver Middle School. He's Pro-Black. He's a Taurus.

Patricia Skinner – *the feminist* - in her late-20s. She has a demanding presence. She's very intellectual, beautiful, and dresses afro-centrically. She has a counseling spirit that people confide themselves in. She is antisocial. She's frugal but loves the finer things that are on sale. She's the librarian at W.E.B Dubois Middle School. She has her bachelor's degree in library science and received her master's degree in library science. She's a Cancer. She's dynamic. She's guarded. She's pro-Black. She has a passion for helping young Black women and teaching young girls about who they are. She does not give men any type of ego-satisfaction. She's very sarcastic. She's a feminist. Her mother was not around, so her father raised her to be outspoken, brilliant, and tough.

Tony Givens – *the anointed sinner* - in his mid-20s. He's helpful, smooth, spiritual, and speaks prophetically. He dresses like an adventurer and has a magnetic aura. He graduated from Newton University. He's a graduate student that is getting his Master's in African American Studies. He is conscious and scripture mixed. He is street and book smart. He's a Taurus.

JaTrina Williams – *the realest* - in her mid-20s. She dresses either sexy or preppy. She's down-to-earth and funny. She's a realist and real outspoken. Though she didn't go to college, she's street and book smart. She's twin sister of Jalisa Williams. She's a bartender at Kemet. She used to dance, hates her mother, and loves her private life. She's an Aries.

Anthony Crawford, Jr.

Jules Williams, Jr. – *the caregiver* - in his early 20s, dresses preppy. He is very understanding. He's very intuitive, argumentative, and investigative. He's the younger brother of Trina and Jalisa. He works as a CNA and looks after his mother, Mary Ann Ethel-Williams, while she's in a nursing home. He's a Sagittarius.

Jazmine Knight – *distress* - in her early-20s, pretty. She dresses very churchy. She very inspective but is very deceitful. She's the mother of Miracle. She is a CNA. She's in grad-school. She's a Scorpio.

Rayven Little – *Proverbs 7*– in her early-20s, classy, sexual, religious, and demanding. She dresses like a churchy girl. She works at an insurance call center. She gets mentored by Tiffany. She's a Gemini.

Alvin Johnson – *the secret* - in his late-20s, handsome, educated, dark-aura, and mysterious. He dresses corporately. He's a manager at a fortune 500 company. He's a sports fanatic. He's a Gemini.

Jalisa Williams – *the dancer* – beautiful, smart, classy, judgmental though she carries a graceful presence. She has an artsy-dress style. She's the twin sister of JaTrina; she's an artistic dancer and displays a great deal of business etiquette. She owns her own dance program full of young girls called DYSO (Dance Your Soul Out). She owns and rents out her auditorium. She owns her own dance studio. She's an Aries.

David Thomas, Sr. – *the deacon* – in his mid-30s, dark-brown-skinned, groomed, charming, sings, preaches, and stays suited and booted. He's a husband, a father, and a deacon at 18th St. Missionary Baptist Church. He's a Leo.

Tabitha Harris-Thomas – *Proverbs 31* – in her mid-30s, very graceful, beautiful, dresses like a churchy. She's the wife of David Thomas, Sr. and the mother of David Thomas, Jr., and Talitha Thomas. Tabitha comes from a religious background and has dedicated her life to Jesus Christ. She's very loyal, faithful, and religious. She's a Sagittarius.

Dr. Phillip Carson – *the professor* –His voice is strong and dynamic. He dresses corporately. He's a graduate school-professor at Turner University (TU) and one of the Thesis and Dissertation Department Heads. He's Darryl's mentor. He's a Libra.

Terrance Robins –*the "good" guy* – in his mid 20s, He's handsome, sensitive, supportive, patient, and has a high understanding of life and love. He dresses like a Hip-Hop Street artist; he is an artist. He's groomed but has some hood-like qualities. He can sing. Has self-control and compromises often. He's an Aquarius. He's a freelance writer that also writes verses and songs for another artist.

Tiffany Freeman – *the investigator* –in her late 20's. She dresses vibrantly. She's a middle school English teacher at W.E. Dubois Middle School. She's nosey, very investigative, and very beautiful. She sees through people and situations. She has expensive taste. She's a Pisces.

Mary Ann Ethel-Williams - Mother of JaTrina, Jalisa, and Jules Jr., elderly lady, wrinkled, but beautiful and polite. She hates being and feeling alone. She's sensitive. She is the widow of Jules Williams Sr. She has a distinct relationship with Jazmine Knight. She's a Capricorn.

David Thomas, Jr. - son of David Sr. and Tabitha; he's in Mr. Darryl Jones's class.

Talitha Thomas - daughter of David Sr. and Tabitha, she dances for Jalisa's youth dance program.

Mrs. Debra Townsend – Jazmine's therapist

Anthony Crawford, Jr.

Ms. Luna Hall – *the science teacher* - She's Darryl's coworker at George Washington Carver Middle School. She's very beautiful. She dresses like a businesswoman. She loves science, nature, and people.

Miracle Knight – Jazmine's daughter

Abbyielle Johnson – Patricia's mentee

Aaron James – *Love* – Aaron is the speaker that everyone comes to see. He's in his late 20's with a strong and dynamic aura. He dresses like a Hip-Hop Street artist.

Charles Mason – *the trap-her* – He's in his mid-thirties. He works at the Department of Mental Health. He's a pretty boy with a great fashion sense. His father is black, and his mother is white. He's Tiffany's ex-boyfriend. He's Ella's baby-father.

Ella Franklin - *the fuck-boy lover* – Ella is Jazmine's high school friend. She's high maintenance. Always wearing sew-ins. She's beautiful and she dresses sexy.

Dennis – *the narcissistic abuser* – College dropout but went to vocational school for welding; Patricia's ex-boyfriend; narcissistic, misogynistic, abusive, charming, and habitual liar.

Kenneth Franklin – Choir Director at 18th Street Missionary Baptist Church. He is in a music fraternity. Nosy and sort of knows about David Sr. and Rayven.

Shyla Johnson – Dr. Phillip Carson's ex-wife. Cunning, very attractive, smart, and adventurous. She's not afraid of taking risk and exploring.

Black Pain't, Vol. I

Brittany – *Darryl's match* - very beautiful. She's very opinionated, courageous, sexual, and unremorseful. She loves hanging out, drinking, smoking weed, and dancing.

Dionte Anderson – *the nurse* – He's in his mid-20s. He's the only Black nurse that works at The People's Hospital.

Pastor Washington – *the pastor* – He is the pastor at 18th St. Missionary Baptist Church. He is David Sr.'s mentor. He is always in a three-piece suit during church services and church events. He wears lots of jewelry.

Made in the USA
Columbia, SC
18 January 2025